CARDIGAN BAY

By the same author

Fell the Angels
Hurricane Hole

CARDIGAN BAY

John Kerr

ROBERT HALE · LONDON

ISBN 978-0-7198-1417-4

Robert Hale Limited
Clerkenwell House
Clerkenwell Green
London EC1R 0HT

www.halebooks.com

2 4 6 8 10 9 7 5 3 1

Typeset in Sabon
Printed in Great Britain by Berforts Information Press Ltd

CHAPTER ONE

THE MAJOR QUIETLY placed one boot on the fire-step, eased to the top of the parapet, and elbows on the ledge, raised the binoculars to the black sky. The stars shone brilliantly and, after a moment, an almost incandescent object filled the lens, hanging just above the horizon like a yellow lamplight. Venus, he thought. Aurora, goddess of the dawn. He rested the glasses on the sandbag and gazed past the double line of wire at the faint sliver of the moon. The familiar verses came to mind. *With what sad steps O moon thou climbst the skies, how silently and with how wan a face.* Stepping down, he peered at the luminous dial of his watch. Within the half-hour, the first pale pink should appear on the eastern horizon. Shivering, he pulled the khaki jacket tightly around himself and leaned his head against the sandbags, closing his eyes, trying to detect any sound in the distance.

Despite the pre-dawn desert chill, tiny rivulets of perspiration slid down Major Charles Davenport's back. He was acutely aware of the peril facing his men. The 25,000 troops of the British garrison, South Africans for the most part, were hemmed in with their backs to the sea. For days Rommel had relentlessly pounded the fortifications in preparation for the final armoured assault on Tobruk. Davenport's company was holding the outer perimeter of the British line, guarding the one escape route. He understood the untenable nature of their position and appreciated the strength and determination of the Afrika Korps troops. Many would die this day, he reflected, as surely as the rising of the sun.

'Excuse me, sir.'

Davenport opened his eyes and stood erect. 'Yes, Corporal,' he said softly.

'Your tea, sir.' A young corporal held out a thermos.

'Thanks.' Davenport took the thermos, unscrewed the lid and said, 'Send for Mr Jameson and the sar-major.'

'Right away, sir.'

Davenport poured a piping hot cup of tea and let the vapours warm his face. After a moment, he took a swallow and savoured the sweetness and warmth. Two dim shapes appeared in the narrow trench, their faces obscured by the brim of their steel helmets. Lieutenant Jameson saluted and stood silently before the major.

'I'm almost certain they're coming,' said Davenport.

'I'm afraid you're right,' said Jameson quietly.

'Have all the dispositions been made?' asked Davenport.

'Yes, sir,' answered the sergeant gruffly. 'Believe me, sir, the boys are ready.'

Davenport took another swallow of tea, and then said, 'Our artillery won't be much help. They're short of ammo, and we'll be lucky if they fire a few rounds. And so, if the Jerries come in force – and if I know Rommel they will – the best we'll be able to do is delay their advance.' Davenport paused. 'Understood?' Both men nodded. Davenport detected a faint lightening of the sky and glanced at his watch. 'Well, gentlemen,' he said slowly. 'If it appears our line is going to be broken, I'll give the order to fall back. There.' He pointed into the blackness to the right and rear. 'Take the company to the second line, toward battalion HQ. There's a way out there, toward the only open road. Leave one squad as a rear-guard. Is that clear?'

'Yes, sir,' both men answered in unison.

'Good luck, then.' Davenport watched them disappear down the trench. He climbed back up on the fire-step and stretched his tall frame to the top. Straining to make out any sound in the distance, he watched the eastern sky slowly begin to glow. Dawn in the desert was a time of utter silence. The wind flinging the sand from the rim of the dunes, the constant buzzing of the black flies, would begin with the sun and the oven-heat. Davenport reached into his pocket for a small leather case. In the faint light he opened it and peered at the faded photograph of a pretty woman with stylishly curled hair. Goodbye, darling, he thought, this time it may really be goodbye. He closed his eyes, concentrating on her face, and offered a silent prayer. Davenport noted the time: ten to six. Suddenly he heard the droning of aircraft. A line of Stuka dive-bombers banked high in the pale sky and commenced a near vertical dive. The brilliant flash of high explosives coincided with a deafening roar, sending a pillar of smoke and ash from the centre of the garrison. Davenport turned back to the darkness and in the next instant detected a metallic clank.

He leapt from the parapet and, crouching on one knee, shuddered with the ear-splitting explosions of the artillery barrage. The darkness suddenly filled with bright light, and amid the hellish din his rational mind reasoned that the shells were falling harmlessly between the two sections of British lines. Rommel's short on ammunition too, Davenport thought, as he was rocked again by explosions. In the interval between the exploding shells he could hear the shouts of the sergeants, cursing the men to stay down and ready themselves. As quickly as the barrage began it was over. The first rays of the sun streamed from the eastern horizon. Davenport jumped to his feet and scaled the parapet. A thousand yards beyond the dannert wire he could just make out the silhouettes of moving objects and hear the deep roar of diesels and clang of wheels and treads. Tanks, perhaps as many as thirty in his estimate. As the black objects slowly advanced, the leading edge of the sun rose, illuminating the battlefield with faint, orange light. Raising the binoculars, he could distinguish clumps of infantrymen sheltering in the lee of the panzers, advancing slowly in a forward crouch. Davenport felt oddly detached, watching the advancing men and machines with a strange fascination. He counted slowly to ten and then shouted, 'Fire at will!'

The anti-tank gunners immediately responded with a loud blast, sending up balls of flame and smoke in the midst of the German line. One tank was hit, erupting into an orange fireball, 'brewing up' as the Tommies called it, and then another. What sounded like a flying train roared overhead and a heavy artillery shell crashed into the enemy line, sending up an enormous plume of smoke and debris. Amid the guns and scream of shells, the men raised themselves on the sandbag ledge and opened a steady rifle and machine gun fire into the advancing Germans. Another round tore a large gap in the enemy line and a second burning tank bathed the desert with a lurid glow. For a moment it seemed that the German infantrymen were falling back under the relentless pounding. But the brief British artillery fire had ceased, and Davenport watched as the German tankers ranged their cannons on the British line. Flames erupted from the cannons' muzzles, and rounds slammed into the sandbagged trench, throwing up clouds of sand and debris, filling the trench with dense black smoke. Amid the screams of the wounded, he could hear the harsh shouts of the sar-major: 'Keep up the fire, boys! Pour it on the bastards!'

Another round from an advancing tank struck not ten yards from Davenport, knocking him to the ground. He reckoned that the first line of tanks would reach the ditch at any moment and climbed back to the top of the parapet just as the lead panzer dipped into it. Turning to the young soldier at his left, he yelled, 'Send for Mr Jameson!' The soldier disappeared into the choking dust and returned after a brief moment.

'Sorry sir,' he cried. 'The lieutenant's dead! But the sergeant's coming!' The sar-major shortly appeared with a bloody bandage around one arm and saluted.

'Take the men out,' Davenport ordered calmly, ducking at another shell-burst. 'Leave one squad behind for cover.'

'Yes sir,' said the sergeant in a loud voice and turned on his heel.

After another moment the boyish-looking corporal who had brought Davenport his tea raced past carrying a 9-millimete sten machine carbine. As he clambered up the fire-step he turned to Davenport and said, 'Don't worry, sir. We'll hold them off.'

'Right,' said Davenport as he jumped down. The corporal lowered the sten to his shoulder and loosed a burst of automatic fire. Davenport made his way in a crouch down the trench, littered with wounded and dying men. As he neared the end of the trench, he reached to the top and vaulted over. With a quick glance to assess the position of the Germans, Davenport strode rapidly toward the knot of men half-running in a crouch behind the lead of the sergeant. All at once Davenport felt a terrific impact. He sprawled on his back in the hot sand, staring up into the blue sky, watching wisps of smoke float past, the stench of cordite filling his nostrils. Taking a deep breath, he raised himself on one elbow and tried to stand but found, to his surprise, he was unable to move his right leg. Gasping from a bolt of searing pain, he clutched his thigh and felt the warm, sticky blood spreading through the khaki. Oh my God, he thought, collapsing on his back. Within seconds a medical corpsman was kneeling at his side with a morphine syrette, which he jabbed in Davenport's thigh. As the din of battle faded, he felt himself being lifted, a sensation almost like floating, and the dirty blue sky dissolved into blackness.

Davenport awakened in the casualty clearing station. The morphine was wearing off, and the slightest movement of his leg brought more blinding pain. He stared at the canvas overhead and listened to the rumble of lorries. A nurse wearing a khaki blouse and blood-stained shorts appeared at his side and checked his pulse. 'How bad is it?' asked Davenport.

'You're a lucky man,' she said, casting an appraising look over the length of her patient. 'You've taken a 50-calibre machine-gun round through the thigh. But clean through. Missed the bone and artery.' She smiled briefly. 'But it will be quite a while, Major, before you're walking again.' She poured water from a carafe into a cup and lowered it to his lips.

'From the sound of it,' said Davenport after swallowing, 'what's left of the army's moving out.'

The nurse looked out the tent flap at the column of lorries. 'A bloody disaster,' she said with an exhausted sigh. 'Jerry's overrun our lines and trapped the entire garrison. The only ones getting out are the battalion HQ and what's left of your company. It was a miracle you were able to escape.'

Listening uneasily to the heavy firing, Davenport said, 'What about us?'

'We're leaving as soon as the ambulance arrives.' She inserted a syringe into an ampoule, flicked it with her index finger, and injected his arm. 'You'll be needing this,' she said. 'The road to Cairo is a bumpy one.'

'One last thing,' said Davenport, feeling instantly woozy. 'Were they able to evacuate many of my men?'

She looked grimly into Davenport's searching eyes and said, 'No. Only a handful.'

'Was a young corporal, with reddish hair, among them?'

The nurse merely shook her head.

'I see,' said Davenport, closing his eyes and succumbing to the narcotic sleep.

Standing at the precipice, Mary Malone Kennedy stared down at the angry sea on the rocks below. For a moment, buffeted by the wind, she imagined she was falling. Too many hopes washed away, too much pain, nothing to be gained by merely surviving day after day. And so she stood at the top of the cliffs, tempting fate. Backing away to safety, she wanted to scream into the whipping wind that she already knew the worst it could do, since the day, the hour, the very minute, her life had changed forever. The day they had explained that her tiny Anna's heart would never be strong enough to sustain her. Her baby was just over a year old, delicate like the finest porcelain. Mary had held her and held her, praying for miracles, but in the end her heart had simply stopped. At the time, Mary and David Kennedy, her husband of four years, were living on the outskirts of Boston, not far from her parents. She was born in Ireland but raised in Boston.

David was a charming young Irishman, tall with curly, dark hair. His accent, his attitude, everything about him recommended him to her. David was in Boston on a visit to his American aunts when he decided to lengthen his stay. He had found work with Mary's father and that was how they met. A simple case of love at first sight led to the discovery that David's large family was scattered among the very same villages in County Wexford as Mary's own ancestors. Her father had fled Ireland in 1920 under the threat of assassination by the dreaded Black and Tans. He and her mother had found America to their liking, feeling almost as much at home in Boston as Dublin but with a new world of opportunity. Indeed her father had prospered, using the skills he'd acquired as a radical pamphleteer during the Rebellion to found an Irish-American weekly, which, through determination and hard work, he had turned into a daily.

Mary and David had walked and talked and worked at getting beyond the pain of the empty place where Anna ought to be. They had found a peace between them that neither imagined they would ever manage. Then God had another word with Mary and took David as well. 'A freak accident,' said the officers who appeared at her door. A head-on crash with a delivery truck rounding a curve on an icy January morning. There were no words for the strangeness or the pain. This time she would suffer it alone. Although an insurance settlement would provide a comfortable life, Mary would gladly have exchanged every penny for just one more day with David. She was suffocating under the weight of her family's steady outpourings of condolences. 'Poor Mary' echoed in her ears.

And so, despite the protests of her parents, she sailed for Ireland, which she'd left at the age of four, and moved to her late grandparents' stone and clapboard cottage at Kilmichael Point, a rocky promontory south of Dublin, overlooking the Irish Sea. Craving solitude, it was the perfect place, standing alone at the end of a rutted track some three miles from the nearest village. Surrounding her were farms, intersected with hedgerows and ancient stone walls, separating her from her neighbours, who, though polite, kept to themselves and afforded her the anonymity she wanted. And she had the good fortune that the cottage had electricity, one of the last in the area to be connected before the rural electrification programme was abruptly halted with the advent of the war, without which the kitchen stove would have been fuelled with wood, the well water pumped by hand, and she would have lacked a radio, her vital connection to the outside world.

When she first arrived the war seemed a distant thing, like far-off thunder, especially considering that Ireland clung to its neutrality. But in no time the Japanese had attacked Pearl Harbor and the newspapers were filled with the battles raging in Russia and North Africa. Unlike her Irish neighbours, who professed indifference to the plight of the hated British, Mary loathed Hitler and the Nazis and had an intense interest in the war. Growing up in the newspaper business, it was news the family discussed across the dinner table each evening. Let her neighbours content themselves to believe that the Nazi threat could never reach their shores. Despite what they had done to her father, Mary desperately wanted the British to survive the German onslaught.

And thus a small notice in the London newspaper attracted her attention. The Red Cross was calling for volunteers on the home front to write to the boys of the British military. At first the inertia of her grief would not allow it. Then, in the end, she did write. It took several weeks, but she received a simple response from a young soldier by the name of Ian James Duthie. In no time, they began a steady correspondence. The homesickness of this 19-year-old from a Scottish village, and his constant fear of death fighting in the North African desert emerged from his crudely scrawled and misspelled letters. She was so much older at 26 that it seemed somehow inappropriate, but she knew the letters had nothing to do with romance, but only comforting a young soldier in a faraway place. Given the wartime postal situation, mail delivery was haphazard at best, though hardly a week passed without one if not several of the army envelopes waiting at the village post office. Caring for someone else, she eventually realized, was the perfect antidote for the pity – of her family, friends, but especially her self-pity – that for so long had trapped her on the edge of despair.

Most days the ritual was the same. Mary would wait until late morning and then, weather permitting, would bicycle the few miles to the village. The early summer days had been exceptionally beautiful, the sky washed a gentle blue by the morning showers, and the spongy turf a shade of emerald that Mary believed existed nowhere else on earth. Her heart was filled with anticipation when she dismounted the cycle at the post office and stepped inside.

'Hello, Mary,' said the old clerk. 'Lovely day.'

'Yes it is, Mr Coggins,' agreed Mary. 'Any mail?'

The old man rested his arms on the worn counter and gazed at her pretty face. 'Yes,' he said, 'but I'm sorry to say there's nothing for you.'

'I see,' said Mary softly. Smiling, she added, 'Perhaps tomorrow.' As she walked out into the sunlight she waved to Sarah McClendon, a young woman of about Mary's age from a nearby farm.

Sarah crossed the road and fell into step beside Mary, pushing her bicycle along the road. 'Coming to the picnic on Sunday?' asked Sarah. 'We could go together.'

'The church picnic?' said Mary. 'I hadn't given it much thought.'

'I happen to know there's a certain someone who's hoping to see you there.' Mary halted and gave Sarah a disapproving look. 'My brother says Jack Healy asks about you all the time,' said Sarah as they resumed walking.

'Sarah,' said Mary as they approached a small shop with the word 'Sundries' over the bright green door. 'How many times do I have to tell you. . . .'

'Fine,' said Sarah with a smile. 'But come with me to the picnic anyway.'

Bidding Sarah goodbye, Mary left her cycle and entered the shop. As she walked up to the counter, Mr McDonough, the proprietor, placed two newspapers in front of her.

'There you are, Mary,' he said. '*The Times* and the *Daily Telegraph*. Will there be anythin' else today?'

'Just these,' said Mary, as she placed a box of candles on the counter and fished in her purse for a few coins. A tall boy suddenly appeared from behind the shelves of tinned goods and shot past Mary with a box of sweets.

'And this,' he announced.

'Now, Donald,' said his father sternly. 'Put that back. . . .'

'It's all right,' said Mary with a smile, 'with all the chores Donald does for me.'

'Thanks,' said the boy, giving Mary a brief, adoring look before tearing out of the store. Mary followed him out, secured her purchases in the basket, and bicycled back home. She left the newspapers on the kitchen table, lit the fire in the stove, and filled the kettle. As she waited for the water to boil, she glanced at the front page of the London paper. Her eyes were immediately drawn to the far right headline:

TOBRUK FALLS
Garrison surrenders at loss of 25,000 men

Oh my God, thought Mary. Tobruk . . . the British Army in North
Africa. Her heart skipped a beat. Had Jamie been at Tobruk? She
couldn't say. With censors reading every letter, he never revealed his
whereabouts. But he was somewhere in the desert in North Africa. As
the kettle whistled, she scolded herself for always thinking the worst.
There were so many other places he might be, and even if he were at
Tobruk, the paper merely reported that the garrison had surrendered
and the troops were now prisoners.

Home. To England. Davenport could scarcely believe it. As he peered
out into the fog he reassured himself that within the hour the ship
should be safely within the Solent, where no U-boat would venture,
and that for now the fog rendered them virtually invisible. Having
survived the harrowing voyage through the submarine-infested
Mediterranean, he was confident they would arrive safely at
Southampton. Listening to the boom of the foghorn, Davenport
pulled the blanket more tightly around himself and thought of his
childhood home, a simple cottage with the midsummer roses spilling over the worn garden wall. His thoughts then turned to his
wife Frances and the telegram she'd sent him. The usual army cable
advising that he'd been wounded would have reached her within
days. And, as soon as he'd been able, he'd written from hospital in
Alexandria, assuring her that he would be fine and would be sent to
recuperate in England as soon as a ship could be found. Yet it seemed
an unnaturally long time before she responded with the telegram that
reached him the day before the ship sailed. For perhaps the hundredth
time, he considered the words she had chosen: delighted by his prospect for a full recovery . . . not to return home on her account . . .
put the war and his duty ahead of personal considerations. '*Duty*,'
Davenport said softly as he stared into the fogbank.
    A nurse appeared at his side and said, 'May I offer you a cup of
hot bouillon?'
    'That would be marvellous.'
    In a moment she returned with a tray and , bracing herself against
the gentle roll of the deck, poured him a cup of the dark broth.
Davenport inhaled the rich aroma before taking a small sip. The taste
of bouillon reminded him of his childhood, seated at the table in the

kitchen with his mother. He was relieved his mother had not lived to see him return in a wheelchair. She had been too sweet for war. The thought of the cosy kitchen of his childhood brought to mind images of the English countryside, the dark-green fields, hedgerows, and stately oaks, so vastly different from the tree-less wasteland of the Libyan desert. How he had longed for England. He took another sip of the rich broth and, peering into the fog, at last could see the faint outline of the Isle of Wight a mile or so in the distance. In a few short hours he would be home.

The midday sun had burned away the fog as Davenport waited at the top of the gangway for an orderly, savouring the warmth and fresh salt air. At the sight of the enormous stores of war *matériel* piled on the pier for the return trip to Egypt his wound seemed inconsequential. England was no longer alone. The vast resources of America could now be brought to bear.

'Ready, sir?'

Davenport smiled and said, 'Roll away, Corporal.' A small group of soldiers and civilians were waiting on the pier but Davenport scanned the faces without interest, certain that Frances was not among them. Perhaps she thought her appeal to his sense of duty might have succeeded in changing his mind – and the army's – about his returning home to convalesce. Before long he was on the train. Though most of the wounded were bed-ridden and had been transferred from stretchers to sleeping compartments, Davenport was still in his wheelchair, secured next to a window in the Pullman car, transfixed by the beauty of the midsummer English countryside. He forgot about Frances, forgot about the war and his wound, and let his gaze fall on a leafy oak *'which erst from heat did canopy the herd,'* in the words of Shakespeare's sonnet. Yes, it was a dream waking: home to England. With the gentle rocking of the train, he soon fell peacefully asleep.

CHAPTER TWO

DAVENPORT GAZED OUT the window at the faces on the platform – for the most part women with anxious expressions – as he waited for the orderly, who soon appeared, released the wheelchair and manoeuvered it into the space between the carriages. 'This is the tricky bit,' he said, as he placed one arm under Davenport's legs and the other around his shoulders, gently lifted him and carried him down the steps. Davenport winced at the pain and sought to avoid the stares of the people crowding around him. Not often since Dunkirk had the public endured the sight of wounded men returning from the field of defeat. The sergeant lowered him into a waiting wheelchair attended by a nurse in a long, grey cloak. He scanned the faces in the slender hope of finding Frances. As the nurse wheeled him past trolleys of luggage and throngs of soldiers, Davenport considered how strange it was to be back in London. He felt as if he might simply hail a taxi to his flat in South Kensington. He visualized Frances in the sitting-room, dark hair stylishly curled, soft cashmere revealing the curve of her breasts. The image stirred a fleeting moment of desire. God, he reflected, it had been so long. As they went inside the terminal, Davenport motioned to a telephone box and said, 'Nurse, I'd like to make a call.'

'Certainly, Major.' She rolled the chair to the box, opened the door, and angled it inside. Davenport reached for a coin, cradled the receiver, and dialled the familiar number, listening as the phone rang and rang. Despite the fact that Frances could not possibly have known the date of his arrival and, that for all he knew, she was merely outside in the garden, his heart sank. He turned to the nurse with a wan smile and said, 'No one home.' Taking the handles of the wheelchair, she manoeuvered him to the exit, where a line of drab green ambulances had taken the place of the usual queue of black taxis. The ambulances had attracted a small crowd. Davenport sat ramrod straight as two orderlies helped him onto a waiting stretcher, which they loaded into the back of an ambulance. The doors closed, engines started, and the caravan wound its way through London and onto a wide thoroughfare heading south.

Davenport dozed in the mid-afternoon warmth, waking to peer out at the green fields and hedgerows of the Kent countryside. Passing over a bridge he observed a sign for the town of Tunbridge Wells. After navigating its streets, the ambulances continued down a country lane, turning at a sign for 'Abbey's Gate.' A quarter-mile down a tree-lined drive, they arrived at the ivy-covered Rushlake Auxiliary Hospital. The Royal Army Medical Corps had built the hospital in 1916 to deal with the flood of wounded from the Battle of the Somme. It was a large structure with a central administrative building and two identical wings, one for enlisted men and the other for officers. At the sound of the arriving ambulances, a tall, grey-haired officer emerged, followed by nurses in crisp uniforms, with tall, white caps. After the more serious cases were dealt with, Davenport was helped into a wheelchair and pushed along the walkway to the arched entrance.

'Welcome to Rushlake Auxiliary,' said the grey-haired officer. 'I understand you've come a long distance, all the way from Alexandria.'

'Yes,' replied Davenport, 'it's quite a relief to be here.' The nurse wheeled him to the front desk, where an older woman with an air of seniority stood behind the counter.

'Good afternoon, Major,' she said. 'Your name?'

'Charles Davenport.'

Consulting her chart, she said to the nurse, 'Room 309. Oh, and Major Davenport, you have a letter and a telegram.' She produced the items from a drawer and handed them across the counter.

'Thanks,' said Davenport, stuffing the envelopes in his jacket without a glance as the nurse turned the wheelchair and rolled him down a long corridor. They shortly arrived at a ground floor room with two beds, separated by a cloth screen, and a window that looked out on the courtyard. The bed on the left appeared to be occupied, but its occupant was absent. The nurse helped him out of the chair and to sit on the bed. Lightly massaging his wounded thigh, he sighed audibly. Meeting the young nurse's eyes, he said, 'Long day.'

'Well, Major,' she said with a smile intended to brighten his mood, 'I'm afraid you're going to be under our supervision for a time.'

Davenport thought back to the dingy room in Alexandria and the heavy-set, older nurse who'd cared for him there. 'I can imagine worse,' he said, returning the smile.

After arranging the pillows, the nurse helped Davenport to lie down. 'You should rest for a while,' she said. 'I'll look in on you after a bit.' Once alone, Davenport unbuttoned his jacket and removed the two envelopes. He studied the familiar cursive on the cream-coloured envelope and, taking a deep breath, extracted the letter and slowly began to read:

6 July 1942
London

Dear Charles,

Several weeks have now passed since I was notified you were

16

wounded and I have finally ascertained that you are being evacu-
ated to an army hospital in Sussex, where I'm hoping this letter
will be awaiting you upon your arrival. From your letter I was
greatly relieved to learn that your injury is not serious and that
you should be able to return to your regiment.

Davenport put the letter aside and stared at the whitewashed
ceiling. He patted the bandage beneath his trouser-leg. With a sigh,
he continued to read:

I hate the war, Charles, not only for what it has done to you
but for my miserable existence with you away. There's nothing
decent to eat, I'm forced to wear the same worn-out clothes day
after day, and the city is dark and depressing thanks to the blackout and the blitz. And unlike the other army wives, I can't quite
bring myself to help out in the war effort sewing bandages or
volunteering at the canteen. I often wonder if things might have
been different for us if, with all our connections, you might have
arranged a staff posting somewhere nearby rather than plunging
off to North Africa.

There's something I must tell you, Charles, and, painful as it
is, I know no other way than to say it straight out. With you so
far away, and for so long, and I so lonely . . .

Davenport put the letter aside, conscious of the pounding of his
heart. No, he thought, not this. Biting his lip, he turned back to her
letter:

– I began seeing someone else. And, though I was determined not
to let it happen, well, it did and, frankly, I'm in love with him.

Davenport choked back a sob and rubbed a tear from his eye.
With a trembling hand, he quickly finished reading:

– When I learned you'd been wounded, I thought you would stay
with the army in Egypt and it wouldn't come to this. But now that
you're here, there's no getting round it. The truth is, it's made me
realize how little we really have in common.

Charles, I know it's a shock but I must ask you for a divorce.
The fault is entirely mine, but sadly these things happen. I've

spoken to a solicitor who assures me it can all be arranged quietly and without a lot of fuss. As soon as you're able, please come for your things. I pray for your full and speedy recovery.

Warmly,

Frances

Davenport tossed the letter aside with a groan. Warmly? Surely she could have chosen a more fitting valediction. He buried his face in the pillow, convulsed with sobs. It was in this wretched condition that he was startled by a cheerful male voice calling out, 'Halloo.'

The same young nurse stood in the doorway grasping the handles of a wheelchair in which a young man, wearing standard issue, blue cotton pyjamas and a dark-blue robe, was seated. Davenport quickly noted that his right sleeve was pinned to his robe: his right leg was also missing, and a black patch covered one eye. The young man flashed an easy smile and said, 'I'm Evan Hockaday, First Lieutenant. And who would you be?'

'Charles. Charles Davenport.'

'Well, Charles, sorry about the leg and all that, but it's dashed good having you here.' The nurse rolled the wheelchair to Hockaday's bedside and helped him out.

'There you are,' she said, as Evan settled on the bed. 'Major Davenport, how are you getting along?'

'Very well, thank you.'

'Then I'll be going.' The nurse closed the door behind her.

Evan cast an appraising glance at Davenport and continued to smile in an open, cheerful way. 'I wonder if you'd mind,' he said, 'calling me by my Christian name?'

'Of course,' said Davenport. He glanced at Evan's youthful face, with fine flaxen hair and an almost pink complexion. His good eye was cornflower blue.

'What happened to you?' asked Evan.

'Took a machine-gun round in the thigh at Tobruk.'

'Bloody disaster, Tobruk.'

'Indeed. And what about you?'

'I was wounded at Gazala as soon as our unit came into the line. I was an FOO with the 4/14 Field Battery. Direct hit from a 105.' He flashed a boyish grin. 'Rommel's gunners had excellent aim.'

Davenport nodded and said, 'Sorry. Tough break.' Leaning back on the pillow, he stared up at the ceiling, absently tapping Frances's letter on his palm.

'Bad news?' said Evan.

Davenport looked at him with a frown and said, 'You might say so.' He closed his eyes, feeling suddenly exhausted, and dozed. When he awoke, he remembered the telegram on the bedside table. He reached for it and tore it open. As he read it, he ran a hand through his hair and whistled softly.

'More news?' asked Evan

'Yes,' said Davenport bitterly. 'I've been reassigned. To a desk job in the War Office, as soon as I'm discharged.'

Ever since Jamie's last letter, with its obscure, dark comment about the desperateness of the British position, Mary had waited and watched for the post. With the news of the fall of Tobruk and the passing of weeks, she grew increasingly frantic. She wrote to the Red Cross in London but received no reply. She even cabled an enquiry to the Army Office of Personnel and received a terse response that such information was restricted to next of kin. Mary soon lost hope of ever learning Jamie's fate. Venturing back to the rim of the cliffs on another blustery day, an idea suddenly came to her. Mary thought of the officer of whom Jamie had often written . . . but what was the name? Returning to the neat bundle of letters, she found it: Major Charles Davenport. Perhaps if she could get a letter to him, he might be able to explain. She settled at the kitchen table and, taking a sheet of pale blue stationery, she thought for a moment and then wrote:

20 July 1942
Kilmichael Point
County Wexford
Ireland

Dear Major Davenport,

Through my participation in the Red Cross letter-writing programme, I befriended a young man, Cpl Ian James Duthie, who served under your command in North Africa. I corresponded with Cpl Duthie on a regular basis, and then suddenly his letters stopped. I've tried contacting the Red Cross and the army, but no one will tell me what has become of him, as I am not family.

Sir, I simply must find out what has happened to Jamie. If you can remember this soldier, who wrote so admiringly of you, can you tell me of his fate? Please understand that this is not a romantic matter. He is simply a friend who has become very important to me. You truly are my last hope.

Sincerely,

Mary Kennedy

Though there was no more reason to think the major had survived the disaster at Tobruk or escaped captivity than Jamie had, Mary felt that somehow her letter might reach him. With some effort she learned the general delivery address for the British Army, and, in the slender hope that the letter might find its way, she dropped it in the slot at the post office.

It took about two weeks to receive a reply and, by the look of the envelope, it had been half way around the world. She gave Mr Coggins an expectant look as he slid it across the counter. For a moment she thought it might be from Jamie, but a quick glance at the neat handwriting indicated otherwise. She was conscious of Mr Coggins's stare.

'Another letter from the young lad?' he asked.

'No, it's from his . . . well, from an officer.' She slipped the letter in her purse.

Mr Coggins pursed his lips and nodded. 'Well, Good day to you Mary.'

She pedaled home as quickly as possible. Her heart pounding, Mary sat at the table and briefly studied the envelope. Tearing it open, she carefully extracted a single sheet of and began to read:

26 July 1942
Abbey's Gate
Sussex

Dear Miss Kennedy,

Thank you for your enquiry regarding Cpl. James Duthie, who served in my company. While it is the usual policy of the service to restrict communications to the next of kin, I have obtained permission to respond to your letter. It is with deepest sympathy that I must inform you that Cpl. Duthie was listed as missing in action and presumed dead. He fell on 21 June, in the Battle for Tobruk. Cpl. Duthie fought valiantly, defending his post when it fell under determined attack. He was a fine soldier, a good man and it was my privilege to serve with him. Please accept my condolences.

Yours truly,

Charles Davenport

Mary slumped on the table and pushed the paper away. She'd kept alive the hope that the letter would tell her of a young soldier recuperating in an army hospital or held as a German prisoner. But the words *presumed dead* echoed in her mind. She felt utterly alone, overwhelmed by the familiar, black despair. Feeling as if she couldn't breathe, she squeezed her eyes shut, trying to cry, but the tears wouldn't come. Perhaps, she thought, she had no tears left. After a few moments, she sat up and reread the simple letter over and over again, wishing somehow to draw a different conclusion. But there would be no more post . . . There was no more Jamie.

After several hours Mary finally summoned the strength to brew a cup of chamomile tea, her only means of stretching out the pitiful wartime ration. Returning to the kitchen table, she blew across the surface of the liquid, glanced at the return address on the letter and compared it to the postmark on the envelope. As she took a sip, she considered whether there might be a way to visit this Major Davenport, to learn more about Jamie and how he had died. For several months now she'd been considering a trip to London, taking up a standing invitation to visit a former college roommate who was living in London and urging her to enjoy what the city, even in wartime, had to offer. Making a note of the simple address on the letter, Mary pictured a map of England, trying to remember the location of Sussex. In the south . . . south of London, she was sure of that. Once she reached London, surely she could get a road map and find this Abbey's Gate. Mary penned a quick note to her friend, suggesting a trip to London a week hence and asking her to respond by telegram.

After what seemed an interminable four days, Mary bicycled into town in the glorious August weather, feeling an intense wave of emotion as she entered the tiny post office where Mr Coggins was seated behind the counter. 'Hello, Mary,' he said with a knowing smile.

'Hello, Mr Coggins. I don't suppose—'

'I'm sorry about the lad. War is a terrible thing.'

'Yes,' she said, blushing.

'But you do have this.' Reaching below the counter, he produced a telegram, which he handed to her. 'You saved me a trip to deliver it.'

'Thanks very much,' said Mary, placing the envelope in her bag.

'Goodbye, Mary,' he called to her as she hurried out the door.

She rose early and dressed for the journey. From her porch, she watched the first rays of the sun streaming across the rolling, silver-grey sea, and then she strapped her suitcase on her bicycle and rode into the village, where she hitched a ride on a horse-drawn wagon to the nearby town of Arklow and boarded the bus for Kingstown, the terminus for the ferry to Wales. As she stood at the railing, she was surprised by the small number of passengers until she considered the fact of Irish neutrality in the war. No doubt few Irish would be welcome in England on summer holiday. Once the ferry was under-way, she stepped inside the almost empty cabin and bought a cup of tea and a biscuit. Mary sat on a bench, looking out over the bow, and tried to concentrate on the visit to London, but her thoughts kept returning to Jamie and tracking down this British major. Was she a fool to think she could find him? What sort of man would he be? She imagined an older officer, with a thick neck and iron-grey hair, close-cropped military style.

The foghorn sounded as the famous headland of the Great Orme came into view. Mary rose from the bench and gazed at the lush green Welsh countryside, dotted with sheep, anxious to disembark and find her way to the train station for the long trip to London.

CHAPTER THREE

DESPITE HER FRIEND'S determined cheerfulness as she gave Mary a whirlwind tour of London, and their lively if superficial conversa-tions, Mary felt oddly estranged, unable to bridge the gap from their carefree college days to her present reality: widowed at 24, suffering the loss of a child, and living alone, far from home, older than her years. And, despite the typical Londoner's nonchalance about the destruction and privations, Mary found the bombed-out ruins, the queues and the shortages deeply depressing after two years in rural simplicity, untouched by the distant war. No matter how she worked at enjoying what little shopping was available, her thoughts kept returning to the possibility of learning the circumstances of Jamie's presumed death. It was therefore with relief that they parted company on the pretext of her visiting an old family friend in the south. She found a road map at a second-hand bookseller's, on which she finally located the village of Abbey's Gate several miles outside Tunbridge Wells. At Charing Cross Station she fought her way through the sea of soldiers and purchased a ticket for the 5.10 train to Hastings, with an intermediate stop at Tunbridge Wells. After spending the night at an inn, Mary persuaded the proprietor to give her a lift to Abbey's Gate, where she expected to find an army base of some kind. Instead, she found herself on the side of a country lane at the entrance to a gravel drive. With a frown, she squared her shoulders and started up the drive. When she rounded the last turn, her arm aching from the suitcase, she was brought up short by the sight in front of her. At the top of a slight rise, a large, ivy-covered brick building stood at the centre of a neatly manicured lawn. The shadow of a transient cloud passed slowly by. She must have taken a wrong turn, though she couldn't imagine how. Well, she would have to ask, and continued on to the curve of the drive and up the steps. Taking a deep breath she rapped the bronze doorknocker.

After a few moments a heavy-set woman in a dull grey uniform swung open the door and glared at Mary with a frown. 'Good morning,' the woman said sceptically. 'Is there something we can do for you?'

'Yes,' said Mary with a smile. 'I'm afraid I'm lost. I'm looking for an army–ah, what I think is an army—'

'Hospital?'

'No, not hospital. A base called Rushlake, I believe it is.'

'This is Rushlake,' said the woman, eyeing Mary curiously. 'Rushlake Auxiliary Hospital.'

'Oh,' said Mary, feeling utterly discouraged. 'I'm afraid I've made a mistake. Is there an army base near the village of Abbey's Gate?'

'I'm afraid not, miss,' answered the woman impatiently. 'There's scarcely anything at Abbey's Gate. Is there someone you're looking for?'

Charles Davenport sat before an old Steinway grand. He played a rich chord and then a melody he had composed long ago. There was a time when he had considered it a special song for Frances. Now it merely evoked deep sadness and longing. He was aware of a young nurse standing at the entrance to the room.

'What a lovely melody,' she said. 'What is it?'

'Oh, nothing, really,' replied Davenport with a self-conscious smile.

'Nurse Phillips asked me to tell you that you have a visitor. A young woman. Should I show her in?'

Davenport nodded and said, 'Of course.' Oh God, he thought. Frances had obviously decided to come after all. He felt a momentary sensation of panic, not sure he wanted to see her. He turned back to the keyboard and played a series of chords followed by an especially difficult passage. Mary stood at the entrance and stared at the man playing the piano. She walked slowly across the room, drawn to the beautiful, lilting melody. As she came nearer, she could see that he was sitting in a wheelchair.

'Excuse me,' she said softly. 'I'm sorry to interrupt.'

Davenport stopped playing and looked up at her with a strange look of disappointment mingled with relief. 'Hello,' he said with a slight smile, noticing her pretty face, bright blue eyes, and thick, dark hair.

'Major Davenport?' she asked quietly.

'Yes.' He gave her a curious look. 'And who might you be?'

Mary took a deep breath and slowly exhaled. 'Well,' she began, 'I'm sure you'll think this is very strange, and I apologize for just dropping in, without writing or calling, but—'

'Don't,' said Davenport. 'Apologize, that is. I hardly ever see a soul except these other chaps, and the nurses, of course, and frankly I thought for a moment you might be someone else.' He grasped the wheels of the chair and angled it away from the piano to look at her.

She braced herself against the back of a chair, feeling it was a miracle she'd found the officer, though he was not at all what she expected. 'I'm Mary Kennedy,' she began again. 'I wrote to you, enquiring about . . . ah, a young man named—'

'Yes, of course,' he said. 'But, please, Miss Kennedy, why don't you sit?' He waited for her to settle in the chair. 'I recall your letter now,' he continued. 'You wrote about Corporal Duthie. From Ireland, if I remember correctly.'

'Yes,' said Mary with a nod. 'That's right.'

'How in the name of heaven did you find me here?' asked

Davenport.

'From the address on your letter,' said Mary with a diffident smile. 'I'll admit it wasn't easy.'

'I expect not. I'm sorry if I seem a bit lost,' he added, amazed that she had gone to such lengths to see him but delighted to have a visitor. With an encouraging smile, he said, 'Is there something I can do for you?'

'To tell you the truth, I was expecting someone, well, different . . . older.' She looked into her lap, gathering her thoughts.

'Let me make a suggestion,' he said, 'I learned from a good friend the day I arrived here. It's Mary, isn't it?' She nodded. 'Well, Mary, why don't you call me Charles.'

'All right. You see . . . Charles . . . I had become quite attached to Jamie, to Corporal Duthie and, when his letters stopped, I was desperate to find out what had happened, and so I wrote to you.' Davenport nodded, staring into her eyes. 'And when you wrote back,' she continued, 'to explain that he was missing, and presumed dead. . . .' Mary swallowed hard, fighting back the tightness in her throat and the moistness in her eyes. 'Well, I thought that perhaps if I could see you, you might be able to tell me . . . to help me understand.'

Mary took a deep breath, struggling to maintain her composure. What a fool she must seem, baring her emotions to a stranger about a young soldier whom she'd never met.

'Are you all right?' asked Davenport with a concerned look.

'Yes, I'm fine.' Sitting erect, she began again. 'You see, I was counting on Jamie. Not so much on him, really, but on the chance to help someone. Looking back, I realize that it probably was a mistake, with the war, but I didn't allow myself to think about it. And now that there aren't any more letters, I. . . .' Reaching into her purse for the bundle of letters, she said, 'These are all I have left.' The words caught in her throat, and she tried to suppress an anguished sob. The room fell silent except for the twittering of the songbirds outside the windows.

Davenport stared at her forlorn expression, trying to make sense out of her words. 'Mary,' he said after a moment, reaching out to touch her lightly on the arm. When he caught her red-rimmed eyes, he said, 'Let's get you a cup of tea. And then you can tell me how I might be able to help.' She nodded thankfully, balling a handkerchief in her lap. 'Nurse!' called out Davenport. The same young nurse who had commented on his music appeared in the doorway. 'Could you bring us two cups of tea please?'

After the nurse returned with a tray, Mary sat for a few minutes silently drinking the soothing liquid. She put her cup and saucer aside and said, 'Thanks. You must forgive my . . .' She halted awkwardly, feeling embarrassed and wondering what he must be thinking.

Davenport responded with an encouraging smile. 'Perhaps it would help,' he said, 'as you've come all this way, to tell you a bit more about this young man and –' He paused to consider – 'and what happened to him.'

Mary nodded and said, 'Yes. I would like that very much.'

Looking into the distance, Davenport said, 'I remember that last morning quite clearly, indelibly, in fact. It was Duthie – your Jamie – who brought me my Thermos of morning tea. He was that sort of lad, always willing to lend a hand, never a word of complaint. There aren't many like that, you know.' Mary smiled. 'That was before daylight,' he continued. 'The morning of June 21st.'

'His last letter was dated the 16th,' said Mary.

'Yes, well, we were pretty well boxed in by then. And short of ammunition. At any rate, it wasn't long after Duthie fetched my tea that Rommel attacked. Just before daylight. I remember looking at my watch.' Mary sat erect in her chair, listening with rapt attention. 'First came the Stukas, then the artillery opened up, and not long after, the tanks.' Davenport paused to take a deep breath. 'You see, Mary, we were on the perimeter, the outermost line. We did our best to stop them, but with so little ammunition . . . The tanks were taking a terrific toll on our position, and I'd made up my mind to try to save as much of the company as possible if we were going to be overrun.' Davenport stopped and ran a hand through his thick hair. 'So I gave the order,' he said quietly, 'to fall back. But to leave one squad in position, to cover our retreat.' He searched Mary's eyes.

'I understand,' she said, nodding.

'Corporal Duthie was among the men who stayed back,' said Davenport. 'I remember passing him in the trench, carrying a sten gun. I remember his boyish grin. He was a redheaded Scot, with freckles.' A tear appeared in the corner of Mary's eye. 'I recall that he spoke to me,' continued Davenport. 'Something like, don't worry, we'll hold them off. It was the last I saw of him. I followed the men out of the trench, and then I was hit. A machine gun round, to the thigh.' He paused to massage his leg. 'But then I blacked out. I was one of the lucky few who got out. When I woke up at the clearing station I asked after the others. After Jamie. None of them made it.'

'I see,' said Mary.

'You might say he saved my life,' said Davenport. 'Mine and a good many others, with that extra bit of time. I'm sure the ones who stayed behind were overrun and almost certainly killed, with the fire they were taking. But there is a chance . . .' He stopped and looked Mary in the eye. 'A chance, a slim one, that he was taken prisoner.'

'Do you really think so?' asked Mary, sitting on the edge of her chair.

'There's no way of knowing, of course. I'm almost certain he was killed, but there is the chance.'

'Well,' said Mary, 'I should be going. You've no idea how helpful this has been.'

'I hope so,' he said with a smile. 'I'm glad you came.'

Taking her handbag she stood up and reached out to give him an awkward handshake. 'Thanks,' she said, 'for being so understanding.'

He gave her a last, long look, wanting to capture the image of her lovely pale face and her brave smile. 'Goodbye,' he said. 'Have a safe journey.'

Mary's trip seemed to last forever, waiting to board the trains in Tunbridge Wells and London and the tedious journey to the northern Welsh coast in a cramped second-class compartment, unable to sleep, left to her troubled thoughts. In a way, she reflected, she was a changed person from the distraught woman who'd made the trip to London a few days before. Emotionally and physically exhausted when she at last reached Wales, she found an inexpensive room for the night. The next morning she boarded the ferry across the Irish Sea, leaning against the railing in the salt air as the distant Wicklow Mountains came into view. At last Mary retrieved her bicycle from behind the post office, strapped down her suitcase and pedalled down the overgrown track the last few miles to her cottage. She had barely rounded the first bend when a flash of rust and white darted across the path under her wheels. Oh my God, she thought, I've killed someone's dog! She could hear the puppy's yelping and crying. Mary felt sick, but, as she approached, she realized the puppy wasn't hurt but huddling in terror. Taking its tiny body into her arms was a sensation Mary hadn't known in a long time. When Mrs McIlney arrived on the scene she was certain the puppy was dead, the way Mary was carrying on. When she realized that the dog was unharmed, she was simply angry at the ball of fur sheltering in Mary's arms. 'I've only three pups left,' she exclaimed in her thick brogue, 'from a litter we never expected, and if I'm going to spend my time chasing after them, I'll drown the lot of them!'

Mary smiled at the idle threat, and then, in a flash, the words registered, and she asked, 'Might I keep this one? I'll pay, of course. And tell me, Mrs McIlney, such a beautiful little spaniel. What's the breed?'

'Ah, Mary. Don't you know your history?' answered the older woman. 'She's the breed of royalty. Cavalier King Charles.' In no time Mrs McIlney was walking away with a satisfied smile, and Mary was riding on, her suitcase left behind for now and her coat bunched in the basket, the little spaniel within it, completely content, big brown eyes on her strange new owner.

Mary decided she'd best find a name for the puppy. She glanced at its pale pink belly rising with each little breath and her sparkling white fur broken by patches of rusty brown. Rolling past a break in the lane, Mary glimpsed the sea, and, at that moment, the word, the name, *Chelsea,* came to mind. She looked at her soft droopy ears, shiny black nose and big brown eyes and decided it suited her perfectly. As the last, golden rays of the setting sun bathed the side of her cottage, Mary and Chelsea arrived home, exhausted yet content.

The first thing Mary had done on her arrival in County Wexford was to wrap her grandmother's bric-a-brac and carefully store it away in the cellar. What was left was pleasantly large, low-ceilinged rooms. Sturdy, old furniture, and the things from the past that meant the most to Mary. The living room ran half the length of the front of the house, and the kitchen was typical of houses from the last century, with a large, old-fashioned range, a white enameled sink, and well-worn wooden table and chairs. Beyond that, a single bathroom, the master bedroom, and the small upstairs dormer bedroom. The heart of the house, though, was the living room, with whitewashed plaster walls and dark oak dado rails and almost no decoration. Her grandfather's ancient shillelagh hung above the wide cobblestone fireplace. Three windows with her grandmother's lace curtains faced the sea.

As soon as Mary brought the puppy into the house, she discovered the box for kindling next to the hearth and struggled to hoist herself over the side. 'Aha,' said Mary, 'you've chosen a home.' Removing the papers and kindling, she scooped Chelsea into her arms, folded her coat in the box, and lowered the puppy on top. Mary plumped a chintz pillow on the sofa and surveyed the room, thinking how much more like home it felt now that she had a partner with whom to share it.

As she turned to go to her bedroom, Mary paused at her grand-mother's upright piano and glanced at the framed photographs on its top of the people who had mattered most: Anna and David, and the faded army snapshot Jamie had sent her. Her heart broke to see them. Running her fingers down the filigree frames, she knew she was letting go of wishes and dreams, ones she could never have. The piano brought to mind the handsome young officer in his wheelchair in the hospital and the anguished look she had caused him. Seating herself, Mary played several notes on the yellowed keys, thinking about the lovely music he was playing when she entered the room. The melody stayed with her as she tidied things, preparing for bed.

CHAPTER FOUR

EVAN HOCKADAY SAT in a square of warm sunshine on the edge of the lawn with a worn, leather-bound Bible open in his lap. He looked up to observe Charles Davenport walking slowly toward him aided by a pair of crutches. Davenport leaned the crutches against a wooden bench next to Hockaday's wheelchair and lowered himself onto it.

'From the look of it,' said Evan, 'you won't be needing those much longer.'

Davenport reached his hand down to the muscle of his right thigh. 'Sawbones tells me if I keep working at it, perhaps in a week I should be walking with only a cane.'

'Well, then,' said Evan, 'I suppose that means you'll be leaving us.'

Davenport gazed at his friend. Hockaday took pains to dress in uniform whenever possible, with the empty right sleeve pinned to his chest and the right trouser leg carefully folded under him. 'Yes, Evan, I believe that's right,' Davenport said. 'I only wish that meant returning to Egypt rather than this bloody assignment in London.'

'You're a strange contradiction,' said Evan. Davenport waited for an explanation. 'Well,' Evan continued, 'it strikes me as a bit odd that someone like you, with your—'

'Education?'

'Yes, education,' Evan agreed, 'but more than that. Your interests. Your love of poetry, for example. I should have thought you'd rather be back in the cloisters with your cherished Shakespeare than returning to the front. Seriously, Charles, you *should* be on the planning staff, not back in the bloody desert.'

Davenport listened to the hum of the insects in the rose bushes and absently massaged his thigh. 'Strange as it may seem,' he said after a while, 'I actually miss it. Something about it . . . the intensity . . . everything matters so much more.'

'Well, you'd just get yourself killed,' said Evan with unexpected emotion. 'You know, I never met anyone quite like you in school—whom I would consider your equal as a scholar. I'm curious how Frances's father felt about your academic aspirations.' As usual, Evan chose an oblique tack when touching on the painful topic of Davenport's divorce.

Davenport uttered a short laugh. 'He never cared for me anyway. Told Frances she'd married beneath herself, which, of course, was true. But my choice of a career at the university? Teaching poetry, no less?' Davenport smiled up at the bright blue sky.

'And he, of course,' added Evan, 'a rich banker in the City, would have greatly preferred a well-born if daft son-in-law with aspirations no greater than winning a large wager on the first race at Epsom.' Davenport merely nodded. 'Well, then, Charles. . . .' Hockaday paused. 'Why *did* you marry her?'

Davenport folded his hands in his lap. 'She was a student,' he said, 'when we met. Very bright, very pretty.' Hockaday smiled encouragingly. 'And, as was the fashion in those days among well-born girls, something of a rebel.'

'Raising funds for the Republicans in Spain,' suggested Evan. 'That sort of thing?'

'Yes,' said Davenport. 'And as I was her instructor, she, well. . . .'

'Fell head over heels for the handsome young don.'

'I should have known better,' said Davenport, 'but I convinced myself that she didn't care for the life she'd been born to, that we could live happily in poverty, surrounded by books and ivy-covered walls.' He shook his head. 'And, though I was certain I could help her to become more, well, *interested* in ideas, gradually things began to change. After a year or so,' he concluded with a frown, 'she began complaining. She was desperate to see her old friends and insisted on taking a flat in South Kensington – with funds from her trust – though it meant a long commute for me.'

'I see,' said Evan. 'Tell me something else,' he said in a cheerful tone. 'What is it about these Elizabethan poets you find so captivating?'

'Oh, that's actually quite simple,' said Davenport, leaning forward on his elbows. 'They had the most extraordinary grasp of iambic pentameter. There's nothing equal to it in English literature. It must have simply flowed in their blood.'

Evan opened the Bible in his lap. 'Yes,' he agreed. 'Just as the translators of the Authorized Version were similarly steeped in that noble mere.'

'Really?' remarked Davenport. 'I had no idea.'

Hockaday looked at him seriously for a moment, then broke into another cheerful smile. 'You should try reading it. As I keep telling you, it could save your soul.'

'Tell me something,' said Davenport, 'no doubt you'll be leaving here before long, will you go home to your family?'

'Leave the service, you mean?' asked Evan with surprise. 'Certainly not. I'm sure the army can find something useful for me.' He looked intently at Davenport with his good eye. 'We must win this war, Charles. With all my heart I believe that. I'm sure they'll find a place for me.'

Davenport studied Hockaday. He would spend the rest of his life an invalid, dependent upon others for the most elementary needs. And yet there was not a trace of bitterness or self-pity. Davenport wondered where he came by this remarkable strength and determination, somehow to remain in the army and help defeat the hated Germans. 'Well,' he said. 'you're a brave chap, Evan – or perhaps merely a stubborn one. But who knows? We certainly need every man.'

After a moment Evan said, 'Charles, the woman who was here to see you last week.'

'Yes?'

'I'm curious. She seemed terribly attractive. But terribly unhappy as well.'

Davenport thought about Mary Kennedy, with her flashing blue eyes, suddenly dissolving into unreachable despair. 'Yes, Evan,' he said after a pause, 'she'd been participating in the Red Cross programme, you know, writing to the boys overseas.'

'I'm vaguely familiar with it.'

'Well, she was corresponding with a young lad in my company. He was one of the unfortunate ones who didn't make it out at Tobruk. so when his letters stopped coming, she was desperate to learn what had happened, and eventually wrote to me. Naturally, I sent her the usual note, that he was listed as missing and presumed dead.'

'Was she in love with him?'

'I don't think so. There was more to it, something about the importance of the correspondence that I couldn't quite follow.' Davenport stopped, remembering the way she looked, the pain in her eyes, when she tried to explain. There was something about her sadness he hadn't been able to make sense of. 'At any rate,' he began again, 'she was greatly relieved to learn a few of the details of what happened.'

'I see,' said Evan.

Davenport suddenly stood up from the bench and grabbed his crutches. 'Well,' he said between clenched teeth, 'I'd best get back to work.'

Emerging from sleep to the tap of tiny paws brought a smile to Mary's face. Sitting up, she grabbed her white chenille robe, and with Chelsea yapping at her feet, went out to greet the day. Sitting on the cottage steps, she petted the pup curled in her lap and began again to frame her letter to the officer. Over and over during the night she had searched for a way to explain the intensity of her feelings. Slowly the letter took shape, the words entwined with the dimly remembered melody he was playing when she entered the room. Mary placed Chelsea on the damp grass and looked into her wide, intelligent eyes. 'Don't venture too close to the cliffs,' she warned, pointing toward the top of the thirty-foot drop to the crashing surf. 'I've got a letter to write. Then we'll have our breakfast.'

Mary stared at the sheet of pale blue paper on her writing desk, the nib of her pen suspended just above the surface. Then in her smooth, neat script, she began to write:

20 August 1942
Kilmichael Point

Dear Major Davenport,

I wanted to thank you again for your kindness in taking the time to see me and explain the circumstances of Jamie's apparent death. You have no idea how much better I feel knowing that he died courageously so that others might escape, and that there is at least some possibility that he was taken prisoner. I also feel I owe you an explanation as to why his disappearance caused me so much distress.

You see, Jamie was the last in a series of losses in my life. Several years ago, my husband and I lost our only baby, and shortly afterward my husband was killed in an accident. I came to Ireland from America to escape these painful memories, and my correspondence with Jamie had been helping to restore some purpose to my life. With his disappearance, I'm afraid they caught up with me again. I deeply appreciate your kindness and understanding, which greatly helped me to put things in proper perspective.

With hopes for your speedy recovery and warm regards,
Mary Kennedy

Carefully folding the letter in an envelope and addressing it as before, she felt a great burden had been lifted from her. What she wanted was a long walk on the beach in the delightful weather. But first she would post the letter. Pulling up at the post office, she took Chelsea from the basket and leaned the bicycle against the kerb. With the pup trotting along, she entered the small stone building and joined the queue.

'Good morning, Mrs O'Flaherty,' said Mary brightly to the petite, elderly woman standing in front of her. 'Lovely day.'

'Why, hello, Mary,' she said, turning away from her parcel. 'You must be so lonely, all by yourself out there on the point,' she added. 'Promise me you'll come by for tea.'

'Thanks,' said Mary. 'I will.' When her turn came, Mary placed her envelope on the counter as Mrs O'Flaherty bent down to caress the puppy's silky ears.

'Well, Mary,' said Mr Coggins, 'where have you been of late? I haven't seen hide nor hair of you these many days.'

'I've been away,' said Mary with a happy smile. 'In England.'

'England?' repeated the old man with exaggerated surprise.

'Yes,' said Mary, vaguely aware of Mrs O'Flaherty lingering behind her. 'To London.' Anticipating the question, she added, 'To see an old friend from college.'

'I see,' said Mr Coggins, who was studying the name and address on the envelope.

Glancing from his face to the letter, Mary said, 'And I've been to see the commanding officer of the unit in which the young soldier, with whom I was corresponding. . . .'

'Yes,' said Mr Coggins, taking his eyes from the envelope to meet Mary's.

'To see the officer in the hospital, and get an explanation of what had happened.'

'I see,' said the clerk. 'And now you'll be corresponding with the British officer,' he added, dropping the envelope in the slot. Mary heard the sound of the door swinging shut.

'Why, no,' she said, taken aback. 'I expect not. Come along, Chelsea,' she commanded with a small clap of her hands. 'Good day, Mr Coggins.'

The lazy summer passed, with little more to occupy Mary than tending her garden, walks on the beach, and occasional trips into town for groceries and the Dublin and London newspapers. As usual, she'd arranged for the McDonoughs' boy Donald to deliver her purchases in his dogcart. Chelsea lay curled beside Mary on the sofa, ears drooping on her paws and a sleepy look in her wide brown eyes. All at once, she jumped to the floor and scrambled to the door, barking her puppy bark. 'What is it, girl?' asked Mary as she rose from the sofa. With a low growl in her throat, Chelsea stared through the glass at the big yellow dog yoked to the two-wheeled cart as young Donald McDonough, whistling a tune, walked up to the porch, his face obscured by bags of groceries. 'Hush,' said Mary as she held open the door. 'We don't want to frighten poor Donald.'

'Aye, she's a vicious one,' said the boy, as he walked past her into the kitchen and lowered the sacks to the table. Chelsea ran to greet him, tail wagging happily.

'Wait just one minute,' said Mary as she hurried to her bedroom for her bag. When she returned, the boy was standing beside the table, his freckled face screwed up as though looking into the sun.

'Are you for the British, then?' he asked.

Mary stared at the boy with a bewildered expression. 'Why, Donald,' she said, 'I'm not sure what you mean. I'm an American. Why do you ask?'

'Well,' answered the boy, without missing a beat, 'there's talk in the village that you've been to London. That you're for the British and all.' Before she could answer, he scooped up the tip money and, as quick as a flash, was out the door and gone.

Outside the War Office in London, on an early September morning, Charles Davenport stood on the busy Whitehall pavement and stared at the massive stone building. Despite two years in the service, he'd never been there. With his cane firmly in his right hand, he entered the lobby and made his way through the crowd of uniformed men. Smiling at the pretty receptionist, he said, 'I'm here to see Colonel Rawlinson. The Office of War Plans.'

'Third floor, Room 348,' she said, without looking up from her papers.

Davenport grimaced. Well, he considered as he started for the staircase, that was one way to rebuild the strength in his leg. When he reached the third floor, he paused for a moment to catch his breath before locating a sign on the bare, dun-coloured walls pointing to Rooms 300 – 350. With a glance at his watch he started down the long corridor, paying no heed to the soldiers hurrying past him. Finally, at the far end of the corridor, Davenport reached a door numbered '348' and the words 'Office of War Plans' on the frosted glass. A plain-looking, middle-aged woman stared up at him through gunmetal wire-rimmed glasses.

'How can I help you, Major?' she said with a trace of a smile.

Davenport removed his hat and said, 'I'm Charles Davenport. I'm here to see Colonel Rawlinson.'

'Yes, Major Davenport, we've been expecting you.' She rose from her chair and said, 'Come this way.' At the end of a passageway, she opened a door, leaned inside, and said, 'Major Davenport is here to see you, sir.'

'Hallo, Davenport,' said Colonel Ian Rawlinson as he rose from his chair to give Davenport a quick handshake. 'Have a seat.' He spoke with a clipped, carefully enunciated upper-class accent and appeared to be in his middle forties, with thinning hair and a neatly trimmed moustache. Judging from his girth and carefully manicured nails, Davenport concluded that he was a typical, desk-bound staff officer. He smiled pleasantly at Rawlinson, who'd returned to his swivel chair before a large wall map. 'Well, Major,' Rawlinson began, 'I understand you've been recuperating in hospital. Have you brought your orders?'

'Yes, sir.' Davenport reached into his breast pocket for a folded sheet. 'I was discharged yesterday.'

'I see,' said Rawlinson as he studied the paper. 'All in order,' he said after a moment. He leaned back and steepled his fingertips. 'I understand you were wounded at Tobruk. A hell of a cock-up.' A sheen of hair tonic glistened on Rawlinson's forehead.

Davenport weighed his response to the colonel's vulgar insult. 'It was quite unfortunate, sir,' he said after a pause. 'A great many fine men were lost.'

'Unfortunate?' repeated Rawlinson. 'It was a disgrace.' He leaned his elbows on the desk. 'I suppose that's what one should expect with colonial troops, eh?'

'The South Africans are determined fighters, sir,' said Davenport. 'And their dispositions were, naturally, the responsibility of Eighth Army command.' Without waiting for Rawlinson to object, he added, 'There's only one way to beat Rommel, and that's at his own game. In a battle of manoeuvre, not bottled up with your back to the sea.'

Rawlinson smiled condescendingly. 'Quite the strategist, I see,' he said. 'That's a good thing, Davenport. We'll need strategists in this office. And speaking of Eighth Army command, I assume you've heard that Churchill sacked Auchinleck and Ritchie? Replaced them with Alexander and Montgomery.'

'Yes, sir.'

'Churchill,' said Rawlinson dismissively. 'Damn meddling politicians. In any case, Davenport, in your new assignment you needn't worry about beating Rommel in Africa; we have a far more formidable nut to crack. This is a new unit that's been cobbled together from a number of outfits. There's a briefing at 0800 tomorrow morning. You'll meet the rest of the men and hear what it's all about. In the meantime, see to your living arrangements.'

Davenport reached for his cane, rose, and said, 'Thank you, sir.' He looked Rawlinson in the eye and gave him a brisk salute.

As Davenport turned to leave, Rawlinson said, 'Your superiors at division HQ recommended you highly. General Bradford wrote that you have a fine intellect, quite the scholar at university.'

'Thank you, Colonel,' said Davenport, feeling slightly

embarrassed.

'Oxford or Cambridge?' asked Rawlinson. 'I was Balliol, class of 21.'

'Neither. I'm a graduate of King's College.'

Rawlinson imperceptibly arched an eyebrow and said, 'I see. And what did you study?'

'Literature. I intend to teach.'

Rawlinson briefly studied Davenport and said, 'Well, Major. Goodbye.'

CHAPTER FIVE

THE BACHELOR OFFICERS' Barracks on Wilfred Street was a poor substitute for the comforts of Charles Davenport's flat in South Kensington. Yet he was indifferent to comfort now. The pain of Frances's infidelity and rejection had burned right through his soul, filling his mind with poisonous jealousy and bitterness, robbing him of even the most fleeting happiness. The cold rain caused his thigh to throb painfully. Leaning heavily on his cane, he walked slowly into the barracks foyer. A private at the counter said hesitantly, 'Major Davenport?'

Davenport looked wearily at the young man and said, 'Yes?'

'Here you are, sir,' said the private, handing Davenport a letter.

Davenport was confused, staring at the blue envelope in the boy's outstretched hand. 'Oh,' he said dully as he accepted it. 'Thanks.' He trudged up the stairs and made his way to his room where he stripped off the waterlogged trench coat and slumped on the bed. He studied the envelope, at the unfamiliar stamp and postmark and the neat script, obviously a woman's. Davenport smiled and tore open the letter like a schoolboy. After reading it quickly, he kicked off his shoes, stretched out, and slowly read Mary Kennedy's letter over again, picturing the anguished young woman in the hospital, with tear-stained cheeks and the handkerchief knotted in her lap. Now he understood. No wonder she had sought him out. She was strikingly beautiful, in such a different way than Frances's carefully made up and coiffed good looks. And what about her accent? He imagined her reading the letter out loud. Ah, she was an American. The letter fell on his chest and he closed his eyes.

Later that evening, after returning to his room following supper and a few pints, Davenport switched on the lamp and placed several sheets of ruled paper on the desk and took a fountain-pen from the drawer. After drumming his fingers on the desktop, he wrote:

8 September 1942
London

Dear Mrs Kennedy,

I'm sorry it's taken so long to answer your letter, but it was sent to the hospital and has just now made its way to me. I've been discharged and sent to a new duty post in London. Thank you so much for writing. It saddens me to hear of your other losses. You have suffered far more than your share of life's tragic blows. I certainly understand why you were so upset over the loss of the young man, and I hope the few details I was able to provide were of some comfort to you.

By the way, it may surprise you to learn that your visit actually was one of the highlights of my stay in hospital. I know it was out of your concern for the fate of Corporal Duthie, but it nonetheless did me a world of good to have someone to talk to about our experience. It can be awfully lonely for the injured soldiers recovering far from home and loved ones.

I hope your journey back to Ireland was a safe one, and especially that the pain of your losses may lessen.

Sincerely,
Charles Davenport

PS Should you have any reason to get in touch with me, I may be reached at the address on the envelope.

The map room resembled a schoolroom, with a large wall map that showed in intricate detail the south coast of England, the Channel ports, and the French coastline from the Belgian border to the Cherbourg peninsula. Colonel Rawlinson stood before it with a pointer in one hand, the other casually stuffed into the pocket of his trousers. He surveyed the men, withdrew his hand from his pocket and checked the time. Davenport was in the third row between a heavy-set captain and a diminutive young lieutenant wearing thick glasses.

'Good morning, gentlemen,' Rawlinson began in a loud voice. 'Welcome to Special Planning Group B. Each of you has been carefully selected to participate in what may prove to be the single most important planning operation of the war.' Rawlinson paused as a collective murmur passed through the room.

'This unit has been formed,' Rawlinson continued, 'on the explicit instructions of the Prime Minister and the War Cabinet. Our task is to plan the greatest military operation in modern warfare.' He paused for effect. 'Codenamed Operation Round-up. The cross-Channel invasion of France.' The murmur grew louder.

Rawlinson paced, tapping the pointer on the grey linoleum. 'Prime Minister Churchill and the President of the United States,' he explained, 'have pledged to our Soviet ally that we shall strike Hitler's armies in Continental Europe in 1943. The Americans have committed a million men, twenty-seven divisions, and we shall add another twenty-one divisions, British and Canadian. The combined armies will launch the largest amphibious operation in history to strike the Germans.' Rawlinson looked out at the eager faces. 'Questions?'

'Sir,' said a young captain in the front row, 'has the point of attack been decided? Where will the landings take place?'

'Let me remind you,' said Rawlinson said with a stern look, 'that every word spoken here must be kept in the strictest confidence. Not a word breathed to anyone outside this room. Now, to answer your question.' Rawlinson turned to the map and extended the pointer to the upper right corner. 'The invasion may occur at any point from *here*,' – he tapped the pointer on Calais – 'all the way to *here*.' He ran the pointer along the curve of the Normandy coastline to Cherbourg. 'We won't know the precise location for some time.'

'But, sir,' interjected a somewhat older major, 'how can we possibly plan an invasion on such a massive scale without knowing the length of the crossing, the precise landing conditions, tides, enemy fortifications and a thousand other pertinent factors?'

'Our job, Mr McGrath,' said Rawlinson with a tight-lipped smile, 'will be to evaluate the advantages and disadvantages of various landing sites. With our colleagues in the Royal Navy, and the Americans, of course, we will be sifting through an enormous quantity of information bearing on that fundamental question. But there are several critical considerations.' He began pacing slowly. 'One, proximity to a deep-water port. It's no use landing a large body of men on a heavily defended beach if one lacks the ability to resupply them. And two, the element of surprise. Where is the attack most likely expected? Where is the coastline most heavily defended?'

From that point the questions became increasingly trivial and Rawlinson's answers like those of a bored university professor. Davenport quietly weighed the scale of the undertaking, wondering how a million American troops could possibly arrive in Britain by the following summer. And where would the twenty-one British and Canadian divisions come from, considering that, at the moment, the British Eighth Army was fighting for its life on the border of Egypt and Libya? When at last they were dismissed, Davenport found his way to his assigned office, a small room with two metal desks and a window with a view of Whitehall Place. He walked over to gaze out at a clear September day, pale-blue sky with a layer of thin clouds, that reminded him of rugby and cricket matches at King's College. Davenport reflected on his years at the academically excellent university, though it was certainly not Oxford or Cambridge. How simple those times before the war seemed.

'Hallo, there.'

Davenport turned to face a young captain in the doorway with his hands on his hips.

'It's Davenport, isn't it?' asked the captain.

'That's right,' said Davenport. 'And you are. . . ?'

'Ashton-Gore,' replied the captain as he shook hands with Davenport. 'Leslie Ashton-Gore.' He was of average height and build, with carefully parted dark hair and a thin moustache in the same fashion as Rawlinson's. 'Well, Davenport,' he said, as he took a quick look around, 'it appears we're going to be sharing this, ah, spacious accommodation.'

Davenport studied Ashton-Gore, at most 25, and judging from his pink, rounded cheeks and chubby physique, another staff officer who'd never been in the field.

Ashton-Gore walked behind one of the desks and lowered himself into a swivel chair. 'Tell me, Davenport,' he asked, 'where were you before being assigned to this unit?'

There was something about the man's too-casual attitude as he tilted back in the chair with his hands clasped over his ample middle, and his use of Davenport's last name, that grated 'Well, Leslie,' said Davenport, 'I was the CO of B Company, First Battalion, Sixth Regiment in the Second Armoured Division.'

'I say, old boy,' said Ashton-Gore, leaning forward. 'Second Armoured Division. Eighth Army, in North Africa?'

'That's right,' said Davenport. He walked over to the other desk and sat on the front edge. 'Until I took a German machine-gun round at Tobruk. Since then I've been recuperating in hospital.'

Ashton-Gore sat up straight and blushed slightly, as it was obvious he'd never seen action. 'I see,' he said. 'Tobruk. How frightful. Well, what do you make of this Operation Round-up?'

'I think the politicos have gone off their nuts,' replied Davenport. 'I don't know about you, but for the life of me I can't imagine how the Yanks are going to send us a million trained and armed men in time for an invasion next summer.'

'Well,' said Ashton-Gore, leaning on his elbows, 'I can't see how it's our province to question what the CIGS tells us. I mean, old boy, if they *say* they're coming, well, then, I should think they are coming.'

Davenport smiled at Ashton-Gore's earnest expression and public school manners. 'I learnt a long time ago,' he said, 'that it's one thing sitting here in Whitehall, pushing pins in a map to signify the movement of men and equipment, and quite another in the field, where transports are sunk and lorries sit idle for lack of petrol. A million men.' He shook his head. 'We had trouble enough equipping an army of a hundred thousand. But you're right, Leslie. Ours is not to question why . . .' Davenport slipped off the desk. 'What do you say to some lunch?'

'Damn, damn, damn,' said Mary as the door slammed behind her. She stamped her foot, sending poor Chelsea, paws unable to find purchase on the wooden floor, skittering across the room for cover. How was it that some ridiculous rumour was circulating? Word of her trip to England to see a British officer had somehow spread among the farmers and the few, mostly elderly, inhabitants of the village, and in the telling the story had inevitably been embellished. Returning to the kitchen, with its inviting aroma of cinnamon, she pulled the gingham apron from her neck and wiped her hands before taking the apple pie from the oven and placing it on the cooling rack.

'Anyone home?'

Mary turned to see Sarah McClendon at the door and called, 'In the kitchen.'

'That smells delicious,' said Sarah, untying her scarf and shaking out her thick auburn hair. She walked over to the counter and bent down to sniff. 'Mince?' she asked.

'No, apple. American apple pie.'

'You should bring it to the social. Are you coming?'

'Social? No one's said anything to me . . .'

'It's Friday evening at the church, and you should come,' said Sarah, settling into a chair at the table. 'It might be a way to let people know that you're, well . . .'

'Well, what?' She gazed into Sarah's green eyes.

'You know how people love to talk. And what with the trip to *London*, with Dublin only an hour away. *I've* never been to London.'

'What do you mean?'

'And seeing the officer. The British officer.'

'Oh,' said Mary. 'I see. Well, it's not what you think. I merely wanted to . . .' Sensing that it was useless to explain, Mary let the sentence die. 'All right,' she said. 'I'll come to the social with my apple pie. And I might even let Jack Healy have a bite.'

Later in the day, Mary decided to cycle into town. When she entered the post office, she smiled politely at Mr Coggins behind the counter, slipped the letters from her pocket, and handed them to him. As she turned to go, her presence unacknowledged, Mr Coggins muttered something under his breath.

She stopped and looked back. 'Sorry,' she said, 'did you say something?'

'You have a letter,' he said flatly, sliding an envelope across the counter. Mary walked over and glanced at the postmark before raising her eyes to meet his cold stare, both of them aware of the British army return address. Blushing in spite of herself, Mary took the envelope and hurried out, her haste no doubt a perceived admission of guilt. Once her bicycle was in the shed, Mary took the letter from her pocket, and with Chelsea at her heels, headed for the knoll of wildflowers at the top of the cliffs. Carefully controlling her anticipation, she settled on the soft grass and studied the envelope. The letter was from Major Davenport, of course. She hesitated for a moment, her heart inexplicably pounding, and then, taking a deep breath, she tore it open and quickly read his note. Mary leaned back, feeling the warmth of the autumn sun on her face with a smile of delight. Letting her gaze fall on the vast, irregular shadows spreading on the flat surface of the sea, she thought back to their conversation in the hospital, remembering the major's calm, clear description of the last moments of Jamie's life. That he should write of her visit as a high point of his stay there brought an intense blush of pure pleasure. She felt the need to write to him, to explain about Anna and David and all that had driven her to the hospital that day. Jumping up with a new felt energy, she dusted off the back of her skirt and, giving Chelsea a rub to share her good feelings, was off for paper and pen.

Mary sat on the porch steps to write another explanation to Major Davenport, though this time she wrote with a lighter heart:

14 September 1942
Kilmichael Point

Dear Major Davenport,

I am so glad you wrote! I recognize the impropriety of saying it, but being an American, I will assume that excuses it. It has been difficult here lately as my neighbours have taken it into their heads that I am loyal to the British, and if you know anything of the rural Irish, you will understand what that means. I have felt somewhat isolated, which made your letter doubly welcome.

With the sunshine drying the ink as quickly as the words poured out, Mary wrote of the loss of her baby Anna, describing her bright smile and fair skin and the weak heart that left her dead at one year and ten days old. She went on to tell the story of her husband's death, the insurance settlement, and her decision to flee her family and friends in Boston, seeking refuge in her grandparents' cottage. After pausing to gaze out at the waters sparkling in the midday sun, she finished with an enquiry about the major's new assignment in London, the indifference of the local population to the Nazi menace, and her frustration at having no one with whom she could discuss it. In closing, she wrote:

Since leaving the hospital that day I feel that I have found my way back to the world, thanks in no small part to your kindness. I do hope you will write again.
Sincerely,
Mary Kennedy

With a sigh, she realized she had filled over three pages of her favorite blue stationery. She slipped them in an envelope, all at once aware of an almost forgotten sensation . . . she was happy!

At the end of another long day studying reams of information about transport capacity, landing craft, and other minutiae of military logistics, Charles wearily returned to the barracks on Wilfred Street. As he walked past the desk in the front hall, the young private called out 'Excuse me, major. You have a letter.'

Davenport reached for the envelope and studied the return address, *Smith, Botford & Doakes* on Leadenhall Street. He furrowed his brow and tucked the envelope into his coat pocket. No doubt it was from a firm of solicitors retained by Frances. He walked to his room, fished for his key and let himself in. Leaning his cane against the wall, he sat at the desk and tore open the envelope. *Dear Mr Davenport*, began the letter. *Mr* Davenport, he thought sourly. With a frown, he slowly read the solicitor's letter, requesting Davenport's co-operation but threatening to allege as grounds for the divorce his abandonment and cruel mistreatment of his wife and the filing of a writ to enjoin him from *'entry into her household'*. Davenport carefully reread the letter, shaking his head at the threat of enjoining him from entering his own flat. He thought about the arguments they'd had over it. He had wanted to live near the university, but she insisted on living in South Kensington, to be near friends and fashionable shops. In the end, as with just about everything, she had prevailed, using her own trust funds to furnish the apartment. He stared at the letter. The threatened injunction was just a lawyer's tactic, designed to intimidate him. Tossing the letter aside, he rose and slipped on his jacket. If that's what Frances wants, let her sue him for divorce and parade before the court her adultery while he was fighting Germans in North Africa.

The following day Davenport awoke with a splitting headache. Moving his head cautiously, he dreaded the thought of going to the War Office until it dawned on him that it was Saturday. He tossed the covers aside, trying to reconstruct the evening. But the scene in the smoky pub, after God only knows how many Scotch and sodas, dissolved into a murky darkness. After dressing, he headed out on a brisk walk in the mild weather to the Embankment and, when he returned to the barracks the young private at the desk cheerfully said, 'Morning, sir. You have another letter.' For a moment Davenport feared another letter from the lawyers but then saw the blue envelope. 'Thanks,' he said, staring at the neat handwriting.

Once in his room, he sank on the bed and leaned back on the pillow. He carefully opened the envelope, a smile on his face and a peculiar lightness in his chest. The smile vanished when he read her matter-of-fact account of the deaths of her baby and husband. And what of her life in a small, provincial Irish village? Surrounded by ignorant Irishmen with their blasted neutrality, foolish enough to think the British were more of an adversary than the Germans. But Mary was not so foolish. Davenport was indignant about her mistreatment and surprised by the depth of feeling her simple letter evoked. Of course he would write again. He sprang up from the bed and paced back and forth. Then he sat at the desk, took a sheet of army stationery from the drawer and wrote:

20 September 1942

Dear Mrs Kennedy,

Thanks so much for your letter. I am so sorry to hear about poor Anna and the loss of your husband. I cannot comprehend the pain you have been through. To have faced the death of Corporal Duthie after everything else must have seemed an unendurable blow. Not having children of my own, I can only imagine the depth of your suffering.

I am pleased that you're an American, though Irish born, as I admire the Americans greatly. And though I am sorry you have been drawn into the war, it fills me with hope to know that the vast resources of the United States are now committed with us.

It is such a shame that hatred for the British should blind the Irish to the threat of the Nazis. And that your neighbours should have turned on you merely because you showed compassion for a young soldier is terribly wrong. But, having been brought up in a small town, I am only too well aware of the petty jealousies and prejudices that rule the hearts and minds of so many.

And what of the progress of the war? At the moment I fear we are losing it. If the Germans succeed in their conquest of Russia, I question whether we will ever defeat them on the Continent. Herr Hitler is unquestionably bent on far more than the acquisition of territory. In my opinion, the most sacred values of Western civilization are at stake. We must pray our Russian ally survives, buying us the time needed to build a great Anglo-American army.

I should tell you something about myself, Mary. I am a married man, but not for long. Upon my return from Africa, I learned that my wife is demanding a divorce. And so it seems that we both, through no choice of our own, have found ourselves quite alone. As for returning to the front, for the time being I've been reassigned to staff duty in London.

I hope this letter finds you in good spirits and that you will write again.

Sincerely,

Charles Davenport

Davenport put down the pen and read the letter. Was it too long and full of sentiment? Yet, he was attracted to her and wanted to encourage her to write again. For the first time in months, he forgot completely about his wound, about Frances, and the war.

CHAPTER SIX

BY NOVEMBER THE days were shorter, and despite the fact that the air raids had long since ceased, the charred ruins and the continuing blackout only added to the gloom in the capital. After more than three years, Hitler's grip on the Continent seemed stronger than ever, there was no let up in the appalling losses in the Atlantic and little hope the Russians could survive the *Wehrmacht* onslaught. Nor was there much cause for hope in the vast struggle against Japan that stretched from Burma across the Chinese frontier to the Southwest Pacific, and as far north as the Aleutians. After months at the War Office, Davenport's routine had become depressingly predictable, arriving at his cramped office by eight each morning and working well past dark before walking back to the barracks with a stop along the way at the local pub, or occasionally at the Officers' Club when he felt able to withstand the unspoken social strictures. An inner circle had formed among the men at Special Planning Group B, consisting of those like Leslie Ashton-Gore who shared Colonel Rawlinson's public school, Oxbridge pedigree. They treated Davenport with grudging respect because of his intellect and experience commanding troops, but it always stopped short of comradeship. The constable's visit to the barracks one morning to serve Davenport with a writ had added to his sense of exclusion. When the man appeared at the front desk, Davenport at first felt humiliation, but that had given way to brooding anger. There was a general understanding among the other officers that he had married the socially prominent daughter of a rich banker, and the fact that she was suing him for divorce merely deepened his ostracism.

Davenport took solace in his work, mastering the complexities of logistics, weather, tides, and enemy dispositions that would determine the outcome of any attempt to land hundreds of thousands of men on the French coastline. At the end of long days immersed in these studies, he would usually find himself in a quiet corner of a pub drinking enough whisky to dull the pain and help him to sleep. The only real relief came in the form of the blue envelopes, which arrived with regularity and filled him with such pleasure that he had grown increasingly dependent on them. Though she never complained, the fact that Mary had lost so much always helped Davenport to shake off his troubles. There was something about her quintessentially American attitude – fiercely independent, yet passionately idealistic – that he found so refreshing in contrast to the archly superior, morally vacuous class of officers surrounding him.

And then there had been the unexpected letter from Evan Hockaday, who had written to say that he had been discharged from Rushlake and reported for duty at a new assignment. The letter was strangely obscure, though Evan had mentioned the opportunity to put his university studies to some use other than 'bracketing an enemy battery'. He was anxious for news of Davenport's job and eager to find a time when they might meet. Davenport had looked for a clue in the letter's postmark, the town of Bletchley in Buckinghamshire. He had immediately written that he could think of nothing more appealing than a weekend away from London and a good long meeting, that Evan should merely tell him a time and place. Within days Davenport received a telegram, but it was not what he expected. It merely read:

JOIN ME IF POSSIBLE WEEKEND OF 10 NOV STOP
TAKE 800 TRAIN TO CHELTENHAM STOP YOU WILL
BE MET AT THE STATION STOP YOURS EH

As his train sped along, Davenport gazed out at the Cotswold hills, here and there a flash of orange or yellow in the clumps of trees, and the pastures the colour of pale straw. He closed his eyes, content that he had left behind everything that oppressed him: Frances and her blasted lawyers, the men in his section, even the war itself. In another half-hour the roofs of Cheltenham came into view. When they arrived at the station, Davenport, alighting on the platform, was approached by a man in a chauffeur's uniform.

'Major Davenport, sir?' he asked politely.

'That's right.'

'Right on time, sir,' said the chauffeur, reaching for Davenport's suitcase. 'This way. Master Evan's expecting you.'

Davenport followed the driver to a Bentley. Within minutes they left the streets of Cheltenham and were speeding through a thick forest that rose to a high ridge. After another half-hour, the driver turned onto a gravel drive flanked by massive oaks and elms. Rounding a curve, Davenport was surprised by the sight of a magnificent stone castle, with square, Saxon towers at each end and a reflecting pond in front. The driver brought the Bentley to a stop before the entrance, where a grey-whiskered old Lab bounded down the steps to greet them. Evan Hockaday waved from his wheelchair at the top of the steps. 'Halloo, Charles,' he sang out. 'Welcome to Marsden Hall.' Davenport climbed out and reached down to nuzzle the dog panting at his feet. 'Let's go inside,' said Evan as Davenport mounted the steps. 'Father is so looking forward to meeting you.' Davenport held the heavy oak door as a servant turned the wheelchair and steered Evan inside. They passed through a large hall, the walls of which were adorned with escutcheons and portraits of Evan's ancestors, into a spacious library. At the far end Evan's father sat by an arched stone fireplace with a plaid blanket on his lap. Davenport paused to survey the room. Bookshelves reached almost to the ceiling and leaded windows commanded a view of the rose gardens on the lawn and blue hills in the distance. Davenport followed behind Evan and, as they drew nearer, could see that Evan's father was very old, with blue-veined hands folded in his lap and skin the texture of parchment.

'Father,' said Evan as his wheelchair came to a stop, 'this is Major Davenport.' Davenport stepped forward, smiling awkwardly. 'Charles,' said Evan, 'my father, Lord Hockaday.'

'Hello, sir,' said Davenport. 'Pleasure.' For a moment he was unsure whether the old man had heard him, for he merely looked at him with a faintly benevolent smile.

Lord Hockaday then reached a hand to take Davenport's and, in a surprisingly strong voice, said, 'You've no idea, Major, how grateful I am for your kindness to Evan. I'm pleased you were able to come.' The servant drew up another chair, and Davenport sat. The sunlight streaming in the tall windows formed a bright square on the carpet between them, adding to the warmth from the embers in the fireplace. Lord Hockaday looked at Davenport with penetrating blue eyes and said, 'Evan tells me you're a scholar of Elizabethan poetry. That you taught at university.'

'Yes, your lordship,' replied Davenport, 'at King's.'

'Ah, the Elizabethans,' said the Lord Hockaday. 'I'm so fond of Wyatt and Sidney.'

Davenport beamed and said, 'How splendid. They happen to be two of my favourites.'

'Well,' interjected Evan, 'I feared if I got the two of you together, the rest of our time would be taken up with a discussion of long-dead poets, a subject I find . . . how should I say it? Positively soporific.'

Davenport smiled at Evan and said, 'We should hate to put you to sleep. Perhaps your father and I can continue our discussion over tea.'

'I should welcome it, Major,' said the old gentleman. 'But now, I shall leave the two of you and enjoy my afternoon nap.' A servant stepped from the shadows and helped him to his feet and slowly out of the room.

'Goodbye, Father,' called out Evan. 'Rest well.'

The earl excused himself after an excellent dinner, leaving Davenport and Evan to enjoy a bottle of vintage port in the study, where a fire crackled in a corner fireplace. Davenport sat in an armchair opposite Evan, whose wheelchair was parked beside the fireplace. Lightning flashed outside followed by a reverberating clap of thunder.

Evan started and said, 'I'm not quite used to unexpected crashes.'

A servant appeared with a salver, the bottle of port and two crystal glasses. Bowing to Evan, he asked, 'Shall I pour, sir?'

'Yes, please,' said Evan, now relaxed.

Once they were served, Davenport swirled the liquid to film the sides of the glass and took a sip. 'Umm,' he said, 'that's wonderful. Must be older than we are.'

'I shouldn't be surprised,' said Evan. 'I suppose you've been wondering about . . . all this.' He gestured vaguely with his one hand. Davenport merely nodded. 'Well,' said Evan, 'it's a bit embarrassing, but, there it is, and there's nothing to be done about it.'

'Don't be absurd,' said Davenport. 'Why should you feel embarrassed?'

'Well, I certainly wouldn't want you to think I invited you here to *impress* you. And I'm sorry I never said anything about all this when we were at Rushlake.'

'I understand. But this really is a magnificent place. How did it happen to come into your family's possession?'

Evan appeared to relax and took a swallow of port. 'Marsden Hall is the estate of the Earls of Hockaday,' he explained, 'as the result of a royal grant by George III in 1763. My father, a truly kind and generous man, is the seventh in the line.'

'I see,' said Davenport, 'which would make you, Evan, the eighth . . .'

'No,' said Evan with a smile. 'That makes me the younger brother of the eighth earl. My brother, Rob, will inherit the title. Which frankly suits me, as I have more important things to do than look after all of *this*.' He sipped his port and said, 'Now, you must tell me about your new assignment.'

'I'm in the Office of War Plans,' said Davenport. 'To be perfectly honest, I detest the place. With a few exceptions, they're all staff officers who've never been close to combat. Our CO, a colonel named Rawlinson, is a soft, arrogant man who favours the public-school men no matter how lacking they are in ability.'

'But what exactly is it you're doing?' asked Evan.

Davenport stared into the fire for a moment. 'Well,' he said at length, 'the truth is, I'm not supposed to discuss it.' He looked into Evan's good eye and smiled. 'But I know anything I tell you will be held in the strictest confidence. I've been assigned to something called Special Planning Group B. About twenty chaps working out of nondescript offices in the War Office.'

'I see,' said Hockaday. 'And what does Special Planning Group B do?'

Davenport paused and then said, 'We're planning the invasion of France.'

Evan drained his glass. 'Are you really?' he said with an admiring look. 'How exceptional. Tell me, how long before this invasion takes place?'

Davenport reached for the decanter. 'Churchill has committed to sometime next year,' he answered. 'I can't say as I blame him. After all, the Russians are fighting for their lives, and if they're gone from the picture, the situation is hopeless, as far as I'm concerned. So the timetable is set for the summer of '43, assuming the Red Army can hold on till then. But . . .' Davenport paused. 'I've been studying the logistics. I can't see how we could possibly mount an invasion until 1944.'

Evan stared pensively into the fire, listening to the rain dripping from the trees outside the windows and the occasional rumble of far-off thunder. Davenport took another swallow of port before rising and walking over to stir the fire. He turned back to Evan and said, 'I was certainly pleased to see that you've returned to active duty. Tell me about your new assignment. Just what is the army up to in the village of Bletchley?'

'When I invited you here,' Evan began slowly, 'I decided to concoct some cover story about my new job.' Davenport responded with a puzzled look. 'Well,' Evan continued, 'I've changed my mind. What I'm about to share with you is so confidential that I shall carry it to my grave, and you must do likewise.'

Davenport returned to his chair and said, 'Very well.'

'When I reported to Bletchley Park, I had no idea what it was all about – something to do with my having taken a degree in mathematics at Oxford.' He paused to sip his drink. 'What I am about to say you must never repeat to a soul.'

'You may depend on it,' said Davenport.

'There are several hundred of us at Bletchley, working in an old manor house in a secluded wood, each one a mathematician.' Davenport nodded and sipped his port. 'The Germans, clever fellows, have built this contraption that looks like a typewriter in a box. In fact, it's a highly sophisticated cipher machine.'

'A cipher machine?' said Davenport.

'Yes, for encoding secret messages. And we happened to pinch one,' said Evan with a slight smile, 'in perfect condition, from one of their U-boats. They call it Enigma.'

'Enigma,' repeated Davenport. 'How romantic.'

'The Germans,' said Evan, 'cocky bastards, believe the code can't be broken. Well, we've proved them wrong.'

'Good heavens, Evan. You mean to say you've broken their code?'

'Precisely. Every single order from the OKW, the Luftwaffe, and the Kriegsmarine to the entire fleet is first encoded by Enigma and then decoded with an Enigma machine in the field or on board ship.

And, Charles,' – Evan's bright blue eye sparkled – 'we've developed the means to intercept and decode *almost every message*, right at Bletchley Park.'

'Think of it,' said Davenport in an excited voice. 'What this could mean for planning the invasion.'

'That's the precise reason – the only reason – I decided to tell you,' said Evan with a satisfied smile.

The days turned to weeks, the weeks to months. Summer was long past. The crunch of fallen leaves on the lane had been silenced by the rains and winds of autumn. Mary now awakened each day to the sight of lacy frost curling from the corners of her window. Her garden had been turned and mulched, bulbs patted in place to herald the arrival of spring. Then suddenly it was almost Christmas, Mary's second away from America and her family. A wagonload of freshly cut fir trees had been brought to town from the mountains, and Mary had chosen a sturdy one. With the help of young Donald McDonough, she had hauled it into the living room and raised it by the stone hearth. Mary had fashioned pine boughs into a wreath for the front door and decorated the tree with her grandmother's collection of glass ornaments. Her mother had written, imploring her to come home, but the time to book passage on a steamer to America was past. With the U-boat sinkings in the Atlantic, and every available ship convoying troops and supplies, it was a virtual impossibility. Mary would face Christmas, and the winter, alone. She struggled to be cheerful, to look forward, not back, and, when the decorating was finally completed and the packages on their way to Boston, she surveyed her surroundings with something like satisfaction.

It was 23 December, and the steady, cold rain of the night before had turned to sleet clattering on her roof. By afternoon, snow had piled into drifts by her porch, the storm had moved out to sea and the smoke from her chimney curled into a sky of pure cobalt. Evening found Mary seated on the sofa by the fire, caressing Chelsea as she reflected on the small bundle of letters in her lap. Charles . . . Charles Davenport. At first his style had been formal, somewhat stilted, but before long she had become 'Mary', and she found herself waiting and hoping for his letters. He had vaguely described his new position in London and filled pages with his views of the war's progress. But eventually Charles wrote to her about his personal life; about his childhood, his mother, now dead, and his father, whom he hoped to visit soon . . . and, at last, his anguish over his failed marriage. Mary had been deeply shocked when he'd confided to her how he had learned, on the day of his arrival at Rushlake Hospital, that his wife had been unfaithful and was demanding a divorce. Through all of his letters a composite picture had slowly taken shape until she felt that she knew Charles Davenport, and, what was more, cared about him.

She rose from the sofa and stood with her back to the fire, watching the reflection of the flames in the glass ornaments, smiling to herself as she thought how fortunate she was to have made such a fine friend. Then she realized with a start that friend was the wrong word. The image of him at the piano flashed into her mind, the strains of his music playing in her head, and for the first time Mary admitted that she longed for far more than a friend. The admission troubled her. No man since David had elicited even a second glance. Yet now, to her surprise, she found herself thinking about a man she had met only once, with whom she exchanged weekly letters. She remembered his face, his smile, his kind manner as he explained about Jamie. She remembered every movement, every nuance . . . 'Enough of this wool gathering,' she said to the puppy following her down the hall as she returned the bundle of letters to their special drawer. 'I'm certain the man would think I'm off my rocker.' She looked Chelsea in the eye. 'And quite rightly so.'

Christmas morning dawned bitterly cold. Weak sunlight filtered through the lace curtains as Mary, wearing her heavy coat over her nightgown, struggled to kindle a fire. Standing with her arms tightly around her, she watched as the fire caught at last and spread quickly. The room seemed terribly empty with the beautifully decorated tree in the corner and the few carefully wrapped packages on a tartan rug. After a cup of chamomile tea before the fire, Mary dressed in her warmest clothes, shrugged on her coat, and, with Chelsea shut inside, carefully made her way down the treacherous path to the rocky shore. When she reached the ledge above the green sea, she sat cross-legged, her arms folded in front of her, staring at the horizon and listening to the waves surging on the rocks. After a while she unbuttoned her coat and reached inside for her silver locket. Peeling off a glove, she opened the clasp and studied the tiny photographs: David, so young and handsome, and baby Anna. She closed it and held it tight in her palm, shutting her eyes, concentrating on the images as she murmured a prayer. She sat there for a long time, oblivious to the wind and cold, just letting them go.

Climbing back up the cliff seemed almost impossible, but she made it, the icy wind pushing her back to the house. When she opened the door and knelt down, Chelsea threw herself into her arms. As Chelsea licked away the last of her tears, Mary smiled at the power of the dog to bring her back from her sadness. After warming herself before the fire, they sat by the tree and opened the few presents from home. With another log on the fire and Chelsea settled in her box, she whiled away the day in quiet contemplation.

CHAPTER SEVEN

THE LONELINESS OF Christmas took days to drift away. On the 29th, young Donald McDonough paid Mary a visit, enjoying the fresh-baked sweets and encouraging Mary to stop by the gathering at the Golden Anchor on New Year's Eve. Most people from the village and surrounding farms would be there, and with spirits high and spirits flowing, Donald was sure this was her way back into the life of the community. After much agonizing, she decided she would go. Though the bitter cold had abated, the snow had turned to slush, and Mary decided this was one of the rare occasions to drive her grandfather's aged saloon. With the wartime ban on the sale of petrol, she had only the ten-gallon jerry can in the shed; once it was gone, there would be no more driving. After a few lethargic revolutions, the engine coughed to life. It was long past dark when she arrived at the village crossroads. Wearing her long coat and rubber boots, she was not much to look at. As Mary approached the pub she could make out the sound of music and loud voices and the illuminated sign of the anchor over the door. She hesitated at the entrance, thinking for a moment she had made a mistake. But when she took a deep breath and pulled open the door, her spirits were lifted by the strains of fiddle and penny-whistle that filled the room. Mary hung her coat on the crowded rack, slipped off her boots, and surveyed the room, spotting an empty table at the back. Wearing her best dress, with a strand of pearls and touch of French perfume, a Christmas gift from her aunt, she smiled diffidently as she made her way to the bar and ordered a half-pint of the local ale. As she eased through the raucous crowd, she noticed Sarah McClendon with Jack Healy, who briefly made eye contact with her and then looked away. She sat at the small table, watching the festive goings on, and feeling strangely invisible in the midst of her laughing, joking neighbours, who, when they turned in her direction, seemed to look right through her. Two pretty girls in matching blue dresses appeared with fiddles at the music stand. When they rested their fiddles beneath their chins, they were joined by a teenage boy, who stood nervously before the crowd. In a single motion the girls drew their bows across the strings and the boy began a traditional ballad in a sweet tenor voice, *'Ta mo chleamhnas deanta . . .'* Mary sat transfixed, listening to the hauntingly beautiful melody and thinking only of the handsome smile of her dear husband David. A hush fell over the room and when the final notes died away, there was a moment of silence before the fiddlers broke into a lively jig.

Mary fought to keep her composure against a wave of intense sadness. When she looked across the smoke-filled room she noticed an unfamiliar man at the entrance, wearing a felt hat pulled low and a long coat. After hanging up his coat and hat, he looked in Mary's direction, striking her as sinister, with dark hair glistening with oil and a scar under his right eye. He seemed to have the same effect on the townspeople, who became quiet or looked away when he walked past them to order a drink at the bar. He drained his glass in one swig, ordered another and pushed his way through the packed tables, glancing briefly at Mary, to join a man seated alone at a nearby table with a pint of stout. She feigned interest in her drink as the two men struck up a conversation in voices loud enough to be overheard.

'Well, Tom,' said the stranger. ' 'Ere's to the bloody New Year. Out with the old, in with the new. To 1942!' He poured down his whiskey and slammed the glass on the table.

'Right you are, Sean,' said the other man with nervous perspiration beading his brow. He took a swallow of the chocolate-brown stout and wiped his mouth with his sleeve.

'1943,' the stranger said. 'D'you suppose the Brits can last another year? I'll tell you what, by God, it's the best chance we've had since the year '21. Let the Germans kick the bloody arses of the Brits, and the north is *ours*! There's no way in bloody hell the Ulstermen could last a month without the English. Say,' – he roughly grabbed the elbow of a young fellow in a stained apron picking up glasses from the littered tables – 'fetch me another whisky.'

Mary stared at the scarred surface of the table, afraid to look in the stranger's direction, fighting the impulse to rush from the smoky pub.

'But that's not all, Tom,' the stranger continued in a harsh voice, 'they mean to use the north as a base to strike against us. Make no mistake about it.' He paused as the boy returned with a glass of whiskey. 'Churchill and his gang would love nothing better than to send an army south from Belfast on the pretext of our blessed neutrality. So, do we sit back like a bunch of patsies while the Brits make ready to strike?' Several women at nearby tables cast shocked glances at their husbands, but the men pretended not to notice. 'No,' growled the stranger. 'By God, not the IRA!'

By now the colour had drained from Mary's cheeks. Her heart pounding, she took a sip from her drink and forced herself to sit quietly, pretending to take no notice of the conversation.

'Well, Sean,' said the other man, 'what exactly should we be doing here?' He pulled a handkerchief from his pocket and mopped his brow. The townspeople at the nearby tables fell silent.

The stranger sipped his whiskey before answering. 'There are things we can do,' he said. 'People we can help. Leave that up to me.' He smiled in a menacing way that everyone understood only too well. He started to push back from the table and then said, 'Oh, and the American woman' – he jerked a thumb in Mary's direction – 'who's sweet on the English officer? You'd better keep a sharp eye on *her*.'

Mary was momentarily stunned and then, indignation winning the battle with fear, abruptly stood up and approached the two men. A malevolent smile curled the stranger's lip.

'How dare you?' she said, her voice quivering. 'I will have you know, sir, that my father fought alongside Michael Collins while you were racing round your mother's knee.' Mary stood with her hands on her hips, her blue eyes flashing.

The man grinned up at her and said, 'Oh, she's a feisty one,' with a lascivious wink.

'There was a time,' said Mary in a stronger voice, 'if you bothered to learn your own history, when the Black and Tans had a price on my father's head. He fought for the cause and raised his children with a fierce loyalty to it. My private life is none of your damned business. Nor the business of any of the people of this village,' she said loudly, her eyes ranging around the room. She looked back at the stranger, her heart pounding and a flush on her cheeks. 'And there's one last thing.' She pointed a slender finger at the man. 'I may be the only one with guts enough to say it, but the Germans are the *real* enemy, not the British, and any Irishman fool enough to think otherwise is beneath pity.' Mary turned on her heel, and with her head high, marched from the room, took her coat from the rack, and walked out. Despite the cold, she didn't put on her coat until she was almost at her car. Well I've done it now, she thought, as she let herself in and pressed the starter. 'He had it coming to him,' she muttered. As she pulled out and accelerated toward the road to her cottage, she realized that she had parted the waters and would soon learn on which side her neighbours stood. Turning a bit too sharply onto the track, a dark form suddenly loomed in the headlights, and she slammed on the brakes, swerving in the muddy ruts almost into a tree. A good-looking young man she'd never seen before suddenly appeared at her window. Mary gasped with fright, but looking into his calm, pleasant face, she quickly regained her composure.

'Are you all right?' he asked as she rolled down the window.

'Yes,' she said, 'but you almost scared me to death.'

'I'm sorry, miss,' he said in friendly brogue. 'But you appeared out of nowhere and gave me quite a start.'

Blushing, Mary said, 'I almost never take the car, and in the darkness . . .'

'Well, goodnight, miss,' he said, moving away into the shadows.

'Goodnight,' murmured Mary, as she turned back onto the lane and bumped along the short distance to her darkened cottage. It wasn't until she switched off the ignition that it crossed her mind to question what this charming man was doing out on the country lane on New Year's Eve. The image of the young man was replaced by the menacing leer of the stranger at the pub as she wearily undressed for bed. As she slipped on her nightgown, she reflected sadly that whatever hope there was of restoring friendly relations with her neighbours was almost certainly lost. Perhaps it was time to call an end to her self-imposed exile, to go home to her family and friends. She looked disconsolately around the darkened bedroom. If it weren't for the war, she admitted, she'd be home now. Yet going home would mean giving up, in a way, surrendering to the expectations of her mother, and leaving behind the life she'd made for herself, as lonely as it was . . . and the chance of seeing Charles Davenport again. Besides, she was unable to return home even if she wanted to. As she turned down the covers and climbed into bed, she wondered what Charles would think of her. Thinking of him helped put the calamity of the evening and thoughts of home out of her mind, and she fell asleep.

Unfortunately, it didn't last. She awoke with a start, her mind racing with images of her encounter with the stranger, conscious of being utterly alone in the dark, silent house. She threw back the eiderdown and, wrapping herself in the quilt, walked cautiously through the living room and out onto the porch, settling on the steps to gaze at the stars in the freezing night air. But the night was eerie, the moon and stars obscured by clouds. For a moment the moon shone through a break in the clouds, illuminating the smooth surface of the sea, before disappearing into the scudding mass. And then she saw a dim red light blinking far out in the distance. In an instant it was gone. Mary rubbed her eyes, fearing a German submarine. After a moment she convinced herself it was nothing, perhaps the running lights of a fishing boat. It had been such a terrible night, perhaps she was simply seeing things. And yet she kept looking out into the darkness, wondering what she had seen.

Davenport hunched over his desk and traced a column of figures, squinting at the small print in the glare of the overhead light. Looking up, he stared absently out of the window toward the river in the late afternoon darkness and the gently falling rain. He rose to lower the blackout shade and then returned to a report he had obtained from the Admiralty on the shipping capacities of the British and US navies. In particular, he was studying landing craft and the larger ships designed to transport them. There were surprisingly few standards governing their specifications, which had led to a bewildering assortment of vessels in both navies. But he had discovered that the US Marine Corps had devoted years to studying and training for amphibious warfare, which they were now engaged in against the Japanese in the Pacific. And the Marines favoured a landing craft of their own design, built by Higgins Industries in New Orleans. Thus the Marines had dubbed them Higgins boats. Unlike the larger, steel-hulled landing craft, Higgins boats were only thirty six feet in length and constructed largely of cheap, plentiful plywood. With their flat bottom and shallow draught, they were ideal for ferrying a platoon from its transport ship to wading distance of the beach. Davenport learned that virtually all of them were destined for the Pacific. He stared at his calculations. With plans calling for six divisions to be put ashore on the first day of the invasion, the number of landing craft would easily be in the thousands. Unless the Admiralty was persuaded to look primarily to Higgins boats, and their production diverted from the Pacific, it was inconceivable that there could be an invasion in 1943.

He took several sheets of foolscap and swivelled around to his old Royal. Inserting a sheet with the red 'Most Secret' heading, he began typing. Lost in the clacking of the keys, Davenport failed to notice when the door opened and Leslie Ashton-Gore entered.

'Well, Davenport,' said Ashton-Gore in a loud voice, 'working late again?' He had the habit of leaving the office punctually at five o'clock and resented Davenport's tendency to remain at his desk long after the others had departed.

'Oh, hallo, Leslie,' said Davenport with a yawn, looking up from the typewriter. 'Just trying to finish this damned report.'

Ashton-Gore took the trench coat he had returned for from the back of door and turned to walk out. 'Charles' – he paused with the doorknob in his hand – 'I say, old man, several of us are meeting for drinks in the OC. Why don't you join us for a change?'

'Thanks,' said Davenport. 'This report can wait till tomorrow.'

As usual, the officers' club was packed with young men in a blue haze of cigarette smoke and buzzing with the din of conversation. Davenport and Ashton-Gore ordered drinks at the bar and made their way to the tables occupied by the men of their section, choosing empty chairs at the nearest table. One table over, Colonel Rawlinson sat with a glass of whisky relishing his accustomed role as senior strategist in the eyes of his junior officers.

'Well, it's Davenport,' said one of the men. 'To what do we owe the pleasure of your company?' Davenport ignored the man's sarcastic tone and took a sip of beer.

'I shanghai'd him,' explained Ashton-Gore. 'I found him, as usual, with his nose in a foot-thick book.'

At the next table Rawlinson's clipped voice was audible as he held forth on the Eighth Army's recent string of successes in North Africa. 'And so you see, gentlemen,' he said, 'our old friend Rommel was, in the end, simply *out-generalled*. There's nothing at all superior about the German infantryman, nor the German tank. Simply put, Rommel is no match for Monty.' Expressions of 'hear, hear' and 'quite right' could be heard, and someone raised the toast: 'To the Desert Rats.' Once the toast was drunk, Davenport pushed back from the table. 'Excuse me,' he said, 'I think I'll have another beer.' He crossed the room to the bar as the men resumed their conversation. Resting his elbows on the counter and his foot on the brass railing, he was in no hurry to return to the table. The barman walked over, and Davenport said, 'I'll have another light ale.' Once he was served, he noticed another officer standing with his back to him at the far end of the bar. Though he couldn't see his face, there was something vaguely familiar about him. From the insignia on his collar Davenport could see he was a colonel. Leaving several coins on the counter, Davenport moved three or four paces closer to the man. At that moment the barman handed the man a glass of whisky, and he turned in Davenport's direction to accept it. Davenport stared at him, feeling a flush on his face and his heart pounding. He put down his glass and clenched his fists. He had met him once before, at some high society affair hosted by one of Frances's horsey-set friends. A few years older than Davenport, he was nevertheless too young to have attained the rank of full colonel without some social intervention. With neatly parted, light-brown hair, he was handsome in a cinematic sort of way, but, like many men of his class, he looked soft and fussy about his appearance. The man took a sip of his drink and then casually looked at Davenport and made eye contact, at first a simple look of greeting but then a flicker of recognition. He started slightly and averted his eyes. Davenport came a step closer.

'Well, well,' said Davenport quietly.

The man looked back at him said, 'Yes . . . I say, it's Davenport, isn't it?'

Davenport stared menacingly and said, 'That's right. I should think you could remember the name easily enough.' He moved another step, so that only a foot separated the two men. The colonel inched backwards, a hunted look in his eyes.

'Well,' he began again, 'I've no doubt that you're, well, terribly upset about this . . .' Davenport continued to stare, clenching his fists at his side. 'But of course, these things happen, and frankly, there's really nothing more to say.' He turned away and picked up his drink.

'Oh, I see,' Davenport said in a low voice. 'These things happen, is that it?' He spat out the words. 'So you're enjoying yourself with *my* wife, in *my* house, while I'm picking black flies out of my stinking rations and sand out of my ears—'

'Now, see here—'

'No, *you* see here!' Davenport suddenly grabbed the man by the lapels, lifted him off the ground, and slammed him against the wall, striking the back of his head and his glass shattering on the floor. Davenport let go and watched him crumple back against the bar. The entire room fell silent.

'Damn you,' the man almost shouted, 'I should have you court-martialed!'

Davenport stared at him contemptuously and said, 'I should like to see you try.'

A week had passed since New Year's Eve, and Mary and Chelsea had been forced by the bitter cold to remain indoors. Just when she was beginning to feel desperate, the weak sun emerged and the temperature began to rise. As she donned her heavy coat, hat, and gloves, she silently prayed that the car would start. When the first feeble attempts failed, Mary slapped the steering wheel in the freezing car and bitterly considered the prospect of walking into the village. Then, with luck, the engine laboured one last time and sputtered to life. Mary fought the gearstick into reverse and backed out of the small wooden enclosure. Icicles hung from the eaves and dripped as she started down the slippery track. She thought of the reception she was likely to receive from her neighbours, none of whom she had seen since the dreadful encounter. It was one thing to have stood up to the odious stranger but why, she wondered over and over, had she found it necessary to rebuke virtually the entire community? If she was an outsider before, she was now certain to be treated as a pariah.

Mary carefully slowed to a stop and turned onto the road into Castletown. Much of the snow had melted as she drove past The Forgery, home of the Dillons, the largest landowners for miles. On the side of the road ahead Mrs Dillon was taking advantage of the thaw to walk her retriever. As Mary drove past slowly, Mrs Dillon turned and, with a smile of recognition, gave her a cheerful wave. Mary drove the remaining half-mile to the intersection of two country roads leading into the village where Mrs Fitzgerald, likewise out for some air, called out, 'Good morning, Mary. Thank heaven for the sunshine. On your way into town?'

For a moment, Mary stared in surprise before she smiled and called back, 'Yes, indeed.' After being shut in for so long, Mary piled the counter at McDonough's high with groceries, a large box of puppy food, and lastly, the London and Dublin papers. She frowned at the neatly lettered sign behind the counter: 'Sorry – no tea today'. Donald's father, in shirtsleeves with braces, eyed her coldly as he looked up from his newspaper spread out on the counter. Despite his father's aloofness, Donald was his usual antic self, vying for Mary's attention as he helped pack her purchases and carry them to the car. Even Mr Coggins bade her a sheepish good morning when she stopped at the post office to deposit her neat stack of letters to her family and, of course, to Charles. When she picked up her mail, her heart skipped a beat at the sight of a letter with the familiar army return address. It was only when she was back in the car that an explanation for her neighbours' goodwill occurred to her. Thinking back to her outburst at the pub, she realized that many of them must have agreed with her, sharing her loathing for the Nazis and possibly the outlawed IRA as well. A smile lit up her face as she considered that she might actually have won some of them over. In her ruminations she almost forgot about the intersection, suddenly braking to avoid a tall, young man in the road, the same man, she now could see she had almost run down driving home on New Year's Eve. Wearing a soft tweed cap and heavy corduroy coat, he approached the car as she rolled down the window. 'I'm so sorry,' she said with an embarrassed smile. 'I never saw you.'

'You're a dangerous woman, I think,' he said with a boyish grin. 'I shall have to go round with a bell on my neck.'

Mary thought about saying something about his being more careful but instead extended her hand and said, 'I'm Mary Kennedy.'

He smiled in a pleasant way and took her hand. 'The name's Eamon,' he said. 'Eamon O'Farrell. Pleased to make your acquaintance.'

'Well, goodbye then,' said Mary. She rolled up the window and started for home. He seemed a nice enough fellow, though she was sure she had never seen him in the area. It was curious; one seldom met strangers in rural Ireland, and it was the second time she'd found him out walking near Kilmichael Point and her secluded cottage. The next time she came across him she must remember to ask what brought him to this seldom-travelled track.

Returning to the cottage, she put away her purchases in the larder and went about the day's chores, stopping every so often to pat the pocket in which she carried Charles's letter. She made bread, pleased by the warm yeasty smell of the rising dough. The aroma was like no other, transporting her back to her mother's side on baking day . . . thick loaves of hot bread, watching the slowly melting butter . . . times she had hoped to share with Anna. Waiting for the bread, she set the kettle on the stove and turned on the radio, just in time to catch the BBC news bulletin. The German Sixth Army, the announcer breathlessly reported, was completely encircled at the Russian city of Stalingrad, and the Red Army commander was demanding its immediate surrender. Could it be, thought Mary, the mighty German army defeated? And the Allies' hopes for ultimate victory depended, as Charles had explained, on the Russians repulsing the German onslaught.

Switching off the radio, Mary's thoughts returned to his letter. There was no more running home to tear them open. Now she waited all day, as long as she could, before settling on the sofa in the living room. The salutation 'Dear Mary' alone brought a bright smile. Dated December 28, Charles recounted the Christmas leave he had spent at home with his father, their first time together since his return from North Africa. Mary was moved by his loving description of the kindly man, a retired schoolteacher, living alone after the death of his wife. She was intensely interested in Charles's detailed account of the weekend he'd spent with Evan Hockaday at Marsden Hall; Evan, whom Charles regarded as such an exceptional person. But a frown darkened her face as she read of his 'unfortunate encounter' with the man his wife Frances was seeing, how every man in his section had either witnessed the ugly scene or heard of it within hours. He closed with wishes for the New Year and, in his careful hand, several lines of verse, in his habit of including lines from his favourite poetry in each letter.

She loved his letters . . . perhaps, she mused, she was falling in love with him, although no such thing had been admitted by either of them. They were careful to avoid that territory. Every letter told how wonderful it was to receive the last . . . what it meant to both of them on long, lonely days, but never a word about their feelings.

CHAPTER EIGHT

THE MINUTE HAND clicked on the numeral 12 – eight a.m., on 1 March, 1943. Davenport, at a desk in the centre of the map room, glanced at the clock. Amid the soft murmur of conversation, his mind wandered to the time with his father over Christmas, feeling a pang of regret for his dilatoriness in writing to him. The thought of writing, however, brought to mind the letter he had received the day before from Mary. At the sound of footsteps, he looked up as

Colonel Rawlinson walked briskly to the lectern. Rawlinson cleared his throat and the room fell silent.

'Good morning, gentlemen,' he began.

'Good morning, sir,' the men answered in unison.

Rawlinson surveyed the faces and rearranged the papers on the lectern. 'Today,' he said in a loud, clear voice, 'we have reached a critical juncture in the planning for Round-up: our preliminary report to the Chief of the General Staff, who will in turn be meeting with his American counterpart. The recommendations we put forward will play a large part in the momentous decisions that will soon be made with respect to the conduct of the war. It goes without saying', – Rawlinson paused for effect – 'that these considerations loom very large over our discussion today. I cannot over-state the gravity of these decisions.'

Rawlinson clasped his hands behind his back and began to pace. 'As you are all aware,' he said, 'our task is to submit recommendations on the following issues. *First*, the selection of the landing beaches. *Second*, the timing of the landing. And *third*, the logistical considerations to effectuate the landing and the resupply of men and *matériel* in the days and weeks following.' Rawlinson looked out at the expectant faces. 'We are to assume that six infantry divisions will be put ashore on the first day. Where such men will be found and how they are to be trained and assembled are outside the purview of our report. Now,' – Rawlinson resumed pacing – 'I have received many excellent reports, and you are to be congratulated for your hard work. Mr Smith-Dorrien. Your report on the proposed landing beaches.'

A short, stocky major with wire-rimmed glasses rose from his desk and walked to the lectern. 'Thank you, sir,' he said as he selected his paper from the stack. Rawlinson walked over to the map and picked up his pointer. Davenport drummed the eraser end of a pencil on the desk. What will it be, he wondered? He had submitted his own recommendations to Smith-Dorrien, an intelligent, serious officer. 'Well,' said Smith-Dorrien, 'this has proved to be a most vexing question. For obvious reasons, the logical place to stage a large amphibious landing is the Pas de Calais. Calais has an excellent deep-water port, and the entire area is well within striking distance of our RAF bases in the south-east. The beaches are wide and flat with clearly marked exits accessible to heavy vehicles. The short distance from Dover greatly reduces the likelihood of mishaps at sea for the naval task force. In short, the Pas de Calais is the perfect invasion site. And for that reason we have ruled it out. The Germans have deduced that it's the most likely place for an invasion,' continued Smith-Dorrien, 'and are presently building the most formidable section of the Atlantic Wall at that very place. And their heaviest concentration of forces is located immediately to the rear of Calais.' Smith-Dorrien paused to adjust his glasses. Davenport nodded with satisfaction. So far so good.

'There are two other deep water ports along the French Channel coast,' Smith-Dorrien continued, 'Le Havre and Cherbourg. We have extensive intelligence from both aerial reconnaissance and resistance reports on beach conditions and defensive fortifications the length of the Normandy coastline. The beaches surrounding Le Havre are quite narrow, with rocky, almost vertical, cliffs behind them, making it difficult, if not impossible, to secure a lodgment inland of the landing area. Hence we considered but likewise rejected the Cotentin peninsula.' Davenport sat up straight. 'While Cherbourg is an excellent port, and the beaches on the eastward side of the peninsula would be acceptable for landing a large body of men, we were deeply troubled by two problems: first, the weather – always a concern in any large-scale operation in the Channel. But the Cotentin peninsula bears the brunt of the Atlantic gales, which bear down from the west, which could spell disaster for the invasion force. But even if the landing were successfully executed, the geography of the peninsula, sticking out, as it were, like a thumb into the Channel, makes it susceptible to being sealed off by the defenders in the days following the landing, especially as the low-lying areas are susceptible to flooding.'

'So that left us with the long stretch of Normandy beaches facing north from the mouth of the Seine to the Cotentin peninsula.' As he spoke Rawlinson traced the line of beaches on the wall map. 'The beaches are generally wide and sandy and, with few exceptions, the bluffs which rise up from them are not terribly steep and should be passable by heavy vehicles. The Cotentin peninsula at the western end acts as something of a breakwater to shelter the area from the Atlantic gales. But by far the most important advantage is the fact it's only lightly defended. In contrast to the formidable fortifications the Germans are erecting farther to the north, the beach obstacles and heavy gun emplacements along these beaches are relatively few and far between.' Davenport smiled inwardly. He had arrived at the same conclusions in his own study of possible landing sites and forwarded his views to Smith-Dorrien.

Rawlinson returned to the lectern. 'Well, gentlemen,' he said, with a tight-lipped smile, 'any questions for Mr Smith-Dorrien?'

A young captain at the back spoke up. 'What about the question of a deep-water port? How have you addressed that concern?'

'You've hit on the single greatest weakness in the choice of this landing site,' answered Smith-Dorrien. 'It will be necessary to resupply the invasion force through the port of Cherbourg. The right wing will have to penetrate inland and execute a ninety-degree turn to the northwest to capture Cherbourg. This may prove to be the most difficult aspect of the plan. Other questions?'

The room fell silent.

'Now for the question of timing,' said Rawlinson. 'Your report, Mr Harwood.'

A slender young officer with neatly parted blond hair stood nervously at the lectern. After fumbling for a moment, he read: 'The timing of a cross-Channel assault is an extraordinarily complex question that is largely dependent on weather and tides. The Channel is notorious for the inclemency of its weather, the severity of its gales and the exceptional length of its tides, with intervals of as much as three hundred yards between the mean low and high tides in certain locations and times of the year. Given the obstacles on the beaches and in the shallows designed to thwart landing craft, we determined that the landing should be timed to coincide with the high tide, in order to float these craft above the obstacles and allow the debarkation of troops in water shallow enough to wade ashore. We also concluded that the landings should occur during daylight hours, preferably at sunrise.' The officer paused and appeared to be searching for something in his report.

'Now then,' he continued, 'the weather. From our study of meteorological data over the past twenty years, we concluded that it would be imprudent to hazard a landing across the Channel at any time before the first of May or after the first of October. The probability of gales is simply too great during the six months from October through to April. And consequently, during the six months when weather conditions are favourable, we identified the few intervals when the high tide coincides with the sunrise, offering the most desirable landing conditions. These windows of opportunity exist in the first week of June and July, the second week of August and the third week of September. Lastly, we are mindful that the German construction of the Atlantic Wall is ongoing and, as each week passes, the fortifications become stronger. Our conclusion, therefore, is that the most propitious time for a cross-Channel assault is the second week of August.' August of 1943, Davenport considered. Five months hence. He couldn't quarrel with the man's analysis. Well, he supposed reality would sink in with the discussion of logistics.

'Thank you, Harwood,' said Rawlinson, tapping the end of his pointer on the linoleum. 'And now, Captain MacDonald. Logistics.'

A tall, broad-shouldered Scot with a shock of reddish-brown hair stepped to the lectern. He glanced briefly at his report, and gripping the sides of the lectern, said, 'The initial assault will consist of six fully equipped infantry divisions, approximately a hundred and twenty thousand men, with three hundred and eighty medium tanks, four hundred and twenty-five artillery pieces, motorized transport and so forth. The logistical requirements to support the embarkation and debarkation of a force of this size may be summarized as follows.' As he droned on, Davenport grew increasingly restive. Get to the point, man, he said to himself. But MacDonald didn't get to the point. He described, in painstaking detail, a flotilla of ships and boats that existed on paper only.

'Thank you, MacDonald,' said Rawlinson. 'Questions?' For a moment the room was silent.

Davenport leaned forward and said, 'Sir.'

Rawlinson gazed at him coldly and said, 'Yes, Mr Davenport?'

'What about landing craft?' asked Davenport. 'You've seen my report, sir. We've nowhere near enough to transport a force even a fraction of the size under discussion here.' Davenport was conscious of a number of whispered remarks but he was determined to make his point. 'It's absurd,' he added, 'to think an invasion could take place in 1943.'

'That will do,' said Rawlinson with asperity. 'Your report has been duly noted. A statement will be included in my report to the effect that concerns have been raised with respect to the availability of landing craft, on which any successful operation would naturally be dependent.' There were a few snickers from the back of the room. 'Ultimately,' said Rawlinson, 'the question of landing craft is for the Admiralty to decide.'

*

Mary spent her midwinter days by the fire with books and needle-work, with Chelsea as her constant companion, looking forward always to the letters that awaited her when she was able to make the trip into the village. Soon after the incident on New Year's Eve with the man from the IRA, she had written to Charles about it, including the details she could remember of the man's drunken threats of strikes against the British in the north and claims of British plans to move against the Irish, hoping that Charles might help her understand whether to take these frightful sentiments seriously. He had written to her that the IRA had evolved from the paramilitary organization which had fought the British and secured Irish independence, to a small rabble of violent malcontents who would stop at nothing to secure union with Northern Ireland. She was astonished to think, as Charles suggested, that these men might be so desperate as to ally themselves with the Germans in the hope of securing aid, or that the British might actually contemplate military action against Ireland.

It was mid-March, and there had been several days without rain or the temperature falling below freezing. Mary stood on her porch in a pair of old dungarees, boots, and her rain-proof jacket, determined to descend the cliffs and enjoy a stroll down the sandy beach that stretched for miles to the south of Kilmichael Point. 'Come along, girl,' she said to the pup, who had paused to investigate the first shoots of grass. Standing at the cliffs, the panoramic view stretched from the Wicklow Mountains to the north, across the Irish Sea towards Wales and to the south far into the mist-shrouded distance. The air was spring fresh, as though something had been shaken into the atmosphere when the last, sharp licks of winter had finally succumbed. Mary paused to take a deep breath and listen to the crash of the surf on the rocks. And then she heard another sound, quite close by, a man humming a familiar tune. He suddenly appeared ten feet below her, slowly ascending the path.

'Why, top of the mornin', Mary,' he called out, pausing on a ledge and removing his cap. 'Lovely day.' Chelsea growled threateningly as Mary shaded her eyes.

'It's Mr O'Farrell,' she said politely, 'if I remember correctly.'

'That it is. But please, call me Eamon.' He slipped on his cap and continued up the path to the top. Chelsea barked even more loudly as he approached.

'Hush,' said Mary, reaching down to restrain the dog. 'You'll frighten Mr O'Farrell.'

Eamon smiled and said, 'She's a beautiful young spaniel. What's her name?'

'Chelsea,' said Mary as the dog quieted, her large, intelligent eyes darting between the two of them. 'What brings you to our remote stretch of the coast?' she asked.

'Oh, nothing, really. Just a bit of beachcombing on this glorious morning. You've quite an exceptional view. What do they call this place?'

'Kilmichael Point,' said Mary. 'I can see you're new here, Mr O'Farrell.'

'I do wish you'd call me Eamon,' he said. 'And, yes, I've not been here many months.'

'You're staying in the village?'

'That's right. I've, ah, found work there . . . I was living before up in the hills.' He gestured vaguely toward the distance. 'Well, I should be on my way.' He touched a hand lightly to his cap. 'Perhaps I'll see you again.' Mary waited until he disappeared before making her way down to the beach, her mind filled with an image of the pleasant man who seemed destined to cross her path.

Less than a week later she encountered him again as she was walking with Chelsea on the beach. At first he was a mere dark form in the distance. But, as he came nearer, he smiled and waved a greeting. With Chelsea beside them, they walked together the half-mile to the foot of the cliffs, making small talk about the weather. By the time they started up the pathway to her cottage, Mary was feeling more comfortable with Eamon, to the point of asking his opinion on the progress of the war.

'Not our fight, is it?' he commented. Just as Mary was shaking her head, he added: 'But Hitler's got to be stopped. And now that the British have the Americans on their side, perhaps the tide has turned.'

Mary smiled as they reached the top of the cliffs. 'Won't you come in for a cup of tea?' she asked. It was the first of many times that Eamon O'Farrell would settle on Mary's porch or take a walk along the beach with Chelsea romping along. They spoke often of the war, and she found his views on the subject strangely contradictory. He was quick to point out the moral shortcomings of the British and argued that the ordinary Germans were no more at fault than the British or Americans. His dislike of the Russians seemed almost equal to his contempt for the Nazis. Mary considered him an odd bundle, yet sensed an ally and, more than anything, she simply liked him. After all she had endured from the local townspeople, she willingly forgave some of his questionable opinions.

As the days grew longer, Mary, still shut in for the most part against the March winds, eagerly awaited the first signs of spring. Seated at her kitchen table, she took a last sip of tea and folded her newspaper. Reaching down to stroke Chelsea's soft fur, she said, 'For a change I'm taking the car into town and leaving you behind.' She could swear from the alert look in her large brown eyes that the pup understood every word. 'I won't be long, and I'll bring you a treat.'

As she drove toward the village, Mary dwelled on the question whether, as Charles had written, the Irish insistence on neutrality, and the possibility that the IRA was aiding the Germans, might actually provoke the British to attack Ireland. Despite the recent gains in North Africa and on the Eastern Front, the war was going badly, which might lead desperate men in Ireland to think that this was their one chance to strike against the British in the north. As British shipping losses continued to mount, it was certain that German U-boats would benefit from agents scouting the movement of British ships from the safety of the neutral Irish coastline, which might prompt the British to move against the Irish. As she turned on to the road into the village, these reflections left Mary even more disquieted.

After buying groceries, papers, and a treat for Chelsea at the McDonough's store, she steered the car down the road toward the post office. Driving past the Golden Anchor, she observed a man wearing a long coat and hat pulled low walking out of the pub. Taking her foot from the accelerator, she strained to see the man's face. There was no mistaking it: it was the IRA man, wearing the same hat and coat he'd worn on New Year's Eve. Intensely curious, Mary slowed to a stop, glancing in her rear-view mirror in time to see a second man step outside the pub, clapping a comradely hand on the IRA man's shoulder. It must be the other man, thought Mary – Tom, if she remembered correctly. She turned to get a better look. At that moment the men shook hands and parted, the IRA man walking away as the other man began walking in her direction. To her horror, she recognized Eamon O'Farrell. She quickly looked away and stepped on the accelerator, almost certain that in the brief moment she had not been seen. After dropping her letters at the post office and learning from the dour Mr Coggins that she had no mail, Mary climbed into the car and drove the short distance home, deeply troubled by her strange discovery.

*

Davenport sat at the desk in his room examining one of Mary's latest letters and another from the firm of barristers representing Frances. Putting aside the letter from Mary, he slit open the other envelope. A scowl came over his face as he read it, demanding that he produce a sworn statement with respect to his assets and income. He thought back to the encounter at the officers' club with Frances's lover. The lawyers were apparently proceeding on the assumption that Davenport's army career would require him to show deference to the man. Well, now there was nothing to be risked in exposing the man's adultery. Yes, he decided again, he would have his lawyer file the necessary papers to question him under oath. He quickly read Mary's letter and then took the fountain pen from his pocket and wrote:

25 March 1943
London

My dear Mary,

I was so pleased to read in your last letter that the attitude in your village continues to thaw. Perhaps with the coming of spring the hostility, and I suspect the envy, of some of your neighbours will melt away. And of course you have Chelsea to cheer you up.

I wish I could say that things are more pleasant here. But since my run-in with Frances's colonel, I've felt even more unwelcome among Col. Rawlinson's inner circle, who are the worst type of Englishman, the sort who've given the Irish so much to resent over the centuries. If it weren't for missing you, Mary, I should happily quit this assignment and return to my old division. With the recent victories in Tunisia, however, I wonder where our army will go next.

Do you think about the end of the war, the kind of world this will be? Will it have been worth the sacrifice of so many lives? I find myself thinking about it often these unhappy days. I long to be back at the university and often think how wonderful it would be to have one's own home and to raise a family. And I often wonder what you will do when the war is over.

If I were with you now, in that room you've described looking out on the Irish Sea, I would sit with you and read poetry. This is one of my favourites by Ben Jonson:
I sent thee late a rosy wreath,

Not so much honouring thee
As giving it a hope that there
It could not withered be;
But thou thereon didst only breathe,
And sent'st it back to me;
Since when it grows and smells, I swear,
Not of itself, but thee!

I had better close. Please be careful about the IRA men, as they're deadly serious and their hatred for the English knows no bounds. I shouldn't be the least surprised to learn they're co-operating with German agents operating on Irish soil. And Mary, please write soon.
Affectionately,
Charles

CHAPTER NINE

THE RUMOURS STARTED sometime on Saturday, and by late Sunday they were as thick as bees around a honey-jar. At eight o'clock the following morning the men of Planning Group B took their seats in the map room amid a steady buzz of conversation as they awaited the arrival of the colonel. The room fell silent at the sound of the door and footfalls on the linoleum. Davenport watched expectantly as Rawlinson approached the lectern, his chin thrust forward, followed by a compact man with greying hair and a dark moustache, wearing the red lapel tabs of a general officer. As the two senior officers walked past, the men sat ramrod straight, as quiet as church mice. Rawlinson took his accustomed position facing the men at the lectern while the general stood to one side. Davenport carefully studied Rawlinson, who looked unusually pale and tightly gripped the lectern, as if to steady himself. Peering out at the familiar faces, he said, 'Gentlemen, this is Lieutenant General Frederick Morgan.' Rawlinson coughed into one hand. 'General Morgan,' he began again in his carefully enunciated voice, 'has the distinct honour of having been recently appointed Chief of Staff to the Supreme Allied Commander.' A low murmur passed among the men. 'And as such, has assumed direct responsibility for Operation Round-up. Effective immediately,' Rawlinson paused to straighten his tunic, 'Special Planning Group B is disbanded.' Rawlinson turned to the general and said, 'General Morgan.'

Davenport felt a flutter in his chest. Disbanded! That would possibly mean a return to his old unit and escape from this oppressive clique. He studied the general as he stepped to the lectern, the close-cropped grey hair, penetrating eyes and lean, fit physique. 'Thank you, Colonel,' said Morgan in a gruff voice. His eyes searched the room, seeming to stare at each man. For the briefest moment, he made eye contact with Davenport. 'Let me begin,' he said, 'by thanking you men for your hard work. Much that's been done here will prove very useful to the staff charged with planning the invasion.' Damning with faint praise, thought Davenport. He noticed Rawlinson standing self-consciously to the side, his eyes downcast as though studying his shoes. 'Indeed,' the general continued, 'I found your report very instructive in its analysis of landing areas and the proposed timing of the invasion: with one glaring exception.' He paused to look at the men with the expression of a disappointed schoolmaster. 'It utterly failed to take into account the critical shortage of landing craft, apart from a passing comment, which rendered it useless as a planning document.'

The tension in the room was palpable, as Rawlinson shifted and appeared to sway slightly. 'Now, then,' Morgan said briskly, 'Colonel Rawlinson has been reassigned to a new command, and, with a few exceptions, the rest of you will receive orders to report to various combat units in the Mediterranean theatre where recent losses have resulted in a critical shortage.' Yes, Davenport considered, this would definitely mean a return to action. 'Lastly, the following men are being retained on my staff and will report for duty tomorrow at COSSAC headquarters.' Morgan withdrew a sheet from his tunic. 'Majors Davenport and Smith-Dorrien, Captains MacDonald and Peterson. The rest of you are dismissed.'

Davenport sat in stunned silence as the men around him rose from their desks and began filing out. He looked up at Leslie Ashton-Gore, standing beside him with a bewildered look on his boyish face. 'Well, Charles,' he said, 'I suppose you should be congratulated, and it would appear I'm headed for the front.'

'Good luck to you, Leslie,' said Davenport warmly. After a few minutes, Davenport joined the other officers who were being retained on Morgan's staff at the front of the room. Morgan stood casually before them, one hand in his pocket. 'Well, gentlemen,' he said in a friendlier tone, 'henceforth you'll be on the staff of COSSAC, comprised of both British and American officers. A most interesting group. The work you've done here will carry forward in the detailed planning of the invasion. Ah, Mr Davenport.' He looked Davenport in the eye. 'Your recommendations on the landing craft issue were especially helpful. A pity Colonel Rawlinson ignored them. But based on your conclusions, if I may confide in you men, there will be no cross-Channel invasion in 1943.'

The damp, musty smell of the cellar evoked memories ... Mary sitting backwards on the chair, her knees folded under her and her chin resting on chubby fingers that gripped the chair-back as she watched her grandfather oil his mower. His pipe was in place as he explained the importance of keeping the mower oiled and sharp. It was spring. Bulbs were blooming, trees budding, and now, late in April, the grass was beginning to grow. It was far from needing mowing, yet she couldn't resist the desire to oil and sharpen the old mower exactly as her grandfather had shown her. Mary lifted the heavy old machine and rested it on the scarred bench. Finding the oilcan, she began as she'd been taught, working it into the wheel hubs. Lost in the ratchety clacking as she turned each wheel, she found herself again surveying the cellar; the orderly arrangement of Christmas ornaments Donald had carried down for her and then noticed a dirty bundle of cloth in the shadows. Deciding to investigate, she lifted the cloth cover and discovered an electrical device that resembled an old, cabinet-enclosed Victrola, with vacuum tubes and wires connected to a black base and assorted knobs and dials. Draping the fabric over it, she pulled the chain to extinguish the bulb, ascended the stairs and shut the door behind her.

With the help of young Donald McDonough, Mary had set about a thorough scouring of the house, painting walls, putting new linen on the beds and lace on the windows. The only area of the house yet to be done was the cellar, and Mary decided to tackle that last. They began early on a Saturday, hauling empty bottles up to the shed, oiling the tools and hanging them over the workbench, cleaning the single window for the first time in years. The vegetable bins were taken outside and shaken out, and the musty odour replaced by the scent of lemon oil and soap. After almost nine hours the job was done and Donald paid and on his way.

The following morning, after the previous day's exertions, Mary slept late, and when she rose she briefly considered donning her decent dress and riding into town to attend Mass at the tiny church. With a guilty shake of her head she decided against it, succumbing to the alienation from the church and its teachings she'd felt since the death of her loved ones. She decided instead to make the trip in the delightful spring weather to buy the Sunday newspapers which were sure to be filled with the latest news of the war now overspreading the globe. Piling the papers on the counter before Mr McDonough, she reached for a box of tuppenny nails to add to the supply in her refurbished cellar.

Chelsea was soundly asleep on the porch when Mary returned to the cottage. Hoping not to disturb her, she silently leaned the bicycle against the shed and reached for the newspapers in the basket when she thought of the box of nails. First things first, she decided, slipping the box in her pocket and tugging gently on the door to the cellar stairs. She peered into the blackness and felt for the handrail. Taking one hesitant step down, she considered going to the kitchen for a match. No, she would just blindly feel her way down until she could find the chain for the overhead light bulb. Slowly descending in the dark, she swung her hand through the air, brushing against the chain. Then Mary heard something, the smallest scraping sound and, with a rush of adrenaline, she found the chain and gave it a yank. In the sudden flash of illumination, she gave a short scream at the sight of a man crouching in the shadows with his hands covering his face. He slowly stood up, dropping his hands to his sides. It was Eamon O'Farrell.

'My God, Eamon,' Mary blurted with a pounding heart. 'What are you doing here?'

He raised his palms. 'I'm sorry to have startled you.' Taking a step closer, in a steady voice he said, 'Mary . . . please, let me explain.'

The image of Eamon outside the pub with the IRA man flashed across her mind. She stepped backwards instinctively, feeling the damp cellar wall at her back. Out of the corner of her eye she saw a pair of pruning shears on the bench and quickly grabbed them. 'Don't come near me,' she said, raising them in front of her.

'Put those down,' Eamon said calmly. 'If you'll just listen to me—'

She gave her head a sideways jerk, her eyes full of fear.

'I shouldn't have come here,' said Eamon. 'But I thought—'

'Thought? What did you think?'

'That you wouldn't mind, and as you were out . . .' He took a half step toward her.

'Don't,' she said, tightly gripping the wooden handles. 'Go on with what you were saying.'

'My bike's broken down on the path. Mary, put those down. You've nothing to fear. I just came to borrow some tools, and never thought that you might—'

'Eamon, you scared me half to death,' said Mary with a sigh of relief. She lowered the shears. 'Take what you need and be gone. And I'll thank you to ask before entering my house.'

He raised his hands in a gesture of conciliation. 'Of course,' he said. 'It was foolish, and I'm sorry I frightened you.' He took a wrench and pair of pliers from the shelf and walked quickly past her and up the stairs. He paused at the top and said, 'Goodbye, Mary,' and then was gone. Breathing more easily, Mary laid the shears on the bench, took the nails from her pocket and placed them on the shelf, pulled the chain to extinguish the bulb and hurried up the darkened stairs.

On a clear, cold morning Charles Davenport reported for duty at Norfolk House, home of the Chief of Staff to the Supreme Allied Commander – COSSAC. As he entered St. James's Square, he gazed at the bright green treetops in the privately maintained park and searched for No. 31, a handsome brick building with an elaborate stone façade located on the south-east corner. Within days of reporting for duty, Davenport concluded that the atmosphere at COSSAC was as unlike the suffocating elitism of Special Planning Group B as he could have imagined. From the sentry at the entrance to the high-ranking officers on COSSAC staff, Americans were everywhere. And while they observed the same military etiquette as the British, there was a casual, irreverent quality to the Americans he couldn't quite put his finger on. In his small windowless office during his first week, Davenport drummed a pencil on the desk and struggled to name this distinctive American quality. He decided they simply weren't impressed by the badges and trappings of British rank and status and surmised they possessed a distrust of class and privilege as old as the Revolution. After the seven months he'd endured in the Office of War Plans, the spirit of enthusiasm and confidence that pervaded the COSSAC staff was infectious.

Although COSSAC was dominated by Americans, there were

many British officers, and Davenport found that, with a few exceptions, the men of both countries got along well. Despite their boundless self-confidence, the Americans were slightly in awe of the combat record of the British, especially following the embarrassing American defeat at Kasserine Pass in Tunisia. After long days of tedious work, Davenport would regularly accompany the young staff officers to a neighbourhood pub for pints, darts, and endless discussion of the war, while the senior Americans were often guests of their British counterparts at the exclusive clubs on St. James's or Pall Mall.

Within days of his new assignment, Davenport cabled Evan Hockaday to inform him of events and express his hope that they might find time for another visit. Returning to his room late one evening, Davenport found a telegram, an invitation to join Evan for lunch in the town of Bletchley, suggesting he make arrangements to stay overnight at a hotel. This puzzled Davenport, as he supposed that he would be afforded the usual courtesy of a guest bed in the officers' quarters. On Saturday Davenport boarded the train. Mary, thought Davenport to himself as the train rattled along. My God, he'd only seen the woman once. He thought back to that encounter, which seemed a long time ago, and imagined he could see her face. He felt an extraordinary lightness in his chest, a sensation he hadn't felt in a long time. Was he falling in love? Before long, the spires of Oxford appeared in the distance and, with a shrill whistle the train slowed to a stop at the station. The normally bustling city seemed almost abandoned. Several boyish students in short black gowns whizzed past on bicycles, and a few ageing dons strolled the pavements. After buying a cup of tea at the depot, he slumped on a bench in the waiting room before boarding the bus to Bletchley. The trip along narrow, twisting roads lasted little more than half an hour, during which Davenport reread Mary's last letter. There was a subtle change in her writing that revealed a changed heart. She had seemed so forlorn at first, consumed by her grief, but now there was a certain lightness; describing in long, descriptive paragraphs the pleasure she took in the flowers blooming in her garden, the romps with Chelsea through the new grass along the pathway above the cliffs. But more than anything, he sensed a subtle change in her feelings. Rounding a corner they entered the town of Bletchley. Davenport gazed out, expecting to see men in uniform out walking on a Saturday morning. But to his surprise there was none. The bus pulled into the small bus station, and moments later Davenport was standing on the pavement

you've broken the German code. And I see how carefully this has been kept under wraps. But what's the point of it? It seems almost like, well, a game of chess.'

Evan gave Davenport an affectionate look and said, 'Let me see if I can explain. Take, for example, Monty's recent battle with Rommel at Medenine in Tunisia. A smashing victory, I'm sure you would agree.'

'No question. An absolute rout.'

'We operate in Hut 6,' said Evan. 'Our job is to intercept and decipher communications between German commanders in the field and Wehrmacht headquarters. At the end of February, Monty's lines south of Mareth were very thinly defended, only a single British division.' He paused to sample the soup and said, 'Quite good. Some sort of leek and potato. At any rate, on 28 February, we deciphered an Enigma intercept from Rommel to Berlin stating his intention to attack Medenine with three armoured divisions and thus encircle the British in front of the Mareth Line.'

Davenport put down his spoon and stared at Evan. 'Do you mean to say. . . ?'

'There's more I could tell you,' said Evan, 'but frankly it's not in your interest that I do so. Suffice it to say, Monty had advance notice of the particulars of Rommel's plan and, when the attack came, was able to repulse it with overwhelming force, rushing the New Zealand Division into the line, as well as the 201st Guards, some four hundred tanks and a great mass of guns.'

'Evan,' said Davenport in a hushed voice, 'what you've just told me is unbelievable. It may very well have altered the course of the war. If it weren't for the fact that you were reading Rommel's mail, Monty may have suffered a major defeat. Why, it's almost like cheating at cards.'

'Precisely,' said Evan. 'And the bloody Huns haven't a clue what we're up to, in lovely old Bletchley Park.'

Following lunch, enjoying coffee on the brick terrace, Evan turned to Davenport and said, 'You've told me almost nothing about your new assignment.'

Davenport studied Evan's earnest face, thinking how young and innocent he would look were it not for the black patch over one eye. After taking a sip of coffee, he said, 'The transfer to the staff of COSSAC was a breath of fresh air. Morgan is terribly capable, and he's surrounded himself with a fine group of American and British officers.'

'I'm confused,' said Evan. 'General Morgan is Chief of Staff to the Supreme Allied Commander?'

'That's right.'

'Who *is* the Supreme Allied Commander?'

'There isn't one,' answered Davenport. 'Not yet anyway. At some point before the final planning for Overlord, Churchill and Roosevelt are supposed to name one. In the meantime, General Morgan has the full responsibility.'

'Overlord?'

'Code-name for the cross-Channel invasion. In any case, I've no doubt we'll do a good job of choosing the landing areas, the date for the invasion, and all the logistics. But that's not what keeps me awake at night.' Evan nodded and sipped his coffee. 'If the Germans are ready,' said Davenport, 'if they're fully prepared, we could be trapped on the landing beaches.' Davenport finished his coffee and said, 'I don't suppose there's anything your people could do to lead the Germans astray? To lead them to believe the invasion is coming at Calais, for example?'

Evan scratched his chin thoughtfully. 'Am I to assume,' he asked, 'the landing will occur elsewhere?'

'Hypothetically.'

'Well,' said Evan, 'I'll tell you this: from all the Enigma traffic, the Germans are clearly taking precautions for a landing at Calais.'

'They'd be fools to do otherwise,' said Davenport.

'But you're suggesting something more devious,' said Evan. 'Something to convince them that the landing is certain to occur at Calais. A feint.'

'Precisely.'

Evan's eye shone with intensity. 'What if,' he said, 'we flooded them with obscure radio transmissions concerning the area around Calais? And then listen in on their response and alter the traffic to reinforce the idea that Calais is the target.'

'Very ingenious,' said Davenport, resting his elbows on his knees. 'If you don't object, I'll take this up with my superiors.'

'Sorry,' said Evan, 'but that won't do. As far as your superiors are concerned, or anyone else for that matter, you haven't a clue as to what's going on at Bletchley. But let me handle it at my end. There might be a way we could help.'

'I knew I could depend on you,' said Davenport with a smile.

'There's one other matter,' said Evan, 'I've been meaning to ask about.' Davenport looked at him expectantly. 'How you're getting along in the divorce proceedings?'

Davenport grimaced. 'Well, you may think me a fool, but after my run-in with the colonel who's seeing Frances, I decided to expose the fact. . . .' Davenport hesitated and then said, 'The fact that he was sleeping with my wife while I was in North Africa.'

'And how does one, as you put it, expose this?' asked Evan.

'By taking the man's deposition, as the lawyers call it. Requiring him to testify under oath. Something her high-priced barrister gambled I would never consider.'

'Bully for you,' said Evan. 'I've no doubt *that* turned the tables. And look at what's happened to your career. On the staff of COSSAC!' He smiled broadly. 'Tell me, Charles, what of the lovely young American from Ireland?'

'Mary,' said Davenport. 'It's so odd. Despite the fact that I've only seen her that one time, we've continued to correspond. And I feel . . . very close to her.'

'Then you should see her again.'

'Believe me, Evan, I intend to.'

CHAPTER TEN

TWO MEN SAT facing one another at a corner table in the otherwise empty smoking room aboard the *Queen Mary*. As the sun slid below the horizon, the walls of the tall room, panelled in burl walnut, glowed in the fading light. The taller of the two, elegantly hand-some in expensive tweeds, drew a card from the deck on the table. 'Bezique,' he said simply, withdrawing three cards from his hand and placing them face up.

'Damn you, Harriman,' exclaimed Winston Churchill, expelling a cloud of blue cigar smoke. 'I should know better than to play cards with a man who owns half the railroads in America and presides over a Wall Street banking empire.' Folding his cards, he reached for his glass and downed the last of his drink. 'Waiter,' he said sharply, and a white-jacketed attendant appeared out of the shadows. 'Fetch me another. Averell?' he added, inviting the American Ambassador to the Soviet Union to join him.

'Yes, Winston, I'll have another.' Churchill scooped up the cards in his surprisingly delicate hands and began shuffling the thick, 64-card deck. 'Now, Averell,' he said as he slid three cards from the top of the deck. 'I trust I can depend on your unflinching support in our conversations with the President.' Harriman silently waited for Churchill to finish dealing, then picked up his cards and began sorting them, averting his eyes from Churchill's gaze. 'You heard General Brooke today,' Churchill continued. 'There's no question more American men, ships, and equipment are going to the Pacific than to Europe.'

The waiter returned with a salver bearing two crystal tumblers. 'There you are, sir,' he said with a deferential nod. 'Will there be anything else?'

'Not for the moment,' said Churchill as he drew a card from the top of the deck. 'Spades,' he announced. 'Your support will prove critical, Averell, on the issue of Sicily.'

Harriman continued to study his hand, frowned, and drew from the deck. Looking up, he smiled and said, 'Naturally, Winston, I'll do what I can. I share your view that the defeat of Hitler has priority over Japan. But I can't forget who my boss is.'

An hour or so later, a young British naval officer with a single gold ring on his cuff walked up to Churchill's table. Churchill looked up with an irritated expression and said, 'What is it, lieutenant?'

'Sorry to interrupt, sir, but we've just received a flash cable from the Admiralty. From Admiral Pound.'

'Yes, go on,' said Churchill, his cigar clenched in his teeth.

'A German submarine, which departed Brest two days ago, is believed to be on a course which will cross our path approximately fifteen miles ahead.'

'I see. And what does Admiral Pound suggest we do about it?'

'At our rate of speed, sir, Admiral Pound suggests we are as likely to ram the submarine as it is to see us first.'

Churchill peered out into the blackness beyond the window. 'Very well,' he said at length. 'Thank you, Lieutenant.' The young officer turned and walked from the room.

When they were alone, Harriman put down his cards and said, 'Good heavens, Winston. How can your navy possibly know these things? The course and heading of an enemy submarine?'

'Suffice it to say,' replied Churchill with a devilish look, 'we have our methods. Now, perhaps you don't realize,'– he paused to take a sip of his drink, – 'I've had my lifeboat fitted out with a 50-calibre machine gun. In case we have to abandon ship. You see,' Churchill said, leaning back and thrusting out his chin. 'I don't intend to be captured. The finest way to die' – he took the cigar from his mouth and stabbed it in the air – 'is in the excitement of *fighting the enemy.*'

A look of concern clouded Harriman's face. 'But surely,' he objected, 'I understood that the very worst a torpedo could do to this ship, because of its compartments, is knock out one engine room. Leaving us with sufficient power to steam at twenty knots.'

'Ah, but Averell,' said Churchill with a smile, 'they might put *two* torpedoes in us. In which case you must come with me in the boat and see the fun!'

The following days and nights in the North Atlantic passed without incident, and on the morning of 11 May, 1943, the *Queen Mary* eased into the Cunard berth on the lower west side of Manhattan. By afternoon Churchill and his party were on board a special train bound for Washington, arriving in time for dinner at the White House. The next day, after a leisurely morning working on dictation in his accustomed third floor bedroom, Churchill emerged, rested and filled with determination, for the opening session of the conference. Attired in his usual black jacket and charcoal trousers, a silver fob-chain adorning his black waistcoat, Churchill strolled down the hall to the President's upstairs study. Standing in the entrance, he gazed at Franklin Roosevelt, seated at a large desk flanked by the flags of the United States and the Presidency. As usual, Harry Hopkins was seated in an armchair opposite the President. Roosevelt looked up, flashed his characteristic grin, and said, 'Winston. Come in, come in.'

Churchill strode across the room and reached across the desk to take Roosevelt's outstretched hand. 'Mr President,' he said warmly. 'How good to see you here again. And Harry, a pleasure, as always.'

'Please, Winston, sit down,' said Roosevelt. 'And tell me about your crossing.'

Churchill's eyes were drawn to the boughs of the stately trees outside the tall windows and the lush green lawn. 'I can't help but remember, Mr President, when I was last here.' A far off look came over Churchill's face. 'What striking changes have taken place since I received the news of the fall of Tobruk in this room. I shall never forget' – his voice quaked with emotion – 'the way in which you sustained us in that desperate time.'

Precisely at one o'clock, the President's study began to fill with military and political advisers. Roosevelt remained at his desk with Churchill opposite him while the men from both sides of the Atlantic took their seats in a semicircle before them. 'Let me begin, Mr President,' said Churchill in his slight lisp, 'by congratulating our victorious armies in Tunis. Today, we can proudly say, Torch is over. And the great question now before us, is what shall the next prize be? I submit that it is Sicily. And following its successful capture, all of Italy lies at our feet. There is no question, Mr President, that the cross-Channel invasion must be deferred to the spring of 1944 at the earliest, because of the critical shortage of landing craft. On that point, I believe we are in agreement. And therefore, possessing a mighty, victorious Anglo-American army in North Africa, having triumphed over the hitherto invincible Afrika Korps, what are we to do? Sit idle while we await the liberating invasion of the Continent?' Churchill paused and peered at the impassive faces of his listeners before answering his rhetorical question:

'No, Mr President. We must *strike* against Sicily. And when Sicily is won – and won it shall be – we must move against Italy. Ah, think of it! Italy out of the war. The Italian fleet no longer a danger in the Mediterranean. The Turks, the Balkans . . . The possibilities, Mr President, are intriguing.'

Roosevelt rocked back in his chair with an inscrutable smile. 'But Winston,' he said after a moment, 'should we risk delaying the cross-Channel invasion with an adventure in Italy? Suppose we're bogged down? Certainly we agree there's no possibility of an invasion before the spring of 1944, but we would prefer to set a date and concentrate all of our efforts on ensuring its success.'

After several hours of at times acrimonious discussion of the arguments for and against an invasion of Sicily, General Ismay entered the room and approached Churchill. 'What is it, Ismay?' asked Churchill with a worn expression.

'Two telegrams, Prime Minister. The first is from Station X and the second from Alexander's HQ in Tunis.' He handed two envelopes to Churchill. Donning his reading glasses, Churchill tore open an envelope and read:

PERSONAL STOP MOST SECRET STOP PRIME MINISTER STOP EYES ONLY
THE FOLLOWING COMMUNIQUÉ WAS DECIPHERED THIS DATE FROM GENERAL VON ARMIN TO BERLIN

OKW: 'WE HAVE FIRED OUR LAST CARTRIDGE, WE
ARE CLOSING DOWN FOREVER' STOP

Churchill arched his eyebrows imperceptibly and refolded the
cable in the envelope. He then read Alexander's cable to Ismay: 'The
end is very near. Von Armin has been captured, and prisoners will
most likely be over 150,000. All organized resistance has collapsed.'
Churchill removed his glasses and dropped the telegram in his lap.
'Mr President,' he said in a loud voice.

Roosevelt paused in his conversation with Hopkins, turned to
Churchill and said, 'Yes, Winston?'

Churchill smiled broadly. 'I have just received word of the
Germans' capitulation in Tunisia. We have taken over a hundred and
fifty thousand prisoners.'

At the conclusion of the conference, Roosevelt invited Churchill
to accompany him for a weekend at Shangri-La, the Presidential
retreat in the Catoctin Mountains of Maryland. After a good-
natured debate between Churchill and Eleanor Roosevelt over
which of them should sit next to the President, the motorcade made
its way into the Maryland countryside. As they entered the town of
Frederick, Churchill turned around to face the President and First
Lady. 'I wonder whether it would be out of our way, Mr President,
to drive past the home of that magnificent woman who defied the
Confederates by waving the Union flag from her upstairs bedroom
window?'

'Not at all, Winston,' replied Roosevelt. 'Barbara Frietchie, of
course, the most famous citizen of Frederick. About whom the poet
Whittier wrote,' he added, with schoolboy pride, 'if I remember
correctly, "Shoot if you must this old grey head, but spare your
country's flag, she said."'

Eleanor Roosevelt laughed and said, 'Excellent, Franklin.'

Still facing them, Churchill said, 'Ah, yes, Mr President . . .
"A shade of sadness, a blush of shame, over the face of the leader
came. . . ."' And then, to the Roosevelts' astonishment, Churchill
recited the remaining verses of the famous poem.

Two men sat near the back of the otherwise empty pub on the
outskirts of Castletown. The only sounds besides the low hush of
conversation were the hiss and crackle of the coal in the grate. Sean

Mulcahy hunched over the table opposite Eamon O'Farrell, cradling a glass. Mulcahy took a swallow of straight whiskey and smiled, baring an uneven row of teeth. 'Now, listen to me, Mr Eamon O'Farrell,' he said in a low, threatening tone, 'or whatever your name may be. Let me be perfectly clear.' He wiped his mouth and reached for a pack of cigarettes. 'I've had it up to *here* with your excuses.' He extracted a cigarette and, lighting it with a match, took a deep drag and exhaled a cloud of smoke. 'We need the goddamn rifles, and we need them *now*. How in the name of Jesus do you suppose—'

'Relax, Sean,' interrupted Eamon. 'As I've told you repeatedly, you'll have the rifles and ammunition. And they'll be delivered on schedule.'

Mulcahy drained his glass and glanced around the room. 'Boy,' he called out, and a lad of about fifteen popped up behind the counter where he'd been drying glasses.

'Sir,' the boy responded immediately. Eamon recognized the McDonough boy from the store and made eye contact briefly.

'Bring us another round,' said Mulcahy. 'Now, O'Farrell,' he began again, 'the men are all set for the raid.' He paused as the boy approached the table with the drinks. When he was gone, Mulcahy took a drag on his cigarette and said, 'We'll hit the Armagh garrison at the first light of day. The Brits won't stand a chance. And so you see, Mr O'Farrell . . . we'd better have those rifles. On the 25th and not a day later. I'm not sure we can trust you, with the company you've been keepin'.'

'What company?'

'The American woman. The feisty one,' he added with a wink.

'You can count on me,' said Eamon. 'At all events, you should create quite a sensation. I don't suppose there's been such a daring raid on British soil since the glory days.'

'British soil,' Mulcahy responded angrily. 'British soil my arse. Listen to me, O'Farrell.' He reached inside his worn, black coat for a revolver. Waving it in Eamon's face, he added with a smile, 'No more excuses. Understood?' He sat back and slipped the revolver under his coat. Eamon remained silent, staring calmly. Mulcahy downed his drink in a swig and abruptly stood up. 'Let's go,' he said roughly.

Once outside, Eamon fell into step alongside Mulcahy, whose felt hat was pulled low and whose hands were stretched deep into his pockets. They turned the corner and walked in a steady rain down a side street along a brick wall. Eamon suddenly grabbed Mulcahy by the shoulder and twisted his right arm behind his back, slamming him against the wall. Eamon stood behind him, pinning him against the wall while he twisted his arm behind his back.

'Aargh,' said Mulcahy in a strangled cry. 'You're breakin' my arm!'

Eamon increased the pressure and leaned close.

'Let me go!' Mulcahy pleaded.

Eamon twisted even harder, bringing another howl of pain. 'Now, Sean,' he said, '*you* listen very carefully. Don't ever threaten me again.' Mulcahy tried to nod with his bloody face pressed against the wall. 'All right,' said Eamon, releasing his grip and shoving Mulcahy away from him. Without another word, he turned and walked away.

Pulling the last letter from Charles from her pocket, Mary read it again. She could sense how much happier he was in this new assignment, the excitement and interest it held for him. As usual there was no news of the divorce, which went on endlessly. She smiled at Charles's description of his visit to Evan – what a fine friend he had made in the hospital . . . what two fine friends he had made, she considered. Lost in that thought, she put the letter in her pocket and let her mind wander to how it would feel if they were actually together. After an hour of rest and reflection on the sun-warmed boulder by the sea, Mary summoned Chelsea and together they set off, clambering over smooth rocks, slick with sea-spray, and worked their way around the base of the cliffs to the sandy beach. Chelsea bounded ahead, dragging seaweed ropes and kelp bulbs back for Mary's inspection. She stooped to inspect something in the shallows and gingerly lifted a cardboard box with a distinctive blue cross on one side and the words *Kriegsmarine – Deutschland* on the other. Mary tossed the box aside and gazed out at the tranquil sea, thinking back to the recent storms, her mind filled with images of some poor sailor struggling to stay afloat.

As she walked with the dog along the beach, she noticed someone else far in the distance, dressed in dark colours and walking towards them. As the figure drew within several hundred yards, Chelsea gave a low, throaty growl, and Mary feared it might be Eamon O'Farrell. Deciding to start back for her cottage, she said, 'Chelsea", as the dog continued to growl. The man could no doubt recognize her now, and walking away would be perceived as cowardice. So she continued on in his direction, and shortly he waved and called out: 'Good day to you, Mary.' As Eamon walked up he slipped off his cap and said, 'Still angry about the other day?'

Ignoring the question, Mary said, 'You certainly seem to spend a great deal of time wandering the beach all alone.'

'That's true enough, I suppose. But now that the weather's turned so delightful, it's better than—'

'Holding down an honest job?'

He gave her a look of surprise. 'Now, what makes you think that I—'

'Please, Eamon,' she interrupted, 'don't think you can tell me some sad story, how you're down on your luck. I know more than you may realize about you and your . . .'

Eamon stood listening, scratching his chin. 'Yes, go on,' he said. She turned away angrily and began walking towards the cliffs. After a moment, he trotted after her. 'Mary please,' he said. 'Why don't you tell me what's on your mind?'

She stopped and turned to face him, the freshening sea breeze furling her long, dark hair. 'I know about you and *that man*,' she said. 'I saw you coming out of the Anchor together, very chummy. The man's little more than a . . .'

'So that's it.' He stood with his hands on his hips. Chelsea ran up with something clenched in her mouth, her long ears and underbelly thoroughly wet. 'Listen, Mary,' he said. 'You don't understand.'

'Don't "listen Mary" me!' she said with surprising vehemence. 'Don't you see the kind of men they are?'

Eamon took a step closer. 'Although I don't agree with their bully boy ways, I see no other option to get our land, our country, back. You know the history and the politics. Nothing ever changes, never has, without a bit of pressure.'

'Don't lecture me about my history,' she said hotly. 'This Sean you've been hanging about with and his ilk are no good. They're murdering criminals. Why would you get involved with them?' Eamon looked in exasperation at the gulls wheeling overhead. 'You can't dismiss the terror these men practise,' Mary insisted, 'as *a bit of pressure*.' Her hands in fists, Mary leaned forward and said, 'Eamon, these men are fools enough to think it's in their interest if the Germans win the war! Do they really think Hitler will stop at the Irish Sea?'

Eamon smiled, noticing the sunlight on her face and her flashing blue eyes. 'Well,' he said pleasantly, 'I must say, I admire your fire. A true Irishwoman. But there's one thing you should understand,' he added, his dark eyes narrowing and hard. 'I'll have nothing to do with helping Hitler. Sure, this is neutral soil, and there may be some foolish enough to think the defeat of Britain would aid the Irish cause. But not I.' He slipped on his cap and began walking down the beach away from her.

As she watched him go, for a moment Mary regretted her angry outburst and then chided herself for thinking she could trust him. After waiting until he was no more than a speck in the distance, she summoned Chelsea and started for home.

Davenport paced, a pencil clenched in his teeth, trying to make up his mind. While it was true he was still married, he reasoned, that seemed increasingly irrelevant in the plodding divorce proceedings. And Mary was widowed, without children. Lastly, there was the war, which seemed to confer a sanction born out of desperation on a wide range of otherwise questionable actions. Damn, he thought, just do it! He sat at the desk and after hesitating a few moments, he wrote:

12 June 1943

Dear Mary,

Isn't it exceptional the difference a year can make? Within weeks I'll mark the anniversary of our disastrous defeat at Tobruk and my being shot. To think that today we're preparing for the greatest military operation in history to end the scourge of Hitler. And that my divorce is thankfully almost behind me, and, most of all, that I have found you.

But even with these warm summer days, I am not happy, dear Mary. There is only one thing that will bring me real happiness, and that is being with you. At the risk of being too bold, let me ask you straight out if I may see you. Not in London, nor there, among your prying neighbours. There's a lovely old hotel, high on the side of a hill overlooking Cardigan Bay on the coast of Wales. We went there often when I was a child, when my mother and father were young. Hopefully you could travel by ferry to Holyhead and take the bus down the coast to Barmouth. Would you meet me there the weekend of 22 June?

Dear Mary, I so hope we can see one another again. As strange as it may sound, you've become the most important thing in my life. Please answer me soon.

Affectionately,
Charles

CHAPTER ELEVEN

CURLED ON THE sofa, Mary stared at the neat writing on the plain army stationery. An involuntary sigh escaped her as two fingers came to rest on her partially opened lips. What was the old saying? Be careful what you pray for? There she was, reading the words she'd hoped for, yet somehow her reaction was totally wrong. Of course she wanted to see him; but in her daydreams it had always been a trip to London, meeting for dinner or strolling the parks, not a weekend assignation at a secluded hotel with a man she'd only seen once. The thought both terrified and excited her. Putting the letter aside, Mary took a deep breath, wondering for the umpteenth time what he would think of her if they were actually together, rather than the real but very imagined beings who had taken such intricate shape through their exchange of letters. Would she measure up to the composite picture he had of her? Would he? Mary resolved that there was only one way to find out; that she would see him. With her heart pounding, she went to the bureau and opened the pigeon-hole where she kept the writing paper.

Davenport arrived punctually at 9.00 a.m. at General Morgan's office, responding to the summons he'd received. Taking a deep breath, he knocked and then opened the door. 'Come in, Major,' said Morgan, who was seated at an elaborately carved mahogany desk next to a Union Jack. He reached for a pack of cigarettes and added, 'Sit down,' motioning to an armchair. After pausing to light a cigarette, he said, 'Thank God, Davenport, we've got at least a few men like you.'

During the uneasy silence that followed, Davenport said, 'Well, ah, thank you sir—'

'What I mean,' said Morgan, 'is that the Americans – well, they. . . . You're aware that they virtually dominate this operation.'

'Yes, sir.'

'And they're fine men for the most part. But dammit, we've

borne the brunt of the fighting till now, and I want our people in leadership positions.' Davenport nodded, wondering why he had been summoned for this unusual monologue. 'Well,' said Morgan, fixing him in his intelligent grey eyes, 'you've done an outstanding job, and frankly, you're one of the few officers with any experience commanding men in combat.'

'Thank you, sir.'

Morgan paused to expel a cloud of smoke before saying, 'I'm recommending you for a promotion, to lieutenant colonel, and naming you Section Leader for the British sector in the invasion.'

For a moment Davenport was stunned, and then he smiled and said, 'Thank you, sir. I assure you I'll do my best.'

'Well, that's all,' said Morgan with a smile. Davenport rose and started for the door. 'Oh, there's one other thing,' said Morgan.

Davenport stopped and said, 'Sir?'

'You've been working long hours. Take some leave, get away for a few days. You'll need all your stamina for the final push.'

'Thank you, sir,' said Davenport. 'I intend to do just that.'

Each day Davenport's pulse had quickened as he walked past the young soldier at the desk in the bachelor officers' barracks. Today was no different as he hurried into the building, reasoning that another day or two would pass before he should expect a reply from Mary. But the young private looked up and said, 'Major Davenport.' Davenport stopped and turned. The private handed him two envelopes. Davenport glanced at the familiar blue envelope and looked with curiosity at the cream-coloured envelope addressed to him. After bounding up the stairs two steps at a time, he hurried to his room, dropped on the bed, and tore open Mary's letter:

16 June 1943
Kilmichael Point

Dear Charles,

Your invitation to meet for a weekend in Wales filled me with delight, but I must confess the delight was mixed with some misgivings. Despite the years that have passed, I've never quite got over the feelings of being a wife and a mother, and my first reaction to the thought of spending a weekend with you was guilt. If this were merely a trip to visit you in London, I'm sure I would feel differently. But I find myself forced to come to grips with the truth about myself, and getting on with my life, and about – us.

It probably had been a mistake to invite her to a secluded hotel in the countryside. With a heavy heart, he continued reading:

The old hotel in Wales, far from prying neighbours or the crowds of the city, sounds like a perfect place. And despite the fact that we've only been together once before, over these past months you've become much more to me than a friend, and I've longed to see you. With the war, I feel that we must take what little time is given to us and not waste a moment. So there it is, as direct as I can make it. I will meet you at Barmouth, as you suggested, on the afternoon of the 22nd, trusting in you to make the necessary arrangements. The only question now is, how can I endure the days remaining before we're finally together?
Love,
Mary

Davenport stared at the ceiling. In his mind's eye he envisioned her, trying to remember her exact features. He took a deep breath and slowly exhaled before re-reading her words. At last he allowed himself to believe she might actually be falling in love with him. He stood up and stretched to his full height, imagining the quaint hotel overlooking the Barmouth estuary, filled with a feeling of pure joy. Then he remembered the other envelope on the bedside table, and withdrew an engraved invitation to *The All Services Ball*, hosted by the *Anglo-American Officers' Association*, at the Grand Ballroom of the Langham Hotel on the evening of 20th June, dress uniform or black tie. His impulse was to decline, but glancing at the name of the organization hosting the dance, he reasoned that many of his new American friends would be there, as well as his fellow British officers. It was time to re-enter society. Why not go to a dance, even if it meant wearing a dress uniform?

Many of the officers at COSSAC had regular girlfriends, but not Davenport's friend Major Hanes Butler. Somehow the gregarious North Carolinian had failed to attract the interest of any of the dozens of winsome English girls in the Norfolk House typing pool. Butler had suggested that he and Davenport should go to the ball together, and Davenport was making a final attempt to straighten his collar. He looked approvingly at his reflection, the gold braid on the shoulders of the navy-blue jacket, the brightly polished brass buttons and the scarlet stripe down the navy-blue trousers. Davenport waited at the barracks' entrance, glancing up at the cottony clouds in the pale blue sky in the cool breeze of the late June evening. With a grind of gears and cough of exhaust, an American army jeep pulled up at the kerb with a young private at the wheel and Butler at his side. 'Hop in, Charlie,' Hanes called out cheerfully. Davenport bounded down the steps and into the back seat.

'Don't you look sharp,' said Davenport with a smile.

Butler looked appraisingly at Davenport's dress uniform. 'You don't look too bad yourself,' he said. 'Let's go, Private. The Langham Hotel, Portland Place.'

When Davenport and Butler entered the ballroom, the dance floor was overflowing with couples dancing to the strains of American swing played by a big band orchestra attired in white evening jackets. Crystal chandeliers blazed over tables crowded with officers resplendent in dress uniform and women in long ball gowns, the walls festooned in alternating Union Jacks and Stars and Stripes, with an occasional red and white Maple Leaf. As the two officers made their way through the throng, they passed a number of their fellow officers from COSSAC, who looked enviously at Davenport, as word of his promotion had travelled quickly among the men. When they reached the bar, Davenport and Butler each ordered a Scotch and soda.

Captain MacDonald, one of the few officers who remained from Special Planning Group B, approached Davenport and extended his hand. 'Congratulations, Charles,' he said. 'No one deserves it more than you.'

Drinks in hand, Davenport and Butler made their way to an unoccupied table at the edge of the dance floor. 'Well, Charlie,' said Butler as he lifted his glass, 'Here's to that noble fighting machine, the British Army.'

Davenport smiled. 'And here's to that unruly mob of colonials,' he replied. After taking a sip, he glanced around the ballroom, noticing Colonel Rawlinson leaning against a pillar with one hand on his hip. It occurred to Davenport that his former CO, some fifteen years his senior, now out-ranked him by only the slimmest margin and that he, as Section Leader in one of the most elite units in the Allied Armies, had far greater responsibility than Rawlinson would ever exercise.

With a stroke of the bandleader's baton, the room was filled with the rich tones of trombones, trumpets, and clarinets as the orchestra soared into a spirited rendition of the latest Glenn Miller. Davenport tapped his foot and let his eyes fall on the couples spinning across the dance floor. Butler sang along quietly in a pleasant baritone. 'Say, Charlie,' he said, pointing with drink in hand, 'take a look at that.' A low whistle escaped his lips as a slender woman in a tight red dress cut low in the back, glided past. As she spun around, her dress revealed a suggestive amount of cleavage, and the light of the chandelier illuminated a pale, beautiful face. 'Man, oh man,' said Butler softly. 'That's some beauty.'

'Yes, I know, Hanes,' said Davenport. 'That's my wife.' Butler gave him an astonished look. 'My soon to be ex-wife, Frances,' added Davenport, staring across the dance floor and momentarily making eye contact with her. When the music ended, her partner bowed and walked off in the direction of the bar. Frances stared briefly at Davenport and then began slowly walking toward him. 'Excuse me, Hanes,' said Davenport as he stood up. 'I won't be a minute.' He walked calmly up to her and said, 'Good evening, darling. You're looking well.'

She eyed him coldly and said, 'What do you want?'

Davenport shook his head and said, 'Want? Look, Frances, I merely thought I should say, now that we're almost finished—'

'*Damn* you, Charles,' she said in a low, threatening tone. 'I suppose you're satisfied, now that you've had the satisfaction of humiliating Trevor and me!'

Davenport gave her a thin smile. 'Satisfaction?' he said. 'Not exactly. But you might say you've finally got what you deserve.' He turned and threaded his way back to the table. 'Say, Hanes,' he said, 'I'll stand you another drink.'

Touring the house for a last time before bed, Mary reflected on how accustomed she had become to living alone. It was only at night, with the lights out and facing the empty bed in the darkness, that she admitted how lonely she was. She had grown so used to a warm, welcoming body sharing that space. As she settled under the eiderdown, she felt a shiver of deep longing. Mary closed her eyes and, after listening to the clock, soon fell asleep.

She watched him, lying peacefully beside her on the beach in the warm sunshine. She lightly touched him, not wanting to wake him yet unable to resist the temptation to brush back his hair, exposing his face to the sun. With the sound of the surf in her ears, she settled beside him on the sand. His arms met her movement and enfolded her in a welcoming embrace. All at once, she was in the chair in her bedroom, unsure whether it was evening or morning, listening to the sound of the clock as the breeze stirred the lace at the window. He was lying peacefully on the bed. As he slowly rolled over, a crimson efflorescence suddenly blossomed on his chest, the dark stain spreading across the fabric of his khaki uniform.

Mary sat bolt upright with a gasp in the pitch-black room, her heart pounding. Raising a hand to her mouth, she peered into the darkness, trying to recapture the vivid dream . . . lying on the beach . . . Charles lying beside her, and then something terrible happened. But what was it? She searched her memory, but the fragment had slipped away, leaving her with a sensation of dread and fear so intense that it churned her stomach.

The train departed Paddington promptly at 8.10 a.m. Davenport sat by the window in the crowded carriage as the working class neighborhoods of London gave way to the open countryside, the meadows filled with bright wildflowers. The spell of near perfect weather had lasted for days and, as he watched the livestock grazing under the canopy of ancient oaks, he prayed that it would continue through the weekend. As the train rattled along past the Cotswold villages, he gazed out at the stone cottages and medieval turrets, thinking the timeless beauty of the English countryside seemed so far removed from the war's devastation. There were two worlds now, Davenport considered, of war and the world of peace, and his time in the world of peace could not last, and he was struck by the grim, irrational certainty of this transience. Real peace, for him, could be obtained only by returning to the crucible of war.

At last the spire of the famous Worcester cathedral came into view in the distance. Crossing the trestle bridge over the Severn, the train slowed to a stop with a hiss of steam. After a brief tram ride from the station, the final streets to his house seemed strangely unreal to him, as though somehow the war had never happened, and he was merely returning home from school. He quickened his pace as he turned on to a narrow road with rows of small brick bungalows. A neighbour wearing a sunbonnet as she worked in the garden waved to him as he passed and called out, 'Hallo, Charles! Welcome home.'

'Good afternoon, Mrs Pickford,' he answered with a wave. He walked along the fence and stopped at the gate. As he let himself in, the door swung open and his father appeared on the porch.

Davenport let his bag drop and half walked, half ran, up the brick steps. 'Dad,' he exclaimed, reaching out to embrace him.

The elder Davenport placed his hands on his son's shoulders and leaned back to get a better look. 'My goodness, Son,' he said with a smile. 'What's this?' He motioned to the insignia on Davenport's collar.

'I've been promoted,' said Davenport. 'I'm a lieutenant colonel now.'

'A lieutenant colonel,' said his father at length. 'Your mother would have been so proud. Now, come in, and let's have a cup of tea.'

After passing an hour or more over potted meat sandwiches in the kitchen, Davenport sat with his father in the small parlour at the front of the house. On one side of the room were bookcases filled with cloth-bound volumes and a collection of photographs; his mother on her wedding day; father, mother and son on his graduation day from college; and Davenport in uniform before embarking for Cairo. His father knocked out his briar pipe on the heel of his hand into an ashtray, hunched over with his arms on his knees and said, 'Tell me, Son, what will this new assignment mean?'

'I'll be supervising the detailed planning for the British portion of the invasion.'

'That's a big job.'

'Yes, it is. And most of the work has to be finished before the final planning conference with the Americans in August.'

'Am I right in thinking this means you'll be spared from any more fighting?'

Davenport looked down at the carpet before answering. 'Yes, I suppose so,' he replied. More convincingly, he added, 'It's a staff assignment for me till the war's over.'

'Thank goodness,' said Davenport's father. 'You've done your part, and it's time for the other chaps to do theirs. Well, I know you must be on your way.' He paused, collecting his thoughts. 'There's one other thing, Son,' he said quietly, 'your mother would know how to say this, but I'm on my own now.' Davenport gave him an expectant look. 'After all you've been through, you deserve someone who's right for you. From everything you've written about her, Mary seems very special . . .'

'She is,' said Davenport. 'You'll like her very much.' He stood up to go.

His father rose and said, 'Well, then, good luck, Son.' Reaching into his pocket, he said, 'I almost forgot.' He handed Davenport a small packet. 'Seeds from my best sweet-peas. For Mary's garden.'

Mary stood at the railing, her fingers wrapped around the smooth teak, as the ferry slipped away from the Kingstown dock. The Irish Sea stretched into the distance, the air filled with scents of sea-salt and wet hemp, one shimmering wave after another that scrolled into a long, white crest with flashes of silver and pearl. Leaning back, she let the breeze furl her skirt as she had when she was a child. There was a weightlessness to her mood, so sensitive to the smallest thing that she could feel nothing at all. She couldn't think or plan, so she swayed at the railing in the sharp breeze. Finally the piercing whistle from the stacks signalled their approach to the long pier jutting out from Holyhead, warning her to retrieve her bag and disembark. Her heartbeat quickened with the realization that within a short while she would be there.

Davenport double-declutched his father's Morris and shifted gear, delighting in the unaccustomed pleasure of driving the open country roads. He sped through the gentle hills of Shropshire and passed into Wales, where the change in scenery was almost as striking as the change in language, the unpronounceable string of consonants on the road signs. Densely forested hills, smudged with clouds, rose steeply from the roadsides, and the lush green pastures beyond the rock walls were dotted with sheep. Rounding a sharp turn, the sun broke through the clouds encircling the hilltops, striking the bright green foliage cloaking the ridge. Davenport slowed at the sign for Dolgellau, a name that flooded him with childhood memories, clattering along the same road in the back seat, his father at the wheel with his mother beside him. After passing through the village, he drove the final miles into the centre of town and after a few moments located the bus depot. He hurried to the small waiting room, which was empty except for an elderly woman dozing on one of the wooden benches. He checked the time, fifteen minutes before the scheduled arrival of the bus from Caernarfon. When the clock showed 5.40 he stood up impulsively and walked to the door. Despite the fact that ferries were still running from Ireland, with the wartime restrictions he feared she might have been detained, or worse, the short voyage from Kingstown cancelled. After several minutes he heard the unmistakable rumble of an approaching vehicle and watched as the wide bumper nosed into the bus stand and slowed to a stop a few paces from him. With a final squeal of brakes, the doors swung open. Several older couples slowly descended the steps, followed by a young mother holding the hand of a small boy who stubbornly stopped to inspect the mechanism of the door, and then Mary's slender legs and hips came into view as, clutching her hat and bag, she made the last awkward step down to the pavement. Feeling his heart skip a beat, he pushed past the boy and said, 'Mary.' For a moment he stared into her eyes and then folded her in a warm embrace.

CHAPTER TWELVE

DAVENPORT TOOK A tense, timid Mary by the arm and walked her to the car. In relative silence with the wind rushing in the partially opened windows, they drove off. With her thick, dark hair complementing cornflower-blue eyes, Mary was even prettier than Davenport remembered.

She turned to him and said, 'It's beautiful, Charles. Not at all what I expected. These hills are so steep and so lush. What's that?' She pointed where the roadside fell away toward a wide body of water.

'The Barmouth estuary,' said Davenport with a smile. 'It stretches some fifteen miles into the valley, and at low tide empties all its water into Cardigan Bay. It's quite a sight.' He turned into the drive at Bontddu Hall, a gabled Victorian hotel overlooking the estuary.

'It's *perfect*,' said Mary, as she climbed out and glanced at the drooping boughs of the evergreens and manicured lawn.

Taking her suitcase, Davenport walked with her to the hotel's entrance and held open the door. 'I hope you don't mind,' he said quietly, as they approached the front desk, 'but I made the reservation under the name Miss Mary Kennedy.' She briefly made eye contact and said, 'Of course.' As he struck the bell on the counter to summon the clerk, Davenport placed her suitcase by the counter and said, 'I'm going up to my room. Shall we meet for drinks at, say, seven?' Feeling a wave of embarrassment as two dowagers with shawls emerged from the lounge, Mary responded with a pained nod and forced smile. Touching her lightly on the arm, he turned and walked quickly to the stairs. Was this what the weekend held in store, she wondered, as she waited? Whispered comments, furtive glances, the disapproving stares of the older guests?

After a moment, the elderly clerk appeared at the desk and said coldly, 'Can I help you?'

It dawned on her that she had never registered alone as a hotel guest. There had always been her father, and then David. 'Yes,' she said. 'I'm checking in.'

The clerk raised his eyebrows slightly and said, 'You have a reservation?'

'Oh, yes,' said Mary. 'Under the name Kennedy. Mary Kennedy.'

The clerk harrumphed, opened a worn black book and ran a crooked finger down the entries on the ruled page. 'Kennedy,' he muttered, 'ah, here it is. Miss Mary Kennedy. Two nights, departing on Sunday.' As Mary rested her arm on the counter to sign the register, she was conscious of the man staring at her and glancing at her wedding ring. Looking up to meet his cold stare, she said, 'Oh, you see, my husband is, well, he passed away . . .'

'Terribly sorry, ah, Miss Kennedy.' He took the register, lifted a heavy brass key from its hook and laid it on the counter. 'Room 312,' he said. 'Do you need any help with your luggage?'

'No, thank you, I'll manage,' said Mary as she reached for her suitcase. By the time she reached the third floor, she was out of breath and angry with herself for feeling so ashamed. Was it a sin to be young and alone, a single woman registering as a hotel guest? Charles had made it seem even more awkward when he had simply left her, though she supposed it would have been even worse had he stayed. Finding her room, she unlocked the door and looked in. It was no one's idea of luxury, yet it had an understated elegance that seemed just right, with a brass bed dressed in crisp linens, between tall windows where curtains stirred gently. Mary dropped her bag and tossed her hat on the bed. The faintest hint of lemon scented the oak dressing table, where there was a vase with fresh flowers just beginning to droop. Mary was struck with a sense of déjà vu – remembering an almost identical vase in the hotel room on her honeymoon. The image caught her unaware, triggering a feeling of betrayal. She felt for her wedding ring, gently turning it before slipping it off and placing it on the dressing table then stood before the mirror to see what damage the day's travels had done, studying the tiny lines at the corners of her eyes and outlining her smile. Raising her fingertips to her cheeks, she wondered . . . what would he think? Could she possibly live up to his expectations? Could he live up to hers? Shaking her head, she began getting ready for the evening.

She changed into a simple blue dress, the full skirt of which accentuated her trim waist, and tied back her hair with a ribbon. Adding a hint of colour to her lips and a pat of perfume on her wrists, she was satisfied. With a final look in the mirror and glance at the vase, she started down to the lounge, as nervous as a schoolgirl on her first date. Davenport rose from the sofa as Mary entered the room. Tall and confident in a tweed jacket and charcoal flannels, with a regimental tie and white shirt, he walked toward her and took her hand. For a moment they looked awkwardly at one another.

'You look lovely,' said Davenport at last. 'I trust that your room . . . is all right?'

'The room?' said Mary, letting go of his hand. 'Yes, it's very nice, though I found checking in somewhat humiliating.'

'Really?' said Davenport with a puzzled look. 'Was there a problem. . . ?'

'Why don't we sit?' she said with a forced smile. Without waiting for an answer, she dropped on the sofa and crossed her legs.

He awkwardly sat a few feet from her, resting his arms on his knees, and smiled encouragingly. 'Hard to believe, isn't it?' he began.

'Yes,' said Mary with a nod.

'That we're actually together,' he explained, 'after all these months.'

'It doesn't quite seem real, I suppose,' she said, comparing the sight of him to her memory of the injured soldier at the piano. He was more handsome than she remembered, but looked much more like the university lecturer he'd described in his letters than the uniformed officer she'd expected. In the ensuing silence Mary forced another smile and then said, 'I'm surprised to see you in civilian clothes. I was expecting to see you in uniform.'

'Well, it does seem a bit odd,' he admitted. 'And I've no doubt the old codgers around this place think I'm shirking.' Both of them smiled and seemed to unbend slightly. 'I left the uniform at home with Dad. Which reminds me.' He reached into a pocket for a small envelope and said, 'He wanted you to have these. He swears they're the best sweet-peas in England.' Mary took the packet and shook it to rattle the seeds. Davenport reached down to pick up two neatly wrapped parcels from the floor. 'What's the old saying?' he said. 'Beware of Greeks bearing gifts?'

'Charles,' she said, 'you shouldn't have.' He handed her the smaller parcel, which she opened. 'Chocolate!' she said with a bright smile. 'How did you ever find it?'

'It helps to work with the Yanks . . . sorry, the Americans,' said Davenport. 'They have access to all the delicacies we've been without for years.' He handed her the other package.

She felt the weight of it in her hands, removed the wrapping paper, and said, 'My', holding up a blue leather volume with an embossed gold border. '*The Oxford Book of Sixteenth Century Verse*. Now I can read all the poems you've quoted to me.' She put the book aside and turned to him. Aware that her pent-up apprehension had been suddenly swept away, she impulsively reached for both of his hands and said, 'Oh, Charles, I'm so happy we're together at last.'

Savouring her touch, he said, 'It's been such a long time.' He glanced at his watch. 'We have a dinner reservation here, in the dining room. Shall we go?'

Mary picked up her gifts and rose from the sofa. 'Lead the way, Major,' she said in a loud enough voice to be heard by the elderly couple seated across the room.

Davenport took her by the arm and said, 'It's Lieutenant Colonel, actually.'

Mary stopped to face him. 'A promotion?' she said with a surprised look. 'We'll have to celebrate.'

At the end of a pleasant dinner, despite the limited choices of mutton or fish, they stepped out on the terrace as the light was beginning to fade. Two wooden chairs faced the vista of the estuary and sea. As they walked across the grass, the sun slipped slowly below the horizon, suffusing the cool air with an evanescent glow. 'Look, Mary,' he said, as he sank into one of the chairs. 'Look down below.' She watched in the fading light as the waters of the estuary raced to the west and out to sea, like water emptying from a tub, leaving the estuary empty.

'It's amazing,' she said. 'I've never seen anything like it.' The sky had turned deep violet, and the sliver of moon was visible above the ridge.

'To think,' he said, 'it's the moon drawing the water out to sea.'

Gazing at her in the twilight, he thought just as some irresistible force was drawing them together.

Charles opened his eyes with the pleasant sensation of a cool draught on his face. Sunlight streamed in the windows, and a light breeze furled the net curtains. He stretched out and pulled the covers up to his chin. Closing his eyes, he replayed the scene from the end of the evening, staring into her eyes as they stood at the door, debating whether to kiss her. In the end, he squeezed her hand and bade her goodnight, feeling like an awkward fifteen-year-old.

Over a hearty breakfast of Irish porridge and a pot of coffee, Davenport explained to Mary his plans for the morning. First, they would drive to Barmouth and then up the coastal road to Harlech to explore its magnificent castle, returning in time for lunch. As they sped down the winding road to town, they chattered happily, exchanging stories of his work in London and her solitary existence with Chelsea, like old friends with lots of catching up to do.

Davenport parked at the jetty and said, 'Let's have a look.' Helping Mary out, he put an arm around her waist, and they walked out on the sea wall.

'Exceptional, isn't it?' he said, raising his voice over the wind. It was high tide, and the estuary was full to the brim, a full mile across.

Mary shielded her eyes with her hand. 'Yes,' she said. 'Just last night we watched all that water rush out to sea.' She gazed toward a fogbank obscuring the horizon, pointed, and said, 'There, directly across the bay, is Kilmichael Point. And at the top of the cliffs is my house.' She turned to him and said, 'If you close your eyes you can see it.'

A gust of wind whipped around them, causing him to hold her tight. 'Mary,' he said, 'do you have any idea how happy you make me?' She pulled away and answered with a smile as the stiff breeze tossed her hair. 'Let's go,' he said, taking her hand, 'before we're blown off the breakwater.' Racing back to the car, they scrambled inside and looked at one another, laughing at their wind-tangled locks. When Mary leaned over to muss his hair, their eyes met, and she impulsively kissed him. Reaching an arm around her, he held her close and savored the kiss. 'Mmm' he said as he pressed the ignition and pulled out onto the road. Mary leaned back, allowing the wind to flow over her with a look of deep contentment. They rumbled along the narrow road, bounded by pastures filled with black-faced sheep, enclosed by rock walls that rose steeply toward the cloud-en-shrouded mountaintops. After a half-hour they entered the town of Harlech and, around a curve, the blackened ruin of Harlech Castle came into view. They parked and he took a thermos from the back while Mary tied a scarf over her hair, and they strolled arm-in-arm on the cobblestones to the castle. Entering through a high arch into an interior courtyard, Davenport looked up at the blackened ramparts and turrets and said, 'I remember coming here as a child. Like most boys, I was intrigued by knights and castles.'

He led her by the hand to a spiral stone staircase. When they emerged on the ramparts overlooking the courtyard, a group of school children appeared with their young teacher. 'Listen,' said Davenport, as they pressed against the wall to let the children pass. The guttural sound of the native Welsh on the lips of the children was strangely pleasing. Davenport led Mary to one of the corner turrets facing out to sea. Extending a hand, he helped her up on the smooth stone wall where they could rest their backs on the tower. From their perch they looked out over the dunes to the glittering waves of Cardigan Bay stretching to the horizon. Comfortably ensconced on the ledge with Mary leaning against him, he said, 'Can you imagine the raiders coming ashore to invade this citadel? And the bow-men on these very walls, ready to repel them.' Davenport looked far out to sea. '1283,' he said. 'The year King Edward built this castle to subdue the Celts and conquer Wales.' Mary put her bag on her lap and opened the clasp. 'And I see you've brought your book,' said Charles.

'Yes, Professor, I have,' she said, as she took out the blue volume from her purse. 'And you're going to read me your favorite poems.'

Davenport took the book and leafed through the pages. 'Here's a good place to begin,' he said. 'Andrew Marvell's *To his Coy Mistress*.' As he read aloud, Mary unscrewed the lid of the thermos and poured a cup of hot tea. She relished the warm sun on her face as she sipped her tea and listened to Davenport's carefully enunciated voice. After a while, he put the book aside, lifted her chin, and kissed her, softly at first, and then with an intensity that surprised both of them. She reached her arms around him and moulded her body to his, delighting in the sensation.

Mary finally pulled away and looked up into his eyes. 'Now I want you to read your favorite sonnet from Shakespeare.'

'All right,' he said, turning the pages. 'My favourite is number seventy-three. *"That time of year thou may'st in me behold,"'* he read aloud, '"*when yellow leaves, or none, or few, do hang . . .*"' Reaching the final couplet, he closed the book and recited the verses from memory: '"*This thou perceiv'st, which makes thy love more strong . . . To love that well which thou must leave ere long.*"' Mary held him close and said nothing but silently repeated the closing line of the sonnet. A cloud slid before the sun, casting a shadow that caused Mary to shiver in the cool breeze.

Davenport held her tight, glanced at his watch, and said, 'The time has got away from us. We'd better be going.' He vaulted down from the wall and then reached up to lift her down. With her arm through his, they returned by the narrow winding staircase down to the rectangle of bright green grass.

It was nearing one o'clock when Davenport turned the Morris into the hotel drive. As soon as the car came to a stop, Mary climbed out and said, 'I'm going up to change. I won't be a minute.'

'No hurry,' he said. 'I'll meet you in the dining room.'

He slipped on his blazer and walked to the dining room in a separate building connected to the hotel by a brick path. As he entered, two elderly couples were settling their bill. A black squall was approaching from the north, abruptly blotting out the sun and tossing the boughs of the evergreens at the edge of the lawn. Turning, he saw Mary standing in the entrance, wearing a floral print dress, belted at the waist, and, he noted with approval, nylon stockings, a rare sight in wartime. Davenport rose, held her chair, and said, 'You look smashing.' He bent down and kissed her cheek.

Looking at him happily, she said, 'This is such a treat. I'd almost forgotten what it's like to dine in a nice restaurant, with linen and silver on the table.' Davenport sipped his drink as they studied the menu. 'Lobster bisque,' said Mary. 'I might almost be back in Boston.'

'You shall have it,' said Davenport. 'And whatever else pleases you.' The waiter returned, and they each ordered bisque and Dover sole. 'And the wine list,' said Davenport.

'Sorry, sir, but with the war . . .'

'There's bound to be something in the cellar,' Davenport said encouragingly. 'Would you mind having a look?'

The waiter returned after a few minutes with a bottle and silver ice bucket. 'I'm sorry, sir,' he said, as he held out the bottle for Davenport's inspection, 'I'm afraid it's all we had.'

Examining the label, Davenport said, 'A '36 Montrachet. That should do nicely.' After sampling the wine, he instructed the waiter to pour it, then raised his glass and, looking Mary in the eye, said, 'Your health and happiness.'

'And yours,' said Mary before taking a sip. 'Oh, Charles, I've never felt happier.'

When they had finished lunch and were enjoying the last of the wine, the storm struck, the rain slapping the windows in sheets and the wind shaking the branches of the trees. The lights flickered with another crash of thunder, and Davenport, staring fervently at Mary, said, 'Do you know how much I love you?'

She bowed her head for a moment before raising her eyes. 'And I love you too, Charles,' she murmured. 'Before this weekend, I wasn't sure. But now I know.'

'God, you make me so happy.' He felt her stocking-clad leg against his under the table and a deep stirring of passion. Reaching across the table to take her hand, he said, 'Are you finished?'

She squeezed his hand and said, 'Yes, let's go.' As they rose from the table, the sky outside the window was dark as night. Standing in the doorway, they looked out at the pouring rain. Charles turned to Mary and said, 'Let's make a run for it.' Drenched from the dash across the path, they walked past the somnolent clerk at the front desk and hurried up the three flights of stairs. Standing outside the door to her room, they laughed at the sight of their clinging, rain-soaked clothes and dripping hair. 'Let's get you inside and out of those wet clothes,' he said, as he fumbled with the key. Mary arched an eyebrow. 'Oh,' said Davenport with a smile, 'I suppose that came out wrong.' She followed him into the dark room, clutching her arms around herself with a shiver. Moving past him into the bathroom, she said, 'I won't be long', and closed the door firmly behind her. Davenport hung his jacket on a chair and unbuttoned his shirt, listening to the sound of water pouring into the bath. He tapped lightly on the door. 'Sorry,' he said, 'might I bother you for a towel?' The door opened a crack, and her slender hand appeared with a towel. 'Thanks,' he said, as her hand disappeared behind the door. After switching on the lamp, he stripped off his clothes, dried off, and stood before the mirror with the towel wrapped around him, combing his hair. He watched in the mirror as the bathroom door opened and Mary emerged, wearing a robe with her long, damp hair lying on her shoulders. He put down the comb and turned around. She walked up and took both his hands.

'Oh, Mary,' he said, his heart pounding.

'Shh,' she said, touching his lips with her fingertips.

He bent down and kissed her. After a minute he pulled back and said, 'We shouldn't.'

'I know,' she said, tightly clinging to him. On tiptoe, she kissed him again amid the sounds of rain dripping from the trees.

Mary pressed her cheek against the down pillow, her eyes closed. The bedding was soft and warm on her bare skin, a pleasant contrast to the cool breeze on her face. She blinked into the half-light and reached a hand across the bed. Where was Charles? Modestly pulling the blanket to her chin, she sat up. The room was neat but empty. She blushed at the thought of the passion they'd shared. She threw back the covers and rose from the bed. After splashing water on her face and brushing out her tangled hair, she dressed quickly. Satisfied the hall was empty, she let herself out and walked to the top of the stairs. As she placed her hand on the banister, she could just make out the notes of a piano. The music grew louder as she went down, a lilting, melancholy melody that seemed somehow familiar. Standing at the entrance to the lounge, she could see Charles at the piano with his back to her. Mary listened, staring at him and remembering. As he played the final notes, she brushed the tears from her eyes and walked across the room. 'It's beautiful,' she said as he looked up at her.

He rose from the bench, put his arms around her waist, and said, 'I'm sorry, but I didn't want to wake you.'

Mary pressed her face against his chest. 'What were you playing?' she said. 'It's the same melody you were playing the day we met at the hospital.'

'Yes,' said Davenport. 'It's something I wrote. You remember?' Mary nodded. How could she forget? As he leaned down and kissed her, the fragrance of her face and hair flooded back over him.

'Mmm,' she said, 'we should be careful.'

'Yes,' he agreed with a smile. 'It wouldn't do to spend our entire holiday in bed.'

'Charles, I'm famished,' said Mary. 'Do you suppose they're still serving tea?'

A short time later, an elderly waitress entered with a tray with a teapot, china, milk, sugar, scones, jam, and clotted cream. Davenport poured as Mary spread jam on a scone and took a bite. 'Here's one department,' she said, 'where the British are hands down winners.'

Once he'd poured them a second cup, Davenport sat back

comfortably on the sofa and happily looked at her. 'I've been thinking,' he said, 'there you are, all alone in your cottage.' She crossed her legs and took a sip of tea. 'And there I am, in London in a tiny room in the barracks. And soon to be a free man.'

'Is the divorce about to be final?'

'A matter of weeks, if not days. Mary, there's so much we could enjoy together. If you were in London . . .'

She placed her teacup on the table, her heart pounding. 'I'm not sure,' she said hesitantly. 'This has been wonderful, but it's the first time we've been together.'

'Mary,' said Davenport in a low voice. 'Sure, we haven't been together *physically*, but we've been together in a more special way. Mary . . . I love you.'

Mary brushed back her hair and said, 'And I love you.'

After a moment of uneasy silence, Davenport said, 'Think about it, will you?' Mary nodded. 'Good,' he said. 'We can talk later.'

Following another leisurely dinner in the hotel dining room, Charles and Mary returned to the lounge, where a fire was burning in the hearth, just as an older couple were tottering off to bed. 'Charles,' said Mary as she settled on the sofa, 'you promised to finish telling me about your work.'

Davenport leaned back in the comfortable armchair and said, 'Well, it's top secret, of course,' he said quietly. 'Very hush-hush. Our staff is responsible for the detailed planning for the invasion,' he continued, 'and I'm in charge of the British part in the landings. The Americans will have the lion's share, but our part is quite large and enormously complex.' Mary listened with a look of intense admiration. 'The show will begin with a terrific naval bombardment and aerial attack, designed to knock out the beach-front fortifications. Meanwhile, parachute troops will land further inland, to disrupt enemy communications and blow the bridges. And then the men will come ashore. The tricky part will be getting the landing craft close enough to allow the men to wade in. The Germans are studding the beaches with tens of thousands of obstacles and mines. We've got to have the work finished by August.'

A worried look clouded Mary's face. 'Do you think,' she asked, 'that a great many men will be killed? They seem so helpless, coming ashore in small boats. Isn't there some other way?'

'I'm afraid not,' said Davenport. 'The Admiralty seem to think their ships will knock out the German resistance, and the dazed survivors won't put up much of a fight. But I know the Germans, and they'll be ready. We can do it, but it won't be easy, and many will die going ashore.'

'I'm so sorry,' said Mary. 'So many brave young men. But thank God you won't be going in with them.'

'No, I suppose not,' said Davenport grimly.

'Charles, you've done your part,' said Mary. 'Promise me,' she said urgently, 'you'll stay where you are on General Morgan's staff.'

Davenport looked in her eyes. 'Mary,' he said, 'I have no intention . . . that is, I mean to stay in my present job, but I can't make a promise like that.'

'Why can't you?' she said desperately. 'Please, you *must* promise me!'

'Believe me, I have no intention of putting in for a transfer. But if I'm needed, well. . . I'm sure you understand.' She nodded silently, wiping a tear from her eye. 'Mary,' he began again. 'I want you to come to London. We can find you a flat near the park, so there'll be plenty of room for Chelsea. London's safe now, and you'll feel right at home with Yanks everywhere—'

'But Charles,' she interrupted, 'what about my house? It seems so . . . so sudden.'

'You ran away there, from everything you lost. Now it's time, don't you see? Time to start again. There's nothing there for you. I love you and want you near me. And when the war's over . . .' He paused. 'I want to spend my life with you.'

'Oh God,' she said, 'how I wish the war would end, and then . . .'

'Mary, you *can* come to London. Do you understand what I'm saying? I want you to *marry* me.'

Gazing at his earnest expression, thinking how handsome he was, she was filled with a strange sense of foreboding. She thought briefly about the day, cradled in his arms on the ledge at Harlech . . . the sensation of bare skin and the warm breath of passion. She wanted to say, yes, of course, I'll come to be with you. She gave him a stricken look and murmured, 'If only you knew how happy that would make me.'

'It's late,' he said, 'and it's been a wonderful day. I should let you rest. I know how much it is to think about.'

Moments later they stood at the door to her room. 'Goodnight,' he said simply. He leaned down to kiss her, lingering for a long moment.

'Goodnight.'

'I'll see you in the morning,' he said, letting go of her hand. 'Sweet dreams.'

The room was black and still. Mary turned on the pillow, trying to fall asleep, but a vague unease gnawed at her. After thinking about going with him to London, marrying him, she fell asleep at last. She slept a dreamless sleep and then suddenly was wide awake. She threw back the covers and walked to the window. Staring out in the darkness, she touched her fingertips to the cold glass. An image of Charles lying on the bed as a red stain spread across his khaki shirt flashed into her consciousness. The distant dream was vividly imprinted, and she knew with a sudden, terrible certainty that if she went with him, if he became hers, he would be like the others. It was a curse. In an instant she realized there was only one hope, one chance. She walked slowly back to bed and lay down, burying her face on the pillow and choking back sobs.

When Charles awoke, judging from the brightness of the room, he decided it must be late. Cursing himself, he threw back the covers and fumbled for his watch. He stood up and, as he reached for his robe, noticed the corner of a blue envelope under the door. Stooping to pick it up, he knew in an instant it was from Mary, and he slumped back on the bed to read her brief note:

Dearest Charles,

This is the hardest thing I've ever had to do. I can't possibly explain it, because I don't understand it myself. I love you with all my heart. And no matter what happens, even if you should find someone else, I will always love you.

By the time you read this, I will be gone. During the night I made up my mind to go back to Ireland, knowing that if I stayed I would never have the courage to do what I believe I must, as I can't face losing you. I could never explain and can only say that I will be waiting, however long it takes, when the war is finally over. Yesterday was the happiest day in my life, and the saddest.

I pray, Charles, that some day you'll come for me.

Love,

Mary

CHAPTER THIRTEEN

OH GOD, SIGHED Mary, it felt good to be home. This *is* home, she insisted. On her knees in the garden, she dug a furrow in the damp soil and reached for the packet of seeds. As she carefully tipped the seeds, an image of Charles on the sofa came to mind; so handsome in his tweed jacket with his neatly combed hair. She clutched the packet, not wanting to let the image go, like all the other fragments of the weekend that filled her mind. She didn't know how she could ever explain; everyone she'd loved, she'd lost. Mary bent over to smooth the soil with the back of the trowel. She stood up, leaving the tool, and went to the tap, rinsing her hands and drying them on her tattered apron before slipping it off and tossing it on the porch. She started for the path down to the beach with the dog trotting after her. Standing on the rocks below, Mary stared into the tidal pools and then stepped gingerly onto the sand and slipped off her sandals. As they walked along, Mary allowed the waves to lap over her feet, thinking about Charles, when suddenly it dawned on her that she had not given him the sweater she'd brought as a gift. Mary's whole being crumpled in on itself, and she sank to the sand in misery. She stayed there for what seemed a long time, shuddering sobs racking her body, as the puppy lay unhappily at her side, chin resting on her paws. And that is how Eamon found her, swept away by sadness, simply lost. His shadow was the first sense Mary had of someone standing above her, stepping between her and the sun. She had not even heard Chelsea's bark. Shielding her red, swollen eyes with her hand to look at him, there was a brief, fleeting feeling that it might be Charles. But she recognized Eamon crouching beside her, reaching out a hand to her shoulder in comfort. She instinctively drew back, as though his touch were caustic.

'What is it, Mary?' he asked softly. 'Is there anything I can do?'

She merely shook her head, too distraught to consider the risks of another encounter on the isolated stretch of beach. After a few minutes he eased himself into a sitting position and said, 'It's no use holding it in. Why don't you tell me what's wrong.'

Mary sat up and eyed him warily. 'It's nothing I care to talk about,' she said hoarsely. Not wanting to appear rude, she added, 'But thanks, anyway.' He clasped his arms around his knees, looking at her with an expression of genuine concern. She took a deep breath.

'Oh, God,' she sighed, 'sometimes I feel like such a fool. I'm afraid I've thrown away the thing that matters most to me.'

'It sounds,' he said, 'like a matter of the heart.'

She looked up and, brushing away a wisp of hair, nodded slightly. In the past, she'd told him something about her losses and wondered if he had heard the gossip in the village. 'Yes, you could say that,' she said after a moment. 'There's someone I . . . care about very much. And I'm not sure if I'll ever see him again, because, well, I can't explain it. If only the war would end. . . .'

'Yes, the war,' said Eamon, nodding in agreement. 'Don't worry, Mary, you don't need to explain. They're lucky here, with no war to send their men and boys off to. But I think I understand what you're going through.'

When she tried to speak her voice cracked, and the tears began again, turning to convulsive sobs. Rather than try to comfort her, Eamon merely sat cross-legged on the sand and listened. After a while, exhausted by the intensity of her feelings, the tears stopped. The sun had sunk below the cliffs, leaving a chill in the wet sand and gusty breeze. Eamon stood up, dusted the sand from his knees, and reached down to take her hands. 'We had best get you home,' he said, as he helped her up. He led her like a child along the beach, recovered her sandals, and ascended the twisting path to her cottage.

Standing with one hand on the door, she considered his kindness and said, 'Won't you come in and have a cup of tea?'

'You have tea?' said Eamon with a smile.

'A little.'

They sat in silence at the kitchen table, waiting for the kettle to whistle. 'You might try telling me,' Eamon began, 'now that you're a bit more calm, about your, ah, friend. Has something happened to him?'

Mary rose to take the kettle from the stove, certain that he knew something of the rumours, and poured the steaming water into the pot. 'My friend,' she said, 'as you've no doubt heard, is a British officer.' She placed cups and saucers on the table with the teapot and milk jug. 'And no, nothing has happened to him.' After pouring each of them tea, she sat and took a sip. The heat on the back of her throat was a welcome relief after so much crying. She let the cup nest in her hands, spreading warmth. 'I mean, he was wounded,' she added, after taking another sip, 'but that was some time ago. Actually, that's how we met, in the hospital. And we've just been writing to one another, since he's been in London, on staff assignment.'

'I see,' Eamon nodded, politely pretending to understand.

'But I went to see him in Wales, at a place called Barmouth. And, well, I'm afraid I made a mess of things.'

'And now you're worried,' Eamon suggested, 'that what with the war . . . Listen, Mary, there are thousands and thousands of women just like you whose men are away.'

'Yes, I know,' said Mary, 'but it's not that. I'm afraid I left him, without even saying goodbye. I just couldn't bring myself to face him. I can't possibly explain it.'

Eamon finished his tea and studied Mary's face. 'I think I understand,' he said. 'With all you've lost, that is. But didn't you say that he's on staff assignment in London?'

'Yes, that's right.'

'Well, then, he should be safe, now that the air raids have stopped.'

'I know it doesn't make sense, Eamon, but I just can't get over the feeling. . . .'

'London must be a fascinating place to be stationed,' said Eamon. 'What sort of job does your friend have?'

'Oh, it's very important,' Mary answered with a small smile. 'And he's just been made lieutenant colonel.'

Eamon abruptly stood up. 'Well,' he said, 'you shouldn't worry. I'm sure your colonel will be out of harm's way. And you'd better make sure he understands why you left him the way you did.'

Mary nodded and said, 'Yes, I know.'

'Well, I'd best be on my way,' said Eamon cheerfully. 'Thanks for the tea.'

Mary smiled and said, 'Thanks so much for . . . well, for listening.'

'Don't think of it,' said Eamon. 'Perhaps now you'll realize,' he added, 'that I'm not such a bad fellow.' Before she could answer, he was out the door and on his way. The catharsis had cleared her mind, she realized, for the first time since she'd returned from Wales. She walked to the bureau in the living room and extracted several sheets of paper and her pen from the drawer.

Davenport, seated at the desk in his windowless office, put down his pencil and rubbed his eyes. Oblivious to the voices in the hallway, he studied the large, finely detailed map of the Normandy coast-line. An area stretching from Cabourg at the eastern extremity, to the village of Port-en-Bessin, about midway along the coast toward

Cherbourg, was marked in red pencil. This forty mile section of beaches represented the British and Canadian sector. Further west, from Port-en-Bessin to Quinéville on the Cotentin peninsula, was the American. He sat back and tried to visualize the enlarged intelligence photographs he'd seen. Rows of quaint seaside homes perched just above the wide beaches . . . the tips of steel obstacles protruding ominously above the wave-tops ahead of the breakers. The houses would be full of snipers and machine-gun nests. Behind the houses would be mortar companies and the German 88s, the deadly fire of which Davenport had witnessed in North Africa. The code name for the British sector was Sword Beach. For hours on end, Davenport struggled with the mind-numbing details of planning the British assault. In a scant two weeks, he thought wearily, it had to be finished, in time for the conference in Quebec.

Davenport looked up from his typewriter to see Hanes Butler standing in the open doorway, holding an unlit cigar. 'Give it up, Charlie,' said Butler, waving the cigar at the pile of paper on the desk. 'You're the last sonofabitch still workin'. Let's get a drink.'

'Sorry, Hanes, but I really need to finish this.'

'Suit yourself. But be sure to lock up and turn out the lights.' The door clicked softly as Butler departed. After another hour, Davenport tore the paper from the carriage of his typewriter. Taking his jacket from the back of the door, he flipped the lightswitch and closed and locked the door. After a stop at the pub around the corner from the barracks, Davenport walked heavily up the steps into the foyer. The corporal at the desk was dozing but awakened at the sound of Davenport's footsteps. 'Sir,' he said, sitting up, 'you have a letter.' Davenport accepted a familiar blue envelope from the corporal's out-stretched hand. The sight of Mary's neat handwriting stirred a feeling of deep unease. Wordlessly he tucked the envelope in his pocket and made his way to his room. In the two weeks since he returned from Wales, he'd reread her note dozens of times, searching for insight into her inexplicable departure, and for hours had sat at his desk, pen in hand, trying to find the words to convince her to reconsider, or at least to explain her motives for leaving. But no words would come.

He sat down on the bed and studied the letter. As the days had passed, his fears had grown that he might never hear from her again. Drawing in a deep breath, he opened the envelope, unfolded the sheets it and read:

7 July 1943
Kilmichael Point

Dear Charles,

I went to my garden at first light today, where I found my frequent nocturnal guest, silently nibbling dew-dampened lettuce. He's a black lop-eared bunny, and I've been searching for him for some time. I was certain if I found the culprit I'd take drastic measures. Instead I sank to my knees and watched, my heart breaking.

Davenport put the letter aside, hesitant to read on, and then picked it up again. '*How can I possibly explain?*' she wrote in her neat hand. She apologized for the pain she'd caused him, but insisted that she loved him so much she couldn't possibly be with him in London, that everyone she'd loved, she'd lost and that she '*couldn't be responsible for the destruction of what I hold most dear . . .*' Davenport frowned at the stilted phrase, unable to plumb its meaning. In another obscure reference, she wrote that '*it's just like that line of verse you read to me at Harlech,*' and then closed with:

I will wait, wait forever and more. If this war ever ends I promise I'll be here. Try to understand and write if you will, if you can.
Love,
Mary

Charles felt enormous relief, his despair slipping away. But what was she trying to tell him? He studied the letter. She loved him, and *therefore* she had to leave him? '*The destruction of that which I hold most dear . . .*' It made no sense. And the obscure reference to the line of verse. He thought back to that sunny morning at Harlech. Was it the sonnet? Yes, of course. He recited the verses from memory: *In me thou see'st the glowing of such fire that on the ashes of his youth doth lie, as on the death-bed whereon it must expire. To love that well which thou must leave ere long.* He shook his head as he wearily reached down to unlace his boots.

The following morning Charles walked into Norfolk House with renewed confidence and energy. In a week he would depart for

Quebec, travelling with the top COSSAC staff, the chiefs of the army, navy, and RAF, and the prime minister himself. He stopped at his office to read a memorandum from General Morgan on the details of the trip to Glasgow and the hitherto unknown arrangements for their passage to Quebec on the *Queen Mary*, with a shiver of excitement at the thought of an ocean crossing on the luxurious Cunard liner. He picked up his folder and glanced at his watch; almost 8.30, time for the briefing.

As Davenport entered the room, the assorted staff officers were chatting in twos and threes or taking their seats. Davenport walked to the lectern and opened his folder. After a few moments, he called out, in the manner of a professor addressing his students, 'Gentlemen, be seated. We have a great deal to cover.' Once the men were in their chairs, he began, 'You are all aware that in approximately one week we depart for the Quadrant conference, where we shall be meeting the American high command, including General Marshall and the President himself. I needn't tell you that this is the culmination of all our hard work. The final go-ahead for Overlord. Some of you recall the humble beginnings of this operation in '42 when it was termed Round-up.' Davenport paused and surveyed the attentive faces. 'Lieutenant, the map if you please.' An officer unfurled a large wall map. Davenport leaned his tall frame on the lectern. 'The planning conference commences in Quebec on 17 August. Some of you will be onboard when we sail from Glasgow. It is therefore essential that we complete our work before embarkation, in a scant week. This morning we shall have a full dress rehearsal, beginning with Third Division concentrations at Newhaven and Shoreham and Fiftieth Division at Poole. Then we shall turn to the detailed plans for the landings on Gold and Sword Beaches. Mr Mallory, if you please.'

At the end of the long day, Davenport returned to his office where he discovered among the memoranda in his in-box a letter from his barrister in the divorce proceedings. Leaning back in his chair, Davenport read: '*I am pleased to enclose the final order granting your divorce, entered by the court on 25 July With this order, these proceedings have now been finally concluded.*' He let his eyes fall on the formal legal document enclosed with the letter, which ended, '*Do hereby declare that the marriage of Charles Foster Davenport to Frances Meade Haversham is dissolved.*' Davenport looked up to see Hanes Butler in the doorway.

'Good news?' asked Butler.

'Yes, Hanes, good news. A letter from my lawyer. My divorce is final.'

'Hell, that's *great* news. I'll buy you a drink.'

'All right,' said Davenport. 'A drink to the bloody lawyers.'

Hanes took a sip of beer and said, 'Try one of these,' extracting cigars from his breast pocket. He turned around to pat a passing barmaid on the rear. 'Hey, sweetheart,' he said, returning her disapproving frown with a smile. 'We could use another round. Two pints of bitter.'

Davenport bit the tip from his cigar and struck a match. He drew deeply and expelled a cloud of aromatic smoke. 'Well, Hanes,' he said, 'here's to the single life.' The barmaid returned with a tray and placed two brimming glasses on the scarred table.

'To the single life,' repeated Butler, pausing to take a swallow of beer. 'Wine, women, and song. And to victory.'

Charles sipped his beer and took another drag on his cigar, the effects of which, combined with the alcohol, made him light-headed. Butler rested his elbows on the table and said, 'Another couple of weeks, and this goddamn planning will be finished. I'm so sick of logistics I can't stand it.'

'Yes,' said Davenport. 'And then . . . we sit and wait.'

'Hey, waiting's not all bad,' said Butler.

'What worries me,' said Davenport, 'is the longer we wait, the stronger the Germans become. Especially if they put someone energetic, like Rommel, in command. The big show doesn't come off till May, ten months from now.'

'That's true,' agreed Butler, gesturing with his cigar, 'but the flip side is we've got more time to assemble an even larger force and get those boys ready.'

'That's where you're wrong, Mr Butler. The landing force is already as large as it can be.' Butler shot him a puzzled look. 'We still don't have enough landing craft,' said Davenport, 'to put even six divisions ashore on day one, let alone a larger force. I've seen all the figures and with the demands you Yanks have for the Pacific, there's no way to make a significant increase in the number of boats in time for the May target date. This battle's going to be won or lost,' he continued in a lower voice, 'on the first day. On the beaches.' He sucked on the cigar. 'And if the Germans bring up their armoured reserves, we'll have a helluva fight on our hands.'

'And what do you suppose we can do to avoid that?' asked Butler.

'Surprise, Hanes,' said Davenport without hesitation. 'We've got to make sure the Germans think the invasion's coming somewhere else. At the Pas de Calais,' he said, in almost a whisper. 'So they don't commit their Panzers to Normandy. And I happen to think we've got a bloody good plan for fooling them.'

'I hope you're right,' said Butler. 'Anyhow, to hell with the war. We're here to celebrate.' He finished his beer and said, 'OK, Charlie, tell me about this gal of yours. You haven't said a damn thing since you came back from your weekend.'

'There's very little to tell. Things didn't . . . well, didn't work out.'

'She's an American, right?'

'Yes, from Boston. And she's a very lovely woman. Married, but a widow.'

'Was her husband killed in the war?'

'No, in an accident. Anyway, she moved from Boston to her family's home in Ireland, on the coast south of Dublin.'

'So you didn't hit it off,' said Butler, 'on this weekend together?'

'That wasn't it,' said Davenport. 'I don't know what her problem is. Something about the war.'

'Women,' said Butler. 'How are you supposed to know what they're thinking? And she's not just a woman . . . she's a damn Yankee.' Davenport nodded glumly. 'Well,' said Butler, 'we need to get fixed up with some local beauties. There's just so much competition.'

'You go ahead,' said Davenport, 'but forget about me.'

Butler pushed away his glass and said, 'C'mon, Charlie, let's go,' tossed a ten shilling note on the table and said, 'That should take care of it.'

'But Hanes,' Davenport protested.

'Forget it. You can get the next one.'

A solitary figure walked along the darkened road. As he passed out of the village, Eamon O'Farrell picked up his pace, hoping to make it to the farmhouse before the storm. Arriving at the dilapidated porch just as the cold rain began to fall, he rapped sharply on the door. After a few moments the door opened a crack, revealing the nervous face of Tom O'Connor. 'It's him,' said O'Connor, turning his back to Eamon. The door swung open and Eamon stepped inside.

'Come in, O'Farrell,' said Sean Mulcahy, standing with three rough looking confederates by the remains of a fire. 'Take off your coat.' Mulcahy's legs were planted slightly apart and his hands rested lightly on his hips, close by the pistol in his waistband.

Eamon shrugged off his coat, casually placed it with his hat on a chair, and walked to the centre of the small, squalid room. 'Well, Sean,' he said, 'now that you've summoned me here on this lovely evening, perhaps you'd care to tell me what it's all about?'

Mulcahy stared contemptuously and said, 'What it's all about, *Mr* O'Farrell, as you prefer to call yourself, is that we were *fucked*. And we aim to find out who done it. Who tipped off the bloody Brits. They were waiting for us, and—'

'Listen, Mulcahy,' interrupted Eamon in a tone of feigned indifference. 'It's not my affair. I lived up to my end of the bargain. The rifles were delivered as promised, and God only knows who betrayed you in this land of whispering informers. Or what bungling incompetence on the part of the IRA . . .'

'God knows, all right,' growled Mulcahy, 'and maybe you know, too.' He took a step toward Eamon and raised his fist.

'I wouldn't,' said Eamon calmly, 'if I were you.' The others standing behind Mulcahy shifted uneasily. Mulcahy lowered his fist and took a step back. He walked to a battered pine cupboard and poured a shot glass of whiskey. 'OK, *Mr* O'Farrell,' he said with a crooked smile. 'I'll leave you be. For now that is,' he added, casting a wink at his plainly nervous comrades. 'But from now on, it's a simple business proposition. Cash for arms. Clear enough?'

'Suit yourself,' said Eamon with a shrug. 'The less I know about your intrigues, the better. But don't forget the coast watchers, Mulcahy, on both the southern and northern approaches.'

'Aye,' said Mulcahy, downing the glass of whisky. 'It can be arranged easily enough. Now, boys, pull up a chair for our guest and let's see if we can reach an understanding. We'll be needing another shipment of rifles and ammunition.'

Walking down the path, Mary realized it didn't matter where in the world you were, a fair was still a fair, a day away from the drudgery of everyday living. She had persuaded Sarah to go with her to the County Wicklow fair. The two women had been spending more time together since Mary had confided that she'd spent the weekend in Wales with Charles and wasn't likely to see him again, a frank admission that both shocked Sarah and seemed to soften her disapproving attitude. Sarah, whose father had both a car and an allotment of petrol, had picked up Mary, leaving the dog with neighbours, and driven to the fairgrounds outside the nearby town of Arklow. Mary and Sarah sat down at a rickety wooden table by the merry-go-round, watching the joy on the tiny faces as the old carousel went round and round, listening to the calliope. Mary thought back to a long-ago carousel ride in Boston, astride a big white horse as her father stood close by, one protective arm around her waist . . .

'A penny for your thoughts,' said Sarah.

'I was just thinking about going to the fair with my father,' said Mary. 'And wishing I'd had the chance to share it with my own little girl.'

'It must be so hard,' said Sarah quietly. Rising from the table, she smiled and said, 'Well, perhaps we should look in on the animal tents.'

Eamon had waited patiently for his opportunity, maintaining a discreet surveillance, and was sure his chance had come when Mary departed with the dog in her friend's old saloon. He quickly cycled to her cottage, where, as expected, he found the door unlocked. Certain she would have saved the officer's letters, he first tried the bureau in the living room, where he found her stationery, but no letters. He then crept down the hall and stopped at a pine chest. He found them in the top drawer, a neat bundle tied with a string. Within minutes, he found what he'd come for: the officer's name, Charles Davenport, and, to his great surprise, a reference to his position, serving on the staff of General Frederick Morgan, Chief of Staff to the Supreme Allied Commander – COSSAC. Blessing his good fortune, Eamon hastily jotted down the information, carefully returned the bundle to the chest, and silently departed.

As Mary and Sarah reached the end of the fairground, long shadows were falling and there was a chill in the air. After wandering among the well-groomed livestock, they'd visited the homemakers' displays of cakes and pies, here and there a beautiful blue ribbon. Mary almost collided with a tall, handsome man with the same intense eyes as Eamon O'Farrell. Despite her misgivings, there was something about Eamon she found so appealing. Walking back to the car, she thought of Charles, wondering for the hundredth time if she'd done the right thing. If he were sent into action and never came back, she would have thrown away the precious time they might have had together. By the time Sarah dropped Mary at her cottage the sun was slipping behind the mountains, spreading a band of mauve tinged with pink across the horizon. Enjoying the spectacular view of the sea, Mary realized that the day away had brought her a semblance of peace of mind. In the fading light, she paused at her garden gate and examined the neat rows of ripening vegetables. She had so much to share, but apart from Sarah and Donald, so few to share it with. She thought again about Eamon, alone and on his own, and decided to take him a basket. With a clap of her hands and brief command to the pup, Mary mounted the steps to her porch.

CHAPTER FOURTEEN

IT WAS SATURDAY, 7 August, Davenport's third day at sea. The *Queen Mary* was eerily quiet, almost empty, with only 200-odd men aboard apart from the crew. He was accompanying General Morgan and the senior staff of COSSAC to the all-important conference in Quebec to reach a final agreement with the American high command on the timing and details of the invasion. Churchill and his senior advisers, including General Alan Brooke and Admiral Pound, were on board as well. Good Lord, Davenport reflected, what a prize it would be for the Germans. Leaning on the railing, he could see the Royal Navy lookouts, training their binoculars on the tranquil ocean for any sign of U-boats. The ship was simply too fast for submarines, too fast even for torpedoes, except for an incredibly lucky shot. And hopefully word of their departure had been kept under wraps.

As he stared at the horizon, Davenport's mind wandered to the weekend in Wales, followed by the familiar tightening in his chest. He couldn't keep his mind from Mary, sitting opposite him in the cosy dining room, her beautiful face framed by thick, dark hair, as the afternoon storm lashed the trees beyond the windows. God, what a waste . . . my dear time's waste. *When to the sessions of sweet silent thought*, he silently recited, *I summon up remembrance of things past, I sigh the lack of many a thing I sought, and with old woes new wail my dear time's waste.* Was their brief time together really a waste? No, but why had she left without even saying goodbye? She was running away, but from what? Davenport looked over the side at the deep blue water with swirls of cream. It was as if staying with him meant she would somehow be destined to lose him, which made no sense.

He turned away from the railing and began strolling along the empty promenade deck, absently inspecting the lifeboats suspended on davits. Opening a varnished teak door, he proceeded down narrow stairs to the lower decks, where his way was blocked by a velvet rope and a 'First Class Only' sign. It might just as well have read 'Top Brass Only'. Turning to head for his stateroom, he almost collided with an officer with the red lapel tabs of a brigadier general, K. G. McLean, one of Morgan's senior deputies.

'I say, Davenport,' said McLean, 'I've been looking for you.'

'It's an awfully large ship, sir,' said Davenport. 'I've been enjoying the fresh air on deck.'

'It's a damned good thing I've found you.'

'Really?' said Davenport with surprise. 'What's up?'

'I've been summoned by the old man to present the Overlord plan. And I need your help.'

'The old man?' said Davenport incredulously. 'Churchill?'

'Yes, Churchill,' said McLean irritably.

'But I thought . . .'

'Yes, so did I,' said McLean. 'That the plan was going to be pre-sented at a formal briefing. But you know how Churchill can be. Captain Pim came round and said casually, "Oh General McLean, the PM was wondering if you might drop by his stateroom. And bring your maps. He's keen to hear the plans for the landings." Just like that.'

'When?' asked Davenport nervously.

McLean glanced at his watch. 'In about twenty minutes. So you'd best get into proper uniform and help me with the maps.'

Half an hour later Davenport and McLean stood at the door to the first class stateroom with a young lieutenant. The door was opened by a captain who said, 'Right this way, General.' Winston Churchill was lying on his bed, clad in a multi-coloured dressing gown, propped up on pillows amid a messy pile of papers. A large black cat was curled up next to him pawing at the embroidery on Churchill's black velvet slippers. Captain Pim, Churchill's aide, said, 'Prime Minister, allow me to introduce Brigadier McLean, Lieutenant Colonel Davenport, and Lieutenant Wigby. From General Morgan's staff.'

'Don't mind the cat,' said Churchill, motioning to the animal. 'He loves attacking my feet. Now, I understand you gentlemen are here to tell me all about the plans for the invasion. Operation Overlord,' he growled dramatically.

'Quite right, sir,' said McLean. 'Lieutenant, would you please set up the map and easel.' Wigby snapped open an easel and attached a large coloured map of the Normandy coastline. 'As you know, Prime Minister,' said McLean, 'we've chosen the Normandy coastline for the landings. From this point,' he traced a line on the map, 'at the mouth of the Orne River, to the Cotentin peninsula, a distance of some eighty miles. The force that will be put ashore on the first day will consist of six divisions comprising a hundred and fifty thousand men.'

'When?' asked Churchill. The three officers exchanged puzzled looks. 'When?' Churchill repeated. 'What time of day?'

'Oh, at sunrise,' replied McLean. 'And at high tide. Which demands, of course, the selection of a landing date when sunrise coincides with high tide, to ensure that the landing craft and amphibious vehicles can be floated over the obstacles and mines.'

'Yes, go on,' said Churchill impatiently.

'During the night parachute troops will be dropped behind the coastal defences, here and here, accompanied by glider troops. Their mission will be to sever enemy communications and secure vital bridges and roads.'

Churchill sat up. 'Glider troops?' he asked. 'What, pray tell—'

The young lieutenant spoke up: 'The gliders are towed by cable, Prime Minister, and then released. Each carries a hundred men and glides noiselessly to a pre-selected landing site.'

'Good God, man,' said Churchill. 'You're telling me they're expected to effect a safe landing without power in some open field or meadow? In the dead of night?'

'Yes, sir,' answered the lieutenant meekly.

'Now, then, Prime Minister,' said McLean, 'turning to the main assault. Colonel Davenport, the second map.'

Davenport unfurled a finely detailed map which he hung over the first. Taking a cue from McLean, he said, 'The invasion flotilla will assemble here, offshore Portsmouth, and proceed to this point at 0400 on D-Day. Following naval and air bombardment of the German fortified positions, the first wave will come ashore. The British and Canadian sector, comprised of the Third Division, the

Fiftieth Division, and the Third Canadian Division, will be landed here, on beaches designated Sword, Juno and Gold.' He paused, aware that Churchill was studying the map intently. 'At the same time,' Davenport continued calmly, 'the American First Division will come ashore here, at Omaha Beach, and the American Fourth Division will land here, at the eastern extremity, designated Utah Beach. The mission of the first wave will be to neutralize the German defenders, secure the beaches, and open the exits for the tracked vehicles and trucks. Meanwhile the second wave will land.'

Churchill silently pondered the map. 'Tell me,' he said at length. 'What is the size of the German force defending this sector of the Atlantic Wall?'

'Our intelligence estimate is one division,' replied McLean. 'At the moment. So long as they continue to believe that the likely point of the invasion is the Pas de Calais, it seems unlikely that they will reinforce Normandy.'

'How do you mean to resupply them? You haven't a deep water port anywhere between Le Havre and Cherbourg.'

'Yes, Prime Minister,' said McLean with a tight-lipped smile, 'that's where the mulberries come into play.'

'Mulberries?' asked Churchill.

'Precisely, sir. The name chosen for the artificial harbours you suggested some time ago as a means of getting heavy equipment and supplies ashore.'

'Excellent,' said Churchill, springing up from the bed with surprising agility. He bent over the map and peered at the minute details. 'Very well done, McLean. An excellent presentation. However,' – he paused and cast a significant look at the three men – 'We shall need more men. And for more men, we shall need greater numbers of landing craft. Landing craft,' he repeated solemnly. 'That's been our curse. We simply can't seem to get enough of them.'

Davenport cleared his throat and said, 'Sir, if I may . . .'

Churchill gazed at him. 'Yes, Lieutenant Colonel?'

'To address the shortage of landing craft, sir, what we need are Higgins boats.'

'Higgins boats?' repeated Churchill.

'Yes, sir. The Americans are producing them in great numbers for their Marine Corps in the Pacific. They're plywood, you see, and avoid the critical shortage of steel .'

'I see,' said Churchill. 'I shall have to remember this.'

123

'If I might offer a suggestion, sir,' said Davenport. 'Perhaps it would be useful to mention the possibility of Higgins boats to President Roosevelt.'

'Yes, Davenport,' said Churchill with a smile. 'I shall.'

Following dinner and a tedious evening of cards in the bar, Davenport ventured back out on deck, a drink in hand. All of the lights normally blazing on the *Queen Mary's* upper decks and funnels, the chandeliers illuminating its dining salons and lounges, had been doused or blacked out, leaving the ship a dark, massive ghost on the invisible surface of the sea. A thin layer of cloud drifted across the dark sky, obscuring the rising moon as a billion stars sparkled brilliantly overhead. Clutching his coat tightly, he listened to the water rushing far below the railing. What would it be like, he wondered, to be standing watch on a merchant ship in the middle of the Atlantic on a night like this, when suddenly the ship erupts in the fireball of an exploding torpedo, plunging him into the frigid water, in suffocating bunker fuel? The thought made him queasy. Serving in a staff assignment, enjoying the luxuries of an ocean liner and the amenities of Norfolk House, were a far cry from the perils of ordinary seamen or the poor, miserable sods at the front. Taking a swallow of his drink, feeling the sensation of the whisky spreading through his chilled frame, he thought about the job they were sending the infantry to do, storming the most heavily defended beaches in modern warfare, taking risks so great that even Churchill had seemed shocked. And he would be in London, safe and secure . . .

Davenport smiled at the image of Churchill lying on the bed with the playful cat. He had been in the presence of the great man, actually conversed with him. In his college days it had been fashionable to think of Churchill as a dangerous eccentric whose railings about Hitler had been scornfully mocked. Those sentiments, Davenport considered, had disappeared rather abruptly during the Blitz. Had he been wrong to say something about Higgins boats? He had been taken aback by Churchill's keen grasp of the central problem presented by the shortage of landing craft. And his manner had seemed so informal . . . why not offer his opinion?

Davenport debated a nightcap. How many drinks had he had? Too many. Without thinking, he tossed the glass over the railing. He thought about the letter he'd slipped into the post box the day he left London. Perhaps it was wrong to have pleaded with her, but if she really loved him, it made no sense for her to refuse even to visit him. He worried that her reasoning masked a deeper reluctance. But he had to know, and so he had written, almost begging her to change her mind. Shivering in the cold, he made his way unsteadily way to his stateroom.

The rich Irish soil yielded a bumper crop. Basket after basket of fresh, healthy produce – tomatoes, beans, potatoes, cucumbers and marrows – had been harvested during the warm days of late summer. Now Mary was picking and bottling the last of it. Her life was a blur, passing back and forth between kitchen and garden. What could not be stored in the cool darkness of the cellar had been processed into row upon row of jars neatly aligned on the pantry shelves. Marmalade abutted pickles, followed by an impressive array of vegetables. Mary exhausted herself in an effort to gain sound sleep, free of Charles's face that sometimes haunted her dreams, where other faces sometimes ventured. She lost weight to the point that the trousers she wore in the garden had to be cinched two notches tighter. Her hair, rather than hanging loosely on her shoulders, was bunched up in a knot, and she was forever pushing back the wisps from her face with her callused hands. After cleaning the kitchen for the last time at the end of a long day, she stood on a chair to lift the last jars to the top shelf of the pantry with a scraping clatter. In the morning, she decided, she'd take a selection of fresh and bottled vegetables to Eamon, whom she regarded as another lost soul, living alone in town, without family or friends, or even a job so far as she could tell. She chose a variety of jars from the shelf – bread-and-butter pickles, cut beans, and tomato chutney. Yes, tomorrow she would pay a call on Eamon.

The next morning, Mary added fresh vegetables to the basket, and, fastening a lead to Chelsea's collar, started into town. It was early September, and the wind off the water carried a chill and rattled the drying leaves in the trees. By the time she reached the cluster of humble buildings that was Castletown she felt warm from the exertion. As she strolled past the post office, the few people she passed paid her no notice; what might they say, she wondered, if they knew the overflowing basket on her arm was for Eamon? Well, they were both odd-man-out in the village, so let them talk. Eamon lived in a dilapidated boarding-house on a side street and, as she walked up, she stopped to straighten a dangling wooden post on the fence. After tying Chelsea's lead to the gate, she hesitantly approached the two-storey house. A door opened to a narrow staircase. The name 'O'Farrell' was one of three roughly scrawled on a card indicating the upstairs rooms. Standing at the foot of the stairs with the basket on her arm, Mary thought back to the threat that had been uttered at the Golden Anchor and briefly considered turning back. No, she had come this far and was determined not to allow the petty jealousies of the townspeople, or the threats of the IRA, intimidate her. She slowly ascended the creaking stairs to a hallway lit by a single naked bulb. There were three doors; but which was Eamon's? She examined the door on her left with a grimy smudge around the doorknob. From the end of the hall, she could just make out the sound of a man's voice. Taking a deep breath, she walked slowly and softly to the end of the hall and stopped at the door.

The voice inside the room was muffled and indistinct. Then she heard a different sound, an electronic chirp and scratch. The man began speaking again. It was Eamon's voice, she was sure of it. She placed the basket on the floor and raised her hand to knock. Then she heard the strange electronic sound again. Mary felt oddly apprehensive and gently leaned her ear against the door. Now she could hear clearly; footsteps on a wooden floor, a chair being dragged back, a man's voice, though she couldn't make out the words, and then static followed by a distorted tone . . . a radio signal. Her heart racing, she inched even closer. Now she could hear another man's voice through the static, speaking in a foreign language. '*Ja, ja, ich verstehe,*' said the man. Mary held her breath as she struggled to make out the strange words. '*Bitte, etwas langsamer,*' the man continued.

Mary raised her hand to her mouth. It was German, she was sure of it. And then she heard Eamon's voice again, clear and unmistakable: '*Warten sie ein moment, bitte.*'

Her heart pounding, Mary lifted the basket from the floor and hurried down the hall, praying he hadn't heard her. 'Jesus, Mary and Joseph,' she whispered as she carefully manoeuvered the narrow staircase. At the foot of the stairs she almost stumbled when the basket shifted, every bit as unbalanced as the thoughts in her head. Gasping for air, she was almost out the gate before she heard the whimper from Chelsea. Quickly untying the lead, she hurried through the gate, trying to look as though nothing was amiss. Walking across the street, she turned just once to look back.

*

Eamon leaned forward, speaking directly into the microphone of the short-wave radio transmitter the antenna of which reached almost to the ceiling. *'Ja, ja, natürlich,'* he said. *'Ich bin sicher. Morgan. Leutnant General Frederick Morgan.'* The radio crackled.

'Hans, sie mussen horchen,' said the other man through the static. *'Diese sehr bedeutend ist.'* 'Hans, listen. This is very important. Are you sure of the name of the other officer?'

'Of course,' replied Eamon in his aristocratic, Hannoverian German. 'Lieutenant Colonel Charles Davenport. I believe he and the woman are very close.'

'Hans, do you understand what this could mean? If this Davenport reports to General Morgan, as you think, and General Morgan reports directly to the Supreme Commander . . .'

'Precisely, Herr Trott. Excuse me a moment.' Eamon stood up and slipped his suspenders over his shoulders. He walked to the window and parted the curtains. He could just make out a woman through the branches of a tree, hurrying out the gate with a basket on her arm and a dog on a lead. After a moment, she paused and looked back over her shoulder. Eamon stared at Mary. What was *she* doing there? He returned to his desk, adjusted the dials, and said, 'Now, Herr Trott. You would agree we've acquired the perfect contact. *Ja?* The question is how best to exploit it.'

'Yes, Hans, I agree. You must take care to use your relationship with her to its full advantage. *Und jetzt ich muss diese Sendung enden. Aufwiedersehen.'*

Mary was too frightened to feel angry. Rounding the corner on the main road, the tug of the lead as the dog stopped abruptly caused the basket to shift, spilling its contents on the pavement. An elderly couple stared at her, making no move to help. 'Oh dear,' said Mary as she watched the glass jars roll into the road. 'Chelsea,' she commanded, tugging at the lead. 'Come, girl!' With a stamp of exasperation she walked on, leaving behind the contents of her basket as the couple stared in bewilderment. All Mary could think about was the refuge of her cottage. She had so few friends, many still avoided her, and the authorities had no sympathy for the British. Besides, she wondered, was Eamon even breaking the law? Dark clouds blotted out the sun, and the wind had a sharp edge. Free from the weight of the basket, Mary found herself almost running the last quarter mile, tugging Chelsea along, acutely aware of her predicament.

The roof of her cottage appeared in the distance. As she hurried along the track, the image of Eamon entered her mind, a solitary figure wandering the desolate beach or appearing out of the blue on the pathway below her cottage. With her breath coming in gasps, Mary ran the final yards to the house, finding the door unlocked and all the lights out – another power failure, she supposed with a sigh. She unfastened Chelsea's lead and searched in the kitchen for candles and matches. After lighting one in the brass candlestick on the kitchen table, she took the key from a hook on the wall and locked the door. Shivering in the darkness, she sat at the table, staring into the circle of yellow light from the flickering candle.

Mary thought back to the incident in the cellar. Her pulse pounded remembering her terrified reaction when she had surprised him there. She sprang up, grabbed the paraffin lamp from the pantry and lit the mantle. As she headed for the cellar the wind was blowing hard, the trees swaying as the sky opened. She descended the steps in the lantern's eerie light and placed it on the workbench where it filled the cellar with a bright, incandescent glow. As she feared, on the far side of the room there was an empty space on the shelf where the strange object had been, a fine line in the dust marking where it once sat. The canvas covering had disappeared as well. It was so clear now . . . Eamon had been back, back for his radio transmitter. Mary felt pinpricks of fear on her skin at the terrible realization. He was a German spy, concealing his radio in her cellar. She'd never felt more alone and defenceless. As she turned to go, in the corner of her eye she saw the glint of a smooth metal surface. Leaning against the wall was her grandfather's shotgun. She dimly remembered him showing her how to load it. An unopened box of shells was on the shelf near the gun. She emptied the shells into her pocket, picked up the gun, and then lifted the lantern and hurried upstairs.

She sat in the old rocking chair by the front door, which was locked and bolted, light from the lantern shining from the kitchen. As Mary leaned the shotgun against the wall, the shells rattled in her pocket with each rock of the chair. Charles had warned her, long ago, about the possibility of German spies operating in neutral Ireland, and possibly working with the IRA. And Eamon was evidently involved with the Republicans. But Eamon was Irish. Or was he? Perhaps the man speaking German behind the door wasn't Eamon after all. Look at yourself, she thought, barricaded in a dark house with a loaded shotgun. Waiting for what? She rocked late into the evening, the shotgun propped beside her and Chelsea asleep at her feet. She awoke with a start, unsure what was she doing there until it all flooded over her again. She stood up and stretched, deciding she needed a breath of fresh air before going at last to bed. Unlocking the door and casting a glance at the shotgun, she stepped out on the porch and peered into the darkness. The rain had ceased but the sky was filled with thick clouds, obscuring the moon and stars. The sea was as black as the night. Suddenly a red light blinked in the distance. Twice more it flashed and was gone.

CHAPTER FIFTEEN

CHARLES SAT ALONE on a park bench along the Embankment, staring at the rows of wrecked warehouses and wharves on the opposite bank, stark reminders of the ferocity of the German air raids during the Blitz, three years past. Good Lord, he wondered, how long could the war last? Amid the shouts of deckhands and the gulls' shrill cries, tugs drove their barges against the stiff current of the Thames, trailing an oily swathe. With a glance at his watch he stood up to stretch. Since returning from Quebec everything had changed. The urgency of the work these past six months was gone, replaced by a dull routine of meetings, reports, and idleness. As he began strolling along the Embankment, he decided he needed a change. He had been far too long sitting behind a desk poring over maps and logistics. Boarding a bus, he mounted the steps to the upper deck and dropped heavily into a seat, staring vacantly at the storefronts. Could he endure this for another eight months? When the bus slowed to a stop at Duke Street St. James, he climbed down the stairs and bounded down to the pavement for the short walk to the stately Georgian headquarters of the Supreme Allied Command.

He was uncharacteristically late, so quickened his pace as he entered the lobby of Norfolk House. A strong male voice was audible through the transom above the door to the briefing room as Davenport turned the knob. General Morgan paused briefly and shot him a disapproving look. 'As I was saying,' said Morgan, standing at the lectern, 'now that a date has been agreed upon for D-Day, our task is clear. Until the actual transfer of responsibility to the field commanders, some four months hence, we shall continue to be absorbed with tactical and logistical planning at the minutest level. It will be terribly important not to wind down and lose a sense of the urgency of our mission . . .' Davenport's mind wandered as Morgan droned on, but he forced himself to concentrate, looking straight ahead and tapping his pencil on the armrest. But the familiar daydream began to form in his mind . . . standing at the railing, looking out over the jade green water as the ferry slipped away from the dock . . . the gulls dipping into the foaming wake as the boat churned across the Irish Sea to the terminal at Kingstown, where standing in the crowd he would find her waiting . . .

'I say, Mr Davenport,' said Morgan irritably.

'Sir,' said Davenport, sitting up straight amid muffled laughter.

'Would you be please summarize the discussions at Quadrant with regard to joint naval co-operation in the assembly areas?'

Later, as the men filed out, Hanes Butler walked over to Davenport and clapped an arm around his shoulder. 'You seem to be having a hard time concentrating,' he said with a grin. 'Out last night?'

'Not likely, Hanes,' said Davenport. 'The fact is, I'm sick of the paperwork and endless planning. It's been over a year now.'

'Tell you what,' said Butler. 'When we finish up, let's have a drink. You can tell me all about it.'

The officers' club at Norfolk House was elegantly appointed, with worn Persian rugs, green-shaded lamps on the library tables and thick, red curtains on the windows looking out on the square. Davenport and Butler sat in leather armchairs by the fireplace sipping pint glasses of beer. 'So you're sick of it?' said Butler in his soft Carolina drawl.

'More than,' said Davenport, as he placed his glass on the table beside him. 'I've had it with this bloody desk job. Ever since Quebec I've been thinking about it, and I've made up my mind.'

'To do what?' asked Butler, leaning forward in his chair.

'To request a transfer,' said Davenport.

'A transfer to . . .'

'Third Infantry Division,' said Davenport. 'I want to command a battalion.'

'Jesus, Charlie,' said Butler with a short laugh. 'You've got to be kidding.'

'No, Hanes, I'm not kidding.'

'Even if you ask,' said Butler, 'I doubt Morgan will let you go.

Why should he give up one of his best officers?'

'Well, that may be, but I intend to find out.'

'But what I can't figure out is why, after what you went through in North Africa, you'd give up a great assignment like this?'

'Somebody's got to do it,' said Davenport in a low voice. 'Hell, we both know exactly what's going to be involved in this operation. The most spectacular operation in military history. Rather than sitting here behind a desk, I want to be part of it.'

'Well, it's not for me,' said Butler with a shake of his head. 'If they assigned me to it, that would be different. I'd be just like the next dumb bastard who figured, well, just my luck. And I'd do it, and pray to God I'd live through it. But volunteer? Sorry, not me.'

Davenport took a sip of beer and stared into the distance. After a moment he said, 'Do you believe in God, Hanes?'

'Course I do,' said Butler without hesitation. He gave Davenport a puzzled look.

'I mean really *believe*,' said Davenport. 'Not just in some vague, general way . . .'

'Heck, I don't know,' said Butler defensively. 'I don't know what you're driving at, but, yeah, I believe in God and in Jesus. It's what I was raised to believe. My mother taught Sunday school and Bible classes as long as I can remember, and my dad's a deacon at the same church where my great-grandfather preached. It's all I've known and been taught since I was a boy.'

'But what kind of God would allow all this to happen?' asked Davenport. 'I'm not sure what to believe any more. So many innocent people killed and maimed, and it's a long way from being over. Where's your God in this bloody war?'

'So that's it,' said Butler with quiet anger. 'Blame God? What about Hitler? What about the Japs?'

Davenport raised a hand and said, 'Sorry, Hanes. I didn't mean to start an argument. I just can't seem to make any sense of it .'

'Listen,' said Butler, looking Davenport in the eye. 'I remember something my grandfather told me. He came home from the war with only one arm.'

'The First War?' asked Davenport.

'No, the War Between the States. *Our* war. Said the one thing that got him through all the fighting and killing was his faith. You see, Charlie, it's got to be *real*, not just some general notion. I sometimes think y'all look at God and the church the same way you do the king, like it's just part of your heritage.'

'I suspect you're right,' said Davenport wearily. 'I just wish I had your conviction.' He finished his beer and said, 'Enough of this. On Monday I'm going to see General Morgan.'

Morgan sat at his desk opposite Davenport, tamping a cigarette on the face of his watch. 'What worries me,' he said, 'is the readiness of the men they're sending us.' He took a lighter from his pocket and lit his cigarette.

'Yes, sir,' said Davenport. 'The Americans, you mean.'

Morgan exhaled smoke from his nostrils and said, 'Correct. Conscripted troops who've never been blooded in combat, going up against battle-hardened Germans.'

'Not entirely, sir,' said Davenport. 'A large part of the German forces in France are *Volksgrenadier* divisions comprised of over-age and poorly trained men.'

Morgan smiled abruptly and said, 'You have a point, Colonel. And by the way,' – he paused to take a drag on his cigarette, – 'General Brooke tells me we should be receiving an allotment of those landing craft of yours.'

'Of mine?' said Davenport.

'Higgins boats, I believe you called them. The order evidently came directly from President Roosevelt.' Morgan smiled. "Who the devil is Lieutenant Colonel Davenport?" Brooke wanted to know. It seems you managed to stir up the PM on his favourite subject. Now, what is it you wanted to see me about?'

'Well, sir,' Davenport began, 'you're aware that I was assigned to the original planning team for Round-up.'

'Yes, and one of the few decent men in the lot.'

'That was a year ago, and we've now completed the detailed planning for Overlord . . .' Davenport hesitated.

'Yes?' said Morgan impatiently.

'Well, sir,' said Davenport, 'I've come to request a transfer.' Morgan eyed him coldly. 'To the Third Division.'

'You know, Davenport,' said Morgan, 'we don't get many men of your intellectual depth at the highest levels of our service. It's a damned shame. Too many mediocrities promoted up in the ranks based on schoolboy connections and things of that sort. But I also understand,' Morgan continued, narrowing his steel-grey eyes, 'that promotion to higher rank, in wartime, depends on commanding troops in combat.

You could have a fine career ahead of you in the army.'

'Thank you, sir,' said Davenport, 'but it's not so much that as a feeling that I *ought* to be involved in the landings, having done so much of the planning.'

'Your sense of duty,' suggested Morgan.

'Yes, I suppose so,' said Davenport quietly.

'But this business about the Third Division,' said Morgan with a frown. 'No point in that. I'm willing to recommend you for a battalion command with the Forty-Fourth Guards Division, which is scheduled to reinforce the Fiftieth Division on D-Day plus two.'

'But sir,' Davenport politely objected, 'there's no one more familiar with the details of the landings on Sword Beach. If you're willing to allow me to transfer from your staff, I'd far prefer the opportunity to participate in the landing on Sword with the Third Division.'

General Morgan stared briefly at Davenport and then said, 'Either you're very brave, or foolhardy. Commanding a battalion in the Third Division means going in with the first wave.'

'Yes, sir.'

Morgan said, 'I'll see what I can do.'

When Davenport arrived at his office two personal letters were in the in-box, one in Mary's familiar hand writing and the other with the return address 'Marsden Hall, Gloucestershire.' He looked at the letter from Mary with a feeling of self-reproach. His last letter had been so lacking in feeling, filled with anecdotes about the trip to Quebec and his encounter with Churchill. The raw emotion of his earlier letters, begging her to reconsider, had been expended. Nor had he hinted, even obliquely, at his request to be transferred. Putting the blue envelope aside, Davenport sank in his chair and read the letter from Evan Hockaday. After vaguely alluding to his mysterious duties at Bletchley Park, Evan wrote that he was planning a weekend at home in October and invited Charles to join him. Davenport smiled; he could think of nothing more appealing than a weekend with Evan at the lovely castle in the Cotswolds. He glanced up at the sound of singing, Hanes Butler's pleasant Southern baritone echoing in the hallway. Butler opened the door, poked his head inside, and said, 'Lieutenant Colonel Davenport, *sir.* Top o' the morning.'

'To what do we owe this sudden outburst of cheerfulness?' said Davenport with a grimace.

Butler slid into a chair and said, 'I'm afraid it's a simple case of insanity.'

'Insanity?'

'As in girl crazy. Can you believe it? I've got a girl.'

'A girl,' said Davenport. 'How extraordinary.'

'Yep, by the name of Peg. Peg o' my heart.' Davenport clasped his hands behind his head and leaned back. 'This buddy of mine from back home,' Butler continued, 'took me to this dance hall over in Lambeth. And, sure enough, I met Peg. Sweet as could be.'

'That's great, Hanes. I'm happy for you.'

Butler sprang up and leaned his hands on the desk. 'Listen, Charlie,' he said. 'You've got to meet her.'

'Sure. Some day—'

'No, I mean tonight. There's some kind of benefit dance, for the orphans in the East End, you know, from the Blitz. I promised Peg we'd come.'

'No, Hanes,' said Davenport, 'I'd prefer—'

'We'll have a ball,' Butler insisted, 'and there'll be lots of cute girls, and none of these high-falutin' West End types.' Butler stood up and turned to go. 'I'll come by for you at seven,' he said over his shoulder. 'Look sharp, Charlie.'

The Lambeth pavements were crowded with soldiers and sailors and their girls queuing up beneath a garishly lit marquee as a US Army jeep, driven by a sergeant with Butler and Davenport in the passenger seats, slowed to a stop. Butler jumped out and said, 'Here's a couple of quid, Sarge. Have yourself a good time and come back for us at eleven.' The bold letters beneath the sign 'Roxy' announced the Saturday night benefit dance. Butler and Davenport fell into line with the enlisted men, almost all with their arms around young women in tight dresses. Butler slid a few coins across the counter to the woman in the booth in exchange for two tickets. 'OK, Charlie,' he said. 'Follow me.' A banner reading *Lambeth Benevolent Association* was suspended from the ceiling at the far end of the dark, cavernous dance hall. For now the band was silent, and only a few couples milled on the dance floor. 'Over there,' said Hanes, raising his voice. 'Peg promised to come early and save us a booth.' One side of the room was lined with booths while the space surrounding the dance floor was jammed with tables and chairs. 'There she is,' said Butler, turning toward Davenport with a smile. Davenport followed Butler through the crowd to a booth midway along the wall where a young woman with stylishly curled dark hair was waiting.

She flashed a happy smile and said, 'Oh, Hanes, you look *so* handsome.' She rose from her seat to take his hands and accept a peck on the cheek. She was short and plump but cute nevertheless.

'Peg,' said Butler, as he slipped into the booth beside her, 'allow me to introduce Lieutenant Colonel Charles Davenport, in the service of His Majesty, King George the Sixth.'

Peg smiled again, revealing a row of crooked teeth, and said, ''Ow do you do,' in a Cockney accent.

'My pleasure,' said Davenport, sliding onto the seat opposite them. 'Hanes has told me all about you.'

'Oh 'e has, has 'e?' she said, with a look of mock disapproval.

'Well, not quite *all*, sweetie,' drawled Butler.

Peg squeezed his hand and said, 'Don't you *love* the way 'e talks?'

Davenport smiled pleasantly, thinking how effortlessly the Americans shifted among classes. 'There she is,' said Peg, tugging on Butler's sleeve and pointing. Davenport followed her outstretched hand to a young woman on the far side of the dance floor. Unlike Peg, she was tall and thin, with one hand at her slender waist and the other shading her eyes from the glare of the spotlight. 'Jenny. Over here,' Peg called out. With a smile of recognition, the woman threaded past the tables towards them.

'We've got a little surprise for you, Charlie,' said Butler with a grin, 'this is Peg's friend, Jenny Wilcox. Jenny, meet Charlie Davenport.' The girl gave Davenport a diffident smile and squeezed into the booth beside him. Static crackled in the loudspeakers and, as the lights dimmed, the band members rose in unison and played a fanfare accompanied by a drum-roll. A short man wearing a wide-shouldered evening jacket bounded onto the stage and strode to the microphone. 'Ladeeees and gentlemen,' he announced. 'Welcome to the Roxy . . .'

'I know 'im,' said Peg excitedly. 'What's 'is name?'

'The famous music hall singer,' said Butler. 'Eddie somethin' or other.'

With a tap of the bandleader's baton, the orchestra played the opening bars of a familiar show tune. 'When you're down in Lambeth way,' sang the emcee in a lilting Cockney accent, 'anytime or any day . . . you'll find them all . . . doin' the Lambeth walk. *Hey!*' As the dance floor filled with swirling couples, the mirror-studded globe overhead began to turn in the spotlight, and thousands of pinpoints danced across the room.

'What'll you girls have to drink?' asked Butler.

'Oh, a lemonade would be lovely,' replied Jenny, while Peg asked for a beer.

'Charlie's a colonel,' said Peg proudly, as Butler disappeared into the throng.

Jenny turned toward him with an awkward glance and said, 'All the army boys I know are in the ranks, off some place fightin' the Germans or the Japs.'

'I was in North Africa,' said Davenport, 'until I was wounded and sent home. I've been stuck behind a desk ever since.'

'Wounded?' said Jenny in an apologetic tone. 'What happened?'

'Oh, the usual,' said Davenport. 'Took a machine-gun round in the thigh.'

Jenny let her gaze fall on his leg. 'Are . . . you all right?'

'Sure. Just dying of boredom, in the desk job, that is.' He smiled at her encouragingly.

Butler returned with a tray and carefully slid three glasses of ale and a lemonade across the table. During a pause in the music, he lifted his glass and said, 'To Peg and Jenny. And victory, of course.' They all raised their glasses.

When the band started into a lively melody, Peg leaned against Butler's shoulder and said, 'C'mon, Hanes, let's dance.'

After Butler led her away, Davenport turned to Jenny, who said, 'Well, Colonel . . .'

'It's Charles.'

'Charles,' she repeated softly. 'It seems a bit odd to see . . . well, an officer like yourself in a dance hall.'

'Does it?' he asked, though the ballroom was overflowing with enlisted men. 'Hanes and I work together,' he explained. 'He asked me to come along.'

Jenny sipped her drink. 'Still and all,' she said, 'it seems a bit strange.'

'I don't see why. After all, Hanes is an officer.'

'Hanes is a Yank,' she said, with a short, dismissive laugh. 'Yanks are . . . well, different.'

'Now there's a point we can agree upon,' said Davenport with a smile. 'But despite what you may think, I'm just an ordinary chap.'

'Really? Not like the ordinary chaps I know.' She seemed to be studying his face.

'Tell me about yourself, Jenny,' said Davenport.

'Not much to tell,' she said with a slight toss of her hair. 'Live alone with me mum and sister since dad was killed in the Blitz.'

'Sorry,' said Davenport.

'He worked in the dockyards,' Jenny explained. 'It's been a bit of a struggle with 'im gone and my brothers off in the navy. It's just a shop-girl's life for me.'

Davenport smiled self-consciously, feeling an attraction to the shy young woman. 'What sort of shop?' he asked.

'Millinery,' she said with a frown. 'You know, ladies' hats and such.' The band began to play a slow Cole Porter favourite.

Davenport sat silently for a moment, watching pinpoints of light play across Jenny's pretty face, and then said, 'Would you care to dance?'

The rhythmic creak of the rocking chair on the loose flooring had always been comforting to Mary but lately it had begun to bother her. In the days that had passed since she walked into town with the basket for Eamon, she had been worrying endlessly. She wanted to report her discovery to *someone*, but to whom? Considering Ireland's neutrality, was there anything illegal about a German intelligence agent in their midst? If not illegal, potentially scandalous to the de Valera government, considering the outcry it would provoke on the other side of the Irish Sea. It would do no good to report Eamon to the local authorities, she reasoned, but perhaps to the government in Dublin, but that would necessitate a trip into the city. Damn, she swore, as she listened to the annoying creak. She felt trapped in her own house, afraid to venture into town or go for a stroll on the beach while the mild weather lasted. At the sound of whistling outside, Mary observed Donald as he walked up on the porch. He must have grown six inches, and though he was still affectionate, a quiet earnestness had taken the place of his boyish capering.

'Morning, Mary,' he called.

'Hello, Donald,' she said as she held open the door. 'What brings you out?'

'As you haven't been by the shop for awhile, I thought I'd look in on you.' He slipped off his cap and, with a self-conscious smile, stepped inside.

With a questioning look, she said, 'Well, come into the kitchen. I've baked some cookies.' As Mary poured him a glass of milk,

Donald studied the headlines on the week-old London paper. 'What do you make of this?' he asked, pointing to the map of the Allied landings at Salerno.

She handed him the glass and then bent over to study the map. 'They've decided to invade Italy proper, now that the government's changed sides.'

'Looks like the Allies will be stuck fighting the Germans in Italy,' said Donald, helping himself to an oatmeal biscuit, 'rather than going after them in France.'

'Yes, I'm afraid so.' Mary gave Donald an encouraging smile, eliciting the slightest blush, and added, 'I'm glad you're keeping up with the news.'

Wiping his mouth, he said, 'You've been all right, have you?'

'Of course. Why do you ask?'

'There's something I ought to tell you,' said Donald, leaning on the countertop.

'All right,' she said, taking a seat at the table.

'I was working at the Anchor a while back, cleaning up during closing hours.' Mary nodded, feeling a spasm of fear. 'Those men were there talking. You know, the IRA.'

'Oh my God, Donald.'

'I couldn't quite make it out, but they were threatening the other one, the nice-looking fellow.'

'Eamon?'

'That's the one.' Mary massaged her forehead. 'The rough one had me bring him a whiskey. That's when I overheard.' Donald hesitated.

'Overheard what?'

'The IRA man warned Eamon about . . . well, about seeing you. He said, the one who's sweet on the British officer. I remember that.'

'What else did he say?'

'I don't remember. But then he pulled a gun and waved it at Eamon. I was scared and slipped out when they weren't looking.'

'Oh, Donald.'

'It worried me, Mary. I just wanted to make sure you were safe.'

Mary stood up and gave him a hug. 'Thank you, Donald. I'll be fine. And believe me, I'm careful to stay away from those men. All of them.'

'Well,' he said, as he slipped on his cap, 'I'd best be on my way.' She walked outside with him and watched with an affectionate look as the boy disappeared down the track.

Mary returned to the rocker with the last letter from Charles and one from home. Charles's letter upset her almost as much as her discovery about Eamon. For the first time in all the months of correspondence she couldn't feel him in his words. His carefully written descriptions seemed contrived somehow, as though he was writing to someone else. The last letter from her mother contained the distressing news that her father, always the picture of ruddy good health, had suffered a mild heart attack. Her mother was worried sick about her brother Bill, serving on a destroyer in the Pacific, and implored Mary to come home. Well, Mary considered unhappily, the chances of booking a passage to America were virtually non-existent at this feverish stage of the war. And the thought of leaving the house, with all the care she'd put into it, and the cliffs and the sea, sickened her as much as the guilt she felt for not being with her poor mother. After penning a quick note to her brother, which she enclosed with a letter to her parents, she gazed out at the angry sea, afraid they were in for a bout of heavy weather. The sky was the shade of old pewter and the sea as turbulent as her thoughts. As much as she dreaded an encounter with Eamon, the visit from Donald had made her feel slightly ridiculous. It might be her best chance to make a quick run into town. Walking the bicycle from the shed, she lowered her head against the wind and began to pedal.

CHAPTER SIXTEEN

EAMON O'FARRELL WATCHED from his vantage point at the front window of the Golden Anchor. At four o'clock, he had the darkened pub to himself, seated behind the half-curtains that provided an unobstructed view of the intersection of the two country roads leading into the village. Ever since he'd observed Mary hurrying from his boarding house, he'd been waiting and watching, certain she would come, forced out of hiding by a need for supplies. With the dark clouds signalling an approaching storm, he suspected that today might be the day. He watched a small mongrel playing with a group of boys, and then suddenly she appeared, a blur on a bicycle swiftly gliding past. There was no mistaking her thick black hair and trim waistline. After fifteen minutes, Mary reappeared on her bicycle, the basket filled with groceries, which she parked at the post office before disappearing inside the stone building. Moments later she emerged, clutching a letter, with a smile on her pretty face. Eamon let himself out the back door of the pub, seen by no one. Mary tucked the letter in her pocket, mounted the bicycle, and pushed off as the first drops of cold rain stung her face. A sudden wind gust brought brittle leaves swirling down the lane, and she pedalled hard, determined to get home before the downpour.

He had chosen a thick gorse bush, twisted by the steady sea breeze, at a turn in the well-worn track. He crouched, listening for her approaching bicycle. Squinting to avoid the rain, Mary's breath came in gasps, knowing that the safety of her cottage was only several hundred yards in the distance. As she sped past the bend in the track she was dimly aware of a figure who suddenly appeared from behind the shrub. Her heart pounding, she pedalled even harder, too frightened to scream as she listened to the footfalls close behind her. Over the rushing wind she heard him call out, 'Mary! Stop!'

In the darkness she could see the lights shining in her windows. The racing steps drew even closer. All at once the storm broke and, blinded by the rain, she pedalled furiously, but rounding the final turn, her tyre caught the edge of a rut. A strong arm encircled her waist just as the bicycle crashed into the thick gorse. They fell heavily together onto the muddy track. Momentarily dazed, her mind could not keep up with what was happening, lying beneath his weight. Eamon struggled to his feet and, taking her hands, hauled her up to face him. Above the shrieking wind and rain, he shouted, 'We must get out of the storm!' She drew back with a terror-stricken look. 'Mary,' he shouted, 'I promise I won't hurt you!'

'My things . . . my letter,' she stammered at last. A bolt of lightning, far too close for comfort, illuminated her pale face.

'Go on, Mary!' he yelled. 'I'll bring your things!' He gave her a push in the direction of the cottage and reached for the handlebars of the twisted bicycle. Soaked through, she stepped under the protection of her porch with Eamon close behind her, hearing Chelsea's shrill bark and the scratch of her paws. He placed those of Mary's purchases he was able to salvage on the porch and knelt down to unlace his shoes. 'Take off your shoes,' he calmly instructed, 'and as many of your other things as you will.' He stripped off his coat and socks as Mary kicked off her shoes. Clutching her arms around herself in the cold wind, she opened the door and stepped inside. Despite the dog's threatening growl, Eamon stayed close to her, placing his hand on her arm.

Looking up into his eyes, she said, 'What are you going to do?'

'I simply need to talk to you,' said Eamon calmly.

Mary forced herself to think. 'There's a towel in the bathroom,' she said, 'down the hall.' He nodded, casting a quick look around the darkened house, as the power had failed. As soon he was gone, she hurried to the pantry for her grandfather's shotgun. She broke it open, inserted two shells, and snapped it shut with a reassuring click. Within moments she heard his bare feet on the floor and raised the gun to her shoulder.

Eamon froze. He was still wearing his wet trousers, with a towel draped over his bare shoulders. To Mary's surprise, a small gold cross hung on his chest from a thin chain. He smiled and said, 'I suppose you're going to shoot me.' Mary stood motionless, nervously fingering the trigger-guard. 'Put the gun aside, Mary,' said Eamon, 'before there's some foolish accident.'

'No, I won't,' she said in a strong voice, though a tear appeared at the corner of her eye.

'All right, then. Have it your way.' He pulled back a chair and sat at the table. 'I've come here to talk,' he said. 'To explain.'

'Who are you?' she blurted out. 'You're a spy, aren't you? A German spy.'

'In a manner of speaking,' he said evenly. 'An agent, actually, of the Abwehr, the military intelligence department.'

Mary tightened her grip on the shotgun and said, 'I knew it. But I don't understand. You're Irish.'

'No, actually, I'm not. My real name is Hans von Oldenburg. I'm from Hanover. Mary, this would be so much easier if you would brew us a pot of tea and let me get a fire going. It's so cold and draughty in here.'

Mary shook her head in bewilderment. 'I don't understand,' she mumbled.

'*For God's sake*, Mary, that's why I came, to explain.' He rose abruptly and started for the living room. 'Now,' he said over his shoulder, 'would you please make us some tea? Keep the shotgun if you like.'

After a few minutes they were seated by the fire, cradling cups of hot, sugared tea. The shotgun lay across Mary's lap, pointing safely at the wall. Eamon managed a small smile and said, 'Now, as I was saying, my father and mother met at the Sorbonne, before the First War. She came from a family of landowners in County Mayo. Landed gentry, I suppose you could say. And my father was an aristocrat, Count Hasso von Oldenburg, though at heart he was a republican. Loathed the Kaiser and any form of autocracy. She was young and beautiful, it was Paris and, naturally, they fell in love.'

'And so your mother is Irish.'

'Yes. Her Irish heritage meant a great deal to her. They were married in 1913. Sadly for them, the war came along, my father joined his old regiment and Mother found herself living among her own country's sworn enemy. She was so cut off from her family during those years that she was determined her son would grow up knowing Ireland.' He smiled and said, 'Might I bother you for a bit more tea?'

Mary lifted the shotgun from her lap and began to lean it against the wall but suddenly changed her mind. 'No,' she said. 'This isn't like before . . . *Herr* Oldenburg. And besides, the tea's gone. Now, why are you telling me all this?'

He studied her, admiring the fire in her eyes. 'Because it's important to me that you understand who I am.'

'I know who you are,' she said angrily. 'You're a German spy. And you've got something to do with those IRA toughs.' Mary tightened her grip on the shotgun. 'When I think back on those chats of ours, in this very house, listening to you carry on about Hitler. God, what a fool I was!' Mary tried to stifle a sob. 'Now why don't you just get out, and leave me alone!'

'Please, Mary,' he said calmly, 'just give me another minute, and I'll be gone.' She pressed her lips tightly together and motioned with the gun for him to continue. 'Yes, I work for German intelligence,' he continued, 'but Ireland's neutral, like Spain and Sweden, and all of the parties have networks here. I was sent here to gather information. On the movement of British forces—'

'And ships, no doubt,' she interrupted. 'So that your U-boats can blow them out of the water. Innocent seamen with wives and children at home, dying by the tens of thousands. And you expect me . . .' Her words trailed away as Eamon hung his head and pulled the towel around his shoulders. The wind was moaning through cracks in the walls.

Eamon spoke in a soft voice without looking up. 'Yes, and to co-operate with the IRA. They're dreamers and fools, and worse.

But they care about one thing only, and that's beating the British, whatever it takes. And so we have a simple bargain: we sell them arms, and in return they help us watch the coast. But I tell you, Mary, I despise those men—'

'Sure you do,' she said hotly. 'Just as you hate Hitler. God if only you knew . . . If only *they* knew.'

Eamon looked up at her. 'I'll be on my way now,' he said sadly. 'I simply wanted you to know the truth. So now you know, and I won't be botherin' you again.' He rose wearily from his chair. 'But there is one other thing: my grandfather, my mother's father, whom I adored as a boy. The IRA murdered him in cold blood, before my poor grandmother's eyes, to settle some score. So that's what I think of the bloody IRA. Now, if I can get my things.'

Mary watched silently, cradling the shotgun, as he emerged from the hall wearing his rain-soaked clothes and pulled on his coat. He turned toward the door, then stopped and said, 'I almost forgot. Your things are on the porch, except for the newspapers, of course. And I'm sure you'll want this.' He took an envelope from his coat pocket, wet through, the blue ink streaked, and handed it to her. Without another word he walked to the door and let himself out into the storm.

Standing in the rain, Charles clutched his suitcase as a black saloon pulled up and the driver rolled down the window. 'Sir,' said the driver, 'you should have waited on the platform.' Davenport recognized the elderly chauffeur who had met him on his last visit. He walked quickly around to the passenger side, tossed his bag in the back, and climbed in beside the driver. 'Sorry to make a mess,' he said as the water dripped from his hat on to the leather seat.

The chauffeur said, 'Quite all right, sir. Shall we be off?' The rain slackened as they drove in silence along the winding road. The gentle Cotswolds, clad in wildflowers in the summer, were now a dull grey against an even darker sky. As they turned into the drive, Davenport glanced at the stark, black boughs of the leafless trees, reminded of the verses: *When yellow leaves, or none, or few, do hang upon those boughs which shake against the cold . . .*

'You'll be staying the weekend, sir?' asked the driver

'Yes,' replied Davenport, 'till Sunday afternoon.' As they rounded a curve on the brow of a hill, the magnificent castle appeared in the distance. A shaft of sunlight broke through the clouds and shone briefly on the honey-coloured stone towers. Davenport pictured Evan Hockaday as he remembered him on his first visit, sitting cheerfully in his wheelchair as the dog bounded down the steps to greet him.

As if reading his thoughts, the driver said, 'Master Evan is staying in the south wing. It would be best to take the servants' entrance, if you don't mind, sir.'

'Of course,' said Davenport. When the car came to a stop, he let himself out and retrieved his bag from the back.

'Allow me, sir,' said the driver, reaching for Davenport's suitcase. 'Right this way.' Davenport followed the old man up a flagstone path to the entrance at the rear of the building where they were greeted by an immaculately dressed young man with neatly parted hair.

'I'm Smith, sir,' he said. 'Master Evan's valet. He's expecting you.' As the chauffeur disappeared up a staircase, Davenport followed the young man to a book-lined study, where Evan Hockaday was seated by the fireplace, a plaid wool blanket on his lap. Pivoting his wheelchair, he smiled and said, 'Hallo, Charles. Come in.'

Davenport took Evan's outstretched hand, and said, 'It's wonderful to see you, Evan.'

'And you're looking well,' said Hockaday. 'Smith, would you please ask Maggie to bring us a pot of tea? And some of those biscuits?'

'Of course, sir.'

'Oh, and Smith, the fire could use a bit of stirring.'

Seated opposite Evan before the fire, Davenport held his cup and saucer in his lap and said, 'How is your father getting along?'

With a frown Evan said, 'Father is unwell. He seldom leaves his room. It was a shock when I first arrived.'

'Sorry,' said Davenport, 'but it's to be expected at his age.'

'It's more than that, I'm afraid,' said Evan.

Davenport studied Evan. In the dim light he seemed to have aged and the cheerful sparkle in his good eye had turned to a look of deep sadness. 'How do you mean, Evan?'

'Since I last wrote to you we have received word about Robert.' Evan glanced at an oil portrait of a handsome young man above the writing desk. His hair was thick and dark, unlike Evan's fine flax, but the pale blue eyes and confident smile were identical.

Davenport put his tea aside, leaned forward and said, 'What about Robert?'

'Killed in action,' said Evan. 'In Burma, with Wingate's Chindits.'

'My God, Evan. I'm so sorry. Damn the war.'

'Father naturally assumed that Robert . . . that Robert would be the one to carry on, to take his rightful place. Especially since what happened . . .' Hockaday paused to compose himself. 'Since what happened to me, Father was hoping for so much from Robert. It's almost as if he died with him.'

The two men sat silently, staring into the fire. Davenport stood up abruptly and walked to the fireplace, resting an arm on the mantel. 'I'm truly sorry about your brother,' he said, 'but there's no finer man than you, Evan, and you mustn't—'

'Don't worry, Charles,' said Evan with a surprising smile. 'You've no idea how grateful I am to be alive. It's Father I'm worried about.'

Bright sunshine woke him. At the sound of a tap on the door Davenport lifted his head from the pillow and called, 'Come in.'

The door swung open, admitting a maid with a tray. 'Your coffee, sir,' she said and then withdrew. He threw back the covers and, after donning a dressing-gown, poured a cup. Opening the curtains, he gazed out on the lawn, blanketed with fresh snow. He was admiring the view and sipping his coffee, when the door behind him creaked open.

'Splendid, isn't it?'

Davenport turned to Evan in his wheelchair, attended by Smith, his valet, who departed, closing the door behind him. 'I heard the storm during the night,' said Davenport, placing his coffee on the bedside table. 'The grounds are lovely with a fresh coat of snow.'

'I thought we might take a look round the country in Father's Bentley.'

'An excellent idea.'

They spent the morning touring the Cotswold countryside, enjoying the views of the snow-dusted fields and stone cottages from the back seat of the car with the elderly chauffeur behind the wheel, travelling along the arrow-straight Roman road from Cirencester to Bourton-on-the-Water, thence to Broadway in time for lunch at the Lygon Arms, overlooking the distant Vale of Evesham. At a quiet table in the hotel dining room, Davenport folded his napkin and said, 'So Robert was with Wingate in Burma?'

'Yes, General Orde Wingate,' said Evan bitterly, 'and his scheme to operate behind the Japanese lines. Some say the man's a lunatic, others a genius, but not many of his men made their way out of that God-forsaken jungle.'

'I've actually met the man,' said Charles. Evan looked at him with surprise. 'On board the *Queen Mary*,' said Davenport, *'en route* to Quebec. Churchill was quite taken with him and dragged him along. Odd looking chap with a beard and gleam in his eye.'

'You astonish me, Charles,' said Evan. 'The *Queen Mary*, Churchill, and the mysterious General Wingate. Pretty heady stuff. I'm desperate to hear all about the plans to win the war. Later, of course,' he added quietly.

Davenport finished his coffee and said, 'And I'm anxious to learn more about your work, which, frankly, is far more important than my lowly staff work.'

'Lowly staff work,' said Evan. 'At the right hand of General Morgan, no less. Tell me, Charles, what's the latest in your divorce proceedings?'

'Well, I'm single again, thank God. No more of Frances and her barristers.'

'I should think that's terrific. And what about that lovely American girl Mary? You've been to see her, haven't you?'

'Yes,' said Davenport. He paused to take a sip of coffee. 'Well, we're still friends.'

'Friends?' said Evan with a curious expression. 'Perhaps there's someone else?'

'Oh well, I've met a girl, if that's what you mean. One of the men on my staff, an American, lined me up with a girl from Lambeth.'

'From Lambeth,' said Evan. 'I see.'

'It's nothing, Evan. She's pretty ... no education, of course.' Abruptly Davenport pushed back his chair and said, 'It's nearly three. I suppose we should be getting back.'

A half-empty bottle of port sat on the table next to Evan's wheel-chair. Davenport was warming himself by the fire with a glass in his hand. 'It was all settled at Quebec,' he said. 'The invasion is definitely set for Normandy.'

'Have they set a date?'

Davenport nodded and gave Evan an inscrutable look, thinking there were some things he should not divulge, even to someone as thoroughly trusted as Evan. 'Normandy,' he continued, 'has the great advantage of surprise. At the moment, the beaches are only lightly defended. But it suffers from one great disadvantage.'

'Yes,' said Evan, 'it lacks a deep-water port. There's none between Le Havre and Cherbourg.'

'Churchill has this daft scheme for an artificial harbour,' said Davenport. 'Anchoring a massive breakwater to a line of ships sunk off the landing beaches. It actually might work. But the trick,' he continued, 'is to convince Hitler's generals that the invasion is coming at the Pas de Calais.'

'Well,' said Evan, 'I believe my colleagues at Bletchley can help with the deception. We're planning to launch a steadily mounting pattern of radio traffic directly opposite Calais. And then we'll monitor the Ultra intercepts from the German high command in response to the perceived build-up. A simple matter of reinforcing their impression that the main attack will be at Calais.'

'Excellent,' said Davenport. 'I knew we could count on your group.'

'I needn't remind you,' said Evan, 'that you mustn't mention a word of this to a soul.'

'You have my word.'

'Well, then,' said Evan, 'it looks as though we'll have to sit back till spring and hope for the best.'

Davenport sipped his port and said, 'It's a good enough plan. But what if the Germans were to put someone really energetic in charge of the Atlantic defences? What if the number of troops defending Normandy were doubled? We can't put any more men ashore on the first day. I worry that the right commander would bring his armoured divisions into action to hold our men on the beaches. It could be a bloody disaster.'

'Yes,' Evan agreed. 'And we could only stand one go at it. If that fails, I doubt we'd have the nerve to make another try. Where would that leave us?'

'Precisely,' said Davenport. 'We've got to get our men in control of the beachhead on the first day. It's our only chance.' He looked Evan in the eye. 'There's something I should tell you,' he said in a serious tone. 'I don't intend to watch this show from the grandstands.'

'What do you mean?'

'I've asked General Morgan for a transfer,' said Davenport. 'To command a battalion in the Third Division.'

'What role have they been assigned?'

'Sword Beach, on the far left of the landing area. The first wave on D-Day.'

Evan seemed lost in his reflections, staring at the fire. 'Has General Morgan given you his answer?' he asked at length.

'He supported my request. I'm waiting to hear.'

'I must say, it doesn't really surprise me. You've been in combat and know what it's all about. But you've asked for an awfully dangerous assignment. Surely there's some other place you might . . .'

After a moment, Davenport said, 'I oversaw the planning for Sword Beach. I'd like to take part in the actual landing. And besides, with my marriage finished, and what happened with Mary, I've got no one—'

'Don't be a fool,' said Evan with surprising vehemence. 'You're talking rot. I know there's one special girl who cares very much for you. I only wish . . .' – Evan hesitated. Davenport studied his slender, broken frame, the eye patch and limp sleeve pinned to his jacket – 'That there was a woman in my life,' Evan said quietly. 'I'd like to think that perhaps someday . . .' He turned to Davenport and said, 'I don't know what happened between you and Mary, but I'm certain she cares a great deal about you. After losing her husband, don't you suppose she fears something will happen to you? Don't give up on her.'

'I don't know, Evan,' said Davenport morosely, before downing the rest of his drink. 'I mean, she left me there in Wales. Simply up and left.' Both men silently stared into the fire. After a while he looked at Evan and said, 'How do you manage the way you do? Where does your strength come from?'

'You know about my faith,' Evan said quietly.

'Yes,' said Davenport, 'but you're not like these other chaps who . . . well, what I mean is, you've got an education. And look at the war. God only knows how many more are going to die. Considering all that's happened, not only with Hitler, but in the First War as well, how do you make any sense out of it? In terms of *God*, that is?'

'I grew up very much as you did, I suppose,' Evan replied. 'Services on Sunday mornings. But things changed for me at the university, thanks to one man. And I began to read the Bible, the Gospels and St. Paul. And, just as Jesus promised, I found a new life.'

Davenport stared at Evan, trying to understand. 'I'm sorry, Evan. I'd best go up to bed.'

CHAPTER SEVENTEEN

WITH THE CLOSING door, Mary's world changed again. How could Eamon have left so quietly after all that had gone before? Even passing her the smeared, rain-soaked letter had seemed almost an act of contrition. Suddenly he had seemed so sad. Trembling again, she lifted the gun from her lap, broke open the barrel, and carefully removed the shells, slipping them into her pocket with shaking hands. She awoke the next morning to the pungent smell of the wool clothing she had laid across a chair in front of the fire before going to bed. There was a surreal feel to things, as though the events of the last evening had never happened. Only after stirring the milk and sugar into the single cup of tea she allowed herself did she return to the letter she'd left on the kitchen table to dry. She carefully extracted the pages, as crisp as fallen leaves, but it was apparent that little would be salvaged from its drenching.

'Mary, how are you my . . .' was legible, and then the words disappeared in a blur of blue ink until her eyes fell on the phrase 'with a heavy heart'. Without reading another word she assumed he was about to tell her goodbye. With a long sigh, she tried to make out the next words, but only the phrase 'try to get leave to see him' was legible, presumably a reference to Charles's father. She thought of her own father, seriously ill in Boston, and the fact there was no way to return home to be with him. Resting her forehead on the heel of her hand, Mary carefully studied the last page. Almost all of the words were washed away, but she could make out just enough to follow the thread. 'So many months . . .' followed by a string of blotted words, and then 'after endless hours our planning . . . essentially complete'. The next fragment, 'hoping to find something more challenging', was a puzzle. She briefly closed her eyes, and when she looked again at the wrinkled page, a ray of sunlight shone through the curtain, forming a square on the table. She stared at the words *love you* in the bright square of light. It was enough. She sipped her tea and stared at the words, daring to hope again.

Only later, after writing a long letter to her father and mother, did she sit at her bureau and begin a brief note to Charles, but after a moment she stopped, caught up in memories of the weekend in Wales, the way the breeze had worried the curtains, the scent of fresh flowers, how he hushed her when they made love. After finishing the letters, she read a long piece in the *Irish Times* about the confusing situation in Italy. The thought of American troops battling the Germans in the streets of Naples or, like her brother Bill, fighting the Japanese in the Pacific, made her feel so isolated, with no one to talk to, surrounded by the rural Irish, untouched by, and largely indifferent to, the war raging around the world. If only she were in London with Charles. With a heavy sigh, she rose from the kitchen table and clapped her hands to summon Chelsea.

Standing at the top of the cliffs in the cold, clear aftermath of the storm, Eamon O'Farrell suddenly sprang into her consciousness. Mary shivered in the wind, glancing uneasily at the drop to the rocks below. It wasn't really Eamon, anyway. The name was as false as everything else about him. What had he said? Hans ... Hans von Oldenburg. It didn't seem possible. Mary forced herself to think back, how calmly he'd sat by the fire drinking his tea. For a moment he had seemed her friend and confidante again. He must have been telling the truth about his mother and the summers in Ireland, considering that he spoke flawless English with as natural a brogue as she had ever heard. But why had he chased her down on the track? He'd openly admitted that he was a German intelligence agent, even explaining his bargain with the outlawed IRA. But why tell her? She couldn't help feeling that somehow he was a good and decent man. Her head and her heart were at war. No, she decided, he was her enemy, and she vowed not to forget it.

'Come in, Mr Davenport,' said General Morgan, 'and have a seat.' Davenport crossed the carpet to the general's immaculate desk and sat in an armchair. Morgan eyed him with a tight-lipped smile and said, 'Well, it looks as though you've got your orders.' He tossed an envelope across the desk.

Davenport quickly removed a sheet from the envelope and scanned its few lines. He was ordered to report on 15 December 1943 to Third Division headquarters in Scotland, to assume command of the Second Battalion, King's Shropshire Light Infantry. He looked up and said, 'Thank you, sir. I know this wouldn't have been possible without your support.'

'I suppose I should say you're welcome,' said Morgan, 'but the truth is, I'd far rather keep you on my staff, and God only knows what fate I've consigned you to. But if this enterprise is going to succeed, we'll need the very best men in command. And, frankly, the

Third Division hasn't seen combat since Dunkirk. Green as a summer apple.'

Davenport said, 'I'm deeply appreciative, sir.'

'Well, good luck. Do your best and perhaps some day you'll have one of these.' Morgan lightly touched the red tab on his lapel.

Davenport rose and stood at attention. 'It has been a great privilege,' he said, 'to serve under your command.' He hurried along the crowded corridors of Norfolk House like a schoolboy, making his way to a small interior office with 'Major H. Butler' stencilled on the door. Flinging it open, he looked at Hanes with a foolish grin.

Butler leaned back, put his feet on the desk, revealing the holes wearing through the soles of his shoes, and languidly dropped a document. 'Well, well,' he drawled. 'You look like the cat that swallowed the canary.'

'Have a look at this, Hanes,' said Davenport, taking a folded sheet from his pocket and handing it across the desk.

Butler studied it briefly and said 'I'll be damned. Looks like you got it. The King's Shropshire Light Infantry. Sounds pretty damned impressive, if you ask me.'

'I don't know a thing about the regiment,' said Davenport, 'other than the fact that it's attached to the Third Division. That's all that matters.'

'Well Charlie,' said Butler, swinging his legs from the desk, 'this calls for a celebration. A night on the town with the girls.'

'Right you are,' said Davenport with a smile. 'Something special.'

'I'll call Peg and she can find Jenny. Let's show these Lambeth gals the way the other half lives.'

'Tell Peg to take the Tube to Green Park , and meet us in the bar at the Ritz. And wear something nice.' He turned to walk out.

'Say, Charlie,' said Butler. 'Guess what I heard today?'

Davenport stopped and turned.

'Hitler's canned the general in charge of the defence of France,' said Butler, 'and named Rommel to take his place.'

'Rommel? Are you sure?'

Butler nodded and said, 'Yep. The Desert Fox.' '

'Well,' muttered Davenport, 'that's exactly what I've been worried about.'

Davenport sat on the bed rereading the letter from his father. *Please son*, he wrote, *if there's any way, come before Christmas. I have to confess it's lonely here.* Davenport put the letter aside and thought about his father. When he was younger, engaged to Frances, he had felt slightly embarrassed by his father, comparing him to the bankers and lawyers whose sons attended college with him. He was a life-long schoolteacher and above all he was devoted to his wife and only child. He was in truth, Davenport reflected, a far better man than almost any he had known. Realizing he should write to tell him about his transfer, he felt a pang of guilt that he'd assured him he would remain on Morgan's staff, just as, he wretchedly conceded, he'd assured Mary. He was conscious of a flutter of anticipation at the thought of seeing Jenny. They'd been out several times since that first night at the dancehall, doubling up with Hanes and Peg at the pub or cinema. Despite her lack of education and clumsy manner-isms, there was something appealing about her. At first he'd likened her to one of those sad but noble characters out of a Dickens novel, but then decided there was more to her than that. Unlike Peg, who was, more or less, content with her lot, Jenny was determined to find a way out of her grim working-class existence. Davenport stood up from the bed and, locking the door, hurried down to the street, where Hanes was waiting in his jeep.

'Don't you look swell,' said Hanes. 'Hop in and let's go.'

The hotel bar was packed with servicemen and their dates, American officers in drab olive and tan predominating. 'The girls are bound to be late,' said Butler. 'Let's get a drink.' After a few minutes they found two seats at the bar and ordered whiskies and soda. Once the bartender slid the glasses across the counter, Butler looked at Davenport and said, 'There they are.' Peg and Jenny stood nerv-ously on the far side of the room, peering at the crowd. Nervousness accentuated Peg's rough features, but Jenny was luminous in a dark, tight-fitting dress that showed off her figure to its full advantage, her lips a dark, moist red in contrast to her pale complexion. 'Sonofagun,' said Hanes softly. 'Would you look at Jenny.'

Davenport slid off his stool and straightened his tunic. 'Good evening, Jenny,' he said as she walked up. She smiled and leaned over for a kiss on the cheek.

'Let's find a table,' said Butler, 'and get y'all something to drink.' Once they were seated, he summoned a waiter. 'What'll it be, Peg?' said Butler.

Looking nervously around the ornate room, Peg said, 'Oh, Hanes, I dunno. A be-ahh.'

The waiter deferentially inclined his head and said, 'Excuse me, madam?'

'Bring the lady a beer,' instructed Butler. 'Jenny?'

She looked at Davenport with an expression of childish delight and said, 'Charlie – what do you think? Something *special*.'

'A champagne cocktail?' suggested Davenport. 'And we'll have another round.'

'Very well, sir.'

When the waiter returned, Jenny held up the fluted glass and studied the tiny bubbles. Taking a sip, she smiled and said, 'Mmm. That's lovely. Would you look at us, Peg? Who would 'ave thought. Out for a night at the Ritz.'

'A bit on the fancy side for me,' said Peg with a self-conscious smile, revealing her uneven teeth. She took a swallow of beer.

'Aw, c'mon, Peg,' said Butler cheerfully. 'Relax. We're here to celebrate.'

'Really?' said Jenny, taking a sip of her cocktail. 'What's to celebrate?'

'The lieutenant colonel here,' said Butler, 'is movin' on to bigger and better things. He's being transferred to the Third Infantry Division.'

Jenny shot a worried look at Davenport. 'Does that mean you'll be leaving?' she asked softly.

'Yes,' said Davenport with a nod. 'We'll be training in Scotland.'

'A toast,' said Butler merrily. 'To the King's Shropshire Light Infantry.'

Jenny raised her glass as Davenport held her in his steady gaze.

'What's that, Hanes?' asked Peg after taking a slosh of beer and wiping her mouth with the back of her hand.

'Charlie's new regiment,' said Hanes. 'Anyway, we need to give him a proper send off. What sounds good?'

'I dunno,' said Peg. 'We could go dancin' . . .'

'No, let's go someplace special,' said Jenny with a sparkle in her eyes. 'Charlie , I'm sure you know a place?'

Davenport thought for a moment and then said, 'We could try Scott's. The best seafood in town.' He thought of his frequent dinners there with Frances before the war.

'Fish,' said Peg in a disappointed voice. 'I was 'opin' for roast beef.'

'Beef?' said Jenny with a roll of her eyes. 'Mutton, more likely.'

'Bottoms up,' said Davenport. 'Let's be on our way.' Standing in the blacked-out street, he peered at an oncoming vehicle. 'Taxi,' he called out, raising a hand. A black Austin veered over and came to a stop.

'Dear, dear,' said Peg, 'ain't we ritzy tonight, ridin' in a taxicab.'

As Davenport watched her ample behind disappear into the back, he leaned down to the driver and said, 'Scott's on Mount Street.'

They were seated at a banquette in the crowded dining room, a half-empty bottle of cheap South African bubbly resting in an ice bucket. Next to Charles, Jenny pretended to listen to the joke Hanes Butler was telling as she watched him out of the corner of her eye, observing the way he held his silverware and wineglass. All evening she'd paid close attention to the way he spoke, the way he enunciated the words, the words themselves – though he wasn't aware of it, she was sure of that. When a smile appeared on his lips at the punch line to the joke, she smiled back at him, thinking him not only the handsomest man she'd ever known, but the *finest*, a man who could teach her, show her how to act proper. A waiter appeared at the table and asked, 'Will there be anything else? Dessert, perhaps, or a liqueur? We have an excellent trifle.'

'Sure,' said Butler, 'for the ladies. And I'll have a cup of coffee.'

'No, thanks,' said Davenport. After the trifle and coffee were served, he sipped his champagne and watched as Peg happily attacked the creamy dessert. 'Champagne and trifle,' he said mildly. 'Who could ask for more?' Jenny looked up and gave him a pretty smile, thinking *I could . . . there's so much more I could ask for.*

When they had finished, Butler downed the last of his coffee and reached into his pocket for a roll of bills. Counting several out on the table, he said, 'That should take care of it. This one's on me. C'mon, Peg, let's take a stroll around the block. We'll see y'all later.'

Once they were alone, Davenport turned to Jenny and said, 'I suppose we should be going. I've got an early start in the morning.'

Looking down into her lap, she said, 'Will I be seeing you again?'

'Why, I'm sure . . .'

'But you'll be leaving.'

'I should be back from time to time. I'm sure we'll see one another . . .'

'Oh, Charlie,' Jenny said softly, impulsively taking his hand. 'I wish you weren't going! We was just getting started. Can't you change your mind?'

'Of course not,' he admonished her, immediately regretting his schoolmaster tone. 'It's the war, Jenny,' he said gently. 'I haven't any choice.'

'I suppose not,' she said, thinking, *he's moving on . . . the good ones always do.*

Outside, in the cold December air, Davenport put his arm around Jenny's slender waist. Unexpectedly, she threw her arms around him, silently embracing him with her face pressing against the scratchy wool of his coat. For a moment, inhaling her perfume and feeling her soft curls on his face, he imagined she was Mary. She pulled away and looked up at him. 'I never knew anyone like you, Charlie,' she said softly. 'You're so . . . I don't know how to say it. Such a gentleman.' Standing on tiptoes, she lightly kissed him. After a few seconds, he broke away, staring at her on the blacked-out pavement.

The jeep slewed in the mud as the tyres fought for traction, the driver bidding the machine to keep moving through the deep, rain-filled ruts. Ahead through the unrelenting downpour, a column of troops appeared out of the hedgerow, slogging forward under the weight of rifles and heavy-laden packs. 'It's no use, sir,' said the driver, turning to look back.

Davenport stared through the mud-spattered windshield. 'The question is,' he said, 'if we'll ever get moving again.' Davenport watched the column of soldiers staggering across the road. With few exceptions, they were young and seemed surprisingly small. Well, he thought, perhaps it's just the amount of gear on their backs that made them seem so diminutive. When the last stragglers crossed, the driver revved the engine and released the clutch, but it was pointless. 'Forget it, Sergeant,' said Davenport. 'Let's give it a push.'

By the time the jeep rounded the last bend, the broad expanse of canvas tents and wooden huts was enveloped in a thick, grey murk. The words 'Whitekirk 2 miles' were barely legible on a road sign. The driver pulled to a stop before a low structure with 'HQ Second Battalion – KSLI' stencilled over the door. As he entered the hut, the corporal on duty snapped to attention. Davenport briefly raised his hand to his hat and muttered 'At ease'. The rain kept up a steady drumbeat on the roof. 'If anyone should ask,' said Davenport, 'I've gone to wash and get into some dry clothes.'

Later, after a dinner of beans and lamb stew, Davenport turned to the two officers at his table and said, 'What do you say to a drink at the O.C.?'

'An excellent idea, Charles,' said the young captain seated beside him.

'Not for me,' said the third man. 'I've got that report to finish.'

'Fine,' said Davenport. 'We'll see you at 0500.' He took his greatcoat from the rack and stepped outside into the winter darkness. A thick layer of cloud blotted out any star light, making it difficult to see the duckboard from the mess hall to the Officers' Club, a simple wooden hut warmed by a wood-burning stove. Davenport and the young captain hung up their jackets and walked to the bar. 'What will it be, Alfred?' asked Davenport.

'Half and half,' said Alfred Pearson, resting his elbows on the bar, cheeks glowing pink from the cold.

'I'll have a whisky and soda,' said Davenport. Once they were served the two men moved to a table near the stove.

Pearson lifted his pint glass and said, 'Cheers.'

Davenport repeated the toast and sipped his drink. Pearson leaned forward and said, 'Tell me, Charles, what's your opinion of General Eisenhower?'

'I was surprised when he was given the command,' said Davenport. 'Not that I wasn't impressed by him at our planning conferences, but he hasn't any experience commanding troops in combat. I will give him this, though,' he paused to take another sip. 'Ike took one look at our plan and immediately insisted on more men.'

'Why weren't more men, more divisions, provided for in the plan?'

'In our scheme?' said Davenport. 'No way to get them on the beaches. As simple as that. We were constrained by available landing craft.'

'And how does Eisenhower plan to deal with that?'

'Through adroit political tactics, I expect. He'll find a way to pressure the politicos to divert more landing craft to Overlord, from Italy or the Pacific.'

'Well, we've got Monty,' said Pearson. 'That should more than compensate.'

'Montgomery,' said Davenport after taking a sip, 'is a careful general, I'll give him that, but what an egotist. And some of his victories in Africa weren't as spectacular as they appeared.'

'But, Charles,' said Pearson, 'he chased Rommel all the way across the desert. And look what he did in Sicily.'

'Well, let's just say he had some unusual help. At any rate, he strikes me as a cautious, methodical commander. And frankly,

I'm not sure that's what we need. Especially now that we're facing Rommel.' Pearson gave Davenport a questioning look. 'We'll need daring and surprise,' explained Davenport. 'We won't catch Rommel with his trousers down, I assure you.' He downed his drink and stood up abruptly. 'We should turn in. We've got an early morning.'

Later he sat on his bed staring at a small, framed photograph. He wasn't sure why he had chosen this particular one – his father standing by the front steps, holding his pipe in one hand and his small hand in the other – to keep with him. Like most little boys, he hadn't liked being photographed and looked away from the camera. But his father wore a proud expression, his face still young and strong. Davenport carefully placed the photograph on an empty crate, turned off the light, and slipped under the covers. Closing his eyes, he tried to focus on the next morning's exercise, but his thoughts turned to Mary. He knew he should write to her and confess that he'd been transferred, but how could he? He turned his face to the wall and drifted into a dreamless sleep.

Adjusting his helmet he glanced at his watch. Tugging at the shoulder harness, he walked to the head of the column, his boots cracking the thin glaze of ice on the Scottish mud. The thousand men of the K.S.L.I. stood in formation, six abreast, the column stretching far out of sight in the early morning darkness. 'Sar-major,' commanded Davenport in a loud voice. The burly sergeant stood rigidly at attention at the head of the column. 'You may give the command.'

'Yes, *sir*. Battalion!' shouted the sergeant. 'Forward . . . *march*!'

As the men moved along the narrow lane, the sound of jangling gear and the tramp of boots filled the air. Davenport set a brisk pace, straining against the weight of his sixty-pound pack. From the rear of the column the gruff exhortations of the sergeants could be heard. The weight of the pack burned into his shoulders. The clank of equipment on the men's belts was loud above the thump of a thousand footfalls. Over the brow of a small hill, rooftops and steeples came into view in the misty dawn, with the North Sea in the distance. He glanced back at the column trailing far behind him, with gaps where men had been unable to keep up. After another ten minutes the van of the column entered the outskirts of a small village, passing the brick walls, neatly tended gardens and flower-boxes of homes similar to those in which most of the boys had grown up. Davenport looked at his watch. They'd covered the four miles from the camp in an hour and twelve minutes.

The battalion embarked in five landing craft which bobbed like corks in the choppy sea, and sailed four miles out accompanied by two destroyers and a corvette. A fine mist obscured the beach, two miles in the distance. Davenport checked his watch. Two minutes till H-hour.

'Sergeant, pass the word,' he said. 'When the destroyers finish firing, we're going in.' All at once the destroyers unleashed a volley, the shells roaring overhead and crashing on the beaches, sending plumes of smoke and debris into the air. A split second later, rocket fire streaked overhead, erupting in fireballs on the beach. The petty officers swung the bows of the LCIs toward the beach, throttling the engines. The stench of cordite, seasickness, and the unnerving roar of the shells was too much for many of the green troops, who retched over the sides as the narrow vessels pounded toward the surf. Anti-tank traps and rolls of razor wire were clearly visible beyond the breakers. The bow pitched high on a roller and, at the moment it crashed back down, the gates opened, lowering the steel ramps into the sea. In the front row, Davenport rose from the bench, his rifle slung over his shoulder, and called out, 'Follow me, men!' As the troops splashed into the waist-deep, freezing water, orange tracers from the destroyers' 50-calibre guns sang overhead, and the *whump* of mortars drowned out the din of the surf and the chug of the idling diesels.

'Form up!' yelled the sergeants, at clusters of men fighting their way through the surf under the weight of their packs. As the battalion's thousand men huddled on the beach, teams of combat engineers exploded gaps in the wire. Regaining some semblance of order, the platoons slogged forward toward the flags marking the exits for the landing exercise.

Davenport unslung his pack and let it drop. Settling on the cold soil, he removed his helmet and leaned his aching back against the pack, staring vacantly over the tops of his boots. In the distance he could hear the rumble of lorries that would transport his exhausted men back to camp. In another few hours, there would be hot food, dry clothes, and a warming glass of whisky. The men were exhausted, but they had made it. With a satisfied smile, he considered that the boys were becoming soldiers.

CHAPTER EIGHTEEN

EAMON O'FARRELL FLIPPED the toggle and removed the earphones. He had been relieved to report his improving relationship with Mary as well as to hear, in carefully coded phrases, of the progress his cohorts were making both within the ministry and the Wehrmacht in the recruitment of men allied to the cause. Everything hinged on the timing of the Allied invasion, which they expected when the Atlantic gales abated. He stood up and lowered the antenna. Glancing at his watch, he realized that he would have to hurry. Something about this rendezvous disquieted him. He had bluffed his way through their accusations about the failed IRA raid on the British compound, but the recent capture in Dublin of the man he knew only as 'Smith' within days after Mulcahy had harboured him in Castletown, undoubtedly aroused their suspicions. Of course Eamon had met the senior IRA man to conclude the terms of another arms sale. They could think what they might, but they had no proof. Slipping a switchblade in his coat pocket, he hurried from the boarding house to the Golden Anchor, arriving as the last of the patrons filed out at closing time. He waited a few minutes and then walked to the door and tapped on the glass. A single light was shining behind the bar. Sean Mulcahy appeared out of the shadows and turned the key in the lock.

'Come in, O'Farrell,' he said with a smile as he held open the door. 'Have a drink.'

Eamon glanced around the empty room. He walked behind the counter, patting the knife in his pocket. After pouring a glass of Irish whiskey, he turned to Mulcahy. 'To your health, Sean,' he said, raising his glass. 'And to your bloody cause.'

Mulcahy smiled and took a long swallow of whiskey. 'Have a seat, Mr O'Farrell,' he said. 'Let's have a little chat.' Eamon unbuttoned his coat and slipped off his cap. The two men sat facing one another in the dark, empty room. 'Pity about Smith,' Mulcahy began.

'What about him?' said Eamon casually.

'Strange coincidence, I should say. Very strange.'

Eamon remained silent, sipping his drink.

'There was no one else saw him, O'Farrell. No one besides you.'

Eamon shrugged and said, 'It's none of my affair, as you well know. Something happen to your friend? An accident?'

'You might say that,' said Mulcahy with a menacing glare.

'What was it you wanted to see me about? I don't have all night.'

'You know, O'Farrell, I'm not sure we've got much use for you anymore. We've got all the rifles and ammunition we need, and our boys are sick of doing the Nazis' bidding. Looks to me like you're losin' the war, and to the sorry goddamn Brits. So it's been nice knowin' you, but it's time to call it quits.'

'So that's it.' Eamon finished his drink in a single swig. 'Have it your way. I'm sure I can find some other shills.' He stood up and pulled on his cap. 'Now if you don't mind. . . .'

'The front door's locked,' said Mulcahy. 'You'll have to go out the back.'

'After you, Sean.' Eamon waited as Mulcahy shrugged on his coat, then followed him to the door at the back. After Mulcahy opened the door and disappeared down the steps, Eamon stood in the doorway holding the knife in his pocket as he searched the small enclosure behind the building in the darkness. As he started down the steps he sensed motion and spun around, pulling the knife and snapping open the five-inch blade. The sight of the glinting knife caused the men who appeared out of the shadows to hesitate. There were three of them, including Mulcahy, armed with clubs and chains. The first man lunged at Eamon, swinging a short, thick shillelagh. Ducking to one side, Eamon slashed the man's outstretched arm. 'C'mon, man,' said Eamon hoarsely. 'Have at it.'

The other two circled slowly, keeping their distance. All at once they both rushed in, one of them swinging a chain hard at Eamon's knees while the other attacked with the club. Deflecting the blow with his arm, Eamon drove the knife into the man's ribs with a hard, slapping sound. For an instant they were frozen in a silent embrace, until the third man fell on Eamon with the fury of a wounded animal. One sharp blow with the shillelagh found its mark on the side of Eamon's head. Down now, sinking into unconsciousness, the blows fell on him again and again.

'That's enough,' said Mulcahy, clutching his side with dark blood running between his fingers. 'Get him into the car.' As they drove out of the village, the only sounds were Eamon's groans as he lay on the back seat. 'There,' said Mulcahy, 'on the right. Take that track.' They bumped a quarter-mile along the lane before coming to a stop. 'Hurry, damn it,' said Mulcahy, 'before I bleed to death!' The other two dragged Eamon from the car and dumped his limp form under a thick shrub. 'That should do it,' said Mulcahy as he gazed at the motionless body in the moonlight. 'Let's go.' They piled into the car and disappeared.

Mary fished in the lukewarm water for the last fork. It had been a strange morning, watching the snow fall in wispy flurries from the kitchen window, surrounded by so many sensual pleasures, her hands deep in soapy water, the warm scent of spice cake filling the room, beautiful music on the gramophone. For some reason, desire had plaited itself to every fibre of her being, moving like honey through all her thoughts. She drew up a chair close to the fire, enjoying the warmth that spread from the blazing logs that had finally caught after considerable effort with the poker and bellows. Her face was obscured by the pages of the *Irish Times* as she absorbed a long piece on the bloody fighting in the Pacific. She put the paper aside, thinking about her brother at sea on the other side of the world. Bright winter sunshine shone through the lace, and Chelsea slept contentedly on the rug by the fender. The calm orderliness seemed so at odds with the chaos raging across the world . . . the exotic places like Mandalay, the Irrawaddy, Port Moresby. She was desperate to make sense out of it, to understand what was coming next and how it might finally end. If only she had Charles to talk to.

She stirred the embers with the poker. It had been a long time since his last letter. He had seemed detached, so careful, almost as though he was guarding some secret. Each time she had resolved to write him, she found herself staring at a blank sheet, unable to make up her mind how to begin. And so for many weeks no letters had passed between them. She studied her hands, smudged with ink from the newsprint, and raised them to her nose, the subtle scent reminding her of home. Closing her eyes, she could almost imagine herself back in those simple times. She walked distractedly to the kitchen, followed by Chelsea, eagerly wagging her tail. She knew the dog would do almost anything to get out into the cold, jumping into the air to snap at a solitary snowflake.

It was a crisp, cold morning, not really snowing, though the occasional flake floated down. Grabbing her heavy coat, she looped a long scarf around her neck and they were off. It was too windy for the path along the cliffs, so they took the garden path that wandered through the gorse back to the lane. The freeze overnight had left thick mantles of frost clinging to the long stems of wild grass. She had walked about a quarter-mile when she heard the dog barking in the distance. She quickened her pace, fearing that Chelsea had cornered some creature. The dog was off the path in the gorse, standing rigidly with her forelegs extended and a low, threatening growl in her throat. Standing at the edge of the path, not wanting to go into the thick shrub, Mary called, but the dog refused to obey. Growing cold and wanting to return to the warmth of her kitchen, Mary took two steps, intent on grabbing the dog by her collar, when she froze. A man was sprawled face down in the brush. From his still, contorted position she was certain he was dead. She looked away instinctively, fighting a wave of nausea, and then forced herself to look back. Dried, black blood was everywhere, matting his hair and covering his face. On one leg, where the trousers had hiked up, was a deep purple bruise and a long gash edged in fresh, satiny red.

Oh my God, she thought, red, red blood . . . he was bleeding . Perhaps he wasn't dead after all? She bent closer, afraid to touch him, watching for some movement in his chest when the glint of gold caught her eye. It was a cross. Jesus, Mary and Joseph . . . it was Eamon's cross! She set off running as fast as she could to the house with Chelsea at her heels. She flung open the door of the shed and grabbed a wheelbarrow, which she shoved, slipping on the ice-encrusted ruts, along the lane until, exhausted from the exertion, she was back to the place where he lay. As she tried to catch her breath, her mind was racing. He was too big to move by herself. In an instant she was running again, tears blurring her vision, when she very nearly collided with Donald, strolling down the track. 'Help me . . . please . . .' she managed to say before turning and starting back, looking on occasion to see that the boy was following her. When he caught up, she was kneeling beside Eamon.

'Oh, my God, Mary!' cried Donald as he dropped to one knee. Together they half carried, half dragged him into the barrow, which they pushed and pulled along the bumpy lane to the cottage. After propping open the door, Donald slipped his arms under Eamon's while Mary firmly grabbed his ankles, and on the count of three, they hauled him into the house, and, with an almost superhuman effort, laid him on Mary's bed. Gasping for breath, she hurried to her desk for a pair of scissors. Donald stood helplessly at the bedside, unable to look away from the blood-caked body. 'Hurry, Donald,' said Mary as she re-entered the room. 'Light the stove and put on a kettle of water to boil.' She placed her fingertips on Eamon's cold wrist, barely able to detect a pulse, and then took the scissors and carefully began cutting away the blood-soaked clothing. When Donald returned with a steaming pan and clean towel, Mary motioned to him to place them at the foot of the bed. 'You must go for the doctor,' she said quietly. 'Take my bicycle and go as fast as you can for Doctor Fraser, but, Donald . . . tell no one else.'

After placing clean sheets to warm in the oven, Mary studied Eamon's almost unrecognizable face, a black mask of bruises and dried blood, his eyes swollen shut, scalp split, and a large clot on the side of his head she dared not disturb. She cleaned and bound the wound on his leg and, when she cut away the black sweater, it was clear that his shoulder was dislocated. Were it not for the small, beautiful cross dangling from his neck she would never have known him. 'Oh God, Eamon,' she muttered, as she washed and bandaged him, 'who did this to you?' She worked steadily, covering him at last with the warmed sheets. He was deathly still, breathing in shallow gasps, and what skin was not battered or bruised was ghostly white. Mary looked up at the sound of car doors slamming and entered the living room just as Donald held open the door for an erect gentleman with a shock of white hair, clutching a black bag.

'Well, Mrs Kennedy,' he said, dispensing with the usual pleasantries, 'where is the man?'

'In my bedroom,' she said, leading the doctor with Donald trailing behind sheepishly. Dr Fraser stood over Eamon's motionless form gazing intently at the ugly wound above the left temple. He snapped opened his bag and turned to Mary. 'Bring me more clean towels,' he said, 'boiling water, gauze, and plasters, if you have them. Look lively, lad, and give Mrs Kennedy a hand.' Ten minutes later Mary stood at the doctor's side as he probed the open wounds. 'You've done a fine job,' he said, laying the stainless steel instrument on the bedside table. 'Now, let's see about that shoulder.' As Mary and Donald held him from one side of the bed, the doctor firmly grasped Eamon's upper arm and popped it back into the socket, muttering something about the blessing of his being unconscious. 'Broken ribs,' he explained, as he bound Eamon's chest with tape. He stitched the gashes on Eamon's face and leg in silence and covered the clotted wound at his temple with a dressing. 'Skull fracture,' he said in a matter-of-fact tone. It was when he was stitching the gash on his leg that Eamon stirred for the first time. Mary stifled a sob. When at last the doctor was finished, he motioned to Mary and Donald to follow him to the kitchen. He sat at the table and said, 'Shocking isn't it? What humans will do to one another.' Looking Mary in the eye, he asked, 'How did this happen?'

'I found him,' she said quietly, 'on the side of the path. I don't know how it happened. He was just lying there.'

The doctor looked up at the boy and said, 'And you, Master Donald?'

'I was out walking when Mary near knocked me down. I ran after her and helped bring him here. I know nothing about it.'

'Do you know this man?' the doctor asked Mary. 'I've not seen him about in the village.'

She hesitated and said, 'Yes, I know him. He's a friend.'

The doctor sat silently for a moment. 'Well,' he said, 'he mustn't be moved. You'll have to care for him here. I can't say if he'll live. The blow to his head has left him in a coma, and the next forty-eight hours will be critical. But he was near enough frozen, and that may have saved him. Stopped the bleeding for the most part.' With that, he stood up and went back to the bedroom.

As Donald helped Mary wash the bloody linens, staring as the water turned wine-red, he suddenly looked up at her, lips trembling, and burst into tears. 'Shh,' she said, tenderly taking him in her arms like a child, though he stood four inches taller than she. 'Don't worry,' she said, gently patting his back. 'It's going to be all right.'

The doctor finally snapped shut his bag and stood with them at the door. 'You should be going home,' he said to Donald. 'Someone has given this man a terrible beating. It had best be kept quiet that they didn't succeed in killing him. Can you keep it to yourself?'

Donald nodded and stepped outside. Mary followed him out on the porch and said, 'Thank you, Donald.' She touched his arm lightly. 'You were a man today.' He responded with a modest smile.

Later that evening the doctor returned to check on his patient and joined Mary in a simple supper of lamb stew and soda bread. They were sitting in comfortable silence in the kitchen when an anguished groan drew them to the bedroom. The doctor withdrew a syringe and a vial of morphine from his bag. He drew some of the drug into the syringe, explaining they would use it sparingly, and carefully showed Mary how to inject the upper arm, asking her to make careful notes. Once Eamon was sleeping calmly, he said, 'It's in God's hands now. Just follow my instructions, and I'll be back before noon.'

When she was alone with Eamon, Mary settled in the rocker

beside the bed listening to his laboured breathing and wondering why he'd been left to die on the track leading to her cottage. The first light of day found her curled up in the rocker wrapped in a quilt, sound asleep. When Donald arrived she went to wash. As she caught sight of herself in the mirror, she realized she'd spent the past twenty-four hours in the same dishevelled, bloodstained clothes.

Despite the unceasing rain, ankle-deep mud, and temperatures hovering just above freezing, there was an electricity in the air and a growing confidence in the men of Second Battalion, K.S.L.I. Davenport had proved an excellent commanding officer, intuitively knowing that more was accomplished by example than exhortation, by earning the men's respect rather than their submission to discipline or intimidation. He had been right; they *were* small and many of them frail to begin with. But the conditioning had produced remarkable results. The young men of his battalion had proved to be the equals of the Ox and Bucks, the Guards, and other elite units in the gruelling exercises conducted day after day. It was Saturday. The men had been given a twelve-hour leave, so long as they ventured no further than Edinburgh, twenty-five miles to the north west along the North Sea coastline. He was at his desk, completing the hated fitness reports. The private on duty answered the telephone: 'Yes, sir. Right here, sir. Colonel Davenport?'

Charles glanced up with an annoyed expression and said, 'Who is it?'

'The brass, sir,' replied the private. 'In London. General Eisenhower's staff.'

Davenport snatched the phone and said, 'Lieutenant Colonel Davenport.'

'Charlie, you son of a bitch!'

'Hanes? Is that you, Hanes?'

''Course it is. Dammit it, Charlie, how in the world are you?'

'Jesus, Hanes,' said Davenport irritably, 'I should've known. Eisenhower's staff.'

'Well, close enough,' said Hanes Butler. 'Listen Charlie, I've got a weekend pass. I was thinkin', what if I came up with the gals? We can find a place to stay in Edinburgh. Have a night out on the town. What do you say?'

'Well, I suppose so,' said Davenport hesitantly. 'Peg and Jenny, you mean. But how do you think you can—'

'No problem. I managed tickets on the express. We should get in by six.'

'Six? Six this evening?' said Davenport in an amazed tone.

'That's right,' said Butler. 'If you say the word.'

'Well,' said Davenport, 'we're quite a way out from Edinburgh. Perhaps we can meet—'

'Name the place. I'll get a car somehow.'

'You never cease to amaze me. Let me think. There's an old hotel on the strand at Dunbar. The Victoria, I think it's called, half an hour from Edinburgh. We could meet for dinner.'

'You got it. The Victoria Hotel, at seven. And look sharp. Jenny's dying to see you.'

Thanks to the mid-February thaw and respite from the constant rain, Charles was able to walk on the duck-boards without sinking into a morass of icy mud. Despite the relative warmth of the afternoon, his room in the temporary barracks was cold and dark. Pulling the chain to light the single bulb, he sat on the bed and unlaced his boots. Next to the framed photograph on top of a crate was a blue envelope, Mary's last letter. A wave of guilt passed like a shadow over him as he thought of her and the plans he'd made to see Jenny. Shrugging it off, he took his dark-green uniform, smartly pressed from the laundry, from its hanger, and laid it across the bed. Then he took his kit to the adjoining hut to wash and shave. Half an hour later, he stood before the mirror combing his damp hair. He felt a school-boy excitement at the memory of Jenny's kiss and embrace outside the London restaurant. As he thought back, a knot of anxiety tightened in his gut at the memory of the afternoon in Wales, and making love to Mary. *Be careful about Jenny*, cautioned a small voice as he adjusted his tie. He slung his coat over his arm and hurried to the bus. After a fifteen-minute ride, the coach rolled at dusk into Dunbar. The pavements were crowded with soldiers and sailors, though few of them had girls on their arms, passing in and out of the pubs and amusement arcade. An old wooden structure, with bay windows facing the sandy beach, occupied the end of the road, with a dilapidated sign for the Hotel Victoria. As Davenport entered the foyer, he observed that, like everything else in town, it had seen better days. The carpets were worn, and the upholstered furniture, like the potted palms, was a throwback to an earlier era. The sedate hotel, fragrant with the floral perfume worn by elderly matrons, seemed an unlikely place for rowdy soldiers out on the town. Above a bevelled-glass door were the words 'Old Vic', Davenport smiled and entered the bar.

He chose a stool at the empty bar and ordered a whisky and soda, wondering whether Hanes had lost his way, or, more likely, their train was delayed. Just as he was about to return to the lobby, the door swung open and Butler strode in, looking sharp in his uniform, Peg on his arm, with her usual dumbstruck expression. Jenny followed behind, in a coat that reached to mid-calf and a rather plain hat, looking more like the simple shop girl than the attractive woman he remembered from their last encounter.

'I figured we'd find you here,' said Butler with a grin. He shook Davenport's hand warmly. 'How the heck are you?'

'Splendid,' said Davenport. He looked expectantly at Jenny, who responded with a nervous smile. 'Hello, Jenny,' he said. 'Let me help you with your coat.'

'Thank you,' she said, casting a glance around the bar.

'C'mon, you two,' said Butler as he squeezed into a booth with Peg. Seeming to gain confidence, Jenny slid daintily across the seat opposite Peg.

'You've had a long day,' said Davenport.

'Long day!' exclaimed Peg. 'I'll say. Thought we was never goin' to get here.'

'Why don't I get us a beer?' suggested Hanes. Charles sat next to Jenny and stole a glance at her. She slipped off her hat and shook out her curls, which bounced on the shoulders of her polka-dot dress.

'Your hair,' he said. 'You've let it grow.'

'Yes,' she said. 'Do you like it?'

'Yes, actually, I do,' he said, aware of her fragrance, something exotic and sultry. 'Lovely perfume,' he added with a smile.

'Did you miss me, Charlie?' she asked unexpectedly.

'Miss you? Er, yes.'

'Life's been so dull since you've been away,' said Jenny. As soon as she learned that Hanes had somehow managed to arrange the trip to Scotland, she'd made up her mind to seize the chance, practising her enunciation and the words she would say.

Hanes returned with a tray, which he carefully lowered to the table. As he slid back into this seat, he said, 'By the way, I checked us into rooms here at the hotel. No point in driving all the way back to Edinburgh. Now, tell me, how are things with the real army?'

'Lots of mud and marching. But the boys are coming around. It's a fine outfit.'

Peg lifted her glass, took a sip, and said, 'Ooh, that's good.'

Jenny stared at Davenport. 'With all that marchin,' she said, 'you must be awfully fit.' Gazing into her hazel eyes, Davenport placed his hand on hers on the seat cushion and took a swallow of whisky.

'OK, Charlie,' said Butler. 'Where are you taking us for dinner?'

'Let's finish these drinks,' said Davenport, 'and then walk down to a restaurant on the quay. The Crown; nothing fancy, but quite decent.'

Jenny sipped her beer and said, 'What's the rush? A girl's got more on her mind than a plate of sausage and mash, after all the way we've come.' She gently placed Davenport's hand on her thigh. 'Gosh,' she said dreamily, 'it's been *such* a long time.'

'Yes,' he responded quietly, taken aback but feeling a wave of excitement at her soft flesh beneath the fabric of her dress.

Peg reached for her glass and said, 'It's too bad, Charlie, that you're stuck way up 'ere. You know, just practisin' with these lads.'

'How do you mean?' asked Davenport.

'Well, *I* don't 'ave to tell *you*,' she said with the air of someone who's in on a secret. 'I mean, the *real* army, the one goin' across' – she lowered her voice – 'is down at Dover. I know – my brother told me.'

Davenport and Butler exchanged a brief look. 'It's just as well, Peg,' said Butler with a smile. 'We don't want Charlie gettin' shot at, do we?'

'No, we don't,' said Jenny, squeezing Davenport's hand. 'We want 'im safe and sound.'

'And Hanes too,' said Peg. 'Let the other stiffs be the 'eros, I say.'

The tables at the Crown were packed with British officers, a violinist and cellist were playing sentimental favourites, and the lights were low and candles flickered on the linen-covered tables. 'You were right about the salmon,' said Butler. 'How were your chops, Peg?'

'Lov-a-ly,' she said with a contented smile. 'And I saved room for pudding.'

Davenport, feeling the effects of the wine, stared at Jenny. Beneath the table, her ankle lightly touched his. She seemed to give him the slightest wink as she raised her wineglass to her lips. She wasn't as pretty as he remembered; in fact, in her polka-dot dress she looked downright plain.

'Charlie,' said Jenny. 'I'm feeling sleepy. Would you walk me to the hotel?'

'Yes, of course,' he said. He finished his wine and said, 'We can settle up later.'

'Sure,' said Butler with a knowing look.

Outside on the pavement, he draped his long coat over Jenny's shoulders. She placed her arm around his waist and leaned against him. 'Charlie,' she said, 'do you care for me?'

He looked in her eyes and said, 'Of course I do.'

'God, I'm crazy about you.' They passed out of the lamplight into the darkness. He stopped, put his arms around her, and kissed her. 'Mmm,' she murmured, pressing her thigh gently against him. He kissed her neck, breathing the exotic perfume and letting his hand fall to the curve of her hip. 'Oh,' she whispered, 'let's go back to the hotel.'

He looked into her eyes, dimly aware of an inner voice of warning. 'Jenny,' he said. 'I—'

'Oh, Charlie,' she breathed, 'please.'

Pulling away, he said, 'I'm sorry, but, well . . . we shouldn't .'

She held a finger to his lips and said, 'Shh,' with a tipsy giggle. 'We should be getting this soldier home.' With her arm through his, they began walking to the hotel.

CHAPTER NINETEEN

MARY STOOD AT the door and listened to the snap of sheets drying in the winter wind. They were not nearly so stiff as on summer days when they hung straight and dried quickly. Closing the door with a shiver, she returned to the kitchen, debating whether to go back to Eamon's bedside or find something else to occupy her. With his dressings changed, she decided to get the laundry out of the way. Then she knocked down the dough she had set to rise.

Returning to her bedroom, the scent of the lavender sachets she had made now competed with the sickroom smells of Dettol and adhesive. Vials of iodine and morphine had taken the place on the dressing-table of the blue bottle of Evening in Paris and her silver hairbrush. She walked softly to Eamon's bedside and gazed at his bruised and bandaged face. Who was he, she wondered, and why had this terrible thing been done to him? Had someone else discovered that he was a German agent? Two days had passed and still he remained unconscious, his breathing laboured. As she pulled up the chair, he suddenly stirred and uttered a low moan. She placed her hand on his forehead, calming him.

'*Bitte*,' he said softly. '*Sie müssen . . . ahhh.*'

She stroked his forehead lightly. 'Shh,' she whispered. 'It's all right.' The suggestion of a smile formed at the corner of his mouth. Mary sank back in the chair and closed her eyes. Listening to his rhythmic breathing, she began to doze but was startled awake by his voice. 'Yes,' he said in a loud voice. 'I'm sure of it. But . . . ahhhh . . .' '*Nein . . .*' he said, '*ich kann nicht hören . . .*'

Mary rose and poured water on a flannel from a pitcher, wrung it out and placed it on his forehead. Though his eyes were firmly shut, he seemed to be struggling with something. 'Time,' he muttered. 'Soon . . . yes, I'm certain . . . Mary will help us.' She raised a hand to her lips as she struggled to make out his words. '*Adam*,' he said, '*wir müssen . . . wir müssen Hitler töten . . .*' Hitler? Mary leaned closer. 'Soon,' Eamon whispered and fell silent. She hurried to the bureau for her notebook and pen. Returning to his bedside, she sat, listening intently. He moaned and said, '*Ahh . . . Schwartze Kapelle.*' Mary jotted down what she thought she had heard, ending with 'capella'. 'A letter,' said Eamon. 'Mary . . . Mary can take the letter.' She scribbled his words on the pad furiously. 'Trust Mary . . . the officer . . . our only chance.' She shook her head and sounded out the words, writing them phonetically.

Please, Eamon, she said to herself, speak English. 'The officer,' he repeated. 'Davenport . . .' Mary put down the pen and stared. 'Our only chance . . . Morgan . . . *der general.*' Eamon fell silent, his breathing shallow and irregular. Mary stared at the strange words on the page. Dear God, what did it mean? She heard a firm rap on the front door, Dr Fraser arriving, precisely at midday, as promised. After placing the notebook on the table she hurried to let him in.

'I gather he made it through another night?' asked the doctor.

'Yes. But he's still unconscious and has a fever. He's delirious.'

'I see. Well, let's have a look at him.' Dr Fraser moved his stethoscope across Eamon's chest above the tape binding his ribs. Mary stood beside him anxiously, praying that no more German phrases would escape Eamon's lips. 'Well,' said the doctor, standing erect, 'his heart is strong and his lungs are clear. You can never tell with these head injuries. If he regains consciousness, he'll be in a great deal of pain, but he mustn't have any more morphine.' She followed the doctor from the room. After slipping on his coat and hat, he turned for the door, then paused. 'Mrs Kennedy,' he said, 'I've been meaning to ask. What's this man's name?'

'It's . . . O'Farrell. Eamon O'Farrell.'

The doctor shrugged and said, 'Must be new to town. Well, I'll be on my way then.'

Mary spent most of the afternoon by the bed, the notebook and pen close at hand, but Eamon never stirred. The doctor had said that unless he regained consciousness in the first forty-eight hours his odds of surviving were greatly diminished. Chelsea lay unhappily on the bare floor, her face on her paws and an anxious expression in her large, brown eyes. The room was growing dim with the early winter dusk. Mary watched Eamon's gently rising chest. Perhaps she should get supper. She gave the dog a pat and then rose and walked to the door.

'Mary.' She turned. One of Eamon's bruised and blood-shot eyes was partly open. He managed a small smile and said, 'Could I have some water?' She reached for the glass on the bedside table and held it to his lips. 'Thank you,' he whispered.

'Be still,' said Mary. 'I'm going to get you a good cup of broth.'

Though Eamon grew stronger with each passing day, Dr Fraser cautioned it would be weeks before he would be well enough to leave. 'His mind's not right, Mary,' he advised after one of his visits. 'He remembers little and is deeply troubled. It would be best not to question him.' The doctor was pleased with Eamon's recovery, and the day he told Mary he could use her as his nurse she beamed for hours. After the first two nights in the chair by his bed, Mary moved to the upstairs bedroom, the dormer window of which looked out to sea beyond the cliffs. She enjoyed the breezes even in the cold of the long winter nights. She spent the late evenings upstairs, reading or listening to the sound of the sea with Chelsea curled at her feet. Twice, awakening late at night to look out from the darkened window, she glimpsed the flashing red light far out on the water.

By the end of the first week Eamon had begun making comments about leaving. 'I'm responsible, Mary. You don't understand . . .'

'I won't allow it,' she said firmly. 'You're not well.' She leaned over to help him sit up, propped against the pillows.

'Oh God,' he moaned, reaching with his good arm to cover his ear. 'A thousand sounds clanging all at once in my head.'

At the end of the second week, when dinner was done and Mary had taken Chelsea for a walk, they settled in Eamon's room, with Mary in the rocking-chair, Eamon propped up in bed, and Chelsea a patch of fur on the rug. Mary held her notebook in her lap. Only a trace of Eamon's bruises remained, and, with the exception of the pink scar at his hairline, his handsome face had returned. 'You've no idea how grateful I am,' he said with a smile. 'I owe my life to you.'

'I only did what any other self-respecting Christian would have done.' He raised his hand to protest. 'But,' Mary continued, 'I must ask you about the circumstances. Can you remember how this happened? Who did it?'

Eamon shook his head and said, 'I can't remember anything after leaving the Anchor with that man Mulcahy. But I have a pretty clear notion . . .'

'Eamon, there's something else I must ask you,' said Mary. He nodded. 'During those first days when you were unconscious, you said some things. Mostly unintelligible, as you were speaking German and delirious.' He narrowed his gaze. 'In any case,' she said, 'I wrote down some of what you said. On this pad.' She held up the notebook.

'And what did you write?' he asked calmly.

'The name Adam. You seemed to be trying to speak to him, in German and then in English.'

'Yes. What else?'

'A German phrase. I haven't any idea how to spell it, but I sounded it out – *s'vart-zah capella*. Something like that.'

'I see.'

'But then you told this man Adam, "Mary can take the letter." You said, "Trust Mary".'

'I've no doubt I was raving, Mary. God knows what I—'

'Listen to me,' insisted Mary. 'I wrote it down.' She studied her notes. 'Then you said, "The officer. . . Davenport." Sorry, I know this is difficult but I'm almost finished. You said, "Our only chance . . . Morgan . . . *der general*".'

Eamon closed his eyes briefly and smiled. When he reopened them, he said, 'And so now you know.'

'Know what?'

'That I know about your relationship with Lieutenant Colonel

Davenport, who reports to General Morgan, the head of COSSAC.'

Mary felt fear welling up inside her. 'But what does it all mean?' she said softly.

Eamon fingered the gold cross on his chest and said, 'The German phrase you wrote down – *Schwartze Kapelle*? It's how the Gestapo refers to our conspiracy. It means the Black Chapel.'

'Your conspiracy?' repeated Mary, her eyes wide. 'What conspiracy?'

'Our conspiracy to kill Adolf Hitler and end the war.'

Davenport awoke to the faint light filtering through the curtains and the rain beating on the corrugated roof. He eased his legs over the side of the bed and sat for a moment with his head in his hands before rising to dress and wash. The raw air on the way to the lavatory and the ice-cold water splashed on his face did wonders. As he towelled off, the scene at the end of the evening suddenly came to mind. Sloppily drunk in the hotel bar, he'd fought the temptation to go with Jenny to her room. He was almost certain, but the memory faded, leaving a blank gap until the vague recollection of his arrival at the camp in Hanes's car. Back in his room, buttoning his shirt, he thought about the power of lust. He reached for the worn volume of Shakespeare's *Sonnets* he kept among his few belongings. He slumped on the bed and leafed through the pages until he found the one he was looking for. '*How like a winter hath my absence been,*' he read silently, '*from thee, the pleasure of the fleeting year!*' Shivering in the draughty room, he continued reading: '*What freezings have I felt, what dark days seen! What old December's bareness everywhere!*' He looked up at the leafless branch shaking outside the window. Old December's bareness everywhere. He scanned the remaining verses, '*And, thou away, the very birds are mute; if they sing, 'tis with so dull a cheer that leaves look pale, dreading the winter's near.*' He closed the book and listened, but no birds were singing. What he would give to see Mary again, to hold her in his arms. All at once he realized he couldn't go on like this, caught somewhere between telling her the truth about his feelings and his situation, and pretending that it didn't matter and training for the coming battle. It wasn't working, and he couldn't rationalize it any longer. He had to tell her and hope for the best. Taking a few sheets of paper and a pen from his pouch, he leaned on the crate and wrote:

24 February 1944

Dearest Mary,

As you can see from the postmark, I have left London. I've also left the staff of COSSAC and am now commanding a battalion in the Third Infantry Division. My regiment is presently training. The truth is I've been here for some time, but have been unable to bring myself to tell you.

You will no doubt feel hurt and betrayed by this news, as I'm keenly aware how much you have worried for my safety. It would be false to suggest that my transfer was the result of the fortunes of war. The simple truth is that I sought it, for reasons that are difficult to put in words. My staff job at COSSAC was complete, and I acted on my deepest desire to do what I can to play a real part in our ultimate victory, as trite as that may sound.

There's only one thing that matters more to me than seeing this through. You've no idea how desperately I've missed you, how empty my life has seen since we've been apart. I love you, and I would do anything to see you again. Events are moving toward a crucial moment and, if I survive, I promise I'll be here for you, if you'll wait for me. I think of the lines from Donne: 'Our two souls, therefore, which are one, though I must go, endure not yet a breach, but an expansion.' In my heart, our two souls are one, and though I must go – and Mary, I must – they will endure. Dearest Mary, forgive me for not telling you sooner. Write soon.

Love,
Charles

He lifted the pages and blew softly on the drying ink. When he stood up, another arc of pain split his head. A drink, he realized, was probably the only cure. He saluted the sentry at the guardhouse and crossed the road to the only pub for miles. Once his eyes adjusted to the dim light, he realized he had the place to himself, apart from an older gentlemen seated by the grate. He sat at the bar and ordered a pint. The barman wordlessly drew the tap, paddled off the foam, and slid the glass across the worn counter. After taking a swallow, Davenport moved to a table by the hissing fire, nodding politely to the old gentleman, sitting alone with a glass of whisky. Davenport took another sip and noticed a guitar leaning against the wall. 'You play?' he asked.

'Aye. Mostly ballads from home.'

'And where would that be?'

'Dublin,' he said with a smile. 'You seem a lonely lad,' he added, 'like so many of the boys in the army.' He played a series of chords and then in a rich baritone sang: 'Must I go by, as she goes free, must I love the girl who won't love me . . .' As Davenport sipped his beer, a wave of intense sadness passed over him, thoughts of his father, mother, and Mary combined into a single moment of longing and loneliness. 'Must I then act the foolish part,' sang the old man, 'and love the girl who'd break my heart . . .' After a moment, Davenport stood up, smiled briefly at the old man, and turned to go, the ballad echoing in his mind.

Mary stared at Eamon with a look of utter disbelief. 'A plot to kill Hitler,' she repeated. 'Surely you don't expect me to—'

'I do,' said Eamon earnestly.

'What am I supposed to think?' said Mary with a shake of her head. 'That you're an Irishman or a German? A friend or an enemy?'

'Please listen to me,' he said wearily.

Mary nodded, brushing a wisp of hair from her face, and said, 'All right.'

'When you overheard me speaking on the radio, I was talking with Adam von Trott, a senior official in the Abwehr. Like me, he concluded long ago that Hitler is a madman, leading Germany to destruction. The simple truth is that we're preparing to act. Hitler must be killed.'

'You expect me to believe that you and your friends are going to try to kill the most powerful man in the world?' asked Mary.

'Some very influential Germans have joined our cause.' Eamon paused to prop himself up. 'Senior army officers,' he continued, 'high ranking government officials, men from leading families. Let me explain about the Abwehr. We're the intelligence arm for the army and the Foreign Service.'

'Spies, you mean,' Mary interrupted.

'Yes,' Eamon agreed. 'But there's another organization in Germany today, the *Reichsicherheitshauptamt*, or RSHA.' A strange look – fear mingled with hatred – crossed his face. 'A creature of Himmler, head of the SS,' he explained, 'and run by the dreaded

Reinhard Heydrich until he was assassinated by the Czechs in '42.'

Mary stared with fascination and said, 'Go on.'

'Himmler never trusted the Abwehr, and with good reason,' said Eamon with a grim expression. 'So he created the RSHA as his own security and espionage organization, a rival of the Abwehr. But the Abwehr had access to certain RSHA files. If you like, spying on *them*. And, as a consequence, we discovered a secret so appalling that it defies belief.' Mary hunched forward on the edge of her chair as he slumped on his pillows. 'What we've learned,' said Eamon, 'is that Himmler's SS, no doubt on direct orders from Hitler, is rounding up and slaughtering millions of innocent people across Europe. Jews, for the most part. The scale of the killings is so vast that it would be impossible to believe were it not for the evidence we've obtained.' Eamon paused to take a deep breath. 'I've seen the photographs myself,' he said softly. 'Enormous camps in Poland where hundreds of thousands of men, women, and children are sent by the trainload. Bodies stacked like fire-wood before being burned in ovens . . .'

Raising her hand to her mouth, Mary said, 'Oh, my God, Eamon, how awful. Why haven't the British and the Americans done something? The world would be outraged—'

'You've no idea how carefully this secret is being guarded. No one knows, or very few know, anything of this in Germany, let alone outside of Germany. We've tried to get the word out, through the church, and other channels, but no one will listen.' Straining to sit up, Eamon said, 'Hitler's not only a madman, he's bent on mass murder and he *must* be stopped.' He slumped heavily on the pillows and closed his eyes.

Mary's mind was spinning. 'Would you care for something to drink?' she said. 'There's a bottle of whiskey in the pantry.'

Eamon opened his eyes and gave her an appreciative smile. 'That would be wonderful. Mixed with a bit of water.'

She returned with a glass and placed it on the bedside table. 'My grandfather's whiskey,' she said. 'I assume it's all right.'

Eamon picked up the glass, took a sip, and said, 'It's excellent.'

Mary sat down. 'Eamon,' she said in a halting voice, 'I wish you'd explain how you got mixed up in all this. Here you are, spying on the British, and – as you put it – trading arms with the IRA.' He looked at her with intense interest. 'And so if you're involved in this conspiracy to kill Hitler and stop the war, why would you be here in this small Irish village? It seems so strange.'

'You're very astute, Mary,' said Eamon. 'Naturally the Abwehr maintains networks in the neutral countries, including Ireland. To keep an eye on the British. And the arrangement with the IRA, trading guns for assistance watching the coastline, was a logical thing to do. With my background, half-Irish, speaking the language fluently, I was the obvious choice. But—'

'Are you suggesting there's some other reason you were sent here?' interjected Mary. 'That the other was a—'

'Pretext,' said Eamon. 'Exactly.' He sipped his drink. 'Our plan is to end the war. With Britain and America, that is. What's the use of killing Hitler if one of his contemptible underlings, like the pig Göring, simply took his place? We would have accomplished nothing.'

'What does this have to do with your being in Ireland?'

'I was sent by Adam von Trott to Ireland on the pretext of spying on the British and co-operating with the IRA. But Adam's real purpose . . .' Eamon paused. 'My real assignment was to find a way to deliver a message.'

'A message,' Mary repeated, spellbound.

Eamon nodded. 'Surely you wondered why I was spending so much time wandering nearby, close to your cottage . . .'

'Well, I assumed it was to use your radio transmitter, hidden in the cellar.'

'That's true, but mainly I was hoping to befriend you.' She blinked at him uncomprehendingly. 'For a reason,' he continued. 'I'd heard you had a relationship with a British officer, and when you told me he had a staff assignment in London . . .' He hesitated.

'Please keep talking,' she said.

'I took a look around one day when you were away, and discovered that your Charles reported to General Morgan. To COSSAC.'

Mary slumped in her chair. Rubbing her forehead, she said, 'And how did you discover that?'

'From his letters,' replied Eamon. 'I found them in the chest in the hall.'

'Oh, Eamon,' sighed Mary.

'Remember why I was sent here, Mary. To find a way to deliver a message to the British and American high command. Davenport is the perfect contact, reporting to the Supreme Allied Commander.'

'So all this time,' she said almost to herself. 'Do you mean as far back as last year you were merely befriending me in order to take advantage—'

'No!' he said loudly, expending his little strength. 'No,' he whispered. 'You were so full of despair, so lonely. I wanted to help. But when I learned about Charles, and COSSAC . . .'

'I see,' said Mary, sitting up straight. 'I understand.'

He looked at her affectionately and said, 'Of course I was attracted to you. But you see, there's someone waiting for me at home.'

'Your girl?' asked Mary, wondering why she'd never considered that this handsome man had a girlfriend.

'No,' said Eamon quietly. 'My wife.'

'Your wife,' said Mary with an amazed look. 'Oh, Eamon, so many secrets. But you were about to tell me about the message, and Charles . . .'

'Once our plan is about to be put into action,' he explained in a stronger voice, 'when we're ready to strike, it's critical that we communicate to the Allies our intention to kill Hitler, arrest the Nazi leadership, and sue for peace with Britain and the United States. That's the message I was sent to deliver.'

Mary sat in stunned silence, gently rocking back and forth. 'Eamon,' she said at length. 'Oh, my God.'

Mary knew it was only a matter of time before he would be well enough to leave, but she forced herself not to dwell on it. The admiration she felt for him and the fear for his likely fate were so great that she knew she would have difficulty managing her emotions. She had no idea where he would go, or how he would elude the men who had nearly beaten him to death. As on most late afternoons, she made a pot of chamomile tea, which she served in her grandmother's Belleek china, which helped to compensate for the flavourless concoction. Eamon was in the comfortable chair by the hearth, watching her with a contented look, a worn leather Bible in his lap. Though his wounds had healed, he walked with a slight limp, and his vision was blurred. 'There we are,' she said, handing him a cup before sitting on the sofa. After taking a sip, she said, 'Now I suppose you would like me to read to you.'

'You know how much I enjoy listening to you read scripture.' He leaned over to hand her the family Bible she'd found among her grandmother's books.

Putting her tea aside, she opened the Bible and said, 'And what will it be today?'

'I was thinking just now about St. Paul's letter to the church in

Philippi. The King James translation is so beautiful.'

'Chapter and verse?' asked Mary. She was no longer surprised by his encyclopaedic knowledge of scripture.

'Let me see,' he said. 'Beginning with the tenth verse of the third chapter.'

Mary read aloud: *'That I may know him, and the power of his resurrection, and the fellowship of his sufferings, being made conformable unto his death; if by any means I might attain unto the resurrection from the dead ... but this one thing I do, forgetting those things which are behind, and reaching forth unto those things which are before, I press toward the mark for the prize of the high calling of God in Christ Jesus ...'* She paused and said, 'May I ask a question?'

'Of course.'

'It seems to me that you and the others in your conspiracy have this conviction of sharing in Christ's sufferings, even if it means your own deaths.'

'Persecution, suffering, death even, in the service of God are an aspect of our faith.' Mary nodded. 'And now read the eighth and ninth verses of the fourth chapter.'

'Finally, brethren,' she began, *'whatsoever things are true, whatsoever things are honest, whatsoever things are just, whatsoever things are pure, whatsoever things are lovely, whatsoever things are of good report, if there be any virtue, and if there be any praise – think on these things.'* She gently closed the volume. 'Oh, Eamon,' she said, 'if only I had your faith.' There was more she wanted to say, but she'd never spoken to him about her religious beliefs and felt ashamed in the presence of his unpretentious devotion.

'Tell me what happened to your faith,' he said simply.

'Well,' she began nervously, 'I was raised a Catholic, and I was a good girl growing up.' She laughed self-consciously, which somehow caught in her throat. 'But then, when my baby was taken away, and David was killed ...' She hesitated, composing herself.

'You were angry with God,' suggested Eamon.

'Yes,' she said with a nod. 'Very angry, though I knew it was wrong. I couldn't believe that a God I'd been taught *loved* me would do such a thing. And ever since, I've given up trying. I just don't understand how God could have let all this happen.'

'You see, Mary,' said Eamon calmly, 'believing in God doesn't mean things are going to turn out the way you hope or even the way you pray. And when you suffer as great a loss as you have, it doesn't mean that God doesn't love you.'

'Then what does it mean?' she asked, fighting back tears.

'Faith in God,' said Eamon, 'gives you the strength to *endure*. To carry on, in the face of these losses. But first you must see the world through a different lens.'

Mary dabbed at her eyes and said, 'Maybe I've been wanting the wrong things.'

'Yes,' he agreed. 'Perhaps you have.'

CHAPTER TWENTY

MARY STOOD ON tiptoe, reaching far back on the pantry shelf. She could have sworn that there was one last unopened bag of flour, but with all the baking of late she realized it was gone. As she untied her apron, she made a mental list of the items she needed from town, wondering whether there might be a letter waiting at the post office. Leaving the apron on the kitchen table, she stepped into the sun-dappled living room where Eamon was reading in his accustomed chair. 'I'm off to town for supplies,' she said cheerfully.

Eamon looked up with a smile and said, 'Take care, Mary. What's the old Irish blessing? May the road rise to meet you and the wind be always at your back.'

She considered the traditional valediction as she shrugged on her coat. 'Yes, well, goodbye,' she said, as she reached down to pat Chelsea. Taking advantage of the mild early spring weather, many of Mary's neighbours were out and about as she cycled into town. Mrs Dillon, walking her retriever, stopped her to enquire about the status of the O'Leary twins, in whose birth Mary had assisted Doctor Fraser. Her new role as the doctor's occasional nurse had elevated Mary in the eyes of the villagers and increased their curiosity about the American woman on Kilmichael Point. 'Mary,' called out Katy Fitzgerald, a young woman pushing a pram past the old stone church. 'Will you be seein' the doctor today? It's the baby's ears acting up again.'

'I'll pass the word,' said Mary, starting off again, the wind furling her hair. At McDonough's store, young Donald sprang to her assistance with unusual alacrity, reaching for items on the upper shelves, showing off his height, now just shy of six feet. Still guarding the secret of Eamon, Donald showered Mary with attention at every opportunity.

'And the newspaper, of course,' he said, as he placed the heavy bag on the counter and reached for the *Irish Times*. 'Filled, as usual with news of the fightin'.'

'Why, thank you, Donald,' said Mary with a pretty smile.

'If I was an American,' he said.

'If I *were* an American,' she corrected him.

'Yah, well, if I *were*, I think I'd be joinin' up. The navy, I suppose, like your brother.'

'Yes,' said Mary, hoisting her bag, 'and break your poor mother's heart.' She saved the post office for last, leaning her bicycle against the building. Mr Coggins gave her the slightest suggestion of a smile as he slid two envelopes across the counter and said, 'I was wondering when you were going to claim these.'

Mary saw at once that one was a letter from Charles and the other from home. Restraining the impulse to tear open the envelopes, she smiled and placed them in her handbag. 'Thank you, Mr Coggins,' she said brightly. 'Have a lovely day.'

The dog pawed at the door with more than her usual enthusiasm at the sight of her mistress. 'Hush, Chelsea,' said Mary as she placed her groceries and newspaper on the kitchen counter. 'What's got into you?' She reached for the envelopes in her purse and carefully examined the postmark on the letter from Charles. Tearing it open, her eyes fell on the opening paragraph. With an exaggerated sigh, she slumped in the chair. The sheet of paper quivered in her hand and then swam before her eyes. He was returning to combat. It was what she had sensed for months but refused, absolutely, to admit since the tone of his letters had taken that strange turn. She had tried blaming it on her irrational fears, but deep in her heart she had known. Mary dropped the letter on the table with a groan, unable to read past the first paragraph. In the silence she could hear nothing but the pounding of her heart and the old, dreaded voice in her mind, whispering to her of death . . .

Mary rubbed her eyes and got up, concerned that Eamon might have heard her. But when she walked into the living room it was empty. The bedroom was empty as well. Without so much as a word of farewell, he had vanished. During the weeks she had patiently laboured to heal his broken body, Eamon, she now realized, had been working to mend her broken soul. She had been needed, with a purpose and meaning she hadn't felt since Anna had nursed at her breast. Though she had been preparing for the end – Eamon had spoken of leaving almost since the first week – she was unprepared for his sudden departure. Her initial reaction would once have been tears, but that would dishonour all he had taught her. If only she had one more chance to talk with him, to seek his counsel about this news from Charles. What was it Eamon had said? That she'd been wanting the wrong things and must learn to see the world through a different lens? She stood by the old bureau, staring out the windows at the jade green sea. Glancing down, she saw a small envelope with the inscription 'Mary'. Inside she found a plain white card with the words:

Dear Mary,

Thank you for giving me back my life. I will never forget you. Remember that we *'rejoice in our sufferings, because we know that suffering produces perseverance, perseverance, character, and character, hope. And hope does not disappoint us.'*
    Trust in God,
    Eamon

Mary wiped away a tear. She wondered where Eamon would go, how he would evade the men who had very nearly killed him. She knew he would keep himself alive to see his plan through to the end. She only wished there had been a goodbye. No, she did not. He had slipped away just as he had first appeared on the path below her cottage. No long, tearful goodbyes. Simply gone. Only later, after she had steadied herself, did she read the rest of Charles's letter. Again she cried, not the crying she might have indulged weeks ago, but tears of acceptance. The words from the poem were so perfect: *Our two souls, therefore, which are one.* Now all that mattered was that he loved her, and she loved him and, trusting in God as Eamon counselled, that some day they would be together again.

At the end of the day, Mary sat in the rocking chair rereading the simple note from her mother. For months she had been dogged by guilt for failing to return home, fearing her father might be gone before she could tell him goodbye, but thankfully he'd made a full recovery. And her mother had enclosed a letter from her brother Bill, full of confidence. Mary inhaled deeply, thinking of Charles and her far-off brother and the perils they were facing as she watched the fading light. These were issues of faith, exactly as Eamon had taught her. She must stop screaming at God about what had gone and ask His help in understanding what she now faced.

She awoke to the sun streaming in the bedroom window, momentarily forgetting that Eamon had left. The realization that she was alone forced her to consider how empty her life had become. Later she went to her bedroom, savouring the smell of antiseptic, the last trace of him, before turning the mattress and remaking the bed. After placing her silver hair brushes and perfumes on the dressing table, she surveyed the room. It was as if Eamon had never been there. But in the weeks she had nursed Eamon O'Farrell back to life, she had begun to find her way.

The men of the Third Division had been encamped along the Scottish coast since January, training endlessly for the amphibious landings. At the end of March, without warning, orders arrived to abandon winter quarters and prepare to move out. The King's Shropshire Light Infantry travelled by lorry to Newcastle where they entrained for their final encampment fifteen miles inland from the Channel. The convoy of drab green lorries stretched as far as the eye could see. Village children stood clinging to the fences, listening to the deep reverberations of the engines, acknowledging the drivers' waves with tentative smiles and extended hands. It seemed the whole of the vast British and American armies was crowding into the south of England. Tens of thousands of vehicles bearing equipment and supplies that beggared description, hundreds of thousands of men, tramped endlessly along the lanes in their steel helmets, heavy packs and rifles slung over their shoulders.

Davenport sat at his desk in the battalion HQ rereading the fitness reports of his company commanders. With the advent of spring, the number of sick cases had declined to the point that they were now at full strength. And, he noted with satisfaction, after the months of training, the men were fit, eager, and spoiling for a fight. Putting the reports aside, Davenport unfolded the letter from Evan Hockaday with its remarkable news that Evan had fallen in love with a young woman who worked with him at Bletchley and that they were planning to be married at a small ceremony at Marsden Hall. The thought filled him with happiness, along with a twinge of envy. Putting the letter aside, Davenport picked up a pink envelope, fragrant with the sickly-sweet smell of Jenny's perfume. He was aware that the perfume-scented envelopes, addressed in her wide scrawl, were something of a joke among the enlisted men. With a frown, he reread the letter, noting the poor handwriting, the occasional misspelled word. But he admitted to feeling admiration for her pluck and determination. She was saving her earnings from the shop, living at home, sewing her own clothes when she was able to find fabric, so that she could go back to school. '*Not to college, of course,*' she'd written, '*but to learn a trade.*' He imagined her learning the skills of the efficient secretaries in the typing pool at Norfolk House. With a bit of help, she might even shed the Cockney accent, considering how determined she was to leave behind the shop-girl's life. He tossed the letter on his desk with a heavy heart. He had led her on, willingly responding to her advances, however clumsy, and he'd been attracted, not only by her looks but by her spirit. But from the moment he'd finally resolved to tell Mary that he'd given up the safety of his desk job and would be leading men into combat, his only thoughts had been about the coming invasion and surviving it so that he could be with Mary again. He'd been a fool to entangle himself with Jenny, and it was time that he told her the truth. Taking a sheet of army stationery and his pen, he wrote quickly:

Dear Jenny,

I've just finished reading your last letter. I truly admire your ambition to go back to school and have no doubt that you'll succeed and find a professional position. As for me, we've left our training camp, and though I'm not at liberty to divulge our whereabouts . . .

He paused and considered striking out the word 'divulge'. With a frown, he continued:

This may be my last opportunity to write for the foreseeable future, as momentous events lie ahead. I've enjoyed our time together and think you're a wonderful girl, but there's something I must tell you. I'm involved in a relationship with someone else, and we're promised to one another. I should have explained this sooner, but it's best that you know. I will remember you fondly and have no doubt that with your looks, personality, and drive you will do well. I do hope you understand.

Sincerely,

Charles

Davenport shook his head as he reread the letter, thinking it stilted and full of clichés. But he doubted he could do much better. It would be awfully complicated if he were still in London – Jenny remonstrating with him in some tearful scene. But the impenetrable curtain of the quarantine had been drawn across the coastal counties, and it was impossible for a civilian to gain access to their camp or even to telephone. The time would pass, and she would find someone else. After folding the letter into an envelope and dashing off her address, he pushed back from his desk, handed the envelope to a young sergeant, and said, 'See to it this gets in today's post.'

He hurried to the briefing in a large tent with the Union Jack and divisional flag hanging behind the podium. The CO of the division, wearing a casual green sweater and the protocol jaunty beret, strode briskly to the podium. 'Very well, gentlemen,' he began. 'The reports on the latest round of exercises were acceptable, but no better. Now that we've got some decent weather, the men simply must be pushed. Live fire exercise wherever possible. As you are no doubt aware, SHAEF have pushed back the date for D-Day. May 1 is out, officially. So we've got at least another month to prepare and we'll need every day.'

'Well now, would you believe it?' said Mr McDonough as he slid the newspaper across the counter.

Mary glanced at the bold headline. 'Oh, my God!' she exclaimed. 'Beg pardon,' she added with a blush as she gathered her things and dashed out the door. Once she was home, she spread out the paper on her kitchen table and quickly read the sensational news:

BORDERS CLOSED
All Traffic to and from Ireland Suspended Indefinitely

LONDON. 28 March, 1944. Reuters. British authorities announced today that all travel to and from the Irish Republic from Great Britain would be henceforth prohibited. Irish citizens present in Britain will be given twenty-four hours in which to return home by means of public transportation. Thereafter all public and private transportation between the two nations will be immediately and indefinitely suspended, such moratorium to be strictly enforced by the Royal Navy. According to the Home Secretary, such drastic measures were required by a 'heightened climate of security and continuing Irish neutrality in the war'. The British action prompted a strongly worded protest from the de Valera government. A note released by the president declared the British measures 'illegal in contravention of international law and an affront to the law-abiding Irish people'. Government officials warned that the travel ban could have disastrous implications for coastal industries and result in acts of violence. An unnamed critic of Irish neutrality, however, expressed the view that the border closure was a 'justifiable reaction' to the unwillingness of the Irish Government to 'lend even the slightest support to the British people in time of war.'

'Jesus, Mary, and Joseph, wouldn't you know it,' muttered Mary as she slumped in a chair.

Later, at the end of a dreary day watching the April rain, Mary considered her situation. Only now, at last free from the irrational fears that had kept her from Charles, she was prohibited from travelling to see him, even if only to ask his forgiveness, to tell him goodbye, and that she loved him. Surely it was only a matter of weeks before the long-awaited invasion. She felt certain Charles would be taking part in it, though he'd stopped short of saying so. And with the invasion, she reflected, Eamon and his colleagues would act. Feeling a sudden chill, she rose from the sofa and walked to the glowing remains of the fire. Where was Eamon now? Had he vanished on the dark sea, to the blinking red light off her coast, to return to his homeland? Was it really possible that his fantastic conspiracy, the *Scwartze Kapelle*, might actually succeed, bringing an early end to the war? All at once, she realized that she was facing these grim, immutable facts – the coming invasion, with Charles going ashore in the assault, quite possibly never to return, Eamon's participation in what must surely be a virtual suicide mission – with something like calm acceptance. No more tears, or desperation, or railing at God. Looking around the empty room, growing dark, she imagined Eamon in place, Bible open in his lap, which in a way Mary realized, he was. And with his help, she was looking at the world beyond the windows through a different lens.

Sitting on the bed in her small but tidy room, Jenny stared vacantly at the wall, clutching Charles's letter. Peg stood at the end of the bed, nervously grasping the brass rail. 'Oh, Jenny,' she said. 'You poor thing. And Charlie seemed, well, such a fine fella.'

Jenny nodded glumly and said, 'Too fine for the likes of me. And I thought . . .' The sentence died in a rueful sigh. Tossing the letter aside, Jenny, wearing only a slip, stood up and stared at her reflection in the mirror. She turned to one side and studied the curve of her belly with detached fascination. Lightly touching the small mound of her abdomen, she said, 'And now this.'

'Are you sure, Jenny?'

''Course I'm sure,' said Jenny, fighting back tears. 'It's not just that I'm late, though it's over three weeks. There's a bun in the oven, no doubt of it.'

Peg with a shook her head. 'What are you goin' to do?'

Jenny stared at her pale reflection in the glass. 'I don't know,' she said, in a voice just above a whisper. 'What can I do? Oh, God,' she sobbed, slumping heavily on the bed.

Sitting beside her and gently placing a hand on her shoulder, Peg said, 'I heard tell of these doctors who can . . . well, you know, fix things up.'

Jenny raised her red-rimmed eyes, her lips trembling. 'I don't know,' she said softly, brushing away her tears. 'It frightens me. I've heard terrible stories . . .'

'It's such a pity about Charlie, but now to turn up preggers!' Jenny nodded. 'Well,' said Peg after a moment, 'does 'e know?'

'Does who know?'

Peg eyed her expectantly. 'The father,' she said. 'The one who done it.'

Jenny gave her a curious, far-off look. 'No,' she said. 'I 'aven't spoken to him.'

'Well, I suppose he's gone away by now,' said Peg. 'Back to sea.'

'Who?' said Jenny.

'Why, your sea-captain friend is who,' said Peg with a surprised expression. 'With the merchant marine. Seemed a nice enough bloke when 'e came round with those sweets, and the perfume and all.'

'What makes you think it was him?'

'But Jenny . . .'

'If only I could see Charlie again,' said Jenny dejectedly. 'He's everything I ever wanted, Peg. I could make him love me, I swear it!'

'Hanes says they've closed off all the army posts.' Looking her in the eye, Peg said, 'I'd forget about 'im if I was you. Charlie's got another gal. At least 'e told you the truth.'

Jenny abruptly stood up and said, 'No. I won't! Charlie's my only chance!'

The jeep rattled to a stop at the headquarters hut. The driver climbed out and patted the change in his pocket. 'Two sovereigns,' he said with a smile, as he mounted the steps and entered the wooden structure. 'I've got a message for the colonel,' he said to the young corporal on duty.

'I'll take it, Sarge,' said the corporal, extending his hand.

'Sorry, lad. This is a personal message. I need to deliver it myself.'

'Well, if you insist,' said the corporal as he rose. 'I'll go and look for him.'

A few minutes later Davenport, wearing a perturbed expression, trailed into the room behind the corporal. 'What's this all about, Sergeant?' Davenport asked curtly.

'Well, sir,' he said, 'it's a personal message.' Davenport eyed him warily. The sergeant tactfully took a few steps toward the window and extracted a folded note from his breast pocket. 'I was asked to see to it you personally received this, sir,' he said, 'by a young lady.'

Davenport accepted the note with a puzzled look. He quickly scanned the typewritten message:

Personally deliver to: Lt.Col. Charles Davenport
Second Battalion, King's Shropshire Light Infantry

It is terribly important that I see you as soon as possible. The messenger will know where to find me. Please come without delay.

He ran a hand through his hair and asked, 'Who sent this, Sergeant?'

'As I said, sir,' the sergeant replied in almost a whisper, 'a lady. Quite attractive, if I may say so. And she seemed to be quite distressed, anxious to see you.'

Davenport's mind was racing. Was it possible? After what he had written, and the invasion less than a month away, that Mary had changed her mind? 'Where is she, Sergeant?' he asked excitedly. 'Where does she want me to meet her?'

'At the Russell. A hotel, sir. I know the way and could drive you.'

Davenport reached for his coat and hat. 'If anyone should ask,' he told the bewildered corporal, 'I've gone to attend to some urgent family business. I'll be back by evening.'

'Just another mile, sir,' said the driver, 'till we reach the checkpoint. What should I tell them?'

'Leave it to me, Sergeant,' replied Davenport. 'I'll bullshit our way through this, as the Yanks would say.' The jeep slowed to a stop at a guardhouse, where a red-and-white striped gate barred their way. A burly sentry with a rifle slung over his shoulder stepped out from the enclosure.

'Papers,' he demanded sternly. Davenport handed the driver his army ID from his days on staff at COSSAC, who passed it along to the sentry. After briefly studying it, the sentry peered into the back and said, 'Returning to London are we, sir?'

'Just a quick trip,' said Davenport mildly. 'Very well, sir,' said the sentry. 'I'll make a note on the log.' He gestured to a comrade, and the heavy gate swung into the air.

'Let's go,' said Davenport. 'Before he changes his mind.'

With few vehicles on the roads outside the quarantine, they made excellent time, and on the outskirts of Tunbridge Wells passed a sign for Abbey's Gate. Davenport thought back to Mary's visit to Rushlake Auxiliary Hospital, a mile or so in the distance, which filled him with a warm glow. Before long the driver was navigating the streets of the town, coming to a stop at a two-storey brick structure with a sign for 'The Russell' over the entrance. 'Make yourself comfortable at the pub across the way,' said Davenport. 'Drinks and dinner on me, and a quid for the trip.'

The lobby was empty except for an elderly couple having tea. Davenport enquired at the front desk and was directed to the dining room. Davenport approached the *maitre d'* and said, 'I'm meeting someone.'

'A young lady?'

'That's right.'

The man gestured to the centre of the room and said, 'Behind the screen there, on the banquette.'

Davenport mussed his hair and took a deep breath. As he stepped around the screen he stopped in his tracks at the sight of Jenny. With her light-brown hair resting on the fox stole draped over her shoulders, she smiled and said, 'Oh, Charlie, I knew you would come.'

CHAPTER TWENTY-ONE

JENNY . . .' SAID Davenport with an astonished look. 'What are you doing here?'

She gave him a hopeful smile and said, 'Oh, Charlie, won't you at least sit down? After I've come all this way?'

Weakly he pulled back a chair and sat, avoiding her eyes. 'I'm sorry,' he said. 'It's just that this is, well . . . such a surprise.' He saw that she had knotted her napkin and guessed that she'd been crying. 'How the devil did you find me?' he asked quietly.

'It took quite a bit of doin', I can tell you that, and cost me a pretty penny.'

A waiter appeared and Davenport said, 'Would you care for something? A cup of tea?'

'Yes, thank you,' she said softly.

'We'll have tea,' said Davenport. Folding his hands on the table, Davenport looked Jenny in the eye and said, 'You know you shouldn't have done this. I've put myself at considerable risk coming here.'

'I had to see you,' she said, leaning across the table.

'But why like this, out of the blue?' Looking in her intense, red-rimmed eyes, his letter came to mind, and a wave of shame passed over him.

Jenny fought back tears and said, 'I needed to see you.' The waiter reappeared with their tea and a plate of scones.

'Thanks,' said Davenport. As he poured Jenny a cup he noticed that she'd dressed for the occasion, a stylish navy-blue suit and matching hat. 'I'm sorry about the letter,' he said. 'I would have preferred to have told you in person, but the fact remains . . .'

'I was savin' up my money,' she interrupted. 'For school.'

'Yes, I think that's wonderful.'

'But now I've gone and spent it,' she said with a toss of her hair. 'On these.' She ran a hand over her fox stole and jacket. 'And makin' my way here to find you.'

'But why?'

'I know what you're thinking,' she continued, determined to have her say. 'I don't have an education, I don't know how to do things proper, how to speak. But you could teach me. Oh, Charlie, there's so much you could show me.'

Nervously glancing at his watch, Davenport said, 'It's not that. There's nothing wrong with you, Jenny. It's just that I—'

'Please,' she interrupted, her eyes flashing. 'You've got to help me!'

Staring into her moist eyes, he was conscious of a strange feeling of foreboding.

'You see,' she said in a voice just above a whisper, 'I'm in the family way.'

'What? Jenny . . . what did you say?'

Raising her eyes to meet his, she said, 'I'm 'avin' a baby.'

For a moment Davenport stared at her, his stomach churning. 'A baby,' he murmured.

'Charlie, we could be happy together.' She impulsively reached across the table for his hand. 'It's nobody's fault,' she said in a stronger voice. 'Things just happen.'

'But Jenny . . . I don't understand . . . What are you saying?'

Her lower lip began to quiver, and then the tears came as an elderly couple at a nearby table turned to watch. 'Oh, Jesus,' she sobbed. 'What am I goin' to do?'

Davenport fought the sensation that the room was spinning. 'I . . . I don't know what to say,' he stammered. His voice sounded strange, as though someone else were speaking. 'Here,' he said, reaching for a handkerchief and handing it to her. 'But Jenny,' he said, 'I could swear—'

She looked imploringly at him, the tears streaking her rouged cheeks. 'We could get married,' she said softly. 'We could be happy, I know we could.'

'Married. . . ? he repeated hoarsely. 'But Jenny, we don't. . . .'

She stared into her lap. 'I'm sorry,' she said after a moment. 'I know I shouldn't have come here like this.' Looking back at him, she said, 'You're going across, aren't you? With the landings?' Davenport nodded. 'I'll wait for you, Charlie,' she said. 'I swear I will.'

After the muffled hush of winter, the Irish countryside was bursting with activity: creatures scurrying in the underbrush, nests with tiny beaks amid the new, green foliage; even the wind sang as it swished through the long winter-dried grass. The anaemic pallor was replaced with a brilliant array of greens and yellow. As she set out on her morning walk with Chelsea, Mary stood still for a moment, absorbing the sights and sounds. They had started down the lane when she stopped abruptly and whistled for the dog, deciding instead to take the path down the cliffs to the beach. As she began the descent, she thought back to the times she had stood so sorrowfully at the top staring out to sea. Once she was on the beach with Chelsea beside her, she was delighted with her decision. It was a glorious day, with lines of white-capped breakers filling her ears with a gentle roar as the gulls soared on the thermals. She walked a long way down the half-moon beach, as far as the next bend on the shoreline before turning back. It was then that she saw a tall man in the distance, with dark hair and dressed in dark colours. Her heart skipped, thinking that it might be Eamon. But Eamon was gone, she reflected, her hands deep in the pockets of her warm coat. It was only when Chelsea streaked off in his direction that Mary began to wonder, and quickened her pace to try to catch up. When she had covered half the distance between them she knew that it *was* Eamon, and she ran right into his welcoming arms.

'Oh, Eamon,' she said breathlessly, taking his hands. 'I thought you had gone for good.'

He gave her an appraising look and said, 'No, not for now. You look wonderful, Mary. And goodday to you,' he added, bending down to scratch the dog's ears.

Mary glanced briefly at the faint, pink scar at Eamon's hairline. 'And you're looking well,' she said. 'Fully recovered?'

He smiled. 'Yes, thanks to you.' He let go of her hands, and they began walking.

'How long will you be here?' she asked. 'Will you stay with me a while?'

He scanned the beach briefly, satisfied that no one else was about, and said, 'Oh, Mary, would that I could.'

'Won't you just stay just a while? The doctor will be by later, and you should let him take a look.' When he responded with a sidelong look beneath a long lock of dark hair, she knew it was pointless. 'Oh, Eamon,' she sighed. 'I've been so lonely since you left.' She took his arm with both of hers and leaned on his shoulder.

He stopped and turned to face her, looking in her eyes. Thinking he might kiss her, she closed them. Instead, he put his arms around her waist and said, 'Mary . . .' She looked back up at him. 'You mean the world to me,' he said. 'But I can't risk being seen, not even by the doctor.'

'Will I ever see you again?'

'You have my word.' And then he pulled her close, pressing his lips to her forehead for one long moment before releasing her and walking away.

Davenport wandered the camp with a heart like stone. No matter how hard he tried he couldn't rid his mind of the image of Jenny. The thought of marrying her was so abhorrent that the prospect of going into combat seemed almost inviting by comparison. He was oblivious to the incessant clamour, columns of men everywhere, vehicles of every description bumping along the rutted roads. Above it all he was aware of the songbirds' warbling, the incongruous verdancy of spring, and the riot of wildflowers as the blackness of despair settled over his soul. He stopped at the railing of an old fence, gazing out on what had been a pasture, but was now a sea of tents. Closing his eyes, he tried once more to bring back to conscious memory the events of that winter night. He dimly remembered the scene in the hotel bar, gently pushing her away, shaking his head. But no matter how hard he tried, the scene dissolved into nothingness. God, it was driving him mad. Then there was Hanes, loud, drunk, hauling him up from the booth. 'Time to get you back . . .' Hanes had said. Davenport could have sworn it never happened, and yet he knew that a part of that fateful night had disappeared into an alcohol-induced haze.

Walking slowly in the general direction of his tent, he could make out the sound of men singing, borne along by the gentle spring breeze, a familiar, comforting tune. As he drew closer, the voices were more distinct, the words clear. Fifty yards in the distance, the Sunday morning regimental church service was underway in a large tent, open at the sides. He couldn't remember the last time he had attended church. But the music evoked pleasant memories, of sitting in the pew with his parents in the ancient Saxon church at home. He felt strangely drawn, and soon found himself standing at the very back of the tent, just under the flap, looking over the heads of the men packed tightly in rows beneath the canvas canopy to hear what might be the last sermon of their young lives. An Anglican priest stood in his vestments before a simple table where a loaf of bread and a silver chalice were arranged on a square of white cloth. Taking the loaf in one hand and the chalice in the other, the priest recited the words of invitation: 'The Lord Jesus, the same night in which he was betrayed, took bread, and when he had given thanks, he broke it and said, Take, eat; this is my body which is broken for you.'

The men rose in succession and filed to the front, to kneel with heads bowed. As he watched them, Davenport was conscious of an overwhelming sensation of wanting to surrender to some hitherto unknown call. All his adult life he had relied on his intelligence and the strength of his character to meet the challenges and obstacles he had faced. Now he realized with blinding clarity that none of that would be sufficient for the conflict that was looming. He watched as the men in front of him rose and moved to the aisle, and then fell in behind them as though driven by an irresistible impulse. Just let go, he repeated to himself in a silent incantation. Kneeling on the new spring grass next to the young, frightened soldiers, he felt the tears welling in his eyes as the chalice was lifted to his lips and the warm wine filled his mouth. 'Dear God,' he prayed silently, 'I can't face this alone. Please, dear God, give me the strength. Show me the way.'

Mary was no longer content to wait until she needed groceries to lay her hands on newspapers from Dublin and London. With each passing day she anticipated news of the invasion, the final stroke to liberate France and end the war. And so, each day, she made the short trip to town. In any case she was happy to be out, thankful for the warm sun, the Wicklow Mountains in the distance, and the steady sea breeze at her back. She could think of little else than Charles and the role he would play in the landings, though she had no idea, besides a deep female intuition, whether he would play any role at all. Leaning her bicycle against the kerb, she hurried into the McDonoughs' shop. 'Here you are, Mary,' said Mr McDonough as he slid two newspapers across the counter. 'One shilling, thank you.' As Mary walked out she almost collided with Donald.

'Sorry,' he said, in a voice so deep it elicited a soft laugh from Mary. Blushing, the tall boy hurried inside. She secured the papers in her basket and swung a leg athletically over the seat as she pushed off for home after a quick stop at the post office. There had been no post from Charles since her last, long letter, assuring him that she understood his decision, that she greatly admired him for what he was doing, and that she deeply regretted her own choice, which, in hindsight, seemed so inexplicably wrong. But with the travel ban, could she be sure when, or even whether, her letter had reached him? Once she was back in her kitchen, Mary spread open the papers and searched the headlines. But there was nothing about the expected invasion, only news of the fighting in Italy and the Far East. She went out to the chair on the porch and watched the gulls turn lazy circles beyond the cliffs. After a while, the silence was broken by a distant rumble. She rose and walked to the end of the porch. To the north and west the blue sky merged with a billowing mass of charcoal. At that moment, a sharp gust of wind broke over her, furling her dress and lifting her hair from her shoulders. Shivering, Mary turned and let herself back in the house.

'Well, girl,' she said to Chelsea, who was staring attentively out to sea, 'it looks as though we're in for quite a blow.' The sentence was punctuated with a sharp clap of thunder and another swoosh of wind that set the weather vane spinning. 'I'd better fetch some wood and shut the windows before it hits.' The dog panted after her as she loaded firewood into the barrow and secured the shutters. Within minutes, the sky had darkened, turning the sea from bottle green to slate. The house secure, Mary arranged the logs and kindling on the andirons and struck a match to the balled-up newspaper. The flames leapt in the hearth, casting an eerie light.

After several hours night had fallen and the squall line passed, the driving rain now a steady drumbeat on the roof. After placing another log on the fire, she slipped on her coat and stepped out on the porch to watch as the storm raced out to sea on its way to the coast of Wales. Thinking she heard the cough of an engine above the rain, she looked down the track, where a beam of light flickered through the gorse. Who on earth, she wondered, at this time of night and out in the storm?

An old car of indeterminable make swerved along the muddy track and came to a stop at the side of the cottage, the headlamps shining through the curtain of rain. For a moment Mary considered hurrying inside for the shotgun, but intuition told her there was nothing to fear. A man emerged from the passenger seat, wearing an oilskin hat with a wide brim and a long, matching coat, like the foul weather gear she remembered the Gloucester fishermen wearing back home. He spoke briefly to the driver and walked up on the porch.

'Eamon,' gasped Mary. 'My God . . . it's you.'

Eamon took off his hat and said, 'Sorry to show up like this, without warning.'

'Come inside,' said Mary, with an involuntary shiver, wondering whether it was from the cold. Eamon nodded, peeling off the coat and tossing it on the chair.

'Come, sit by the fire,' said Mary, holding the door, 'and let me bring you a glass of whisky.'

'Thank you,' said Eamon. 'That would be lovely.'

Mary brought not one but two glasses of her grandfather's whiskey to the warming fire. 'Now,' she said, 'what brings you here on this stormy night?'

He waited a moment before answering, looking around the room affectionately. 'Tonight I tell you goodbye, Mary,' he said. 'A U-boat is standing off the coast, waiting to return me to the Fatherland.'

Mary forced a smile. 'Oh, Eamon, I'm going to miss you so much . . .'

'Mary,' he said softly. A determined look crossed his face. 'I've come to ask you a great favour.' She gave him a questioning look. He took a sip of whiskey and then reached into his pocket for an envelope. 'I've brought a letter,' he said. 'And you are the only one . . . the *only* one, I can trust to deliver it.'

'But, Eamon . . .' she interrupted.

'Please,' he said in a low voice, 'take this.' He handed her the envelope. 'I need you to take it to Charles.'

'To Charles?'

'It's our only chance,' he said urgently. 'Davenport can make sure it's delivered to General Morgan . . . and to Eisenhower.'

'This is madness! Charles has left Morgan, and I've no idea where to find him. And besides, the border is closed. There's no way across.'

Eamon rose and stood before the fire. 'The message is written in code,' he said firmly. 'Davenport will know what to do with it. I've made the arrangements to get you across. And I know where he can be found.'

She stared at him in amazement. 'You know?' she said. 'How could you possibly—'

'Please listen to me,' he said evenly. 'I only wish the weather were better, but we have no choice . . .'

'What do you mean?' she said, as a clap of thunder boomed far off in the distance. Pinpricks of fear spread from her chest to her neck. 'Surely, you're not suggesting—'

Eamon took a step toward her and placed a hand on her shoulder. 'Mary, try to understand,' he said. 'You're our only hope.' She stared at him in the flickering light from the fire. 'I promise you'll be safe,' he said reassuringly. 'I've arranged things with some fishermen who . . . well, they're arms runners as well. They've agreed to take you across, and there's a car waiting on the other side to drive you to Davenport. But, please, we must hurry.'

'But, Eamon, I—'

'Goodnight, Mary. You must tell Charles that the end of the war – I swear it – depends on delivering this letter into the right hands.' He released her shoulder and gave her an encouraging smile. 'Goodbye,' he said, 'and God bless.'

CHAPTER TWENTY-TWO

WITHIN A MATTER of minutes, Mary had packed a bag and was pulling on her coat while trying to calm the anxious pup. 'I'll be back as quick as I can,' she said, as she tapped her pocket to make sure the envelope was there. With one last look around the room, she let herself out the door after taping a hurriedly scrawled note to Donald. Hearing the laboured turning of an engine, followed by a deep, throaty exhaust, she stared in the darkness and rain at the man in the driver's seat of the old car. 'Come along, miss,' he called out to her. 'We'd best be on our way.' She squared her shoulders and walked to the passenger door, peering inside at the driver, a complete stranger, with a round, kind face and thick, white hair. When Eamon mentioned the arms runners, she had assumed the worst. But, as soon as she climbed into the cramped seat, she realized she had nothing to fear. After struggling for a moment with the gearstick, the old gentleman made a neat turn and swung onto the muddy track. 'Mary Malone Kennedy, is it?' he said with a sidelong glance.

Mary stared for a moment and then smiled and said, 'That's right. How did you know?'

'It's a great joy,' he said with a twinkle in his eye, 'to meet the granddaughter of Paddy Malone.'

'You knew my grandfather?'

'Knew him?' he said. 'I should say so. We shared a cell at Frongoch during the Rising.' He slowed and turned on the road into town and said, 'Yes, your grandfather and I were great mates right through to the end, side by side. As fine a man as I ever knew.'

Reaching the coastal highway, they rode along in silence, passing through darkened villages and continuing south. Far out to sea Mary could see flashes of lightning. 'I'm so sorry,' she said, 'but in the confusion, I neglected to ask your name.'

'O'Farrell,' he replied. 'Eamon O'Farrell.'

Mary gaped at him and said, 'How strange.'

'The German, you mean,' he said with a smile. 'Your friend, as I understand it. You might say he borrowed my name, Mary. Just as well I'm not well known in these parts.'

Mary stared at the swathe of pavement in the headlamps, turning over the concentric circles of fate . . . her grandfather and the old man . . . the old man and Eamon. 'Well, Mr O'Farrell,' she said at length, 'where are you taking me?'

'In another half-hour we'll turn on a dirt road that leads to a fisherman's cottage. The boys will be waiting.' Mary leaned back, filled with dread at the prospect of crossing the Irish Sea in a small craft on a stormy night. But at the end of the journey – somehow, if she trusted Eamon – would be Charles, and she would endure anything to see him one last time. 'Don't worry, lass,' said the old man. 'These are men of the sea, and it's a fine, seaworthy boat, and *fast*. These lads know their job, and they'll get you safely across.' She nodded and stared into the darkness. 'Ah, here we are,' said the driver as he turned on a rutted track. After a few minutes the headlamps washed across a stone outbuilding, and the car came to a stop. A man appeared out of the shadows, wearing an oilskin coat and hat identical to those Eamon had worn. The driver patted Mary on the arm and said, 'Good luck, my dear,' he said. 'May the good Lord look after you.'

'Thank you, Mr O'Farrell,' said Mary, shivering at the thought he was leaving her in the company of strange men. She took her small bag and climbed out.

'This way,' said a second man from the shadows. 'You're late.' Mary could just make out three men standing beside a stone barn. Not a light was burning in the nearby house. She fell into step behind the men, mere dark shapes in macs, descending steps down to a pier, resonant with the whining of ropes and the scraping of a hull against the pilings. 'Watch your step, miss,' said the nearest man, turning toward her as he started across the wet planks. The yellow beam of a torch flickered, revealing the dark shape of a boat. One of the men disappeared nimbly over the side, returning after a moment clutching something under his arm. He said, 'My name's O'Kelly. We're in for a rough ride, miss, so you'll be wanting these.' He handed her the bundle. 'Now, boys,' he ordered, 'let's get underway.' Mary unfolded the package – an oilskin hat and coat – and put them on. She reached for the hand offered by one of the men, who steadied her as she stepped over the side onto the deck.

Coils of rope, reeking of creosote, were stowed against the transom beyond a squat hold that occupied most of the deck, presumably to stow the day's catch. The air was thick with exhaust from the idling diesels. As the men cast off the lines, there was a deep rumble and shuddering vibration of the engines and the boat lurched forward, its bow knifing through the heavy seas. Mary clung tightly to the railing as the boat gathered way, bucking on the waves. As the captain opened the throttle, it surged forward, planing across the rough seas. Mary wiped the salt spray from her eyes and lowered the brim of her hat. They seemed to be flying into the maw of the storm, now a great mass of black billows directly in their path that blossomed into silver star-shells with the flashes of lightning. She stared ahead, growing queasy as the boat pitched and rolled.

'You'd best come below,' said a man at her side.

'No, thanks,' said Mary, in a voice loud enough to be heard over the engines and crashing waves. She clung to the railing, letting the wind and spray wash over her face. A bolt of lightning arced across the skies, followed by a loud clap of thunder. Fat drops of icy rain stung her face. Dear God, she prayed, take me safely to him and grant that this plan of Eamon's succeeds.

Charles sat at his cluttered desk with a pencil clenched in his teeth. He stared at the blank sheet of paper, trying to think of a way to begin the letter to Mary. Each time he started to write, he was over-whelmed with guilt and despair. The thought that he might have forfeited his one chance at true happiness in a thoughtless lapse of self-control made him almost physically ill. He couldn't begin to tell her about the trap he was in; nor could he pretend, even in a few, simple words of greeting and farewell, that there was any hope left for them. Staring out at the desultory rain, he snapped the pencil in two and tossed the pieces in the wastebasket. With D-Day approach-ing, the tension in the camp was rising, despite the daily films, games of football and cricket and the sudden bounty of eggs, steak, and other long-forgotten delicacies. 'Fatten 'em up for the slaughter,' went the gallows joke among the men. Let's just get on with it, Davenport thought, reflecting the sentiment of the million men encamped in the coastal counties. He looked up at the sound of angry voices, a disturbance in the outer office. God, not another fist fight . . . He rose from his desk and stuck his head out the door. An MP, dripping wet in his long coat and steel helmet with the white stripe, stood pointing in the face of the corporal on duty.

'I've got a mind to write you up,' said the MP angrily. 'Now get the effing colonel—' At the sight of Davenport he halted in midsentence and snapped to attention.

'What's going on?' asked Davenport irritably.

'Sir,' said the corporal. 'I was telling this bloke that you was not to be disturbed, and he was makin' a bloody row about havin' to see you.'

'What's this all about?' Davenport asked the MP.

'What it's about, sir, is a lady we've detained at the guardhouse.'

'A lady?' said Davenport. The MP nodded. 'And what, pray tell,' said Davenport with growing asperity, 'does the fact that you've detained a lady at the guardhouse have to do with me?'

'Well, sir,' said the MP with a nervous glance around the room, 'she insists on seeing you.'

Davenport felt a flush of anger. *Damn,* he said to himself. Jenny's got her nerve. 'Well, Sergeant,' he said calmly, 'you know better than that. It's absolutely prohibited.'

'Yes, sir. But the fact is, she insists on having a word with you.'

'That's nonsense,' said Davenport flatly. 'Tell her I'm out on exercises. Tell her anything. But get rid of her.'

The MP shrugged and said, 'Well, if you say so, sir.' As he started for the door he muttered, 'With pleasure. Bloody Yanks.'

Davenport stared at the man and said, 'What did you say?'

The MP turned to face Davenport and said, 'Ah, she's an American, sir.'

'Wait just a moment,' said Davenport. He shot into his office and returned with his coat and hat. 'Let's go, Sergeant,' he commanded. 'If anyone should ask, Corporal, tell them . . . hell, tell them whatever the hell you like.'

He strained to see in the steady downpour as the jeep slewed through the mud. As the driver pulled up to a small, whitewashed structure, Davenport saw a dark form step out from behind the building, on the other side of the lowered gate. His heart pounding, he leapt from the vehicle. 'Sir,' the MP called after him, 'you mustn't leave the camp!' Davenport ducked under the gate and rushed up to Mary, taking her by the shoulders and staring into her eyes. 'Mary!' he said, 'I can't believe it's really you!' She threw her arms around him and pressed her cheek, glistening with tears and raindrops, tightly against his.

'Oh, Charles,' she murmured. 'Thank God.'

He savoured the sensation for a few seconds and then pulled away, searching her face for an explanation. 'How did you ever find me? And how did you possibly manage to get here, with the border closed and the quarantine—'

'Forgive me, Charles,' she said, her words barely audible above the pouring rain, 'but this all happened so fast. Is there somewhere we can talk?' She was soaked to the skin, her hair in tangled, dripping tendrils.

He glanced back at the guardhouse. 'Our only chance,' he said, 'is a café a few blocks down the road.' He put his arm around her and began walking away from the roadblock. 'Let's just hope they leave us be.' A half-timbered house appeared out of the murk, with a sign over the green door for The Nancy Wren. The small blackboard in the half-curtained window offered tea, crumpets, and scones. Davenport held open the door and they stepped inside. She took off her hat and shook out her hair, and they stripped off their sodden coats and hung them by the entrance. Leading Mary by the arm to a table by the grate radiating warmth from the burning lumps of coal, Charles ushered her to a chair and sat next to her. He reached for her cold, wet hand. 'You've no idea how happy this makes me.'

A waitress appeared and said, 'What can I bring you?'

'Tea,' said Davenport with an encouraging smile, 'and the scones.'

Mary glanced nervously at her watch and said, 'Oh, Charles, if only we had more time.'

It struck him that something was wrong, that she couldn't possibly have managed to find him, evading the ban on travel from Ireland, unless it was a matter of dire necessity. 'What is it, Mary?' he said. 'Please tell me what's wrong.'

She looked into his dark eyes, thinking him even more handsome than she remembered. 'Oh, Lord, Charles, I'm so sorry,' she began. 'What a fool I was. But I'm a different person now, and I'd give any-thing to have the time back.'

He leaned forward and gently squeezed her hand. 'All that mat-ter's now,' he said, 'is that you're here.'

The waitress returned with their order, and, when she was gone, Davenport poured them the tea and said, 'How in the devil did you find me here?'

She took a bite of scone and sip of tea and then said, 'It would be best if I get straight to the point.' He merely nodded and sipped his tea. 'To explain how I found you, and how I was able to travel from Ireland . . .' She hesitated. 'Well,' she said, 'it was arranged by a German intelligence agent. . . .'

'What?' said Davenport. 'You can't be serious—'

'. . . who got me across on a fishing boat,' she continued, 'and another German agent, here in England, knew where to find you.'

Davenport sat in stunned silence, holding his teacup in mid-air. Looking nervously around the empty tearoom, he said, 'But how is that possible?'

She leaned across the table and said quietly, 'I'm sorry, but I've got to explain. There's a man in Ireland, a friend of mine named Eamon, and, believe me, he's a wonderful man.'

'Eamon,' Charles repeated softly.

'Well, that's the name he went by. His real name's Hans. He's a German. And he was helping the IRA, at least so they thought, though in reality he was working against them, but the point is—'

'He was spying?' Davenport interrupted. 'Is that what you're saying?'

'Listen to me!' Mary said desperately. 'It's not what you think. Eamon hates Hitler and the Nazis with a passion. And he sent me here, to see you.'

Davenport shook his head and said, 'He *sent* you to see me?'

'Yes. He works for something called the Abwehr.' Mary looked furtively around the room. 'They've turned on Hitler,' she whispered. 'They've learned some terrible things about him. '

'Haven't we all,' said Davenport, looking at her with a furrowed brow.

'No, some *really* terrible things,' she insisted. 'Unbelievable things. And they plan to kill him and bring down the whole Nazi regime.'

Charles shook his head. 'Surely, you don't believe . . . My God, Mary, do you seriously expect me to—'

After taking another swallow of tea, Mary said calmly, 'These men – Eamon and his colleagues – know the invasion's coming any day now, and they plan to act soon after that. I tell you, Charles, they're going to kill Hitler or die trying, and then they plan to end the war.'

'To end the war?'

'Yes, and that's why they've sent me here.'

Davenport studied her somber expression and said, 'Go on.'

'There's a conspiracy,' she said, leaning close to him. 'Made up of some very powerful men in Germany, decent men, according to Eamon. They loathe Hitler and his gang. The Gestapo has a name for them. Here, I've written it down.' She reached in her pocket for a scrap of paper and handed it to him.

'The *Schwartze Kapelle*,' he said aloud.

'Yes, it means the Black Chapel. And their plan, once Hitler is dead, is to overthrow the Nazis, put them all under arrest, and seize power.'

'A coup, you mean,' said Davenport, utterly fascinated. 'By the army, in all probability.'

'Yes, that's right,' said Mary. 'And then they plan to sue for peace. With Britain and the United States. With the Christian nations, as Eamon put it.'

'God, if only it were true,' said Davenport with a frown.

'It *is* true, Charles,' said Mary. 'I swear it. In any case, they considered it imperative to send a message to the Allies' high command, to convey their plans, now, before the invasion. Eamon sent me with a letter,' said Mary in the same earnest tone. 'It's addressed to General Morgan, but Eamon hopes it will reach Eisenhower. Or even Churchill.'

'To General Morgan?' said Davenport in an angry whisper. 'I can't believe you told a . . . a German agent about *me* and my job at COSSAC. My God, Mary, how could you?'

'I only told Eamon you had a staff assignment in London and never mentioned your name, let alone General Morgan or COSSAC. I thought he was just another Irishman, who happened to share my views on the war. But . . . well, he *is* an intelligence agent, and he looked through your letters one day when I was out.'

'I see,' said Davenport. 'And so this Eamon chap, in reality a German agent, figures I might be a back channel to General Morgan.'

'The *perfect* channel,' interrupted Mary, 'to Morgan, and on to Eisenhower. Charles, don't you see?'

'Yes, I see,' he said. 'And you expect me—'

'To deliver it.' Mary gazed intently into his eyes.

Davenport considered, about to say, *This is madness, lunacy, no one would ever believe a word,* but instead he said, 'May I see the letter?'

Mary rose from the table and went to her coat, returning with a small parcel wrapped in waxed paper. After sitting, she carefully removed the envelope and handed it to him. 'To Lieutenant General Frederick Morgan,' Davenport read aloud. He opened the envelope and extracted a single sheet of paper. After peering at it for a moment, he said, 'But this is written in code.'

'Eamon said it would be,' said Mary. 'He said it would help to prove its, ah, authenticity.'

'But if it can't be read . . .'

'He said you would know someone who could decipher it.'

With a sharp intake of breath, Davenport folded the letter in the envelope. 'Mary,' he said after a pause, 'are you sure?'

She nodded. With a glance at her watch she said, 'I'm almost out of time. Charles, what about you? Are you going to . . . to take part in the invasion?'

'Yes,' he said, squaring his shoulders. 'Yes, Mary, I'm afraid that I am.'

'I understand,' she said softly. 'Please tell me you'll be all right. You know I'll be waiting for you. If you still want me, that is.'

He looked in her eyes and said, 'Of course I still want you. And if I get through it, I'll do everything in my power . . .' With an anguished look, he let the sentence die.

She stood up abruptly and said, 'I have to go. They – the men who brought me – are waiting.' Davenport rose and put his arms around her. 'Oh, Charles,' she cried, as she flung her arms around his neck. 'I love you so much. More than you can ever know. Please, please, come back to me.'

He held her tight, wanting to remember every detail, unwilling to let her go. 'Mary,' he murmured, 'no matter what happens, you must believe me. I will never love anyone but you.'

She pulled away and said, 'I'm afraid it's time.' Wordlessly he helped her into her coat and watched as she tied the belt and put on her hat. Staring into her bright blue eyes, he leaned down for a final kiss. 'Goodbye, Charles,' she murmured. 'I'll be waiting.' She turned and let herself out, starting off in the pouring rain. Davenport leaned against the window, watching her go through the rain-streaked glass.

CHAPTER TWENTY-THREE

DAVENPORT WEIGHED HIS options. He would have considered the letter a hoax if anyone other than Mary had delivered it. It was unthinkable that she could have been taken in by some Irish impostor, or that she would have risked crossing the Irish Sea at night in a gale for anything less than what she claimed. By the time he climbed out of the jeep, he had made up his mind. He hurried past the young corporal to his desk to search in the middle drawer for the scrap of paper he was looking for. He found it, a telephone number and the notation: 'Station X, Hut 6.' With a glance at his watch, Davenport dialled the number. 'Hullo,' answered a young woman. 'May I help you?'

'Is this Station X?' asked Davenport.

After a pause, the operator said, 'With whom do you wish to speak?'

'Captain Evan Hockaday, in Hut 6.' Davenport bit his lip.

'*Major* Hockaday is unavailable,' said the operator firmly. 'Do you wish to leave a message?'

Davenport ran a hand through his hair. 'Listen, Operator,' he said, 'this is urgent. Can you give him a message to call Lieutenant Colonel Charles Davenport?'

'Very well,' she said, followed by a click. Davenport leaned back in his chair, tapping the letter Mary had entrusted to him on his palm, and waited. After twenty minutes that seemed like an hour, the phone rang. He reached for the receiver and said, 'Evan?'

'Yes, Charles. I understand this is urgent.'

'It is. I need to see you.'

'Were you thinking of the weekend, as I've made other plans?'

'No. I was thinking of tonight.'

'Tonight? Surely, you're not serious.'

'I'm absolutely serious, but my problem is I need a pass. Can you get someone to send a telegram to the CO of Third Division requesting my immediate assistance for a twelve-hour leave?'

'It's highly irregular,' said Evan. 'Can you give me some idea what this is about?'

'I'd rather not, on the phone that is.'

'Well, I'll see what I can do. I'll ring you back shortly.' Within a half-hour, following a second brief conversation with Evan,

Davenport received a summons to the division HQ, where he was given the requested pass from the CO's highly sceptical adjutant. As all traffic on or off the base was forbidden, Davenport was able to commandeer a staff car with a full tank of petrol and by nine o'clock was speeding along the virtually empty roads. Stopping at intervals to consult a map, he passed through Reigate, swinging west to Windsor and then north into Buckinghamshire. As he entered the outskirts of Bletchley, the luminous dial of his watch showed a quarter past midnight. After passing through the darkened streets into the forested countryside, he arrived at the entrance to a country estate with a sign for Bletchley Park. As he turned into the drive, he considered the fact that Evan had been promoted, and the operator's tone suggested that he must have a position of some importance. Davenport came to a stop at a guardhouse with a uniformed sentry.

'Your papers, please,' said the sentry. After briefly reviewing the documents, the sentry pointed to a large Victorian structure in the distance and said, 'The main building is on the left, sir.' Unlike the rest of the English countryside, lights were burning in virtually every window of the elaborate building and the car-park was full. After parking, Davenport slipped on his hat and jacket and hurried up to the entrance. He entered the high-ceilinged lobby where a young woman in uniform was seated at a reception desk. She looked at him pleasantly, notwithstanding the late hour.

'I'm here to see Major Hockaday,' said Davenport.

'You must be Colonel Davenport,' she said with a smile. She handed him a clipboard and said, 'Please sign in, and I'll let the major know you're here.'

Davenport would have guessed he was in the lounge of a rather dowdy hotel in the countryside, with its worn floral carpets, over-stuffed sofas, and potted ferns. After a few minutes a young soldier wheeled in Evan Hockaday, looking fresh and sharp in full uniform. The soldier gave Davenport a quick salute and excused himself. Davenport shook Evan's hand warmly and said, 'Evan, thanks so much for seeing me.'

'I presume you've had a long journey – from somewhere near the Channel.'

'Yes, from our camp in Sussex.'

After Davenport was seated on the sofa next to Hockaday's wheelchair, Evan looked at him expectantly and said, 'What's this all about?'

'Is there somewhere we can talk privately?'

'I'm afraid this is as private as it gets,' said Evan. 'The rest of this place is strictly off limits. But at this hour we should have the room to ourselves.'

'Well,' Davenport began, 'you remember Mary?' Evan nodded. 'She appeared out of the blue at the entrance to our camp late this afternoon, insisting on seeing me.'

'How could she possibly have known where to find you?'

Davenport lowered his voice and said, 'Not only that, but she managed to get across from Ireland.' Evan knitted his brow and scratched his chin. 'Seems she had the assistance of the IRA,' Davenport continued, 'and, more importantly, of the Abwehr.'

'The Abwehr?' said Evan incredulously.

'Yes, and to get to the heart of it, Mary says she was sent by a German agent, operating in Ireland, for the purpose of delivering a letter to me.'

Evan frowned and said, 'You've driven here in the middle of the night to tell me that your friend from America managed to cross over from Ireland, assisted by an Abwehr agent, notwithstanding the border closure and the quarantine? Really, Charles, isn't that a bit—'

'It's all true,' interrupted Davenport.

'This letter,' said Evan after a few seconds. 'Do you have it?'

'Yes, right here.' Davenport withdrew the envelope from his breast pocket. 'It's why I had to see you.' He leaned closer to Evan and said, 'Mary insists there's a plot within the Abwehr and the Wehrmacht to assassinate Hitler and overthrow the government. This Abwehr agent apparently befriended Mary and told her he's a part of it. And he sent her with this.' Davenport handed Evan the letter.

'Addressed to General Morgan,' said Evan. 'Your old boss.'

'Yes,' said Davenport. 'This fellow can't have known that I transferred from COSSAC.'

Hockaday looked up from the envelope and said, 'If there's any truth to this tale, it would make eminent good sense to send such a letter to Morgan.' He extracted the single sheet of paper and scanned it. 'Charles,' he said with great solemnity, 'do you have any idea what this is?'

'Well, obviously,' said Davenport, 'it's written in code. And this chap, the German, told Mary that I would know someone who could decipher it.'

Evan's gaze narrowed. 'Did you ever tell Mary about me?' he asked quietly. 'About my work, here at Bletchley?'

'Of course not.'

Evan looked into the distance. 'Well,' he said, 'the Abwehr may know more about things than we've given them credit for. Charles, this letter was encoded on a German Enigma machine. I'm sure of it. And there are prefixes that originate only with the OKW in Berlin. It will be easy enough to determine if they're present to authenticate its origin. I can have this deciphered in half an hour. But what was her explanation? Why the letter?'

Davenport took a deep breath. 'According to Mary,' he said, 'the men behind this conspiracy are high up in the government and the army. They plan to act shortly after the invasion. And if they're successful, they intend to sue for peace with Britain and the US. Hence the letter to Morgan. An overture of some kind.'

Evan massaged his chin with a thoughtful expression. 'We've wondered for a long time whether there might be some such rising against the Nazis from within.'

'That reminds me of something,' said Davenport. 'Mary gave me the name this fellow says the Gestapo uses for the conspiracy.' Davenport handed Evan a slip of paper.

'I don't know anything about this,' said Evan, 'but one of my people might. Wait here, Charles. This shouldn't take long.'

Davenport dozed but awakened at the creak of Evan's wheelchair. He rubbed his eyes, sat up, and said, 'Were you able to make any sense out of it?'

Hockaday waited for his attendant to park the chair and excuse himself. 'This is highly irregular,' he said. 'You must swear that under no circumstances will you divulge the fact that you've seen this.' He then handed Davenport a typewritten sheet.

'Who is General Beck?' asked Davenport, his eyes dropping to the bottom of the page.

'General Ludwig Beck,' said Evan, 'was the only member of the general staff with the courage to speak out against Hitler. He resigned from the army in 1938 rather than serve under him. If there's anyone with the stature to lead a coup, it would be Beck.'

Davenport quickly read the decrypt, looked up, and said, 'This is incredible.' He read aloud: *'Determined to rid the world of the scourge of Hitler and restore Christian civilization to Europe and a legitimate democratic government to the people of Germany*

. . . unalterably opposed to war with the Christian nations and determined to effect an honourable peace with Britain and the United States immediately upon the elimination of the Nazi regime. Good Lord, Evan, do you think it's the real thing?'

'My instincts would say, no, it's another crackpot scheme, except for three things. First, the Enigma prefixes match. There's no getting around the fact that this letter was encoded on an Enigma machine in Berlin. And the name *Schwartze Kapelle* – the Black Chapel. Our man was astonished to see those words. It seems the Gestapo has been trying to penetrate this conspiracy, without much luck, and that's the name they've coined for it. There's no way some lowly Abwehr agent in Ireland would know it.'

'Amazing. To think that Mary . . . But you said there were *three* things.'

'Look at the closing paragraph,' said Evan.

Davenport studied the document. 'You mean this reference in what looks like Latin?'

'It is Latin,' said Evan. 'The translation is, '*By this we shall be known*' with the citation "19 REV 1", a reference to the Revelation of St John, Chapter nineteen, Verse one, the passage that describes the final victory over the Anti-Christ.' Davenport gave Evan a bewildered look. 'I believe these men,' continued Evan, 'are part of a small group of dedicated Christians, led by Dietrich Bonhöffer, the Lutheran theologian, who consider Hitler the Anti-Christ. The reference in Latin is a signature, Charles. I believe them. But the question remains, will they succeed?'

Davenport rose from the sofa, stretched, and said, 'What will you do with the letter?'

'I'll make certain the right people see it. What they do with it will depend on what, if anything, these men are able to accomplish.' Evan took back the paper from Davenport and said, 'Now, tell me one more thing before you go. Are things ready? Are you taking your men across?'

'Yes, we're ready,' said Davenport grimly. 'With any luck Rommel will be expecting us elsewhere.'

Evan smiled. 'I've no doubt of that. We believe they're convinced the blow is going to fall at Calais. And when it's all over will you go back to her?'

'Mary,' he said. 'How remarkable that she brought this letter to us. I'm afraid I've made quite a mess of things.' Evan gave him a concerned look. 'It's out of my hands now. Just promise you'll pray for me. That would mean a great deal.'

'Of course,' said Evan.

Davenport took Evan's hand, looked into his piercing blue eye and said, 'Goodbye.'

On the morning of 1 June 1944, the thousand men of the K.S.L.I. set forth from their six-week encampment near Haywards Heath in Sussex. Loaded in the back of two-and-a-half-ton lorries, they were driven to Lewes, whence they would march to their designated point of embarkation. Under a pale summer sky, the column stretched for half a mile along the road to Newhaven, the men straining under the weight of eighty-pound packs over-filled with ammunition, mines, knives, rations, and Bibles. All along the eight-mile march, the road was lined with clusters of men, women, and children, not cheering, flag-waving crowds, but sober faces expressing pride, hope, and the unuttered prayer that the massive force descending on the coastline might soon bring an end to almost five years of war. The young soldiers marched silently, acknowledging the waves of the children but averting their eyes from the baleful glances of the women too much like their own mothers. Davenport marched at the head of the column. Over the brow of a hill, beyond the rooftops and steeples, he observed a remarkable spectacle: an enormous flotilla arrayed on the sparkling sea. In all the planning and preparation, he had never imagined anything on so vast a scale.

The 17,000 men of the Third Division were converging on the Channel ports, from Newhaven to Portsmouth, where a long line of LCIs, the vessels designed to transport the infantry to the landing beaches, awaited their arrival. 'Well, Sergeant,' said Davenport to the heavy-set Scot at his side, 'there they are. Those sardine tins are going to be home for the next several days.'

'Aye, sir,' said the sergeant with a grimace. 'Though why we should be forced to sit aboard them for days is a mystery to me.' A landsman through and through, the sergeant was deeply disquieted by the prospect of inhabiting a cramped space aboard ship.

'Simple logistics,' explained Davenport. 'First the men must be loaded. Then the amphibious vehicles, tanks and ammunition, and lastly, the escorts. It will take days, and that's just for the troops going ashore on the first day.'

The regiment tramped through the village, past the pubs and

shops and the weathered headstones in the churchyard until at last they reached the quay. Davenport studied the beehive of activity, lorries overflowing with supplies of every description, black coils of telephone line, stacks of jerry cans, and wooden crates packed with grenades and bangalore mines. MPs directed the steady flow of vehicles and tanks clanking across the concrete aprons onto the wide steel ramps of the LCTs. It seemed impossible that such a massive build-up could possibly go unnoticed by the enemy, whose reconnaissance planes still ventured into the RAF-patrolled skies. Davenport looked up at an approaching jeep, recognizing the frowning face of the regimental CO.

The jeep screeched to a halt, and the short, compact brigadier alighted. 'All right, Davenport,' he said briskly, acknowledging the salute with a touch of his hand to his hat, 'you're familiar with the loading procedure. Last on, first off. Take your men to the far pier and report to the loadmaster. We need to get the battalion embarked by noon to make room for the Royal Warwickshire and Royal Norfolk. Battalion commanders' briefing is at 1700 hours.'

The five LCIs assigned to the regiment were berthed in a close-packed row at the end of the Newhaven docks. After receiving their assignments from the loadmaster, Davenport instructed his company commanders to march the men to the ramps and on board the 160-foot vessels. The mood among the men in the queues in the late morning sunshine was almost festive. Despite the obvious perils, they were anxious to be going at last, to get across, and get it over with. Davenport boarded with the officers and men of A Company. Brightly coloured signal flags fluttered on the halyards; the hull and squat, round superstructure wore a fresh coat of dull grey. As the men inched along the line, a naval crewman distributed cartons of cigarettes. There was scarcely room to walk, so jammed were the decks with provisions and equipment. Below, there were only enough bunks for a third of the 200 men, requiring them to sleep in three, eight-hour shifts. They unslung their packs, made themselves as comfortable as possible and settled in for a long wait. Once the loading was complete, the LCIs weighed anchor and steamed out into an assigned place a mile offshore in the midst of the vast Allied armada. There, bobbing on the heavy swells, they would wait . . . and wait. 2 June came and went, then 3 June, and still they waited . . . eating the decent navy rations, fighting boredom with endless games of dice and cards, reading cheap paperback novels as they sat wedged into some nook or cranny of the crowded deck, or in solitary moments in prayer, some of the men reading Bibles.

Davenport awoke on the morning of 4 June with the restless, stomach-churning realization that the time had come at last. Within twenty-four hours they would be on their way to Sword Beach. He crawled out of the cramped bunk and bounded up the gangway. The sky had turned dull grey, and a cold drizzle was falling. His heart sank. Before the assault could be launched, it was crucial for airborne troops to penetrate the enemy's rear, by parachute and glider landings, operations Davenport knew would be scratched by low cloud, rain, or fog. He leaned on the railing and stared through the mist at the line of ships that stretched as far as he could see. Throughout the day the weather worsened, heavy downpours and gale force winds churning the seas and tossing the landing ships like matchsticks on a pond. The men could find no relief from the constant rolling and pitching decks. By nightfall the salt spray and rain mingled with vomit on the slippery decks, the stench only adding to the misery. The storm intensified during the night. Davenport tried sleeping with his face buried in a pillow, but it was no use. He listened to the wind moaning above the groans of his seasick men and the rain lashing the deck. Surely the operation would be cancelled. In the darkness, a sailor appeared and said, 'A message, sir, from General Smith.'

Davenport swung his legs over the side, opened the envelope, and read the note in the blue glare of the ready light: 'To all commanding officers. Due to inclement weather, D-Day is postponed for 24 hours. H-Hour will be 0630 on 6 June 1944.' Davenport took a deep breath and braced himself against the bulkhead as the ship rolled twenty degrees. Well, he considered, the brass hats must know more about the weather than the men riding out the storm. Davenport reached for his coat and steel helmet. The stench was little better in the open air. Passing by crouching forms, Davenport did up his jacket and made his way to the bow, where the fresh breeze filled his nostrils with salt air. As they pitched up and down, he stared at the dark shapes on the black sea. Another day and night, and they were going in. His mind wandered to Mary, her blue eyes against her pale cheeks as she sat beside him in the tearoom, earnestly pleading for his help. She seemed so brave, so noble, in her determination and conviction. He forced himself to think about his options. If he survived, what would he do? It still seemed impossible to him that the baby Jenny was carrying was his. But if he survived – not just the landing, of course – what *would* he do? He stared down at the black water below the railing. There was a chance, he supposed, she might give up the child for adoption, but the idea that someone else might raise his own child seemed totally unacceptable. Besides, she'd begged him to marry her. Poor, pitiful Jenny. Please, dear God, he prayed, show me the way out of this.

The following night Davenport slept fitfully on a hammock slung beneath the canvas near the aft companionway. The wind and rain had relented, giving the men some measure of relief from the seasickness they'd endured for thirty-six hours. As he dozed he could hear the sound of droning, dreaming that the skies were filled with aircraft. His eyes fluttered open. The noise was real enough, and directly overhead. He climbed out of the hammock and stepped out from under the cover. Through a break in the clouds he could clearly see a low-flying formation of C-47 Dakotas. Davenport checked his watch. It was 12.25 on the morning of 6 June.

'Damn, Colonel,' said a young lieutenant standing beside him. 'What the hell is that?'

'The sixth Airborne,' said Davenport as he watched the V-shaped formation. 'They'll be getting things ready for us.' As the last of the aircraft thundered off toward the French coast, he said, 'It's on, Iverson. This means it's really on.' Davenport hurried below to wash and shave. By 0300 the galley stoves were lit, and the navy cooks were preparing breakfast. The men crowded the deck, leaning on the railings and smoking as they watched the black horizon for signs of activity.

The navy skipper stepped out from the bridge on to the platform with Davenport. 'Well, Colonel,' he said, 'time to get underway.' The orders were passed to weigh anchor as the bow swung around and the engines came to life with a deep, vibrating thrum. Somewhere in the distance ahead were the warships – destroyers, cruisers, and ancient battleships – and further beyond them, the line of LCTs, the first to go ashore with their cargo of tanks. The massive armada moved into the centre of the Channel. Breakfast was served at 0400 with a tot of rum. Despite their recent nausea and the fear gripping the heart of every man onboard, the young soldiers filled their steel trays to overflowing and gulped down the grog. At 0430 the chaplain assembled the men in the bow for prayers. Davenport remained on the platform by the bridge. Leaning over the rail, he strained to hear the chaplain's words. The ship churned along at ten knots, the cold breeze lying at the starboard quarter. The pure, clear voice of a young tenor rose from the men assembled in the bow, rendering a hauntingly beautiful version of the hymn *Abide With Me*. Davenport's eyes grew moist as the final refrain died on the breeze: '*In life, in death, O Lord abide with me.*'

'Destroyer dead ahead,' sang out a lookout. 'Five hundred yards and closing.'

The ship's engines slowed and then stopped with a shudder. Davenport checked the time, 0500. Well, he thought, the show's about to begin. The men crowded onto the decks and stared expectantly over the heaving black swells. By 0520 the faint glow of dawn appeared on the horizon. Davenport could just make out the ghost-like warships lying dead ahead. He trained his binoculars on the invisible French shore. Suddenly he saw a faint orange flicker on the black backdrop, followed after a few seconds by the sound of distant thunder. The German batteries were opening fire. All at once a brilliant flash erupted from the muzzles of a nearby cruiser followed by an ear-splitting crash. Within seconds a deafening crescendo engulfed their craft as the entire Allied fleet opened fire on the enemy fortifications and gun emplacements. The blast from the fifteen-inch guns of the battleship *Warspite* was stunning. Up and down the line, destroyers, cruisers, and battleships pounded away, the muzzle flashes brilliantly lighting the sky and the thunder of the guns deafening the almost 200,000 men crammed aboard the landing ships. Above the crash of the guns, Davenport could distinguish the whine and scream of the incoming German shells, sending fountains of spray among the line of ships. Precisely at 0620, the naval guns fell silent. He ranged the binoculars across the horizon. Dense black smoke obscured the beaches. With his heart pounding, he knew that as soon as the minute hand on his watch struck six, the first wave of landing craft, lying five kilometres offshore, would start churning toward the surf to discharge tanks and men.

As the soldiers of A Company made their final preparations, checking gear, cleaning their rifles, and filling their canteens, Davenport remained at his perch above the deck, straining to hear the sounds of battle. He could visualize every detail of Sword Beach: the pastel Victorian villas beyond the shingle, sheltering German machine-guns and mortars and, further to the rear, the lethal

88-millimetre guns. It seemed inconceivable that anyone or anything could have survived the ferocious naval bombardment, but he was certain they had. He pictured the obstacles Rommel had carefully planted on the beach and tidal flats, the ten-foot high Belgian gates studded with mines and the pilings driven into the sand beneath the surf with explosive charges lashed to their tips. The landing was planned to coincide with high tide at first light, to float the landing craft into the shallows and allow the heavy-laden men to wade ashore in waist deep water. But the murderous obstacles submerged by the high tide could pierce the thin hulls of the landing craft and blow the men to pieces before they ever set foot on French soil. Then there were the heavy German guns sited on Sword Beach at Merville and Le Havre. The airborne troops who had landed in the dark of night were assigned to take out those batteries, but if they had failed, the big guns would rain death on the troops traversing the beaches.

Puffs of smoke appeared on the horizon – the British tanks swimming ashore from the LCTs and hammering the German defences. Then Davenport heard the faint rattle of small arms – or was it the chatter of German machine-guns – and the whoosh of the 88s, used by Rommel with murderous effect in North Africa. Davenport gripped the railing and stared at the smoke-shrouded horizon. The first wave, the men of the South Lancs, the Suffolk, and East Yorks Regiments, were in a desperate struggle with the German defenders.

A launch from the nearest destroyer sliced the waves on the starboard bow. 'Take positions,' sounded a voice through a megaphone, 'at co-ordinate X-47. Move up at 0900 hours.' Davenport hurried down to the crowded deck. The men stood rigidly along the rails, staring toward the beaches with pale, frightened faces. Few had experienced combat. Davenport found the captain commanding the company. 'In ten minutes,' Davenport calmly informed him, 'we're moving into position. I want your men ready. Understood?'

The young officer quietly said, 'Yes, sir.' Davenport went below for his pack and rifle. He suddenly recalled the exact moment the attack came on the last day at Tobruk . . . the line of Stukas coming in low from the eastern horizon. Fighting a spasm of fear, he lifted the strap of his pack to one shoulder, grabbed his rifle and hurried up on deck. The sun had broken through the ragged clouds, exposing the vastness of the Allied armada. The LCI surged forward through a narrow lane between the warships. The smoke-filled beaches loomed closer, no more than two kilometres in the distance, and the sounds of the raging battle grew more distinct. 'Form up!' bellowed the sergeant majors. The men formed two lines behind the bow ramps. Davenport looked to the skipper on the bridge. Spotting Davenport in the midst of the men, he signalled that they were going in. A heavy wave slapped the bow. 'Close up!' shouted the sergeants as the men inched forward. A young private, no more than eighteen and five feet four, trembled against a stanchion. Placing his hand on the boy's shoulder, Davenport said, 'Don't worry,' as reassuringly as he was able. 'You'll be all right.' A German shell exploded thirty yards from the LCI, showering the men in a cold spray.

'Oh, Jesus,' moaned the soldier. 'I can't take it.'

Davenport squeezed him lightly on the shoulder and moved down the line. Another young soldier clung to a rosary, softly reciting a Hail Mary in an Irish brogue. Davenport stood on a crate and looked over the railing. They were only 300 yards from the beach, and the breakers, with dark green forms bobbing in the surf, were clearly visible. The mine-studded pilings protruded ominously from the wave tops. Several hundred yards to the starboard an LCI burst into flames with dense black smoke spiralling skyward. All at once the ship ground to a halt. 'Ramps down,' bellowed the crew chief. Twin ramps dropped and the men surged forward.

'C'mon, lads,' shouted the sergeants. 'Let's go, let's go!' As they splashed into the waist-deep surf, machine-gun fire slapped the water around them. Davenport waited until the last platoon was on its way down the ramp. And then, standing at the top, he surveyed the beach. Bodies were floating in the bloody shallows and a tank lay in smoking ruins halfway up the beach. But the beach seemed strangely empty. The sounds of fighting – bursts of rifle fire and the thud of the tanks' cannons – were further inland. Davenport hurried down the ramp and splashed into the receding surf with a feeling like joy. They'd made it! He was certain . . . the battle was won.

'Step lively, boys,' yelled a sergeant. A smile spread across the face of the young private who minutes earlier had been paralysed by fear. The men stood in clumps on the beach, adjusting their packs, smiling at their unexpected good fortune. Davenport took a quick look to his left to observe the rest of the battalion wading ashore. Slinging his rifle over his shoulder, he strode rapidly toward the soldiers loitering on the beach. The mortar shell fell without warning. Exploding shards of steel cut the smiling young soldier nearly in two. Davenport saw only a blinding field of orange, then all was blackness as he cartwheeled backward. He lay motionless, his legs sprawled beneath him, blood seeping into the cold, wet sand.

CHAPTER TWENTY-FOUR

MARY SURVEYED THE neat rows of her garden and the expanse of sea and sky beyond the cliffs. My third summer, she mused, before turning toward the kitchen where the newspapers lay folded on the table. She glanced at the headlines of the *Daily Telegraph*, news of the fighting in Italy but nothing about the impending invasion. The clock on the mantel chimed ten. As she turned on the radio, she was surprised to hear the announcer on the Dublin station rather than the usual music. Through the static she could hear his excited voice: 'We repeat, we have received an urgent bulletin from London. The following communiqué was released by the Supreme Headquarters of the Allied Expeditionary Forces at 9.32 a.m.' Clasping her arms tight across her chest, Mary leaned close to the radio, straining to capture every word. An American voice broke through the static.

'Under the command of General Eisenhower, Allied naval forces, supported by strong air forces, began landing Allied armies this morning on the northern coast of France.' Oh my God, thought Mary.

Then the familiar Irish voice returned, 'We repeat, ladies and gentlemen, the Allied command in London have announced the long awaited invasion of France. Details remain sketchy at this time, although the official German news agency reported earlier today the landing of airborne troops north of the Seine. We will interrupt our regular programming to bring you further developments as they are reported.'

Mary stared at the small, round radio speaker now filling her kitchen with music. She slumped in the chair, massaging her forehead in her hands. She stayed by the radio for the rest of the morning, hoping to learn which units were involved, where the landings had taken place, and the progress of the fighting. But there was no more news. In her mind she heard his words telling her, yes, he would be there. At 11.30, again the music was suspended. The Dublin announcer solemnly informed his listeners: 'We interrupt our scheduled programming for the following live broadcast from His Majesty, King George the Sixth.' A scratchy recording of 'God Save the King' was aired, followed by static-filled silence, and then the carefully enunciated words of the King:

> Four years ago, our Nation and Empire stood alone against an overwhelming enemy, with our backs to the wall. Now once more a supreme test has to be faced. This time the challenge is not to fight to survive but to fight to win the final victory for the good cause. The Queen joins with me in sending you this message. She well understands the anxieties and care of our womenfolk at this time and she knows that many of them will find, as she does herself, fresh strength and comfort in such waiting upon God.
>
> At this historic moment surely not one of us is too busy, too young or too old to play a part in a nation-wide, perchance a world-wide, vigil of prayer as the great crusade sets forth.

Mary prayed, fervently, from the depth of her heart, for Charles, for all the men, that they might succeed and return home safely. . . and for Eamon and his cause, wherever he might be. Music resumed on the radio, and after a few moments lost in thought, Mary returned to her chores. Then once again the announcer broke in: 'It is reported that the British Prime Minister, flashing his usual confident grin and two fingers signalling victory, has just entered the House of Commons to a thundering ovation. Prime Minister Churchill is now addressing the Commons.' Mary closed her eyes, trying to visualize the historic moment.

Winston Churchill surveyed the familiar faces on the green leather benches and assumed his usual oratorical stance, his right hand grasping the lapel of his black jacket. 'Let me begin,' he said, 'with the news from the Italian front. With our recent victory in Rome.' The tension built as Churchill devoted almost fifteen minutes to a discussion of the Allies' capture of the Italian capital. 'Now,' he said at last, 'I have also to announce to the House that during the night and early hours of the morning' – he paused for effect – 'the first of a series of landings in force upon the European Continent has taken place. So far, the commanders report that everything is pro-ceeding according to plan. And what a plan!' The Commons erupted in cheers and applause. 'Landings on the beaches are proceeding at various points at the present time. The fire of shore batteries has been largely quelled. Obstacles which were encountered in the sea have not proved as difficult as was anticipated. There is very much less loss than we expected. The many dangers and difficulties which at this time yesterday appeared extremely formidable are behind us.' The Members rose as one and broke into a long, ringing ovation. Churchill acknowledged the tribute with a nod and strode triumphantly from the chamber.

An American army officer stood in a corridor of St Bartholomew's Hospital, running a finger around his hatband as he waited for the nurse to return. Weak sunlight shone through the windows that looked out on a Georgian quadrangle. Major Hanes Butler watched as a crow landed on the sill, reminding him of the crows in the tall pines of his Carolina home.

'Excuse me, sir.'

He turned to a middle-aged nurse in a long white dress, with a peaked cap perched somewhat precariously atop her thick brown hair. 'Yes, ma'am,' said Butler in his soft drawl.

'You may go in now,' she said. 'Colonel Davenport is on the right-hand side of the ward. But please remember – visits are limited to thirty minutes.'

Butler nodded and said, 'Yes, ma'am.' Rows of iron beds, partially obscured by screens, lined each side of the ward. Butler's shoes tapped on the linoleum as he walked past the beds, averting his eyes from the men, until he was two-thirds of the way down the ward. He paused to look at the man on his right, whose face was obscured by a bandage. His gaze fell on the next man, resting peacefully under the white covers with one leg suspended from a stainless-steel frame and his arms folded across his chest. Despite the bandage on his forehead, Butler recognized Charles Davenport. When he walked up to the bedside he saw that Davenport was sleeping.

'Charlie,' he said softly. He gently shook his shoulder. 'Hey . . . wake up.'

Davenport opened his eyes and a look of happy recognition spread across his face. 'Hanes,' he said in a strong voice. 'Well, I'll be damned.'

'Well, Charlie,' said Butler with a smile, 'y'all did a heckuva job. Whipped ol' Jerry's ass.'

'Yes, it was quite a show,' said Davenport. 'But how are things going now? I never hear anything in here.'

'They're still havin' a tough time breaking out of the beachhead. But I reckon it'll get done soon enough, with the number of men we keep sending across.' He glanced briefly at Davenport's suspended leg, frowned, and said, 'How bad is it?'

Davenport exhaled slowly and said, 'It was a mortar round, right on the beach. I caught the shrapnel in my left shin, and a knock on the head. The docs tried saving it' – he paused and looked at his leg – 'but they had to take it off below the knee.'

Butler shook his head and said, 'Jeez, I'm sorry. What a lousy break.'

'I'm afraid it's the end of the war for me,' said Davenport in a resigned tone, propping himself up on the pillows.

'Was it bad? The landing, I mean.'

'Not by the time we came in. Just an occasional mortar round and some sniper fire.' Davenport sat part way up, leaning on an elbow. 'Listen, Hanes,' he said. 'There's something I need to ask you . . .'

'Shoot,' said Butler.

'Does Jenny know anything about this? I mean, have you said anything?'

Butler gave Davenport a strange look. 'Listen, Charlie,' he said, 'that's one of the reasons I wanted to see you. To talk to you about Jenny.'

'So you know,' said Davenport dejectedly.

'Know what?'

Davenport slumped back on the pillows and said, 'That she's, well, pregnant.'

'Yes, I know, but if you'd let me explain—'

'Please,' interrupted Davenport, raising his hand. 'There's something important I need to ask you. That night in Scotland, after the four of us had dinner?'

'Sure, what about it?'

'Well, I know I was tanked, but for the life of me I can't remember what happened. Did I . . . I mean, did we go up to the room?'

'You were drunk all right, damned near passed out. But *no*, you didn't. That's what I've been trying to tell you. I was there, and I'm telling you, it never happened.'

Davenport lay back on the pillows and closed his eyes. So he'd been right all along.

'But don't be too hard on Jenny,' said Butler. 'Peg says she was pretty broken-hearted when she got the news you had another girl, and then she turned up pregnant.' Davenport nodded, feeling the overwhelming emotion of the condemned man who suddenly learns he's been pardoned. 'She shouldn't have led you to believe,' Butler continued, 'that it was yours. But it sounds like she was desperate.'

'What about Jenny?' asked Davenport. 'What will she do now?'

'She'll be fine. This other fellow, a captain in the merchant marine, came by to see her the other day. Turns out he's crazy about her, and when he realized what had happened, he asked her to marry him. I gather she feels pretty rotten about laying it all on you.' He looked at his watch. 'I better get movin' or that nurse will run me out of here. You need to take it easy and get well. They need you back on Morgan's staff.'

Davenport stared at the far wall. 'Sure, Hanes,' he said thoughtfully. 'And thanks for dropping by.'

Mary was dressed in her Sunday best, anxious to get to church. Despite her exhaustion, she couldn't rest. The days of worrying, walking, and learning to pray again had brought her back to worship. It was the only place she had found any peace. Her attendance had begun soon after Eamon's farewell. The first services had an uneasy feel, like a new suit of clothes, stiff and scratchy, not quite right. But as the weeks passed, the Mass felt more familiar, and there came a sense of rediscovery, of old and welcome feelings, and genuine acceptance by the townspeople as she joined them in Sunday worship. The church was an aged stone structure. It looked small and insignificant, standing alone on the edge of town.

After lighting a candle, she sat on one of the satin-smooth pews and breathed the stone-cooled air, redolent of wood polish and candles. Calm at last, she surrendered herself to the liturgy and ritual, oblivious to the sound of the wooden door scraping open. She sank to the kneeling bench with the rest of the congregation and clasped her hands tightly together. Engrossed in the priest's solemn incantation, she closed her eyes and began to pray, just as she had prayed each day for weeks.

He moved as quietly as he was able, leaning heavily on his crutches and swinging his good leg forward. He searched the pews, gazing into the eyes of the parishioners who looked up at the British officer moving slowly down the centre aisle, pausing to smile at a tall boy, perhaps sixteen, who was watching him with a look of intense

EPILOGUE

ON 20 JULY, 1944, Lieutenant Colonel Count Klaus von Stauffenberg, attending a staff briefing at Wolfschanze, the Führer's East Prussian headquarters, carefully placed his briefcase beneath a heavy oak conference table and excused himself from the meeting. Hurrying to his waiting car, he commanded the driver to take him to the nearby Luftwaffe airfield where a plane was standing by to fly him back to Berlin. At the airfield he telephoned his contact at Wehrmacht headquarters on Friedrichstrasse. As Stauffenberg was contacting his co-conspirators in Berlin, the bomb hidden in his briefcase exploded at 12.37 p.m., ripping apart the fragile wood structure. Stauffenberg heard it himself. The Führer was surely dead. Operation Valkyrie was on.

By the time Stauffenberg's plane landed at Tempelhof, Berlin's airfield, the carefully orchestrated conspiracy to topple the Nazi regime had sprung into action. Troops were on the march to arrest Goering, Goebbels, and the rest of the Nazi leadership. At Wehrmacht headquarters, however, General Friedrich Olbricht, Stauffenberg's key ally in the German Army, received an unexpected telephone call from Wolfschanze. Four men in the conference room had indeed been killed in the blast. But Adolf Hitler had miraculously survived. Olbricht and Stauffenberg were immediately placed under arrest and summarily shot. In the days and weeks that followed, the 20 July conspirators – the *Schwartze Kapelle* – in the plot to assassinate Hitler and topple the Nazi regime, were ruthlessly rooted out by the Gestapo from their positions in the army and civil government. Hauled before the People's Court, they were publicly humiliated before they were shot and suspended from meat hooks with piano wire for the Führer to view. Adam von Trott, Eamon's superior in the Abwehr, was among those rounded up and executed in the weeks following the failed coup. Only later, and out of view of his adoring German public, was Field Marshal Erwin Rommel, commander of the German forces that sought to repel the Normandy invasion, implicated in the conspiracy and forced to take his own life by poison.

There is no known historical record of the response of the British and American governments to the peace overtures of the 20 July plotters or of the action they may have contemplated had the German patriots succeeded in killing Hitler and overthrowing the Nazi regime.